NON SANS DROICT.

*William Shakespeare*

# The History of HENRY IV
## [PART ONE]

With New Dramatic Criticism
and an Updated Bibliography

EDITED BY MAYNARD MACK

*The Signet Classic Shakespeare*
GENERAL EDITOR: SYLVAN BARNET

A SIGNET CLASSIC

SIGNET CLASSIC
Published by the Penguin Group
Penguin Books USA Inc., 375 Hudson Street,
New York, New York 10014, U.S.A.
Penguin Books Ltd, 27 Wrights Lane,
London W8 5TZ, England
Penguin Books Australia Ltd, Ringwood,
Victoria, Australia
Penguin Books Canada Ltd, 10 Alcorn Avenue,
Toronto, Ontario, Canada M4V 3B2
Penguin Books (N.Z.) Ltd, 182–190 Wairau Road,
Auckland 10, New Zealand

Penguin Books Ltd, Registered Offices:
Harmondsworth, Middlesex, England

Published by Signet Classic, an imprint of Dutton Signet,
a division of Penguin Books USA Inc.

30   29   28   27   26   25   24

 REGISTERED TRADEMARK—MARCA REGISTRADA

Library of Congress Catalog Card Number: 86-62299

Printed in the United States of America

# Contents

# Shakespeare: Prefatory Remarks

Between the record of his baptism in Stratford on 26 April 1564 and the record of his burial in Stratford on 25 April 1616, some forty documents name Shakespeare, and many others name his parents, his children, and his grandchildren. More facts are known about William Shakespeare than about any other playwright of the period except Ben Jonson. The facts should, however, be distinguished from the legends. The latter, inevitably more engaging and better known, tell us that the Stratford boy killed a calf in high style, poached deer and rabbits, and was forced to flee to London, where he held horses outside a playhouse. These traditions are only traditions; they may be true, but no evidence supports them, and it is well to stick to the facts.

Mary Arden, the dramatist's mother, was the daughter of a substantial landowner; about 1557 she married John Shakespeare, who was a glove-maker and trader in various farm commodities. In 1557 John Shakespeare was a member of the Council (the governing body of Stratford), in 1558 a constable of the borough, in 1561 one of the two town chamberlains, in 1565 an alderman (entitling him to the appellation "Mr."), in 1568 high bailiff—the town's highest political office, equivalent to mayor. After 1577, for an unknown reason he drops out of local politics. The birthday of William Shakespeare, the eldest son of this locally prominent man, is unrecorded; but the Stratford parish register records that the infant was baptized on 26 April 1564. (It is quite possible that he was born on 23

April, but this date has probably been assigned by tradition because it is the date on which, fifty-two years later, he died.) The attendance records of the Stratford grammar school of the period are not extant, but it is reasonable to assume that the son of a local official attended the school and received substantial training in Latin. The masters of the school from Shakespeare's seventh to fifteenth years held Oxford degrees; the Elizabethan curriculum excluded mathematics and the natural sciences but taught a good deal of Latin rhetoric, logic, and literature. On 27 November 1582 a marriage license was issued to Shakespeare and Anne Hathaway, eight years his senior. The couple had a child in May, 1583. Perhaps the marriage was necessary, but perhaps the couple had earlier engaged in a formal "troth plight" which would render their children legitimate even if no further ceremony were performed. In 1585 Anne Hathaway bore Shakespeare twins.

That Shakespeare was born is excellent; that he married and had children is pleasant; but that we know nothing about his departure from Stratford to London, or about the beginning of his theatrical career, is lamentable and must be admitted. We would gladly sacrifice details about his children's baptism for details about his earliest days on the stage. Perhaps the poaching episode is true (but it is first reported almost a century after Shakespeare's death), or perhaps he first left Stratford to be a schoolteacher, as another tradition holds; perhaps he was moved by

> Such wind as scatters young men through the world,
> To seek their fortunes further than at home
> Where small experience grows.

In 1592, thanks to the cantankerousness of Robert Greene, a rival playwright and a pamphleteer, we have our first reference, a snarling one, to Shakespeare as an actor and playwright. Greene warns those of his own educated friends who wrote for the theater against an actor who has presumed to turn playwright:

> There is an upstart crow, beautified with our feathers,
> that with his *tiger's heart wrapped in a player's hide* sup-
> poses he is as well able to bombast out a blank verse as
> the best of you, and being an absolute Johannes-factotum
> is in his own conceit the only Shake-scene in a country.

The reference to the player, as well as the allusion to
Aesop's crow (who strutted in borrowed plumage, as an
actor struts in fine words not his own), makes it clear
that by this date Shakespeare had both acted and written. That Shakespeare is meant is indicated not only by
"Shake-scene" but by the parody of a line from one of
Shakespeare's plays, *3 Henry VI:* "O, tiger's heart wrapped
in a woman's hide." If Shakespeare in 1592 was prominent enough to be attacked by an envious dramatist, he
probably had served an apprenticeship in the theater for
at least a few years.

In any case, by 1592 Shakespeare had acted and written, and there are a number of subsequent references to
him as an actor: documents indicate that in 1598 he is
a "principal comedian," in 1603 a "principal tragedian,"
in 1608 he is one of the "men players." The profession
of actor was not for a gentleman, and it occasionally drew
the scorn of university men who resented writing speeches
for persons less educated than themselves, but it was respectable enough: players, if prosperous, were in effect
members of the bourgeoisie, and there is nothing to suggest that Stratford considered William Shakespeare less
than a solid citizen. When, in 1596, the Shakespeares
were granted a coat of arms, the grant was made to Shakespeare's father, but probably William Shakespeare (who
the next year bought the second-largest house in town)
had arranged the matter on his own behalf. In subsequent
transactions he is occasionally styled a gentleman.

Although in 1593 and 1594 Shakespeare published two
narrative poems dedicated to the Earl of Southampton,
*Venus and Adonis* and *The Rape of Lucrece,* and may
well have written most or all of his sonnets in the middle nineties, Shakespeare's literary activity seems to have
been almost entirely devoted to the theater. (It may be

significant that the two narrative poems were written in years when the plague closed the theaters for several months.) In 1594 he was a charter member of a theatrical company called the Chamberlain's Men (which in 1603 changed its name to the King's Men); until he retired to Stratford (about 1611, apparently), he was with this remarkably stable company. From 1599 the company acted primarily at the Globe Theatre, in which Shakespeare held a one-tenth interest. Other Elizabethan dramatists are known to have acted, but no other is known also to have been entitled to a share in the profits of the playhouse.

Shakespeare's first eight published plays did not have his name on them, but this is not remarkable; the most popular play of the sixteenth century, Thomas Kyd's *The Spanish Tragedy,* went through many editions without naming Kyd, and Kyd's authorship is known only because a book on the profession of acting happens to quote (and attribute to Kyd) some lines on the interest of Roman emperors in the drama. What is remarkable is that after 1598 Shakespeare's name commonly appears on printed plays—some of which are not his. Another indication of his popularity comes from Francis Meres, author of *Palladis Tamia: Wit's Treasury* (1598): in this anthology of snippets accompanied by an essay on literature, many playwrights are mentioned, but Shakespeare's name occurs more often than any other, and Shakespeare is the only playwright whose plays are listed.

From his acting, playwriting, and share in a theater, Shakespeare seems to have made considerable money. He put it to work, making substantial investments in Stratford real estate. When he made his will (less than a month before he died), he sought to leave his property intact to his descendants. Of small bequests to relatives and to friends (including three actors, Richard Burbage, John Heminges, and Henry Condell), that to his wife of the second-best bed has provoked the most comment; perhaps it was the bed the couple had slept in, the best being reserved for visitors. In any case, had Shakespeare not excepted it, the bed would have gone (with the rest of his household possessions) to his daughter and her husband. On 25 April 1616 he was buried within the chancel of the church at Stratford. An unattractive monument to his memory, placed on a wall near the grave, says he died on 23 April. Over the grave itself are the lines, perhaps by Shakespeare, that (more than his literary fame) have kept his bones undisturbed in the crowded burial ground where old bones were often dislodged to make way for new:

> Good friend, for Jesus' sake forbear
> To dig the dust enclosèd here.
> Blessed be the man that spares these stones
> And cursed be he that moves my bones.

Thirty-seven plays, as well as some nondramatic poems, are held to constitute the Shakespeare canon. The dates of composition of most of the works are highly uncertain, but there is often evidence of a *terminus a quo* (starting point) and/or a *terminus ad quem* (terminal point) that provides a framework for intelligent guessing. For example, *Richard II* cannot be earlier than 1595, the publication date of some material to which it is indebted; *The Merchant of Venice* cannot be later than 1598, the year Francis Meres mentioned it. Sometimes arguments for a date hang on an alleged topical allusion, such as the lines about the unseasonable weather in *A Midsummer Night's Dream*, II.i.81–117, but such an allusion (if indeed it is an allusion) can be variously interpreted, and in any case there is always the possibility that a topical allusion was inserted during a revision, years after the composition of a play. Dates are often attributed on the basis of style, and although conjectures about style usually rest on other conjectures, sooner or later one must rely on one's literary sense. There is no real proof, for example, that *Othello* is not as early as *Romeo and Juliet*, but one feels *Othello* is later, and because the first record of its performance is 1604, one is glad enough to set its composition at that date and not push it back into Shakespeare's early years. The following chronology, then, is as much indebted to informed guesswork and sensitivity as it is to fact. The dates, necessarily imprecise, indicate something like a scholarly consensus.

## PLAYS

| | |
|---|---|
| 1588–93 | *The Comedy of Errors* |
| 1588–94 | *Love's Labor's Lost* |
| 1590–91 | *2 Henry VI* |
| 1590–91 | *3 Henry VI* |
| 1591–92 | *1 Henry VI* |
| 1592–93 | *Richard III* |
| 1592–94 | *Titus Andronicus* |
| 1593–94 | *The Taming of the Shrew* |
| 1593–95 | *The Two Gentlemen of Verona* |
| 1594–96 | *Romeo and Juliet* |
| 1595 | *Richard II* |
| 1594–96 | *A Midsummer Night's Dream* |
| 1596–97 | *King John* |
| 1596–97 | *The Merchant of Venice* |
| 1597 | *1 Henry IV* |
| 1597–98 | *2 Henry IV* |
| 1598–1600 | *Much Ado About Nothing* |
| 1598–99 | *Henry V* |
| 1599 | *Julius Caesar* |
| 1599–1600 | *As You Like It* |
| 1599–1600 | *Twelfth Night* |
| 1600–01 | *Hamlet* |
| 1597–1601 | *The Merry Wives of Windsor* |
| 1601–02 | *Troilus and Cressida* |
| 1602–04 | *All's Well That Ends Well* |
| 1603–04 | *Othello* |
| 1604 | *Measure for Measure* |
| 1605–06 | *King Lear* |
| 1605–06 | *Macbeth* |
| 1606–07 | *Antony and Cleopatra* |
| 1605–08 | *Timon of Athens* |
| 1607–09 | *Coriolanus* |

| 1608–09 | *Pericles* |
| 1609–10 | *Cymbeline* |
| 1610–11 | *The Winter's Tale* |
| 1611 | *The Tempest* |
| 1612–13 | *Henry VIII* |

### POEMS

| 1592 | *Venus and Adonis* |
| 1593–94 | *The Rape of Lucrece* |
| 1593–1600 | *Sonnets* |
| 1600–01 | *The Phoenix and the Turtle* |

## Shakespeare's Theater

In Shakespeare's infancy, Elizabethan actors performed wherever they could—in great halls, at court, in the courtyards of inns. The innyards must have made rather unsatisfactory theaters: on some days they were unavailable because carters bringing goods to London used them as depots; when available, they had to be rented from the innkeeper; perhaps most important, London inns were subject to the Common Council of London, which was not well disposed toward theatricals. In 1574 the Common Council required that plays and playing places in London be licensed. It asserted that

> sundry great disorders and inconveniences have been found to ensue to this city by the inordinate haunting of great multitudes of people, specially youth, to plays, interludes, and shows, namely occasion of frays and quarrels, evil practices of incontinency in great inns having chambers and secret places adjoining to their open stages and galleries,

and ordered that innkeepers who wished licenses to hold performances put up a bond and make contributions to the poor.

The requirement that plays and innyard theaters be licensed, along with the other drawbacks of playing at inns, probably drove James Burbage (a carpenter-turned-actor) to rent in 1576 a plot of land northeast of the city walls and to build here—on property outside the jurisdiction of the city—England's first permanent construction designed for plays. He called it simply the Theatre. About all that is known of its construction is that it was wood. It soon had imitators, the most famous being the Globe (1599), built across the Thames (again outside the city's jurisdiction), out of timbers of the Theatre, which had been dismantled when Burbage's lease ran out.

There are three important sources of information about the structure of Elizabethan playhouses—drawings, a contract, and stage directions in plays. Of drawings, only the so-called De Witt drawing (c. 1596) of the Swan—really a friend's copy of De Witt's drawing—is of much significance. It shows a building of three tiers, with a stage jutting from a wall into the yard or center of the building. The tiers are roofed, and part of the stage is covered by a roof that projects from the rear and is supported at its front on two posts, but the groundlings, who paid a penny to stand in front of the stage, were exposed to the sky. (Performances in such a playhouse were held only in the daytime; artificial illumination was not used.) At the rear of the stage are two doors; above the stage is a gallery. The second major source of information, the contract for the Fortune, specifies that although the Globe is to be the model, the Fortune is to be square, eighty feet outside and fifty-five inside. The stage is to be forty-three feet broad, and is to extend into the middle of the yard (i.e., it is twenty-seven and a half feet deep). For patrons willing to pay more than the general admission charged of the groundlings, there were to be three galleries provided with seats. From the third chief source, stage directions, one learns that entrance to the stage was by doors, presumably spaced widely apart at the rear ("Enter one citizen at one door, and another at the other"), and that in addition to the platform stage there was occasionally some sort of curtained booth or alcove allowing for "discovery" scenes, and some sort of playing space "aloft" or "above" to represent (for example) the top of a city's walls or a room above the street. Doubtless each theater had its own peculiarities, but perhaps we can talk about a "typical" Elizabethan theater if we realize that no theater need exactly have fit the description, just as no father is the typical father with 3.7 children. This hypothetical theater is wooden, round or polygonal (in *Henry V* Shakespeare calls it a "wooden *O*"), capable of holding some eight hundred spectators standing in the yard around the projecting elevated stage and some fifteen hundred additional spectators seated in the three roofed galleries. The stage, protected by a "shadow" or "heavens" or roof, is entered by two doors; behind the doors is the "tiring house" (attiring house, i.e., dressing room), and above the doors is some sort of gallery that may sometimes hold spectators but that can be used (for example) as the bedroom from which Romeo—according to a stage direction in one text—"goeth down." Some evidence suggests that a throne can be lowered onto the platform stage, perhaps from the "shadow"; certainly characters can descend from the stage through a trap or traps into the cellar or "hell." Sometimes this space beneath the platform accommodates a sound-effects man or musician (in *Antony and Cleopatra* "music of the hautboys is under the stage") or an actor (in *Hamlet* the "Ghost cries under the stage"). Most characters simply walk on and off, but because there is no curtain in front of the platform, corpses will have to be carried off (Hamlet must lug Polonius' guts into the neighbor room), or will have to fall at the rear, where the curtain on the alcove or booth can be drawn to conceal them.

Such may have been the so-called "public theater." Another kind of theater, called the "private theater" because its much greater admission charge limited its audience to the wealthy or the prodigal, must be briefly mentioned. The private theater was basically a large room, entirely roofed and therefore artificially illuminated, with a stage at one end. In 1576 one such theater was established in Blackfriars, a Dominican priory in London that had been suppressed in 1538 and confiscated by the Crown and thus was not under the city's jurisdiction. All the actors in the Blackfriars theater were boys about eight to thirteen years old (in the public theaters similar boys played female parts; a boy Lady Macbeth played to a man Macbeth). This private theater had a precarious existence, and ceased operations in 1584. In 1596 James Burbage, who had already made theatrical history by building the Theatre, began to construct a second Blackfriars theater. He died in 1597, and for several years this second Blackfriars theater was used by a troupe of boys, but in 1608 two of Burbage's sons and five other actors (including Shakespeare) became joint operators of the theater, using it in the winter when the open-air Globe was unsuitable. Perhaps such a smaller theater, roofed, artificially illuminated, and with a tradition of a courtly audience, exerted an influence on Shakespeare's late plays.

Performances in the private theaters may well have had intermissions during which music was played, but in the public theaters the action was probably uninterrupted, flowing from scene to scene almost without a break. Actors would enter, speak, exit, and others would immediately enter and establish (if necessary) the new locale by a few properties and by words and gestures. Here are some samples of Shakespeare's scene painting:

> This is Illyria, lady.

> Well, this is the Forest of Arden.

> This castle hath a pleasant seat; the air
> Nimbly and sweetly recommends itself
> Unto our gentle senses.

On the other hand, it is a mistake to conceive of the Elizabethan stage as bare. Although Shakespeare's Chorus in *Henry V* calls the stage an "unworthy scaffold" and urges the spectators to "eke out our performance with your mind," there was considerable spectacle. The last

act of *Macbeth,* for example, has five stage directions
calling for "drum and colors," and another sort of appeal
to the eye is indicated by the stage direction "Enter Mac-
duff, with Macbeth's head." Some scenery and properties
may have been substantial; doubtless a throne was used,
and in one play of the period we encounter this direction:
"Hector takes up a great piece of rock and casts at Ajax,
who tears up a young tree by the roots and assails Hector." The matter is of some importance, and will be
glanced at again in the next section.

## The Texts of Shakespeare

Though eighteen of his plays were published during
his lifetime, Shakespeare seems never to have supervised
their publication. There is nothing unusual here; when a
playwright sold a play to a theatrical company he sur-
rendered his ownership of it. Normally a company would
not publish the play, because to publish it meant to allow
competitors to acquire the piece. Some plays, however,
did get published: apparently treacherous actors sometimes pieced together a play for a publisher, sometimes
a company in need of money sold a play, and sometimes
a company allowed a play to be published that no longer
drew audiences. That Shakespeare did not concern himself with publication, then, is scarcely remarkable; of his
contemporaries only Ben Jonson carefully supervised the
publication of his own plays. In 1623, seven years after
Shakespeare's death, John Heminges and Henry Condell
(two senior members of Shakespeare's company, who had
performed with him for about twenty years) collected his
plays—published and unpublished—into a large volume,
commonly called the First Folio. (A folio is a volume
consisting of sheets that have been folded once, each sheet
thus making two leaves, or four pages. The eighteen plays
published during Shakespeare's lifetime had been issued
one play per volume in small books called quartos. Each
sheet in a quarto has been folded twice, making four
leaves, or eight pages.) The First Folio contains thirty-six

plays; a thirty-seventh, *Pericles,* though not in the Folio is regarded as canonical. Heminges and Condell suggest in an address "To the great variety of readers" that the republished plays are presented in better form than in the quartos: "Before you were abused with diverse stolen and surreptitious copies, maimed and deformed by the frauds and stealths of injurious impostors that exposed them; even those, are now offered to your view cured and perfect of their limbs, and all the rest absolute in their numbers, as he [i.e., Shakespeare] conceived them."

Whoever was assigned to prepare the texts for publication in the First Folio seems to have taken his job seriously and yet not to have performed it with uniform care. The sources of the texts seem to have been, in general, good unpublished copies or the best published copies. The first play in the collection, *The Tempest,* is divided into acts and scenes, has unusually full stage directions and descriptions of spectacle, and concludes with a list of the characters, but the editor was not able (or willing) to present all of the succeeding texts so fully dressed. Later texts occasionally show signs of carelessness: in one scene of *Much Ado About Nothing* the names of actors, instead of characters, appear as speech prefixes, as they had in the quarto, which the Folio reprints; proofreading throughout the Folio is spotty and apparently was done without reference to the printer's copy; the pagination of *Hamlet* jumps from 156 to 257.

A modern editor of Shakespeare must first select his copy; no problem if the play exists only in the Folio, but a considerable problem if the relationship between a quarto and the Folio—or an early quarto and a later one—is unclear. When an editor has chosen what seems to him to be the most authoritative text or texts for his copy, he has not done with making decisions. First of all, he must reckon with Elizabethan spelling. If he is not producing a facsimile, he probably modernizes it, but ought he to preserve the old form of words that apparently were pronounced quite unlike their modern forms—"lanthorn," "alablaster"? If he preserves these forms, is he really preserving Shakespeare's forms or per-

haps those of a compositor in the printing house? What is
one to do when one finds "lanthorn" and "lantern" in ad-
jacent lines? (The editors of this series in general, but not
invariably, assume that words should be spelled in their
modern form.) Elizabethan punctuation, too, presents
problems. For example in the First Folio, the only text
for the play, Macbeth rejects his wife's idea that he can
wash the blood from his hand:

> no: this my Hand will rather
> The multitudinous Seas incarnadine,
> Making the Greene one, Red.

Obviously an editor will remove the superfluous capitals,
and he will probably alter the spelling to "incarnadine,"
but will he leave the comma before "red," letting Macbeth speak of the sea as "the green one," or will he (like
most modern editors) remove the comma and thus have
Macbeth say that his hand will make the ocean *uni-
formly* red?

An editor will sometimes have to change more than
spelling or punctuation. Macbeth says to his wife:

> I dare do all that may become a man,
> Who dares no more, is none.

For two centuries editors have agreed that the second
line is unsatisfactory, and have emended "no" to "do":
"Who dares do more is none." But when in the same
play Ross says that fearful persons

> floate vpon a wilde and violent Sea
> Each way, and moue,

need "move" be emended to "none," as it often is, on the
hunch that the compositor misread the manuscript? The
editors of the Signet Classic Shakespeare have restrained
themselves from making abundant emendations. In their
minds they hear Dr. Johnson on the dangers of emend-
ing: "I have adopted the Roman sentiment, that it is more
honorable to save a citizen than to kill an enemy." Some

departures (in addition to spelling, punctuation, and lineation) from the copy text have of course been made, but the original readings are listed in a note following the play, so that the reader can evaluate them for himself.

The editors of the Signet Classic Shakespeare, following tradition, have added line numbers and in many cases act and scene divisions as well as indications of locale at the beginning of scenes. The Folio divided most of the plays into acts and some into scenes. Early eighteenth-century editors increased the divisions. These divisions, which provide a convenient way of referring to passages in the plays, have been retained, but when not in the text chosen as the basis for the Signet Classic text they are enclosed in square brackets [ ] to indicate that they are editorial additions. Similarly, although no play of Shakespeare's published during his lifetime was equipped with indications of locale at the heads of scene divisions, locales have here been added in square brackets for the convenience of the reader, who lacks the information afforded to spectators by costumes, properties, and gestures. The spectator can tell at a glance he is in the throne room, but without an editorial indication the reader may be puzzled for a while. It should be mentioned, incidentally, that there are a few authentic stage directions —perhaps Shakespeare's, perhaps a prompter's—that suggest locales: for example, "Enter Brutus in his orchard," and "They go up into the Senate house." It is hoped that the bracketed additions provide the reader with the sort of help provided in these two authentic directions, but it is equally hoped that the reader will remember that the stage was not loaded with scenery.

No editor during the course of his work can fail to recollect some words Heminges and Condell prefixed to the Folio:

It had been a thing, we confess, worthy to have been wished, that the author himself had lived to have set forth and overseen his own writings. But since it hath been ordained otherwise, and he by death departed from that right, we pray you do not envy his friends the office of their care and pain to have collected and published them.

Nor can an editor, after he has done his best, forget Heminges and Condell's final words: "And so we leave you to other of his friends, whom if you need can be your guides. If you need them not, you can lead yourselves, and others. And such readers we wish him."

SYLVAN BARNET
*Tufts University*

# Introduction

## I

Readers who come to *Henry IV* [*Part One*] from *Richard II* (and they are well advised who do so) find themselves in a changed world. The new king's second word is "shaken"—"So shaken as we are, so wan with care" (I.i.1). IIis realm's pcacc, "frightcd," pants to catch her breath. The English earth, invoked in vain by Richard in the earlier play for aid against Henry's invading power (III.ii.4ff), like a perverted mother has been sucking "her own children's blood." Englishmen have met Englishmen "in the . . . furious close of civil butchery." The "edge" of war's knife has cut his master.

Though the new king assigns these troubles to the past, we are speedily assured they will not stay there. Present news is equally bloody. In the West, a thousand of Mortimer's men have been "butchered," and afterward mutilated. In the North, ten thousand Scottish corpses were seen by Sir Walter Blunt "balked in their own blood." Throughout the play we shall hear continually of this sort of thing: of "guns and drums and wounds" (I.iii.55) and "many a good tall fellow" destroyed (I.iii.61); of "bloody noses and cracked crowns" (II.iii.93); wearing "a garment all of blood" (III.ii.135); noblemen offered up "hot and bleeding" to "the fire-eyed maid of smoky war" (IV.i.113–14); ragamuffins tossed dead into a pit —"Tut, tut, good enough to toss; food for powder. . . ." (IV.ii. 66–67)—or consigned, maimed, to the town's end,

"to beg during life" (V.iii.38). Richard returned from
wars in Ireland in the earlier play, and the present king,
then Henry Hereford, known as Bolingbroke, invaded
England; but we never heard of doings like these. This
is indeed a changed world: the world of outrage that is
anticipated in the next-to-last scene of *Richard II* by the
brutal murder of the King and, earlier, in the deposition
scene (IV.i.121–49), by the warning of the Bishop of
Carlisle:

> What subject can give sentence on his king?
> And who sits here that is not Richard's subject? . . .
> My Lord of Hereford here, whom you call king,
> Is a foul traitor to proud Hereford's king;
> And if you crown him, let me prophesy
> The blood of English shall manure the ground,
> And future ages groan for this foul act;
> Peace shall go sleep with Turks and infidels,
> And, in this seat of peace, tumultuous wars
> Shall kin with kin, and kind with kind, confound;
> Disorder, horror, fear, and mutiny
> Shall here inhabit, and this land be called
> The field of Golgotha and dead men's skulls.
> O, if you raise this house against this house,
> It will the woefullest division prove
> That ever fell upon this cursèd earth!
> Prevent it, resist it, let it not be so,
> Lest child, child's children, cry against you woe.

The violence predicted by Carlisle takes over immediately in *1 Henry IV*, as we have seen. But the bishop's
enunciation of what is sometimes called "the Tudor myth"
—the thesis that an ever-watchful Providence brings retri-
bution on peoples who displace their lawful sovereigns,
and, specifically, that England's sufferings between the
murder of Richard in 1399 and the accession of the first
Tudor monarch in 1485 were a divinely appointed punishment for the assault on Richard—the enunciation of
this doctrine better suits Shakespeare's earlier treatment
of these disorders in the Henry VI plays and *Richard III*
than the Henry IV plays. The world that produces Henry

is changed in this respect, too. The old scheme of celestial
superintendence hangs loosely over it, to be glanced at
in moments of introspection and anxiety; but to all dramatic intents and purposes, Henry's world, like Henry
himself, is secular. One reason may be that Shakespeare
saw in secularism the necessary condition of a usurper's
success. A more compelling reason, doubtless, is that his
attention had increasingly shifted from the interpretive
moral and theological scheme with which his sources provided him toward the complexities and crosscurrents of
human beings as they act and react on one another: in
Yeats's words, toward "the fury and the mire of human
veins."

The best anticipation of the mood of our play, from
this point of view, is Richard's own warning, addressed
to the man whose betrayal of him enabled Henry to seize
the throne:

> Northumberland, thou ladder wherewithal
> The mounting Bolingbroke ascends my throne,
> The time shall not be many hours of age
> More than it is, ere foul sin, gathering head,
> Shall break into corruption. Thou shalt think,
> Though he divide the realm and give thee half,
> It is too little, helping him to all;
> He shall think that thou which knowest the way
> To plant unrightful kings, wilt know again,
> Being ne'er so little urged another way,
> To pluck him headlong from the usurped throne.
> The love of wicked men converts to fear,
> That fear to hate, and hate turns one or both
> To worthy danger and deservèd death.          (V.i.55–68)

These lines pay tribute to the overall theological scheme
("foul sin, gathering head"), but this fact should not
blind us to the principles of *realpolitik* which they put
forward as the mode of action that will govern in the
hearts of Henry and his associates.

The irony of the new king's position, we soon learn,
springs from these principles. As a successful usurper
with the blood of a predecessor on his conscience, he is

himself a principle of the disorder on which, as Shakespeare's Macbeth will learn at length, no lasting order can be built. Lawlessness springs up about him as if like Jason he had sown the dragon's teeth. It comes not only in the form of the Percys' rebellion and the behavior of his son, but in the knavery of Falstaff and the murky atmosphere of the inn at Rochester (to some extent an image of England), where all order is in decay and no man trusts another. All these are reflections cast by Henry in the mirror of the body politic. If there are highwaymen on the public road and other highwaymen at Glendower's plotting to snatch the Crown, these circumstances cannot be separated from the circumstance that one who has acted like a highwayman is king.

Thus the Tudor theme of the harsh wages of usurpation by no means vanishes from the play. Minimizing it as doctrine, Shakespeare makes it part of the poetic and dramatic texture, while he qualifies and complicates it by presenting to us in Henry a capable and even admirable king—one who, though never granted the security and peace he longs for, maintains his crown by a combination of strength, sagacity, severity, and lenience, and passes it on to an eventually deserving son. The ambivalence of his position is brought out by continual questioning of his title. The rebels question it on many occasions verbally (I.iii.10ff, 143ff; IV.iii.52ff; V.i.30ff) and, subsequently, by force of arms. The King himself seems to cast a doubt on it when he dresses others "in his coats" to confuse the enemy at Shrewsbury, as if royalty were a costume or blazon to be laid on at will. When Falstaff "acts" the King in the tavern, this doubt assumes a compelling visual shape, as does a further doubt whether "that father ruffian," as Hal calls Falstaff when he himself assumes the King's part, is more a ruffian in some respects than the deposer and murderer of Richard. Meantime, in the language of the play, this subject is teased at incessantly: we hear of the "Grace" that Hal will or will not have when he is king; of the "*true*[1] prince" knowable by instinct; of the "heir *apparent*"[1]—

[1] The italics are, of course, the editor's.

with a lurking pun in the second term; of false or cracked coins (bearing the King's image) to be passed current; of "nobles" appreciated to "royals"; and of many forms of "counterfeiting." Perhaps the ambiguities surrounding Henry's claim are expressed most succinctly in two remarks made by the Scottish Douglas during the battle. Douglas is engaged in killing all who wear the King's coats as fast as he can find them. "I fear thou art another counterfeit," he says as he sees Henry approach in the same garb. "And yet, in faith, thou bearest thee like a king." The first sentence suggests the emptiness of Henry's title in that he is not the rightful king; the second suggests the justness of his title in that he is a man who knows how to rule. We notice, however, that the King's life is saved neither by the stratagem of the coats nor by kingly "bearing," but by the chivalry of his son.

## II

The *First Part of Henry IV* was published in 1598; it was probably written and acted in 1596–97. There are some topical allusions in the play to these years, notably the Second Carrier's reference to the high cost of oats that killed Robin Ostler (II.i.12). Topical in a more important sense, during the whole of the 1590's, was the play's general subject matter. Though contemporary concern about succession to the throne need not (though it may) have influenced Shakespeare's choice of materials for his English histories, it inevitably gave them an extra dimension. Elizabeth was now in her sixties, and there was no assured heir, only a multiplicity of candidates, including her sometimes favorite, the Earl of Essex. Many recalled anxiously the chaos in times past when the center of power in the monarchical system had ceased to be sharply defined and clearly visible. This had occurred to an extent after Henry VIII's death, and earlier after Henry V's, and still earlier after the murder of Richard II.

If Shakespeare was at all influenced by these anxieties, his rendering of them is on the whole buoyant and optimistic in his second English tetralogy and especially so in *1 Henry IV*. True, the England seen in this play and its immediate successor is far from reassuring. It has even been described as

> . . . an England, on the one side, of bawdy house and thieves'-kitchen, of waylaid merchants, badgered and bewildered Justices, and a peasantry wretched, betrayed, and recruited for the wars; an England, on the other side, of the chivalrous wolf pack of Hotspur and Douglas, and of state-sponsored treachery in the person of Prince John—the whole presided over by a sick King, hagridden by conscience, dreaming of a Crusade to the Holy Land as M. Remorse [i.e., Falstaff] thinks of slimming and repentance.[2]

But this is only half the picture. Beside it, for the first Henry IV play, we must place the warmth, wit, and high spirits of the tavern scenes, the impetuous charm of Hotspur, the amusing domesticities of Kate and Glendower's daughter, the touching loyalty of Francis, the affections that (along with sponging) bind Falstaff to Hal, and Hal's own magnanimity and self-command. For both the first and second plays, we must weigh heavily into the account the character of the story told. This, the greatest of monarchical success stories in English popular history, traces the evolution of an engaging scapegrace into one of the most admired of English kings. Chicanery and appetite in the first play, apathy and corruption in the second, form an effective theatrical background against which the oncoming sunbright majesty of the future Henry V may shine more brightly—as we are assured precisely that it will do on our first meeting with him (I.ii).

When Shakespeare turned to this subject in 1596–97, he found in his historical sources, mainly Holinshed's *Chronicles,* two dominant motifs. One was the moral and theological interpretation of the troubles attending Henry IV's reign in consequence of his usurpation. This

[2] Danby, J. F., *Shakespeare's Doctrine of Nature: A Study of King Lear.* London: Faber and Faber, 1949, pp. 97–98.

we have already discussed. The other was the legend of the madcap youth of Henry's son and heir—a legend already exploited in an anonymous play of which we have today only a debased and possibly abbreviated text: *The Famous Victories of Henry the Fifth*. The *Famous Victories* contributes to *1 Henry IV* the germ of the robbery incident (though the Prince's involvement in a thieving episode is found in the chronicles as well); the germ of the tavern high jinks and parodying of authority; the germ of the expectation of Hal's reign as a golden age of rascals; and the germ of the reconciliation scene between the Prince and his father. The extent to which these hints are fleshed out and transfigured by Shakespeare's imagination may be seen in the character of Mistress Quickly. Her entire original in the *Famous Victories* is a sentence spoken by the Prince, favoring a rendezvous at "the old tavern in Eastcheap" because "there is a pretty wench that can talk well."

From the *Famous Victories* come also the names Gad's Hill (for the arranger of the robbery), Ned (our Ned Poins), and Jockey Oldcastle. The last was Shakespeare's name for Falstaff when the play was first performed, as references throughout the early seventeenth century show; Hal's addressing him as "my old lad of the castle" in the play as we have it (I.ii.43–44) is a survival from this. By the time the play was printed, the name had been altered to Falstaff for reasons that can now only be guessed at. Possibly there had been a protest by Oldcastle's descendants, one of whom was Lord Chamberlain during part of 1596–97. How the historical Oldcastle (d.1417), a man of character who was made High Sheriff of Herefordshire and eventually Lord Cobham, came to be metamorphosed into the roisterer of the *Famous Victories* is also an unsolved mystery, though no more mysterious than the dramatic imagination that exalted this dull stage roisterer, lacking eloquence, wit, mendacity, thirst, and fat, into the Falstaff we know.

On Holinshed and minor sources like Samuel Daniel's epic *The First Four Books of the Civil Wars between the Two Houses of Lancaster and York* [1595], Shakespeare based his treatment of the Percy rebellion, recasting the materials to give them an inner coherence. The Hotspur of history, for example, was twenty-three years older than Hal and two years older than the King himself, who at the date of the battle of Shrewsbury was only thirty-seven, his eldest son being then sixteen, and Prince John thirteen. Shakespeare followed the lead of Daniel and made Hotspur a youth, in order to establish dramatic rivalry between him and Hal. He then aged Henry rapidly so that by the time of the battle the King can speak of crushing his "old limbs in ungentle steel" and be the more appropriately rescued (this episode is also derived from Daniel) by his vigorous heir. For the same dramatic purpose, he assigned to Hal the triumph over Hotspur—though the inspiration for this may have come from misreading an ambiguous sentence in Holinshed. The reconciliation of Prince and King, touched on in the chronicles and dramatized briefly in the *Famous Victories* as occurring in Henry's latter years, he moved forward to a position before Shrewsbury, in order to enhance the human drama of father and son and further sharpen our anticipation of Hal's meeting with Hotspur. Hotspur's blunt uncourtly humor, the conception of Glendower as scholar and poet fired by a Celtic imagination, the entertaining clash of temperament and mood that this makes possible at Glendower's house, not only between Welshman and Englishman, but between romantic lovers and seasoned man and wife—all this again is Shakespeare's invention. His transformation of Holinshed, like his transformation of the *Famous Victories,* may best be indicated by a specific example. All of Hotspur's deliciously impetuous speech about the popinjay lord who came to Holmedon to demand his prisoners, not to mention the wonderfully ebullient scene in which it occurs, has behind it in Holinshed only seventeen words: "the King demanded of the Earl and his son such Scottish prisoners as were taken at Homeldon. . . ."

Hal's triumphant journey from tippling in taverns to glory on the field of battle derives from one other "source," more influential than any yet mentioned here.

This is the *psychomachia* of the morality plays—that is, the struggle of virtues and vices for possession of a man's soul, a theme acted again and again in the plays of the early sixteenth century, which the drama of Marlowe and Shakespeare superseded. In these plays, youthful virtue is beset by temptations and misleaders but customarily sees the true light at last and is saved. In the same general manner, Prince Hal "has to choose, Morality-fashion, between Sloth or Vanity, to which he is drawn by his bad companions, and Chivalry, to which he is drawn by his father and brothers. And he chooses Chivalry."[3]

## III

The play that Shakespeare built from these miscellaneous materials is simple in its large outlines. It brings before us three contrasting environments at once, each with a commanding personality. The court is Henry's domain; the tavern is Falstaff's; the feudal countryside is Hotspur's. What essentially takes place during the first three acts is the progress of Hal, the one unattached player, from Falstaff's environment to Henry's. Hal then returns in the last scene of Act III to mobilize the tavern world for war, after which Falstaff's environment dissolves. We then have two environments, both military and political in nature, one of them dominated by Hotspur, the other (beginning with Act IV) increasingly by Hal. Falstaff, now in his turn the unattached man, makes appropriate comments on each.

Within this simple framework, Shakespeare accomplishes an articulation of complementary images, cross-references, and ironic contrasts that is without parallel in the history of English stage comedy. The highway robbery comments on the Percys' plot and also on the King's usurpation, as we saw a few moments ago. Gadshill, boasting of the quality of his confederates (II.i), antici-

---

[3] Tillyard, E. M. W. *Shakespeare's History Plays.* London: Chatto and Windus, 1944, p. 265.

pates Hotspur's misplaced confidence in the fidelity of his fellow rebels (II.iii). Falstaff bawling for his horse (II.ii) has satirical affinities with Hotspur chattering to the same purpose (II.iii). Hal describes Hotspur talking to his wife (II.iv) as if he had been an eavesdropper in the scene preceding, and points our attention to a tavern monomania in Francis which is perhaps reminiscent of Hotspur's monomania for "palisadoes, frontiers, parapets." Hotspur describes a presumed but perhaps wholly imaginary fight between Glendower and Mortimer in epic terms (I.iii); Falstaff does the same for a definitely imaginary contest with eleven﹒men in buckram (II.iv). Falstaff keeps telling us he is about to reform; Hal actually does so. Hal's interview with his father (III.ii) is broadened and deepened for us in advance by the burlesque of it (II.iv) and by the failure of Hotspur to achieve a similar self-discipline (III.i). Glendower and Hotspur mirror each other in egoism, contrast vividly in the pedantic refinements of the one, the countrified heartiness of the other. Falstaff's remarks on honor, as everyone knows, complement those we have heard earlier from Hotspur; the comic account of Falstaff's conscripted derelicts corrects and supplements the description of Hal's army by a general who loves parades (IV.i.97ff) and the anticipation of destroying it by a general who loves carnage (IV.i.113ff); Falstaff's cynical "They'll fill a pit as well as better" hangs over the ensuing battle, enveloping especially those who are to fill a pit simply because the King has dressed them in his coats; etc. This list of cross-references could be extended almost indefinitely.

Only through such qualifying optics as these does Shakespeare allow us to view the simple Morality "choice" described by Professor Tillyard. Hotspur is one term in that choice—at first glance, a wholly negative term. He misjudges Henry, seeing only the King's duplicity. He misjudges Hal, seeing only the truant, overlooking Hal's sagacity and versatility. Magnanimity is also beyond his reach. His manners are rude, not courtly. His reaction to Glendower is both impolitic and provincial. Yet the play shows us there is much to be said on behalf of this misguided and hotheaded young man. In many respects, he is set apart from, and above, the company he keeps. In being free of scheming policy, he is differentiated from his uncle Worcester and the King. In fighting (for a time) the nation's battles, he has in the past surpassed Hal. He can be counted on when needed and is thereby distinguished from Glendower, Mortimer, and his father. His valor in battle is total. In this he is unlike Douglas, who makes a fine display of fearlessness but in the pinch flees. And he is naively frank-hearted. Hotspur, Worcester knows, would be moved to meet what seems the King's generous offer of amnesty with equal generosity, and the battle would probably not be fought.

Falstaff, the other term of the choice, is similarly complex. First of all, he is endowed by Shakespeare with a comic imagination that enables him (as Antony will later be enabled by the imagination of Cleopatra) to show his back above the clement he lives in. His shattering of official clichés and stained-glass attitudes throughout the play is a measure of his penetration as well as, sometimes, his irresponsibility: "Why, Hal, 'tis my vocation, Hal. 'Tis no sin for a man to labor in his vocation" (I.ii.108–09); "A plague of sighing and grief, it blows a man up like a bladder" (II.iv.332–33); "Thou knowest in the state of innocency Adam fell, and what should poor Jack Falstaff do in the days of villainy? Thou seest I have more flesh than another man, and therefore more frailty" (III.iii.169–73); "Rebellion lay in his way, and he found it" (V.i.28). These show the same gift of comic insight that enables him to multiply images of himself as a shotten herring or a poulterer's hare, to raise the stock role of *miles gloriosus*, or braggart soldier, into the most rapturous flight of mendacity the comic stage has ever seen (II.iv), and to fling into the tense silence before the robbery one of those searching questions about the nature of man and his societies that a wide-eyed child will sometimes propound: "Zounds, will they not rob *us?*" (II.ii.64). (In *2 Henry IV*, appealing to "law of nature" to account for the way of a pike with a dace, he will make this Hobbist question a proposition).

Falstaff is also set apart by his genuine affections, his joy in his friends: "Gallants, lads, boys, hearts of gold, all the titles of good fellowship come to you!" (II.iv.278–80). He is even set apart by a certain kind of honesty. He will lie to others inexhaustibly, but that life is sweeter to him than honor, sack than killing, money in the pocket more gratifying than a fine squad of soldiers, he never seeks to hide from himself. Yet it would be folly to ignore that his honesty makes him no less a rascal, his affection no less a parasite, his perspicacity about some matters no less willful-blind about the rest. Falstaff is much more than —but he also is—a glutton, drunkard, liar, coward, and thief.

Hotspur and Falstaff are extremes, and we see the gulf that separates them when Hotspur goes down fighting while Falstaff plays dead to save his skin. But extremes (so runs the familiar saying) meet, and we see them meet when Falstaff, having taken Hotspur's body on his back, assures Hal he is "not a double man." The phrase reminds us that he and Hotspur are in some respects outsized versions of the same thing. Both are chivalric figures, Falstaff being, however backslidden, a knight; both exemplify ways in which chivalry may go to seed. "A hare-brained Hotspur, governed by a spleen," as his uncle Worcester describes him, can sacrifice to spleen a true knight's fealty and stain the honor he so prizes by making it the ground his egoism walks on. As for Falstaff, that "huge bombard of sack," that "roast Manningtree ox with the pudding in his belly": in his knight's bosom, "there's no room for faith, truth, nor honesty; . . . it is all filled up with guts and midriff."

Falstaff and Hotspur help us see that Hal's course is a mean between extremes. King Henry helps us see that Hal's mean is not a path of least resistance but a creative will that points toward a new kind of world. A master of appearances, as his description of his behavior in King Richard's time informs us (III.ii), Henry is at the same time their victim. If he seriously imagines that he would ever actually go on that Crusade whose "dear expedience" occupies his council at the opening of the play (I.i), he is obviously self-deceived; if he does not intend to go, it is a calculated charade. The sketches of Hotspur and his son which he draws for us in the same scene are unmistakably sincere; but we soon discover they are wrong —mere stereotypes of martial prowess and libertinism. Henry does not really understand either his son or Hotspur. When he holds up Hotspur for a model in the reconciliation scene (III.ii), when he exhibits his delusion that what he was to King Richard, Hotspur is now to Hal, when he speaks of Hal's "barren pleasures" to us who have just seen the tavern bulge with an energy and feeling never to be matched at Henry's court, we understand how far he has become prisoner of a royalism that is less imaginative than his son's. And when the battle comes, we understand more clearly against this background the meaning of the contrasts there: the King "has many marching in his coats"; the Prince offers to decide the issue by taking the danger on himself alone; the King, thinking in political terms, sends his enemies to execution and within these terms is perfectly right to do so; the Prince thinks in larger terms and spares Douglas, not for political reasons (though doubtless he is aware of these), but because, as in his praise of Hotspur, he can cherish "high deeds/Even in the bosom of our adversaries." Even Falstaff at his most ignominious, wounding Hotspur's corpse and claiming credit for having killed him, the Prince can bring himself to excuse; he will gild his lie "with the happiest terms I have."

Thus by the play's end, Hal casts an inclusive shadow. He has met the claims of Hotspur's world, of Falstaff's, and of Henry's, without narrowing himself to any one. He has practiced mercy as well as justice, politics as well as friendship, shown himself capable of mockery as well as reverence, detachment as well as commitment, and brought into a practicable balance court, field, and tavern. He is on the way to becoming the luminous figure toward whom, in *Henry V*, Welshman, Irishman, Scot, and Englishman will alike be drawn. In this figure, combining valor, courtliness, hard sense, and humor in an ideal image of the potentialities of the English character, Shakespeare seems to have discerned grounds for that optimism about the future of his country which permeates his historical vision in the plays from *Richard II* to *Henry V*. We ourselves may find in it, if not so local and particular an image, glimpses of an ideal form that remains relevant to us—such a form as Socrates and Glaucon, in the ninth book of the *Republic*, allude to in their discussion of the perfect city. Glaucon, the doubter, says: "But the city whose foundation we have been describing has its being only in words; there is no spot on earth where it exists." And Socrates replies: "No; but it is laid up in heaven as a pattern for him who wills to see, and seeing, to found that city in himself. Whether it exists anywhere, or ever will exist, is no matter."

MAYNARD MACK
*Yale University*

# The History of Henry IV
## [PART ONE]

[*Dramatis Personae*

King Henry the Fourth
Henry, Prince of Wales        } the King's sons
Prince John of Lancaster
Earl of Westmoreland
Sir Walter Blunt
Thomas Percy, Earl of Worcester
Henry Percy, Earl of Northumberland
Henry Percy ("Hotspur"), his son
Edmund Mortimer, Earl of March
Richard Scroop, Archbishop of York
Archibald, Earl of Douglas
Owen Glendower
Sir Richard Vernon
Sir John Falstaff
Sir Michael, a friend of the Archbishop of York
Poins
Gadshill
Peto
Bardolph
Francis, a waiter
Lady Percy, Hotspur's wife and Mortimer's sister
Lady Mortimer, Glendower's daughter and Mortimer's wife
Mistress Quickly, hostess of the tavern
Sheriff, Vintner, Chamberlain, two Carriers, Ostler, Messengers, Travelers, Attendants

*Scene:* England and Wales]

# The History of Henry IV

## [PART ONE]

## [ACT I

### Scene I. *London. The palace.*]

*Enter the King, Lord John of Lancaster, Earl of Westmoreland, [Sir Walter Blunt,] with others.*

*King.* So shaken as we are, so wan with care,
  Find we a time for frighted peace to pant°1
  And breathe short-winded accents of new broils
  To be commenced in stronds° afar remote.
  No more the thirsty entrance of this soil      5
  Shall daub her lips with her own children's blood,
  No more shall trenching° war channel her fields,
  Nor bruise her flow'rets with the armèd hoofs
  Of hostile paces. Those opposèd eyes
  Which, like the meteors° of a troubled heaven,    10
  All of one nature, of one substance bred,°
  Did lately meet in the intestine° shock
  And furious close° of civil butchery,
  Shall now in mutual well-beseeming° ranks
  March all one way and be no more opposed    15
  Against acquaintance, kindred, and allies.

---

1 The degree sign (°) indicates a footnote, which is keyed to the text by line number. Text references are printed in **boldface** type; the annotation follows in roman type.
I.i.2 **pant** catch (her) breath   4 **stronds** shores   7 **trenching** (1) cutting (2) encroaching   10 **meteors** atmospheric disturbances   11 **All ... bred** i.e., because believed to originate from vapors   12 **intestine** internal   13 **close** grappling   14 **mutual well-beseeming** interdependent well-ordered

The edge of war, like an ill-sheathèd knife,
No more shall cut his master. Therefore, friends,
As far as to the sepulcher of Christ°—
20  Whose soldier now, under whose blessèd cross
We are impressèd and engaged° to fight—
Forthwith a power° of English shall we levy,
Whose arms were molded in their mother's womb
To chase these pagans in those holy fields
25  Over whose acres walked those blessèd feet
Which fourteen hundred years ago were nailed
For our advantage on the bitter cross.
But this our purpose now is twelvemonth old,
And bootless° 'tis to tell you we will go.
30  Therefor we meet not now.° Then let me hear
Of you, my gentle cousin° Westmoreland,
What yesternight our council did decree
In forwarding this dear expedience.°

*Westmoreland.* My liege, this haste was hot in ques-
        tion°
35  And many limits of the charge° set down
But yesternight; when all athwart° there came
A post° from Wales, loaden with heavy news,
Whose worst was that the noble Mortimer,
Leading the men of Herefordshire to fight
40  Against the irregular and wild° Glendower,
Was by the rude hands of that Welshman taken,
A thousand of his people butcherèd;
Upon whose dead corpse there was such misuse,
Such beastly shameless transformation
45  By those Welshwomen done, as may not be
Without much shame retold or spoken of.°

19 As ... Christ i.e., to Jerusalem  21 impressèd and engaged conscripted and pledged (i.e., by Henry's vow after the murder of
Richard: cf. *Richard II*, V.vi.45–50)  22 power army  29 bootless
useless  30 Therefor ... now that is not the reason we now meet
31 gentle cousin noble kinsman  33 dear expedience urgent enterprise  34 hot in question undergoing hot discussion  35 limits of
the charge apportionings of tasks and costs  36 athwart crosswise,
i.e., interfering  37 post messenger  40 irregular and wild i.e., as
border-raider and guerrilla  43–46 such ... spoken of (the phras-
ing in Holinshed, Shakespeare's source, suggests that the dead English were castrated)

*King.* It seems then that the tidings of this broil
   Brake off our business for the Holy Land.

*Westmoreland.* This, matched with other, did, my
      gracious lord;
   For more uneven° and unwelcome news                    50
   Came from the north, and thus it did import:
   On Holy-rood Day° the gallant Hotspur there,
   Young Harry Percy, and brave Archibald,
   That ever-valiant and approvèd Scot,
   At Holmedon° met, where they did spend                 55
   A sad and bloody hour;
   As by discharge of their artillery
   And shape of likelihood° the news was told;
   For he that brought them,° in the very heat
   And pride of their contention° did take horse,         60
   Uncertain of the issue° any way.

*King.* Here is a dear, a true industrious° friend,
   Sir Walter Blunt, new lighted from his horse,
   Stained with the variation of each soil
   Betwixt that Holmedon and this seat° of ours,          65
   And he hath brought us smooth and welcome news.
   The Earl of Douglas is discomfited;
   Ten thousand bold Scots, two and twenty knights,
   Balked° in their own blood did Sir Walter see
   On Holmedon's plains. Of prisoners, Hotspur took       70
   Mordake, Earl of Fife and eldest son
   To beaten Douglas, and the Earl of Athol,
   Of Murray, Angus, and Menteith.
   And is not this an honorable spoil?
   A gallant prize? Ha, cousin, is it not?                75

*Westmoreland.* In faith it is. A conquest for a prince
      to boast of.

---

50 uneven cf. "smooth," line 66   52 Holy-rood Day September 14
55 Holmedon Humbleton in Northumberland   58 shape of likelihood probability   59 them i.e., the news   59–60 heat . . . conten-
tion peak of battle   61 issue outcome   62 true industrious loyally
zealous   65 seat dwelling, i.e., the palace   69 Balked (1) heaped
(2) thwarted

*King.* Yea, there thou mak'st me sad, and mak'st me
          sin
          In envy that my Lord Northumberland
          Should be the father to so blest a son:
80        A son who is the theme of honor's tongue,
          Amongst a grove the very straightest plant;
          Who is sweet fortune's minion° and her pride;
          Whilst I, by looking on the praise of him,
          See riot and dishonor stain the brow
85        Of my young Harry. O that it could be proved
          That some night-tripping fairy° had exchanged
          In cradle clothes our children where they lay,
          And called mine Percy, his Plantagenet!°
          Then would I have his Harry, and he mine.
90        But let him from my thoughts. What think you, coz,°
          Of this young Percy's pride? The prisoners
          Which he in this adventure hath surprised°
          To his own use he keeps, and sends me word
          I shall have none but Mordake, Earl of Fife.

*Westmoreland.* This is his uncle's teaching, this is
95        Worcester,
          Malevolent to you in all aspects,°
          Which makes him prune° himself and bristle up
          The crest of youth against your dignity.

*King.* But I have sent for him to answer this;
100       And for this cause awhile we must neglect
          Our holy purpose to Jerusalem.
          Cousin, on Wednesday next our council we
          Will hold at Windsor, so inform the lords:
          But come yourself with speed to us again,
105       For more is to be said and to be done
          Than out of anger can be utter°d.°

*Westmoreland.* I will, my liege.          *Exeunt.*

82. **minion** darling  86 **fairy** (fairies were thought sometimes to
steal a beautiful infant, leaving an ugly "changeling" in its place
88 **Plantagenet** family name of Henry IV  90 **coz** kinsman (short
for "cousin")  92 **surprised** taken  96 **Malevolent . . . aspects** (an
astrological expression comparing Worcester to a planet whose influence obstructs Henry's designs)  97 **prune** preen his feathers for
action (like a hawk)  106 **uttered** transacted in public

[Scene II. *London. The Prince's lodging.*]

*Enter Prince of Wales and Sir John Falstaff.*

*Falstaff.* Now, Hal, what time of day is it, lad?

*Prince.* Thou art so fat-witted with drinking of old
sack,° and unbuttoning thee after supper, and sleeping upon benches after noon, that thou hast forgotten to demand that truly which thou wouldest        5
truly know. What a devil hast thou to do with the
time of the day? Unless hours were cups of sack,
and minutes capons, and clocks the tongues of
bawds, and dials° the signs of leaping houses,° and
the blessed sun himself a fair hot wench in flame-    10
colored taffeta, I see no reason why thou shouldst
be so superfluous to° demand the time of the day.

*Falstaff.* Indeed you come near me° now, Hal; for we
that take purses go by° the moon and the seven
stars,° and not by Phoebus,° he, that wand'ring      15
knight so fair.° And I prithee, sweet wag, when thou
art a king, as, God save thy Grace°—Majesty I
should say, for grace thou wilt have none—

*Prince.* What, none?

---

I.ii.3 **sack** Spanish white wine   9 **dials** sundials   9 **leaping houses**
brothels   12 **so superfluous to** so irrelevant as to   13 **near me** i.e.,
close to understanding me (as if Hal were shooting at a mark)
14 **go by** (1) walk under (2) tell time by (3) regulate our lives by
14–15 **seven stars** constellation Pleiades   15 **Phoebus** the sun   15–
16 **he . . . fair** (Falstaff possibly quotes here, or sings, a line of a lost
ballad; the sun was readily thought of as an eternal wanderer or
"knight-errant")   17 **Grace** (Falstaff puns on "your Grace"—a title
which Hal as king will exchange for "your Majesty"—and spiritual
grace and, in lines 20–21, on grace before eating)

20 *Falstaff.* No, by my troth; not so much as will serve to
be prologue to an egg and butter.

*Prince.* Well, how then? Come, roundly, roundly.°

*Falstaff.* Marry,° then, sweet wag, when thou art king,
let not us that are squires of the night's body be
25 called thieves of the day's beauty.° Let us be
Diana's° foresters, gentlemen of the shade, minions°
of the moon; and let men say we be men of good
government,° being governed, as the sea is, by our
noble and chaste mistress the moon, under whose
30 countenance we steal.

*Prince.* Thou sayest well, and it holds well° too; for
the fortune of us that are the moon's men doth ebb
and flow like the sea, being governed as the sea is
by the moon. As, for proof now: a purse of gold
35 most resolutely snatched on Monday night and most
dissolutely spent on Tuesday morning; got with
swearing "Lay by," and spent with crying "Bring
in";° now in as low an ebb as the foot of the ladder,°
and by and by in as high a flow as the ridge of the
40 gallows.

*Falstaff.* By the Lord, thou say'st true, lad—and is not
my hostess of the tavern a most sweet wench?

<hr>

22 **roundly** i.e., get to the point (but possibly with a glance at Falstaff's girth)    23 **Marry** (a mild oath, from "By the Virgin Mary") 24–25 **squires . . . beauty** (Falstaff's puns on "night/knight"—knights were often attended by body-squires—and probably on "body/beauty/booty." The "day's beauty" in one of its senses here is the sun and balances "the night's body," which in one sense is the moon) 26 **Diana** goddess of the moon and the hunt (by identifying the hunt with hunting for "booty"—and "beauty"—Falstaff presents himself and his crew as Diana's companion foresters, her titled "Gentlemen of the Shade," her "minions," who "steal"—i.e., [1] move silently [2] take purses under her "countenance"—i.e., under [1] her face [2] her protection)    26 **minions** servants and favorites    27–28 **of good government** (1) well-behaved (2) ruled by a good ruler    31 **it holds well** it's a good comparison    37–38 **Lay by . . . Bring in** (the highwayman's commands: the first to his victims, the second to the waiter in the tavern where he spends his gains)    38 **ladder** (leading up to the gallows)

*Prince.* As the honey of Hybla,° my old lad of the
castle°—and is not a buff jerkin° a most sweet robe
of durance?                                                    45

*Falstaff.* How now, how now, mad wag? What, in thy
quips and thy quiddities?° What a plague have I to
do with a buff jerkin?

*Prince.* Why, what a pox° have I to do with my hostess
of the tavern?                                                50

*Falstaff.* Well, thou hast called her to a reckoning°
many a time and oft.

*Prince.* Did I ever call for thee to pay thy part?

*Falstaff.* No; I'll give thee thy due, thou hast paid all
there.                                                         55

*Prince.* Yea, and elsewhere, so far as my coin would
stretch; and where it would not, I have used my
credit.

*Falstaff.* Yea, and so used it that, were it not here apparent that thou art heir apparent—But I prithee,   60
sweet wag, shall there be gallows standing in England
when thou art king? And resolution thus fubbed°
as it is with the rusty curb of old father Antic° the
law? Do not thou, when thou art king, hang a thief.

*Prince.* No; thou shalt.                                      65

*Falstaff.* Shall I? O rare! By the Lord, I'll be a brave°
judge.

43 **Hybla** Sicilian source of fine honey   43–44 **old lad of the castle**
rowdy (with pun on "Oldcastle," Falstaff's original name, and probably on "The Castle," a well-known London brothel)   44 **buff
jerkin** tan (leather) jacket (a "robe of durance" because both durable
and suggesting imprisonment [durance] because worn by the
sheriff's officers)   46–47 **What . . . quiddities** "So you're in a witty
mood, are you?"   49 **pox** (the Prince turns Falstaff's "plague" into
a disease more characteristic of tavern hostesses)   51 **called her to a
reckoning** (1) called her to a showdown (2) asked her for the bill
62 **resolution thus fubbed** courage (i.e., in the highwayman) thus
cheated of its reward   63 **old father Antic** i.e., "that old screwball"
66 **brave** (1) excellent (2) handsomely decked out

*Prince.* Thou judgest false already. I mean, thou shalt
have the hanging of the thieves and so become a rare
70    hangman.

*Falstaff.* Well, Hal, well; and in some sort it jumps
with my humor° as well as waiting in the court, I
can tell you.

*Prince.* For obtaining of suits?°

75   *Falstaff.* Yea, for obtaining of suits, whereof the hangman hath no lean wardrobe. 'Sblood,° I am as
melancholy as a gib-cat° or a lugged° bear.

*Prince.* Or an old lion, or a lover's lute.

*Falstaff.* Yea, or the drone° of a Lincolnshire bagpipe.

80   *Prince.* What sayest thou to a hare,° or the melancholy
of Moorditch?°

*Falstaff.* Thou hast the most unsavory similes, and art
indeed the most comparative,° rascalliest, sweet
young prince. But, Hal, I prithee trouble me no
85    more with vanity.° I would to God thou and I knew
where a commodity° of good names were to be
bought. An old lord of the council rated° me the
other day in the street about you, sir, but I marked
him not; and yet he talked very wisely, but I re-
90    garded him not; and yet he talked wisely, and in the
street too.

---

71–72 **jumps with my humor** agrees with my frame of mind   74 **suits**
petitions for court favor (but Falstaff takes it in the sense of the
victim's garments, which were forfeit to the executioner)   76 **'Sblood**
by God's (i.e., Christ's) blood   77 **gib-cat** tomcat   77 **lugged** i.e.,
tied to a stake and baited by dogs, as entertainment   79 **drone**
single note of a bagpipe's bass pipe   80 **hare** (proverbially melancholy)   81 **Moorditch** foul London drainage ditch   83 **comparative**
full of (insulting) comparisons   85 **vanity** i.e., worldly considerations
(Falstaff here takes up one of his favorite humorous roles, assuming
for the next several lines the sanctimonious attitudes and vocabulary
of Elizabethan Puritanism)   86 **commodity** supply   87 **rated** scolded

*Prince.* Thou didst well, for wisdom cries out in the
streets, and no man regards it.°

*Falstaff.* O, thou hast damnable iteration,° and art
indeed able to corrupt a saint. Thou hast done much      *95*
harm upon me, Hal—God forgive thee for it! Before I knew thee, Hal, I knew nothing; and now
am I, if a man should speak truly, little better than
one of the wicked.° I must give over this life, and
I will give it over! By the Lord, and° I do not, I      *100*
am a villain! I'll be damned for never a king's son
in Christendom.

*Prince.* Where shall we take a purse tomorrow, Jack?

*Falstaff.* Zounds,° where thou wilt, lad! I'll make one.
An° I do not, call me villain and baffle° me.      *105*

*Prince.* I see a good amendment of life in thee—from
praying to purse-taking.

*Falstaff.* Why, Hal, 'tis my vocation,° Hal. 'Tis no sin
for a man to labor in his vocation.

*Enter Poins.*

Poins! Now shall we know if Gadshill have set a      *110*
match.° O, if men were to be saved by merit,° what
hole in hell were hot enough for him? This is the
most omnipotent villain that ever cried "Stand!" to
a true° man.

---

92–93 **Thou . . . it** (Hal quotes Proverbs 1:20–24: "Wisdom crieth
without, and putteth forth her voice in the streets . . . saying . . . 'I
have stretched out my hand, and no man regarded' ")      94 **damnable
iteration** i.e., a sinful way of repeating and (mis)applying holy texts
99 **the wicked** (Puritan idiom for those who were not Puritans; cf.
"saint" in 95, which glances at the Puritans' way of referring
collectively to themselves)      100 **and if**      104 **Zounds** by God's
(i.e., Christ's) wounds      105 **An if**      105 **baffle** hang upside down
(a punishment allotted perjured knights)      108 **vocation** calling (with
reference to the Puritan stress on a man's being "called" by God to
his work)      110–11 **set a match** arranged a robbery      111 **merit** i.e.,
good works (in Puritan doctrine wholly insufficient for salvation)
114 **true** honest

115 *Prince.* Good morrow, Ned.

*Poins.* Good morrow, sweet Hal. What says Monsieur
    Remorse? What says Sir John Sack and Sugar?°
    Jack, how agrees the devil and thee about thy soul,
    that thou soldest him on Good Friday last for a cup
120  of Madeira and a cold capon's leg?

*Prince.* Sir John stands to his word, the devil shall
    have his bargain; for he was never yet a breaker of
    proverbs. He will give the devil his due.

*Poins.* Then art thou damned for keeping thy word
125  with the devil.

*Prince.* Else he had been damned for cozening° the
    devil.

*Poins.* But, my lads, my lads, tomorrow morning, by
    four o'clock early, at Gad's Hill!° There are pil-
130  grims going to Canterbury with rich offerings,° and
    traders riding to London with fat purses. I have
    vizards° for you all; you have horses for yourselves.
    Gadshill lies tonight in Rochester. I have bespoke
    supper tomorrow night in Eastcheap.° We may do
135  it as secure as sleep. If you will go, I will stuff your
    purses full of crowns; if you will not, tarry at home
    and be hanged!

*Falstaff.* Hear ye, Yedward:° if I tarry at home and
    go not, I'll hang you for going.

140 *Poins.* You will, chops?°

*Falstaff.* Hal, wilt thou make one?

*Prince.* Who, I rob? I a thief? Not I, by my faith.

*Falstaff.* There's neither honesty, manhood, nor good

---

117 **Sack and Sugar** (sack sweetened with sugar was particularly
the drink of the elderly, but there may be a pun, in this context, on
sackcloth, symbol of penance)    126 **cozening** cheating    129 **Gad's
Hill** (a place notorious for holdups on the road from Rochester to
London)    130 **offerings** i.e., for the shrine of St. Thomas à Becket
132 **vizards** masks    134 **Eastcheap** London street and district    138
**Yedward** (dialect form of Edward)    140 **chops** "fat-face"

fellowship in thee, nor thou cam'st not of the blood
royal° if thou darest not stand for° ten shillings.      *145*

*Prince.* Well then, once in my days I'll be a madcap.

*Falstaff.* Why, that's well said.

*Prince.* Well, come what will, I'll tarry at home.

*Falstaff.* By the Lord, I'll be a traitor then, when thou
art king.                                                *150*

*Prince.* I care not.

*Poins.* Sir John, I prithee, leave the Prince and me
alone. I will lay him down such reasons for this
adventure that he shall go.

*Falstaff.* Well, God give thee the spirit of persuasion    *155*
and him the ears of profiting, that what thou speak-
est may move° and what he hears may be believed,
that the true prince may (for recreation sake) prove
a false thief; for the poor abuses of the time want
countenance.° Farewell; you shall find me in East-    *160*
cheap.

*Prince.* Farewell, the° latter spring! Farewell, All-
hallow summer!°                          [*Exit Falstaff.*]

*Poins.* Now, my good sweet honey lord, ride with us
tomorrow. I have a jest to execute that I cannot    *165*
manage alone. Falstaff, Bardolph, Peto, and Gadshill
shall rob those men that we have already waylaid;°
yourself and I will not be there; and when they have
the booty, if you and I do not rob them, cut this
head off from my shoulders.                              *170*

*Prince.* How shall we part with them in setting forth?

145 **royal** (pun on "royal," a ten-shilling coin)   145 **stand for** (1)
pass for (as a coin) (2) contest for (in a robbery)   155–57 **God . . .
move** (mimicry again of the Puritans, who claimed to act only when
the spirit moved in them)   159–60 **want countenance** lack protection (royal and aristocratic)   162 **the** (sometimes used in the sixteenth century for "thou" and "you")   162–63 **All-hallow summer**
(Poins compares Falstaff's youthfulness in old age to the belated
summer that occurs around All Hallows day)   167 **waylaid** set our
trap for

*Poins.* Why, we will set forth before or after them and
appoint them a place of meeting, wherein it is at our
pleasure to fail; and then will they adventure upon
175   the exploit themselves, which they shall have no
sooner achieved, but we'll set upon them.

*Prince.* Yea, but 'tis like that they will know us by our
horses, by our habits,° and by every other appointment,° to be ourselves.

180   *Poins.* Tut! Our horses they shall not see—I'll tie them
in the wood; our vizards we will change after we
leave them; and, sirrah,° I have cases of buckram
for the nonce,° to immask our noted outward garments.

185   *Prince.* Yea, but I doubt° they will be too hard for us.

*Poins.* Well, for two of them, I know them to be as
true-bred cowards as ever turned back; and for the
third, if he fight longer than he sees reason, I'll
forswear arms. The virtue of this jest will be the
190   incomprehensible° lies that this same fat rogue will
tell us when we meet at supper: how thirty, at least,
he fought with; what wards,° what blows, what ex-
tremities he endured; and in the reproof° of this
lives the jest.

195   *Prince.* Well, I'll go with thee. Provide us all things
necessary and meet me tomorrow night° in Eastcheap. There I'll sup. Farewell.

*Poins.* Farewell, my lord.                                    *Exit.*

*Prince.* I know you all, and will awhile uphold
200       The unyoked humor° of your idleness.

---

178 habits dress   178-79 appointment piece of equipment   182
sirrah (term of address showing great familiarity)   182-183 cases
... nonce outer coverings of coarse linen for the purpose   185 doubt
fear   190 incomprehensible unlimited   192 wards strategies of defense (in swordsmanship)   193 reproof disproof   196 tomorrow
night (they will meet for the robbery tomorrow morning, but Hal
is thinking ahead to the jest on Falstaff that night)   200 unyoked
humor undisciplined inclinations

Yet herein will I imitate the sun,°
Who doth permit the base contagious° clouds
To smother up his beauty from the world,
That, when he please again to be himself,
Being wanted,° he may be more wond'red at     *205*
By breaking through the foul and ugly mists
Of vapors that did seem to strangle him.
If all the year were playing holidays,
To sport would be as tedious as to work;
But when they seldom come, they wished-for come,   *210*
And nothing pleaseth but rare accidents.°
So when this loose behavior I throw off
And pay the debt I never promisèd,
By how much better than my word I am,
By so much shall I falsify men's hopes;°     *215*
And, like bright metal on a sullen° ground,
My reformation, glitt'ring o'er my fault,
Shall show more goodly and attract more eyes
Than that which hath no foil° to set it off.
I'll so offend to make offense a skill,     *220*
Redeeming time° when men think least I will. *Exit*.

201 sun (royalty's traditional symbol)    202 **contagious** (clouds were thought to breed pestilence)    205 **wanted** lacked, missed   211 **rare accidents** unexpected or uncommon events   215 **hopes** expectations   216 **sullen** dull   219 **foil** contrasting background   221 **Redeeming time** making amends (Hal alludes to Ephesians 5:7ff, which bears in a general way on much that has been said in this scene: "Be not ye therefore partakers with them, for ye were sometimes darkness, but now are ye light in the Lord: walk as children of light. . . . See then that ye walk circumspectly, not as fools, but as wise. Redeeming the time, because the days are evil).

[Scene III. *Windsor. The council chamber.*]

*Enter the King, Northumberland, Worcester,
Hotspur, Sir Walter Blunt, with others.*

*King.* My blood hath been too cold and temperate,
　　Unapt to stir at these indignities,
　　And you have found me,° for accordingly
　　You tread upon my patience; but be sure
5　　I will from henceforth rather be myself,°
　　Mighty and to be feared, than my condition,°
　　Which hath been smooth as oil, soft as young down,
　　And therefore lost that title of respect
　　Which the proud soul ne'er pays but to the proud.

*Worcester.* Our house, my sovereign liege, little de-
10　　serves
　　The scourge of greatness to be used on it—
　　And that same greatness too which our own hands
　　Have holp° to make so portly.°

*Northumberland.*　　　　　　My lord—

*King.* Worcester, get thee gone, for I do see
15　　Danger and disobedience in thine eye.
　　O, sir, your presence is too bold and peremptory,
　　And majesty might never yet endure
　　The moody frontier° of a servant brow.
　　You have good leave to leave us: when we need
20　　Your use and counsel, we shall send for you.
　　　　　　　　　　　　　　　　*Exit Worcester.*
　　You were about to speak.

---

I.iii.3 **found me** found me out　5 **myself** i.e., what I am as king
6 **my condition** i.e., what I am by nature　13 **holp** helped　13 **portly**
stately　18 **frontier** rampart (as if Worcester were an enemy fortress)

*Northumberland.*　　　　　　　Yea, my good lord.
　Those prisoners in your Highness' name demanded
　Which Harry Percy here at Holmedon took,
　Were, as he says, not with such strength denied
　As is deliverèd to your Majesty.　　　　　　　　　25
　Either envy,° therefore, or misprision°
　Is guilty of this fault, and not my son.

*Hotspur.* My liege, I did deny no prisoners.
　But I remember, when the fight was done,
　When I was dry with rage and extreme toil,　　　　30
　Breathless and faint, leaning upon my sword,
　Came there a certain lord, neat and trimly dressed,
　Fresh as a bridegroom, and his chin new reaped°
　Showed like a stubble land at harvest home.
　He was perfumèd like a milliner,　　　　　　　　35
　And 'twixt his finger and his thumb he held
　A pouncet box,° which ever and anon
　He gave his nose, and took't away again;
　Who° therewith angry, when it next came there,
　Took it in snuff;° and still he smiled and talked;　40
　And as the soldiers bore dead bodies by,
　He called them untaught knaves, unmannerly,
　To bring a slovenly unhandsome corse°
　Betwixt the wind and his nobility.
　With many holiday and lady° terms　　　　　　　45
　He questioned° me, amongst the rest demanded
　My prisoners in your Majesty's behalf.
　I then, all smarting with my wounds being cold,
　To be so pest'red with a popingay,°
　Out of my grief° and my impatience　　　　　　　50
　Answered neglectingly, I know not what—
　He should, or he should not; for he made me mad
　To see him shine so brisk, and smell so sweet,

---

26 **envy** malice　26 **misprision** misapprehension　33 **reaped** i.e., with the closely clipped beard of a man of fashion　37 **pouncet box** perfume box　39 **Who** i.e., his nose　40 **Took it in snuff** (proverbial, meaning "took offense," but here with pun on "snuffing" the perfume)　43 **corse** corpse　45 **holiday and lady** fastidious and effeminate　46 **questioned** talked to　49 **popingay** parrot (here, one who is gaudy in dress and chatters emptily)　50 **grief** pain

And talk so like a waiting gentlewoman
Of guns and drums and wounds—God save the
55    mark!°—
And telling me the sovereignest° thing on earth
Was parmacity° for an inward bruise,
And that it was great pity, so it was,
This villainous saltpeter should be digged
60    Out of the bowels of the harmless earth,
Which many a good tall° fellow had destroyed
So cowardly, and but for these vile guns,
He would himself have been a soldier.
This bald unjointed chat of his, my lord,
65    I answered indirectly,° as I said,
And I beseech you, let not his report
Come current° for an accusation
Betwixt my love and your high Majesty.

*Blunt.* The circumstance considerèd, good my lord,
70    Whate'er Lord Harry Percy then had said
To such a person, and in such a place,
At such a time, with all the rest retold,
May reasonably die, and never rise
To do him wrong,° or any way impeach
75    What then he said, so° he unsay it now.

*King.* Why, yet he doth deny his prisoners,
But with proviso and exception,
That we at our own charge shall ransom straight
His brother-in-law, the foolish Mortimer;
80    Who, on my soul, hath willfully betrayed
The lives of those that he did lead to fight
Against that great magician, damned Glendower—
Whose daughter, as we hear, that Earl of March
Hath lately married. Shall our coffers, then,
85    Be emptied to redeem a traitor home?

---

**55 God save the mark** (a ritual phrase originally used to invoke a blessing, but here expressing scorn)  **56 sovereignest** best  **57 parmacity** spermaceti (medicinal substance found in sperm whales)  **61 tall** stalwart  **65 indirectly** absently  **67 Come current** (1) be accepted (i.e., as of true coin) (2) intrude  **74 To do him wrong** i.e., to be held against him  **75 so** provided

Shall we buy treason, and indent° with fears°
When they have lost and forfeited themselves?
No, on the barren mountains let him starve!
For I shall never hold that man my friend
Whose tongue shall ask me for one penny cost          90
To ransom home revolted Mortimer.

*Hotspur.* Revolted Mortimer?
He never did fall off, my sovereign liege,
But by the chance of war. To prove that true
Needs no more but one tongue for all those wounds,          95
Those mouthèd wounds,° which valiantly he took
When on the gentle Severn's sedgy bank,
In single opposition hand to hand,
He did confound° the best part of an hour
In changing hardiment° with great Glendower.          100
Three times they breathed,° and three times did they
     drink,
Upon agreement, of swift Severn's flood;
Who° then affrighted with their bloody looks
Ran fearfully among the trembling reeds
And hid his crisp° head in the hollow bank,          105
Bloodstainèd with these valiant combatants.
Never did bare and rotten policy°
Color° her working with such deadly wounds;
Nor never could the noble Mortimer
Receive so many, and all willingly.          110
Then let not him be slanderèd with revolt.°

*King.* Thou dost belie° him, Percy, thou dost belie him!
He never did encounter with Glendower.
I tell thee, he durst as well have met the devil alone
As Owen Glendower for an enemy.          115

86 **indent** bargain   86 **fears** (1) cowards (2) traitors, i.e., those who
by "fear" have yielded to the enemy and so become traitors "to be
feared"   96 **mouthèd wounds** i.e., wounds that speak for him
(based on the likeness of a bloody flesh wound to a mouth)   99 **con-
found** spend   100 **changing hardiment** battling   101 **breathed**
paused for breath   103 **Who** i.e., the river   105 **crisp** (used punningly to mean both "curled" [of a man's head] and "rippling" [of a
river]; "head" also refers punningly to a river's force)   107 **policy**
cunning   108 **Color** (1) disguise (2) redden (i.e., with blood)   111
**revolt** treason   112 **belie** misrepresent

Art thou not ashamed? But, sirrah,° henceforth
Let me not hear you speak of Mortimer.
Send me your prisoners with the speediest means,
Or you shall hear in such a kind from me
120  As will displease you. My Lord Northumberland,
We license your departure with your son.
Send us your prisoners, or you will hear of it.
                    *Exit King, [with Blunt, and train].*

*Hotspur.* And if° the devil come and roar for them,
I will not send them. I will after straight
125  And tell him so, for I will ease my heart,
Albeit I make a hazard of° my head.

*Northumberland.* What, drunk with choler?° Stay, and
    pause awhile.
Here comes your uncle.

                *Enter Worcester.*

*Hotspur.*                Speak of Mortimer?
Zounds, I will speak of him, and let my soul
130  Want mercy if I do not join with him!
Yea, on his part I'll empty all these veins,
And shed my dear blood drop by drop in the dust,
But I will lift the downtrod Mortimer
As high in the air as this unthankful king,
135  As this ingrate and cank'red° Bolingbroke.°

*Northumberland.* Brother, the King hath made your
    nephew mad.

*Worcester.* Who struck this heat up after I was gone?

*Hotspur.* He will forsooth have all my prisoners;
And when I urged the ransom once again
140  Of my wife's brother, then his cheek looked pale,
And on my face he turned an eye of death,
Trembling even at the name of Mortimer.

*Worcester.* I cannot blame him. Was not he pro-
    claimed

116 sirrah (term of address to an inferior, here insulting)   123 And
if if   126 make a hazard of risk   127 choler anger   135 cank'red
infected   135 Bolingbroke i.e., the king

By Richard that dead is, the next of blood?°

*Northumberland.* He was, I heard the proclamation:          *145*
And then it was when the unhappy king
(Whose wrongs in us° God pardon!) did set forth
Upon his Irish expedition;
From whence he intercepted° did return
To be deposed, and shortly murderèd.          *150*

*Worcester.* And for whose death we in the world's wide
    mouth
Live scandalized and foully spoken of.

*Hotspur.* But soft, I pray you, did King Richard then
Proclaim my brother Edmund Mortimer
Heir to the crown?

*Northumberland.*          He did, myself did hear it.          *155*

*Hotspur.* Nay, then I cannot blame his cousin king,
That wished him on the barren mountains starve.
But shall it be that you, that set the crown
Upon the head of this forgetful man,
And for his sake wear the detested blot          *160*
Of murderous subornation°—shall it be
That you a world of curses undergo,
Being the agents or base second means,
The cords, the ladder, or the hangman rather?
O, pardon me that I descend so low          *165*
To show the line° and the predicament°
Wherein you range under this subtle king!
Shall it for shame be spoken in these days,
Or fill up chronicles in time to come,
That men of your nobility and power          *170*
Did gage° them both in an unjust behalf
(As both of you, God pardon it, have done)
To put down Richard, that sweet lovely rose,

144 next of blood i.e., heir to the throne   147 in us at our hands
149 intercepted interrupted   161 murderous subornation confederacy in murder   166 line degree, station (but also "hangman's rope"
[cf. line 164] and "tether" [cf. line 167])   166 predicament category
(but also "perilous position")   171 gage pledge

And plant this thorn, this canker° Bolingbroke?
175 And shall it in more shame be further spoken
That you are fooled, discarded, and shook off
By him for whom these shames ye underwent?
No, yet time serves wherein you may redeem
Your banished honors and restore yourselves
180 Into the good thoughts of the world again;
Revenge the jeering and disdained contempt
Of this proud king, who studies day and night
To answer all the debt he owes to you
Even with the bloody payment of your deaths.
Therefore I say—

185 *Worcester.*          Peace, cousin, say no more;
And now I will unclasp a secret book,
And to your quick-conceiving° discontents
I'll read you matter deep and dangerous,
As full of peril and adventurous spirit
190 As to o'erwalk a current roaring loud
On the unsteadfast footing of a spear.

*Hotspur.* If he fall in, good night, or sink, or swim!°
Send danger from the east unto the west,
So honor cross it from the north to south,
195 And let them grapple. O, the blood more stirs
To rouse a lion than to start a hare!

*Northumberland.* Imagination of some great exploit
Drives him beyond the bounds of patience.

*Hotspur.* By heaven, methinks it were an easy leap
200 To pluck bright honor from the pale-faced moon,
Or dive into the bottom of the deep,
Where fathom line could never touch the ground,
And pluck up drownèd honor by the locks,
So° he that doth redeem her thence might wear
205 Without corrival° all her dignities;
But out upon this half-faced fellowship!°

---

174 **canker** dog-rose (an inferior rose, but with suggestions of "can-
kerworm" and "ulcer")   187 **quick-conceiving** eagerly responsive
192 **good ... swim** i.e., the man is doomed whether he sinks at once
or is swept away by the current   204 **So** provided   205 **corrival**
partner   206 **out ... fellowship** down with this half-and-half sharing
(of honors)

*Worcester.* He apprehends a world of figures° here,
    But not the form of what he should attend.
    Good cousin, give me audience for a while.

*Hotspur.* I cry you mercy.°                        210

*Worcester.* Those same noble Scots that are your
    prisoners—

*Hotspur.* I'll keep them all.
    By God, he shall not have a Scot of them!
    No, if a Scot° would save his soul, he shall not.
    I'll keep them, by this hand!

*Worcester.*               You start away    215
    And lend no ear unto my purposes.
    Those prisoners you shall keep.

*Hotspur.*            Nay, I will! That's flat!
    He said he would not ransom Mortimer,
    Forbade my tongue to speak of Mortimer,
    But I will find him when he lies asleep,    220
    And in his ear I'll hollo "Mortimer."
    Nay, I'll have a starling shall be taught to speak
    Nothing but "Mortimer," and give it him
    To keep his anger still in motion.

*Worcester.* Hear you, cousin, a word.    225

*Hotspur.* All studies° here I solemnly defy°
    Save how to gall and pinch this Bolingbroke;
    And that same sword-and-buckler° Prince of Wales,
    But that I think his father loves him not
    And would be glad he met with some mischance,    230
    I would have him poisonèd with a pot of ale.°

*Worcester.* Farewell, kinsman: I'll talk to you
    When you are better tempered to attend.

---

207 figures (1) figures of speech (2) airy fancies (as opposed
to substantial "form," line 208)   210 cry you mercy beg your
pardon   214 Scot (pun on "scot," meaning "small payment")
226 studies interests   226 defy reject   228 sword-and-buckler "low-
down" (sword and shield were arms of the lower classes)   231 ale
(a further glance at Hal's presumed low tastes, gentlemen's drink
being wine)

*Northumberland.* Why, what a wasp-stung and impatient fool
235  Art thou to break into this woman's mood,
Tying thine ear to no tongue but thine own!

*Hotspur.* Why, look you, I am whipped and scourged
with rods,
Nettled, and stung with pismires,° when I hear
Of this vile politician, Bolingbroke.
240  In Richard's time—what do you call the place?
A plague upon it! It is in Gloucestershire;
'Twas where the madcap duke his uncle kept,°
His uncle York—where I first bowed my knee
Unto this king of smiles, this Bolingbroke—
245  'Sblood!—when you and he came back from Ravens-
purgh°—

*Northumberland.* At Berkeley Castle.

*Hotspur.* You say true.
Why, what a candy deal° of courtesy
This fawning greyhound then did proffer me!
250  "Look when his infant fortune came to age,"
And "gentle Harry Percy," and "kind cousin"—
O, the devil take such cozeners!°—God forgive me!
Good uncle, tell your tale; I have done.

*Worcester.* Nay, if you have not, to it again.
We will stay your leisure.

255  *Hotspur.*                    I have done, i' faith.

*Worcester.* Then once more to your Scottish prisoners:
Deliver them up without their ransom straight,
And make the Douglas' son your only mean
For powers in Scotland—which, for divers reasons
260  Which I shall send you written, be assured
Will easily be granted. [*To Northumberland*] You,
my lord,

238 **pismires** ants   242 **kept** dwelt   245 **Ravenspurgh** harbor in
Yorkshire (where Hotspur's father had gone to take sides with
Bolingbroke—who was returning from exile on the Continent—
against the absent King Richard II)   248 **candy deal** sugared bit
252 **cozeners** cheats (with pun on "cousin" of previous line)

Your son in Scotland being thus employed,
Shall secretly into the bosom creep
Of that same noble prelate well-beloved,
The Archbishop.                                                265

*Hotspur.* Of York, is it not?

*Worcester.* True; who bears hard°
His brother's death at Bristow,° the Lord Scroop.
I speak not this in estimation,°
As what I think might be, but what I know        270
Is ruminated, plotted, and set down,
And only stays but to behold the face
Of that occasion that shall bring it on.

*Hotspur.* I smell it.° Upon my life, it will do well.

*Northumberland.* Before the game is afoot thou still
      let'st slip.°                                                273

*Hotspur.* Why, it cannot choose but be a noble plot.
      And then the power of Scotland and of York
      To join with Mortimer, ha?

*Worcester.*                            And so they shall.

*Hotspur.* In faith, it is exceedingly well aimed.

*Worcester.* And 'tis no little reason bids us speed        280
      To save our heads by raising of a head;°
      For, bear ourselves as even as we can,
      The King will always think him in our debt,
      And think we think ourselves unsatisfied,
      Till he hath found a time to pay us home.°        285
      And see already how he doth begin
      To make us strangers to his looks of love.

*Hotspur.* He does, he does! We'll be revenged on him.

*Worcester.* Cousin, farewell. No further go in this
      Than I by letters shall direct your course.        290

267 **bears hard** (because his brother had been executed by Henry)
268 **Bristow** Bristol  269 **in estimation** as a guess  274 **smell it**
i.e., like a hound catching the scent  275 **let'st slip** let loose (the
dogs)  281 **head** army  285 **home** i.e., with a "home" thrust

When time is ripe, which will be suddenly,°
I'll steal to Glendower and Lord Mortimer,
Where you and Douglas, and our pow'rs at once,
As I will fashion it, shall happily meet,
295 To bear our fortunes in our own strong arms,
Which now we hold at much uncertainty.

*Northumberland.* Farewell, good brother. We shall
thrive, I trust.

*Hotspur.* Uncle, adieu. O, let the hours be short
Till fields and blows and groans applaud our sport!
*Exeunt.*

# [ACT II

## Scene I. *Rochester. An inn yard.*]

*Enter a Carrier with a lantern in his hand.*

*First Carrier.* Heigh-ho! An it be not four by the day,° I'll be hanged. Charles' wain° is over the new chimney, and yet our horse not packed. What, ostler!

*Ostler.* [*Within*] Anon, anon.

*First Carrier.* I prithee, Tom, beat° Cut's saddle, put  5
a few flocks in the point;° poor jade is wrung in the withers° out of all cess.°

### *Enter another Carrier.*

*Second Carrier.* Peas and beans are as dank here as a dog, and that is the next° way to give poor jades the bots.° This house is turned upside down since Robin  10
Ostler died.

*First Carrier.* Poor fellow never joyed since the price of oats rose; it was the death of him.

*Second Carrier.* I think this be the most villainous house in all London road for fleas, I am stung like  15
a tench.°

II.i.1 **by the day** in the morning   2 **Charles' wain** the Great Bear
5 **beat** i.e., to soften it   6 **a few flocks in the point** a little padding
in the pommel   6–7 **wrung in the withers** rubbed raw at the shoulders   7 **out of all cess** to excess   9 **next** nearest   10 **bots** worms
16 **tench** fish with red spots (as if flea-bitten)

*First Carrier.* Like a tench? By the mass, there is ne'er
a king christen could be better bit than I have been°
since the first cock.°

20  *Second Carrier.* Why, they will allow us ne'er a jordan,° and then we leak in your chimney,° and your
chamber-lye° breeds fleas like a loach.°

*First Carrier.* What, ostler! Come away and be hanged!
Come away!

25  *Second Carrier.* I have a gammon° of bacon and two
razes° of ginger, to be delivered as far as Charing
Cross.

*First Carrier.* God's body! The turkeys in my pannier°
are quite starved. What, ostler! A plague on thee,
30  hast thou never an eye in thy head? Canst not hear?
And 'twere not as good deed as drink to break the
pate on thee, I am a very villain. Come, and be
hanged! Hast no faith in thee?

*Enter Gadshill.*

*Gadshill.* Good morrow, carriers, what's o'clock?

35  *First Carrier.* I think it be two o'clock.

*Gadshill.* I prithee lend me thy lantern to see my gelding in the stable.

*First Carrier.* Nay, by God, soft!° I know a trick worth
two of that, i' faith.

40  *Gadshill.* I pray thee lend me thine.

*Second Carrier.* Ay, when? Canst tell?° Lend me thy
lantern, quoth he? Marry, I'll see thee hanged first!

---

17-18 there . . . been i.e., not even a Christian king (though kings
get the best of everything) could have surpassed my record in flea-
bites   19 the first cock midnight   20-21 jordan chamberpot   21
chimney fireplace   22 chamber-lye urine   22 loach fish that breeds
often   25 gammon haunch   26 razes roots   28 pannier basket   38
soft i.e., "listen to him!"   41 Ay, when? Canst tell? (standard retort
to an inopportune request)

*Gadshill.* Sirrah°carrier, what time do you mean to
   come to London?

*Second Carrier.* Time enough to go to bed with a    45
   candle,° I warrant thee. Come, neighbor Mugs, we'll
   call up the gentlemen, they will along with company,
   for they have great charge.°         *Exeunt [Carriers].*

*Gadshill.* What, ho! Chamberlain!

                  *Enter Chamberlain.*

*Chamberlain.* "At hand,° quoth pickpurse."                    50

*Gadshill.* That's even as fair as "at hand, quoth the
   chamberlain"; for thou variest no more from picking
   of purses than giving direction doth from laboring:
   thou layest the plot how.

*Chamberlain.* Good morrow, Master Gadshill. It holds    55
   current° that I told you yesternight: there's a frank-
   lin° in the Wild° of Kent hath brought three hundred marks° with him in gold, I heard him tell it to
   one of his company last night at supper—a kind of
   auditor,° one that hath abundance of charge too,    60
   God knows what. They are up already and call for
   eggs and butter, they will away presently.

*Gadshill.* Sirrah, if they meet not with Saint Nicholas'
   clerks,° I'll give thee this neck.

*Chamberlain.* No, I'll none of it; I pray thee keep that    65
   for the hangman; for I know thou worshippest Saint
   Nicholas as truly as a man of falsehood may.

*Gadshill.* What talkest thou to me of the hangman? If
   I hang, I'll make a fat pair of gallows; for if I hang,

---

45–46 **Time . . . candle** (evasively spoken, the carriers being suspicious of Gadshill)   48 **charge** luggage   50 **At hand** (a popular
tag meaning "Ready, sir!" but relevant here to the Chamberlain's
filching way of life, as Gadshill points out)   56 **current** true   56–
57 **franklin** rich farmer   57 **Wild** weald, open country   57–58 **three
hundred marks** £200 (Elizabethan value)   60 **auditor** revenue officer   63–64 **Saint Nicholas' clerks** highwaymen (St. Nicholas was
reckoned the patron of all travelers, including traveling thieves)

70  old Sir John hangs with me, and thou knowest he is
    no starveling. Tut! There are other Troyans° that
    thou dream'st not of, the which for sport sake are
    content to do the profession some grace; that would
    (if matters should be looked into) for their own
75  credit sake make all whole. I am joined with no foot-
    landrakers,° no long-staff sixpenny strikers,° none
    of these mad mustachio purple-hued maltworms;°
    but with nobility and tranquillity,° burgomasters and
    great oneyers,° such as can hold in,° such as will
80  strike sooner than speak,° and speak sooner than
    drink, and drink sooner than pray—and yet, zounds,
    I lie, for they pray continually to their saint, the com-
    monwealth, or rather, not pray to her, but prey on
    her, for they ride up and down on her and make her
85  their boots.°

*Chamberlain.* What, the commonwealth their boots?
    Will she hold out water in foul way?°

*Gadshill.* She will, she will! Justice hath liquored° her.
    We steal as in a castle, cocksure. We have the re-
90  ceipt of fernseed,° we walk invisible.

*Chamberlain.* Nay, by my faith, I think you are more
    beholding to the night than to fernseed for your
    walking invisible.

*Gadshill.* Give me thy hand. Thou shalt have a share
95  in our purchase,° as I am a true man.

*Chamberlain.* Nay, rather let me have it, as you are a
    false thief.

---

**71 Troyans** good fellows   **75–76 foot-landrakers** footloose vaga-
bonds   **76 long-staff sixpenny strikers** men who would pull you
from your horse with long staves even to steal sixpence   **77 mus-
tachio purple-hued maltworms** big-mustached purple-faced drunk-
ards   **78 tranquillity** (Gadshill's witty coinage, on the analogy of
"nobility": people who don't have to scrounge their living)   **79 one-
yers** ones (?)   **79 hold in** keep confidence   **80 speak** i.e., say "hands
up"   **85 boots** (with pun on "boots/booty")   **87 in foul way** on
muddy roads   **88 liquored** (1) greased (as with boots) (2) made her
drunk   **89–90 receipt of fernseed** recipe of fernseed (popularly
supposed to render one invisible)   **95 purchase** (euphemism for
loot)

*Gadshill.* Go to; "homo" is a common name to all
    men.° Bid the ostler bring my gelding out of the
    stable. Farewell, you muddy knave.    [*Exeunt.*]  *100*


[Scene II. *The highway, near Gad's Hill.*]


*Enter Prince, Poins, and Peto, etc.*

*Poins.* Come, shelter, shelter! I have removed Falstaff's
    horse, and he frets° like a gummed velvet.

*Prince.* Stand close.    [*They step aside.*]

*Enter Falstaff.*

*Falstaff.* Poins! Poins, and be hanged! Poins!

*Prince.* [*Comes forward*] Peace, ye fat-kidneyed rascal!  *5*
    What a brawling dost thou keep!

*Falstaff.* Where's Poins, Hal?

*Prince.* He is walked up to the top of the hill; I'll go
    seek him.    [*Steps aside.*]

*Falstaff.* I am accursed to rob in that thief's company.  *10*
    The rascal hath removed my horse and tied him I
    know not where. If I travel but four foot by the
    squire° further afoot, I shall break my wind. Well,
    I doubt not but to die a fair death for all this, if I
    scape hanging for killing that rogue. I have forsworn  *15*
    his company hourly any time this two and twenty
    years, and yet I am bewitched with the rogue's com-
    pany. If the rascal have not given me medicines to
    make me love him, I'll be hanged. It could not be
    else: I have drunk medicines. Poins! Hal! A plague  *20*

98–99 **homo . . . men** the Latin for man, *homo* is a term that covers
all men, true (i.e., honest) or false   II.ii.2 **frets** chafes (with pun
on the fretting or fraying of velvet as the gum used to stiffen it
wore away)   13 **squire** rule

upon you both! Bardolph! Peto! I'll starve° ere I'll
rob a foot further. And 'twere not as good a deed
as drink to turn true man and to leave these rogues,
I am the veriest varlet that ever chewed with a tooth.
25    Eight yards of uneven ground is threescore and ten
miles afoot with me, and the stony-hearted villains
know it well enough. A plague upon it when thieves
cannot be true one to another! (*They whistle.*)
Whew! A plague upon you all! Give me my horse,
30    you rogues! Give me my horse and be hanged!

*Prince.* [*Comes forward*] Peace, ye fat-guts! Lie down,
lay thine ear close to the ground, and list if thou
canst hear the tread of travelers.

*Falstaff.* Have you any levers to lift me up again, being
35    down? 'Sblood, I'll not bear mine own flesh so far
afoot again for all the coin in thy father's exchequer.
What a plague mean ye to colt° me thus?

*Prince.* Thou liest, thou art not colted, thou art uncolted.°

40    *Falstaff.* I prithee, good Prince Hal, help me to my
horse, good king's son.

*Prince.* Out, ye rogue! Shall I be your ostler?

*Falstaff.* Hang thyself in thine own heir-apparent garters!° If I be ta'en, I'll peach° for this. And I have
45    not ballads made on you all, and sung to filthy tunes,
let a cup of sack be my poison. When a jest is so
forward—and afoot too—I hate it.

*Enter Gadshill* [*and Bardolph*].

*Gadshill.* Stand!

*Falstaff.* So I do, against my will.

---

21 **starve** die   37 **colt** trick   38–39 **uncolted** i.e., unhorsed   43–
44 **heir-apparent garters** (Falstaff adapts a proverbial phrase to fit
a crown prince)   44 **peach** inform on you

*Poins.* O, 'tis our setter;° I know his voice. [*Comes    50
forward*] Bardolph, what news?

*Bardolph.* Case ye, case ye! On with your vizards!
There's money of the King's coming down the hill;
'tis going to the King's exchequer.

*Falstaff.* You lie, ye rogue! 'Tis going to the King's    55
tavern.

*Gadshill.* There's enough to make us all—

*Falstaff.* To be hanged.

*Prince.* Sirs, you four shall front them in the narrow
lane; Ned Poins and I will walk lower: if they scape    60
from your encounter, then they light on us.

*Peto.* How many be there of them?

*Gadshill.* Some eight or ten.

*Falstaff.* Zounds, will they not rob us?

*Prince.* What, a coward, Sir John Paunch?                65

*Falstaff.* Indeed, I am not John of Gaunt° your grandfather, but yet no coward, Hal.

*Prince.* Well, we leave that to the proof.°

*Poins.* Sirrah Jack, thy horse stands behind the hedge.
When thou need'st him, there thou shalt find him.    70
Farewell and stand fast.

*Falstaff.* Now cannot I strike him, if I should be
hanged.

*Prince.* [*Aside to Poins*] Ned, where are our disguises?

*Poins.* [*Aside to Prince*] Here, hard by. Stand close.    75
                    [*Exeunt Prince and Poins.*]

---

50 **setter** one who makes arrangements for a robbery   66 **John of
Gaunt** Hal's grandfather (but in reply to "Sir John Paunch" Falstaff
puns on "gaunt/thin" which Hal evidently is [cf. II.iv.244–48])
68 **proof** test

*Falstaff.* Now, my masters, happy man be his dole,° say I. Every man to his business.

*Enter the Travelers.*

*Traveler.* Come, neighbor. The boy shall lead our horses down the hill; we'll walk afoot awhile and
80  ease our legs.

*Thieves.* Stand!

*Traveler.* Jesus bless us!

*Falstaff.* Strike! Down with them! Cut the villains' throats! Ah, whoreson caterpillars!° Bacon-fed
85  knaves! They hate us youth. Down with them! Fleece them!

*Traveler.* O, we are undone, both we and ours forever!

*Falstaff.* Hang ye, gorbellied° knaves, are ye undone? No, ye fat chuffs;° I would your store° were here!
90  On, bacons, on! What, ye knaves, young men must live. You are grandjurors,° are ye? We'll jure ye, faith!    *Here they rob them and bind them. Exeunt.*

*Enter the Prince and Poins [disguised].*

*Prince.* The thieves have bound the true men. Now could thou and I rob the thieves and go merrily to
95  London, it would be argument° for a week, laughter for a month, and a good jest forever.

*Poins.* Stand close! I hear them coming.
[*They stand aside.*]

*Enter the thieves again.*

*Falstaff.* Come, my masters, let us share, and then to horse before day. And the Prince and Poins be not
100  two arrant° cowards, there's no equity stirring.°

76 **happy man be his dole** may happiness be our lot    84 **whoreson caterpillars** miserable parasites    88 **gorbellied** great-bellied    89 **chuffs** misers    89 **store** total wealth    91 **grandjurors** i.e., men of substance (as required for service on a grand jury)    95 **be argument** make conversation    100 **arrant** thorough    100 **no equity stirring** i.e., no justice left alive

There's no more valor in that Poins than in a wild
duck.

*Prince.* Your money!

*Poins.* Villains!

} *As they are sharing, the Prince
and Poins set upon them.
They all run away, and Falstaff, after a blow or two,
runs away too, leaving the
booty behind them.*

*Prince.* Got with much ease. Now merrily to horse. The    105
thieves are all scattered, and possessed with fear so
strongly that they dare not meet each other: each
takes his fellow for an officer. Away, good Ned. Falstaff sweats to death and lards the lean earth as he
walks along. Were't not for laughing, I should pity    110
him.°

*Poins.* How the fat rogue roared!          *Exeunt.*


[Scene III. *Northumberland. Warkworth Castle.*]


*Enter Hotspur solus,° reading a letter.*


*Hotspur.* "But, for mine own part, my lord, I could be
well contented to be there, in respect of the love I
bear your house."° He could be contented—why is
he not then? In respect of the love he bears our
house! He shows in this he loves his own barn better    5
than he loves our house. Let me see some more. "The
purpose you undertake is dangerous"—why, that's
certain! 'Tis dangerous to take a cold, to sleep, to
drink; but I tell you, my lord fool, out of this nettle,
danger, we pluck this flower, safety. "The purpose    10
you undertake is dangerous, the friends you have

---

105–11 Got . . . him (printed as verse by Pope and many later
editors, with line breaks after "horse/fear/other/officer/death/
along/him")  II.iii.s.d. solus alone (Latin)  3 house family

named uncertain, the time itself unsorted,° and your
whole plot too light for the counterpoise of so great
an opposition." Say you so, say you so? I say unto
15  you again, you are a shallow, cowardly hind,° and
you lie. What a lack-brain is this! By the Lord, our
plot is a good plot as ever was laid; our friends true
and constant: a good plot, good friends, and full of
expectation; an excellent plot, very good friends.
20  What a frosty-spirited rogue is this! Why, my Lord
of York° commends the plot and the general course
of the action. Zounds, and I were now by this rascal,
I could brain him with his lady's fan. Is there not my
father, my uncle, and myself; Lord Edmund Mor-
25  timer, my Lord of York, and Owen Glendower? Is
there not, besides, the Douglas? Have I not all their
letters to meet me in arms by the ninth of the next
month, and are they not some of them set forward
already? What a pagan° rascal is this, an infidel! Ha!
30  you shall see now, in very sincerity of fear and cold
heart will he to the King and lay open all our proceedings. O, I could divide myself and go to buffets°
for moving such a dish of skim milk with so honorable an action! Hang him, let him tell the King! We
35  are prepared. I will set forward tonight.

*Enter his Lady.*

How now, Kate? I must leave you within these two
hours.

*Lady.* O my good lord, why are you thus alone?
For what offense have I this fortnight been
40  A banished woman from my Harry's bed?
Tell me, sweet lord, what is't that takes from thee
Thy stomach,° pleasure, and thy golden sleep?
Why dost thou bend thine eyes upon the earth,
And start so often when thou sit'st alone?

---

12 **unsorted** unsuitable   15 **hind** menial   20–21 **my Lord of York**
the Archbishop of York (cf. I.iii.264 ff)   29 **pagan** faithless   32 **di-**
**vide . . . buffets** split myself into two, and set the halves fighting
42 **stomach** appetite

Why hast thou lost the fresh blood in thy cheeks  45
And given my treasures and my rights of thee
To thick-eyed musing and cursed° melancholy?
In thy faint slumbers I by thee have watched,°
And heard thee murmur tales of iron wars,
Speak terms of manage to thy bounding steed,  50
Cry "Courage! To the field!" And thou hast talked
Of sallies and retires, of trenches, tents,
Of palisadoes,° frontiers,° parapets,
Of basilisks,° of cannon, culverin,°
Of prisoners' ransom, and of soldiers slain,  55
And all the currents° of a heady° fight.
Thy spirit within thee hath been so at war,
And thus hath so bestirred thee in thy sleep,
That beads of sweat have stood upon thy brow
Like bubbles in a late-disturbèd stream,  60
And in thy face strange motions have appeared,
Such as we see when men restrain their breath
On some great sudden hest.° O, what portents are
    these?
Some heavy business hath my lord in hand,
And I must know it, else he loves me not.  65

*Hotspur.* What, ho!

          [*Enter a Servant.*]

              Is Gilliams with the packet gone?

*Servant.* He is, my lord, an hour ago.

*Hotspur.* Hath Butler brought those horses from the
    sheriff?

*Servant.* One horse, my lord, he brought even now.

*Hotspur.* What horse? A roan, a crop-ear, is it not?  70

*Servant.* It is, my lord.

47 cursed peevish  48 watched lain awake  53 palisadoes defenses
made of stakes  53 frontiers fortifications  54 basilisks, culverin
(sizes and types of cannon)  56 currents occurrences  56 heady
violent  63 hest (1) command? (2) resolution?

*Hotspur.* That roan shall be my throne. Well, I will
   back him straight. O Esperance!° Bid Butler lead
   him forth into the park.°

[*Exit Servant.*]

75 *Lady.* But hear you, my lord.

*Hotspur.* What say'st thou, my lady?

*Lady.* What is it carries you away?°

*Hotspur.* Why, my horse, my love—my horse!

*Lady.* Out, you mad-headed ape! A weasel hath not
80   such a deal of spleen° as you are tossed with. In
   faith, I'll know your business, Harry, that I will! I
   fear my brother Mortimer doth stir about his title
   and hath sent for you to line° his enterprise; but if
   you go°—

85 *Hotspur.* So far afoot, I shall be weary, love.

*Lady.* Come, come, you paraquito,° answer me directly
   unto this question that I ask. In faith, I'll break thy
   little finger, Harry, and if thou wilt not tell me all
   things true.°

90 *Hotspur.* Away, away, you trifler! Love? I love thee not;
   I care not for thee, Kate. This is no world
   To play with mammets° and to tilt° with lips.
   We must have bloody noses and cracked crowns,°
   And pass them current too. Gods me,° my horse!
   What say'st thou, Kate? What wouldst thou have
95   with me?

73 **Esperance** hope (part of the Percy motto)   72–74 **That . . . park**
(Pope and many later editors print as verse; with line breaks after
"throne/Esperance/park"   77 **away** (1) i.e., from home (2) from
your usual self   80 **spleen** caprice   83 **line** strengthen   79–84 **Out
. . . go** (printed by Pope and many later editors as verse, but with a
variety of lineations)   86 **paraquito** parrot   86–89 **Come . . . true**
(printed by Pope and many later editors as verse, with line breaks
after "me/ask/Harry/true"   92 **mammets** dolls   92 **tilt** duel   93
**crowns** (1) heads (2) coins—which when "cracked" were hard to
"pass current" (possibly there is an allusion to the "crown" of
kingship, which, though not genuine when usurped, may be passed
current by force)   94 **Gods me** God save me

*Lady.* Do you not love me? Do you not indeed?
  Well, do not then; for since you love me not,
  I will not love myself. Do you not love me?
  Nay, tell me if you speak in jest or no.

*Hotspur.* Come, wilt thou see me ride?                    *100*
  And when I am a-horseback, I will swear
  I love thee infinitely. But hark you, Kate:
  I must not have you henceforth question me
  Whither I go, nor reason whereabout.
  Whither I must, I must, and—to conclude,            *105*
  This evening must I leave you, gentle Kate.
  I know you wise—but yet no farther wise
  Than Harry Percy's wife; constant you are—
  But yet a woman; and for secrecy,
  No lady closer—for I well believe                  *110*
  Thou wilt not utter what thou dost not know,
  And so far will I trust thee, gentle Kate—

*Lady.* How? So far?

*Hotspur.* Not an inch further. But hark you, Kate:
  Whither I go, thither shall you go too;             *115*
  Today will I set forth, tomorrow you.
  Will this content you, Kate?

*Lady.*                           It must of force.° *Exeunt.*


[Scene IV. *Eastcheap. The tavern.°*]


*Enter Prince and Poins.*


*Prince.* Ned, prithee come out of that fat° room and
  lend me thy hand to laugh a little.

*Poins.* Where hast been, Hal?

---

117 **of force** of necessity    II.iv.s.d. **tavern** (the tavern is said to be
in Eastcheap, but it is never explicitly named; references to a boar
in *Henry IV* [*Part Two*] suggest it is the Boar's Head)    1 **fat** hot

*Prince.* With three or four loggerheads° amongst three
or fourscore hogsheads. I have sounded the very
bass-string of humility. Sirrah, I am sworn brother
to a leash° of drawers° and can call them all by their
christen names, as Tom, Dick, and Francis. They
take it already upon their salvation° that, though I
be but Prince of Wales, yet I am the king of courtesy,
and tell me flatly I am no proud Jack° like Falstaff,
but a Corinthian,° a lad of mettle, a good boy (by
the Lord, so they call me!), and when I am King of
England I shall command all the good lads in Eastcheap. They call drinking deep, dyeing scarlet;° and
when you breathe in your watering,° they cry "hem!"
and bid you play it off.° To conclude, I am so good
a proficient in one quarter of an hour that I can drink
with any tinker in his own language during my life.
I tell thee, Ned, thou hast lost much honor that thou
wert not with me in this action. But, sweet Ned—
to sweeten which name of Ned, I give thee this
pennyworth of sugar,° clapped even now into my
hand by an under-skinker,° one that never spake
other English in his life than "Eight shillings and
sixpence," and "You are welcome," with this shrill
addition, "Anon,° anon, sir! Score° a pint of bas-
tard° in the Half-moon,"° or so—but, Ned, to drive
away the time till Falstaff come, I prithee do thou
stand in some by-room while I question my puny
drawer to what end he gave me the sugar; and do
thou never leave calling "Francis!" that his tale to
me may be nothing but "Anon!" Step aside, and I'll
show thee a precedent.°

---

4 **loggerheads** blockheads   7 **leash** trio   7 **drawers** tapsters   9 **take
. . . salvation** pledge their salvation   11 **Jack** fellow   12 **Corinthian** gay blade   15 **dyeing scarlet** i.e., from the complexion it
gives a man   16 **breathe in your watering** pause for breath while
drinking   17 **play it off** down it   23 **sugar** i.e., for sweetening wine
(cf. I.ii.117)   24 **under-skinker** under-tapster   27 **Anon** i.e., (I'm
coming) at once   27 **Score** charge   27–28 **bastard** Spanish wine
28 **Half-moon** one of the inn's rooms   34 **precedent** example

*Poins.* Francis!                                                    35

*Prince.* Thou art perfect.

*Poins.* Francis!                          [*Poins steps aside.*]

       *Enter [Francis, a] Drawer.*

*Francis.* Anon, anon, sir. Look down into the Pomgarnet,° Ralph.

*Prince.* Come hither, Francis.                                     40

*Francis.* My lord?

*Prince.* How long hast thou to serve,° Francis?

*Francis.* Forsooth, five years, and as much as to—

*Poins.* [*Within*] Francis!

*Francis.* Anon, anon, sir.                                         45

*Prince.* Five year! By'r Lady,° a long lease for the clink-
   ing of pewter. But, Francis, darest thou be so valiant
   as to play the coward with thy indenture° and show
   it a fair pair of heels and run from it?

*Francis.* O Lord, sir, I'll be sworn upon all the books      50
   in England I could find in my heart—

*Poins.* [*Within*] Francis!

*Francis.* Anon, sir.

*Prince.* How old art thou, Francis?

*Francis.* Let me see: about Michaelmas° next I shall      55
   be—

*Poins.* [*Within*] Francis!

*Francis.* Anon, sir. Pray stay a little, my lord.

*Prince.* Nay, but hark you, Francis. For the sugar thou
   gavest me—'twas a pennyworth, was't not?              60

38–39 **Pomgarnet** Pomegranate (another of the inn's rooms)   42
**serve** i.e., as an apprentice (apprenticeship ran for seven years)
46 **By'r Lady** by Our Lady (mild oath)   48 **indenture** contract
55 **Michaelmas** September 29

*Francis.* O Lord! I would it had been two!

*Prince.* I will give thee for it a thousand pound. Ask me when thou wilt, and thou shalt have it.

*Poins.* [*Within*] Francis!

65 *Francis.* Anon, anon.

*Prince.* Anon, Francis?° No, Francis; but tomorrow, Francis; or, Francis, a Thursday; or indeed, Francis, when thou wilt. But, Francis—

*Francis.* My lord?

70 *Prince.* Wilt thou rob this leathern-jerkin, crystal-button, not-pated, agate-ring, puke-stocking, caddis-garter, smooth-tongue, Spanish-pouch?°

*Francis.* O Lord, sir, who do you mean?

*Prince.* Why then, your brown bastard is your only
75 drink; for look you, Francis, your white canvas doublet will sully. In Barbary, sir, it cannot come to so much.°

*Francis.* What, sir?

*Poins.* [*Within*] Francis!

80 *Prince.* Away, you rogue! Dost thou not hear them call?

    *Here they both call him. The Drawer stands amazed, not knowing which way to go.*

    *Enter Vintner.*°

*Vintner.* What, stand'st thou still, and hear'st such a calling? Look to the guests within. [*Exit Francis.*]

---

66 **Anon, Francis?** (Hal pretends to take Francis' "anon"—at once—to Poins as meaning he wants the thousand pounds at once)   70–72 **this . . . Spanish-pouch** i.e., the innkeeper, whose middle-class appearance Hal details: leather jacket with crystal buttons, short hair, agate ring, wool stockings, plain worsted (not fancy) garters, ingratiating (and probably unctuous) speech, money pouch of Spanish leather   74–77 **Why . . . much** (semi-nonsense; but the implication seems clear that Francis must stick to his trade)   80 s.d. **Vintner** the innkeeper

My lord, old Sir John, with half a dozen more, are
at the door. Shall I let them in?

*Prince.* Let them alone awhile, and then open the door.    *85*
[*Exit Vintner.*] Poins!

*Poins.* [*Within*] Anon, anon, sir.

*Enter Poins.*

*Prince.* Sirrah, Falstaff and the rest of the thieves are at
the door. Shall we be merry?

*Poins.* As merry as crickets, my lad. But hark ye; what    *90*
cunning match have you made with this jest of the
drawer? Come, what's the issue?°

*Prince.* I am now of all humors that have showed themselves humors since the old days of goodman Adam
to the pupil age of this present twelve o'clock at    *95*
midnight.°

*[Enter Francis.]*

What's o'clock, Francis?

*Francis.* Anon, anon, sir.                         [*Exit.*]

*Prince.* That ever this fellow should have fewer words
than a parrot, and yet the son of a woman! His in-    *100*
dustry is upstairs and downstairs, his eloquence the
parcel of a reckoning.° I am not yet of Percy's mind,
the Hotspur of the North: he that kills me some six
or seven dozen of Scots at a breakfast, washes his
hands, and says to his wife, "Fie upon this quiet    *105*
life! I want work." "O my sweet Harry," says she,
"how many hast thou killed today?" "Give my roan
horse a drench,"° says he, and answers "Some fourteen," an hour after, "a trifle, a trifle." I prithee call
in Falstaff. I'll play Percy, and that damned brawn°    *110*

92 **issue** outcome, point (of the jest)   93–96 **I . . . midnight** I am
ready for every hour of gaiety that men have invented since the
beginning of the world   100–02 **His industry . . . reckoning** his
whole activity is running up and down stairs, his whole conversation
the totaling of bills   108 **drench** dose of medicine   110 **brawn** fat
boar

shall play Dame Mortimer his wife. "Rivo!"° says
the drunkard. Call in Ribs, call in Tallow.

*Enter Falstaff, [Gadshill, Bardolph, and Peto;*

*Francis follows with wine].*

**Poins.** Welcome, Jack. Where hast thou been?

**Falstaff.** A plague of° all cowards, I say, and a ven-
115   geance too! Marry and amen! Give me a cup of sack,
boy. Ere I lead this life long, I'll sew netherstocks,°
and mend them and foot them too. A plague of all
cowards! Give me a cup of sack, rogue. Is there no
virtue extant?                     *He drinketh.*

120 **Prince.** Didst thou never see Titan° kiss a dish of butter
(pitiful-hearted Titan!) that melted at the sweet tale
of the sun's? If thou didst, then behold that compound.

**Falstaff.** You rogue, here's lime° in this sack too! There
125   is nothing but roguery to be found in villainous man.
Yet a coward is worse than a cup of sack with lime
in it—a villainous coward! Go thy ways, old Jack,
die when thou wilt; if manhood, good manhood, be
not forgot upon the face of the earth, then am I a
130   shotten herring.° There lives not three good men un-
hanged in England; and one of them is fat, and grows
old. God help the while! A bad world, I say. I would
I were a weaver; I could sing psalms° or anything. A
plague of all cowards, I say still!

135 **Prince.** How now, woolsack? What mutter you?

**Falstaff.** A king's son! If I do not beat thee out of thy

kingdom with a dagger of lath° and drive all thy
subjects afore thee like a flock of wild geese, I'll never
wear hair on my face more. You Prince of Wales?

*Prince.* Why, you whoreson round man, what's the 140
matter?

*Falstaff.* Are not you a coward? Answer me to that—
and Poins there?

*Poins.* Zounds, ye fat paunch, and ye call me coward,
by the Lord, I'll stab thee.                        145

*Falstaff.* I call thee coward? I'll see thee damned ere I
call thee coward, but I would give a thousand pound
I could run as fast as thou canst. You are straight
enough in the shoulders; you care not who sees your
back. Call you that backing of your friends? A plague 150
upon such backing, give me them that will face me.
Give me a cup of sack. I am a rogue if I drunk today.

*Prince.* O villain, thy lips are scarce wiped since thou
drunk'st last.

*Falstaff.* All is one for that. (*He drinketh.*) A plague 155
of all cowards, still say I.

*Prince.* What's the matter?

*Falstaff.* What's the matter? There be four of us here
have ta'en a thousand pound this day morning.

*Prince.* Where is it, Jack, where is it?               160

*Falstaff.* Where is it? Taken from us it is. A hundred
upon poor four of us!

*Prince.* What, a hundred, man?

*Falstaff.* I am a rogue if I were not at half-sword° with
a dozen of them two hours together. I have scaped 165
by miracle. I am eight times thrust through the dou-

---

137 **dagger of lath** wooden dagger (by this phrase Falstaff associates
himself with a character called "the Vice" in the old religious plays,
who drove the devil offstage by beating him with a wooden dagger)
164 **at half-sword** infighting at close quarters

blet,° four through the hose;° my buckler cut
through and through; my sword hacked like a hand-
saw—*ecce signum!*° I never dealt° better since I was
170   a man. All would not do. A plague of all cowards!
Let them speak. If they speak more or less than
truth, they are villains and the sons of darkness.°

*Prince.* Speak, sirs. How was it?

*Gadshill.* We four set upon some dozen—

175   *Falstaff.* Sixteen at least, my lord.

*Gadshill.* And bound them.

*Peto.* No, no, they were not bound.

*Falstaff.* You rogue, they were bound, every man of
them, or I am a Jew else—an Ebrew Jew.

180   *Gadshill.* As we were sharing, some six or seven fresh
men set upon us—

*Falstaff.* And unbound the rest, and then come in the
other.°

*Prince.* What, fought you with them all?

185   *Falstaff.* All? I know not what you call all, but if I
fought not with fifty of them, I am a bunch of radish!° If there were not two or three and fifty° upon
poor old Jack, then am I no two-legged creature.

*Prince.* Pray God you have not murd'red some of them.

190   *Falstaff.* Nay, that's past praying for. I have peppered
two of them. Two I am sure I have paid,° two rogues
in buckram suits. I tell thee what, Hal—if I tell thee
a lie, spit in my face, call me horse. Thou knowest

166-67 **doublet** Elizabethan upper garment   167 **hose** Elizabethan
breeches.   169 **ecce signum** behold the evidence (Latin; spoken as he
shows his sword)   169 **dealt** i.e., dealt blows   172 **sons of darkness**
i.e., damned (but cf. also I.ii.24)   183 **other** others   186-87 **bunch
of radish** (again an object long and lean)   187 **three and fifty** (fifty-
three was the number of Spanish ships popularly reputed to have
opposed Sir Richard Grenville at the battle of the Azores in 1591;
Falstaff thus humorously claims for his fight the status of a national
epic)   191 **paid** settled with

my old ward:° here I lay, and thus I bore my point.
Four rogues in buckram let drive at me.     *195*

*Prince.* What, four? Thou saidst but two even now.

*Falstaff.* Four, Hal. I told thee four.

*Poins.* Ay, ay, he said four.

*Falstaff.* These four came all afront and mainly° thrust
at me. I made me no more ado but took all their     *200*
seven points in my target, thus.

*Prince.* Seven? Why, there were but four even now.

*Falstaff.* In buckram?

*Poins.* Ay, four, in buckram suits.

*Falstaff.* Seven, by these hilts, or I am a villain else.     *205*

*Prince.* [*Aside to Poins*] Prithee let him alone. We shall
have more anon.

*Falstaff.* Dost thou hear me, Hal?

*Prince.* Ay, and mark° thee too, Jack.

*Falstaff.* Do so, for it is worth the list'ning to. These     *210*
nine in buckram that I told thee of—

*Prince.* So, two more already.

*Falstaff.* Their points being broken—

*Poins.* Down fell their hose.°

*Falstaff.* Began to give me ground; but I followed me     *215*
close, came in, foot and hand, and with a thought°
seven of the eleven I paid.

*Prince.* O monstrous! Eleven buckram men grown out
of two!

*Falstaff.* But, as the devil would have it, three misbe-     *220*

---

194 **ward** fencing posture   199 **mainly** mightily   209 **mark** pay
**close attention to**   214 **Down fell their hose** (Poins wittily takes
"points" in the sense of laces holding the breeches to the doublet)
216 **with a thought** quick as a thought

gotten knaves in Kendal green came at my back and
let drive at me; for it was so dark, Hal, that thou
couldest not see thy hand.

*Prince.* These lies are like their father that begets them
225 —gross as a mountain, open, palpable. Why, thou
clay-brained guts, thou knotty-pated° fool, thou
whoreson obscene greasy tallow-catch°—

*Falstaff.* What, art thou mad? Art thou mad? Is not
the truth the truth?

230 *Prince.* Why, how couldst thou know these men in Kendal green when it was so dark thou couldst not see
thy hand? Come, tell us your reason. What sayest
thou to this?

*Poins.* Come, your reason, Jack, your reason.

235 *Falstaff.* What, upon compulsion? Zounds, and I were
at the strappado° or all the racks in the world, I
would not tell you on compulsion. Give you a reason on compulsion? If reasons° were as plentiful as
blackberries, I would give no man a reason upon
240 compulsion, I.

*Prince.* I'll be no longer guilty of this sin; this sanguine°
coward, this bed-presser, this horseback-breaker,
this huge hill of flesh—

*Falstaff.* 'Sblood, you starveling, you eel-skin, you dried
245 neat's-tongue,° you bull's pizzle,° you stockfish°—
O for breath to utter what is like thee!—you tailor's
yard, you sheath, you bowcase, you vile standing
tuck!°

*Prince.* Well, breathe awhile, and then to it again; and

---

226 **knotty-pated** blockheaded    227 **tallow-catch** (1) pan to catch
drippings under roasting meat? (2) tallow-keech, i.e., roll of fat for
making candles?    236 **strappado** instrument of torture    238 **reasons**
(pronounced like "raisins," and hence comparable to blackberries)
241 **sanguine** ruddy (and hence valorous-seeming)    245 **neat's**
tongue ox-tongue    245 **pizzle** penis    245 **stockfish** dried codfish
247-48 **standing tuck** upright rapier

when thou hast tired thyself in base comparisons, 250
hear me speak but this.

*Poins.* Mark, Jack.

*Prince.* We two saw you four set on four, and bound
them and were masters of their wealth. Mark now
how a plain tale shall put you down. Then did we 255
two set on you four and, with a word,° outfaced you
from your prize, and have it; yea, and can show it
you here in the house. And, Falstaff, you carried your
guts away as nimbly, with as quick dexterity, and
roared for mercy, and still run and roared, as ever 260
I heard bullcalf. What a slave art thou to hack thy
sword as thou hast done, and then say it was in fight!
What trick, what device, what starting hole° canst
thou now find out to hide thee from this open and
apparent shame?                                      265

*Poins.* Come, let's hear, Jack. What trick hast thou
now?

*Falstaff.* By the Lord, I knew ye as well as he that made
ye. Why, hear you, my masters. Was it for me to
kill the heir apparent? Should I turn upon the true 270
prince? Why, thou knowest I am as valiant as Her-
cules, but beware instinct. The lion will not touch
the true prince.° Instinct is a great matter. I was now
a coward on instinct. I shall think the better of myself, and thee, during my life—I for a valiant lion, 275
and thou for a true prince. But, by the Lord, lads,
I am glad you have the money. Hostess, clap to the
doors. Watch tonight, pray tomorrow.° Gallants,
lads, boys, hearts of gold, all the titles of good fellowship come to you! What, shall we be merry? Shall 280
we have a play extempore?

---

256 **with a word** (1) in brief? (2) with a mere shout to scare you?
263 **starting hole** hiding place    272–73 **The lion . . . prince** (a traditional belief about lions)    278 **Watch . . . tomorrow** cf. Matthew
26:41 "Watch and pray, that ye enter not into temptation." (Falstaff
puns on "watch," which means "carouse" as well as "keep vigil")

*Prince.* Content—and the argument° shall be thy running away.

*Falstaff.* Ah, no more of that, Hal, and thou lovest me!

*Enter Hostess.*

285 *Hostess.* O Jesu, my lord the Prince!

*Prince.* How now, my lady the hostess? What say'st thou to me?

*Hostess.* Marry, my lord, there is a nobleman of the court at door would speak with you. He says he
290 comes from your father.

*Prince.* Give him as much as will make him a royal man,° and send him back again to my mother.

*Falstaff.* What manner of man is he?

*Hostess.* An old man.

295 *Falstaff.* What doth gravity° out of his bed at midnight? Shall I give him his answer?

*Prince.* Prithee do, Jack.

*Falstaff.* Faith, and I'll send him packing.     *Exit.*

*Prince.* Now, sirs. By'r Lady, you fought fair; so did
300 you, Peto; so did you, Bardolph. You are lions too, you ran away upon instinct, you will not touch the true prince; no—fie!

*Bardolph.* Faith, I ran when I saw others run.

*Prince.* Faith, tell me now in earnest, how came Fal-
305 staff's sword so hacked?

*Peto.* Why, he hacked it with his dagger, and said he would swear truth out of England but he would make you believe it was done in fight, and persuaded us to do the like.

---

282 **argument** subject   291–92 **royal man** cf. "noble" in the previous speech, but with a pun on the "royal," a coin worth ten shillings, which was of greater value than the "noble," worth six shillings eight pence   295 **gravity** i.e., sober age

*Bardolph.* Yea, and to tickle our noses with speargrass    310
to make them bleed, and then to beslubber our garments with it and swear it was the blood of true men.
I did that° I did not this seven year before—I
blushed to hear his monstrous devices.

*Prince.* O villain! Thou stolest a cup of sack eighteen    315
years ago and wert taken with the manner,° and ever
since thou hast blushed extempore. Thou hadst fire°
and sword on thy side, and yet thou ran'st away.
What instinct hadst thou for it?

*Bardolph.* My lord, do you see these meteors?° Do you    320
behold these exhalations?°

*Prince.* I do.

*Bardolph.* What think you they portend?

*Prince.* Hot livers and cold purses.°

*Bardolph.* Choler,° my lord, if rightly taken.       325

*Prince.* No, if rightly taken, halter.

### *Enter Falstaff.*

Here comes lean Jack; here comes bare-bone. How
now, my sweet creature of bombast?° How long is't
ago, Jack, since thou sawest thine own knee?

*Falstaff.* My own knee? When I was about thy years,    330
Hal, I was not an eagle's talent° in the waist; I could
have crept into any alderman's thumb-ring. A plague
of sighing and grief, it blows a man up like a bladder.
There's villainous news abroad. Here was Sir John
Bracy from your father: you must to the court in    335

---

313 **that** what    316 **taken with the manner** caught with the goods
317 **fire** i.e., the alcoholic hue of Bardolph's face    320, 321 **meteors,
exhalations** i.e., the pimples and other features of Bardolph's face,
spoken of as if they were meteorological portents    324 **Hot livers
and cold purses** (the two notable results of excessive drink)    325
**Choler** anger (Bardolph implies that he is choleric, and therefore no
coward; Hal proceeds to understand "choler" as "collar," which in
Bardolph's case will be—if "rightly taken"—the hangman's noose)
328 **bombast** cotton stuffing    331 **talent** talon

the morning. That same mad fellow of the north,
Percy, and he of Wales that gave Amamon the bas-
tinado, and made Lucifer cuckold, and swore the
devil his true liegeman upon the cross of a Welsh
340 hook°—what a plague call you him?

*Poins.* Owen Glendower.

*Falstaff.* Owen, Owen—the same; and his son-in-law
Mortimer, and old Northumberland, and that
sprightly Scot of Scots, Douglas, that runs a-horse-
345 back up a hill perpendicular—

*Prince.* He that rides at high speed and with his pistol
kills a sparrow flying.

*Falstaff.* You have hit it.

*Prince.* So did he never the sparrow.

350 *Falstaff.* Well, that rascal hath good metal° in him; he
will not run.

*Prince.* Why, what a rascal art thou then, to praise him
so for running!

*Falstaff.* A-horseback, ye cuckoo! But afoot he will not
355 budge a foot.

*Prince.* Yes, Jack, upon instinct.

*Falstaff.* I grant ye, upon instinct. Well, he is there too,
and one Mordake, and a thousand bluecaps° more.
Worcester is stol'n away tonight; thy father's beard
360 is turned white with the news; you may buy land
now as cheap as stinking mack'rel.

*Prince.* Why then, it is like, if there come a hot June,
and this civil buffeting hold, we shall buy maidenheads as they buy hobnails, by the hundreds.°

337–40 **he of Wales . . . hook** (Falstaff alludes to Glendower's supposed magical powers: he has cudgeled a devil named Amamon,
made horns grow on Lucifer, and forced the devil to swear allegiance to him on the cross of a weapon that has no cross)    350 **good
metal** (with pun on "mettle," spirit, courage)    358 **bluecaps** Scots
362–64 **if there . . . hundreds** (the Prince applies the analogy of
selling cheap what won't keep to the reactions of virgins as they
see all the men going off to war)

*Falstaff.* By the mass, lad, thou sayest true; it is like we   365
shall have good trading that way. But tell me, Hal,
art not thou horrible afeard? Thou being heir apparent, could the world pick thee out three such enemies again as that fiend Douglas, that spirit Percy,
and that devil Glendower? Art thou not horribly   370
afraid? Doth not thy blood thrill° at it?

*Prince.* Not a whit, i' faith. I lack some of thy instinct.

*Falstaff.* Well, thou wilt be horribly chid tomorrow
when thou comest to thy father. If thou love me,
practice an answer.   375

*Prince.* Do thou stand for my father and examine me
upon the particulars of my life.

*Falstaff.* Shall I? Content. This chair shall be my state,°
this dagger my scepter, and this cushion my crown.

*Prince.* Thy state is taken for° a joined-stool, thy golden   380
scepter for a leaden dagger, and thy precious rich
crown for a pitiful bald crown.

*Falstaff.* Well, and the fire of grace be not quite out of
thee, now shalt thou be moved. Give me a cup of
sack to make my eyes look red, that it may be   385
thought I have wept; for I must speak in passion,
and I will do it in King Cambyses' vein.°

*Prince.* Well, here is my leg.

*Falstaff.* And here is my speech. Stand aside, nobility.°

*Hostess.* O Jesu, this is excellent sport, i' faith!   390

*Falstaff.* Weep not, sweet queen,° for trickling tears are
    vain.

---

371 thrill shiver (with fear)   378 state chair of state   380 taken for
(either "seen to be merely," or, alternatively, this is a meditative
comment, possibly an aside, in the detached vein of I.ii.199 and
II.iv.481, with "thy" referring to the King)   387 King Cambyses'
vein i.e., the old ranting style of Preston's *King Cambyses* (1569)
389 nobility (addressed to his motley ragamuffins)   391 queen (addressed to the Hostess, who is evidently tearful with laughter; probably with a standard pun on *quean* = tart, prostitute)

*Hostess*. O, the Father, how he holds his countenance!°

*Falstaff*. For God's sake, lords, convey my tristful°
          queen!
     For tears do stop the floodgates of her eyes.

395 *Hostess*. O Jesu, he doth it as like one of these harlotry°
          players as ever I see!

*Falstaff*. Peace, good pintpot. Peace, good tickle-brain.
     Harry, I do not only marvel where thou spendest
     thy time, but also how thou art accompanied. For
400  though the camomile,° the more it is trodden on, the
     faster it grows, so° youth, the more it is wasted, the
     sooner it wears. That thou art my son I have partly
     thy mother's word, partly my own opinion, but
     chiefly a villainous trick° of thine eye and a foolish
405  hanging of thy nether lip that doth warrant me. If
     then thou be son to me, here lies the point: why,
     being son to me, art thou so pointed at? Shall the
     blessed sun of heaven prove a micher and eat black-
     berries?° A question not to be asked. Shall the son°
410  of England prove a thief and take purses? A question
     to be asked. There is a thing, Harry, which thou
     hast often heard of, and it is known to many in our
     land by the name of pitch. This pitch (as ancient
     writers do report) doth defile; so doth the company
415  thou keepest. For, Harry, now I do not speak to
     thee in drink, but in tears; not in pleasure, but in
     passion; not in words only, but in woes also: and
     yet there is a virtuous man whom I have often noted
     in thy company, but I know not his name.

---

392 **holds his countenance** keeps a straight face   393 **tristful** sad
395 **harlotry** rascally   400 **camomile** aromatic herb (Falstaff proceeds to satirize the highflown style of the court by using a manner
of speech called euphuism—from John Lyly's fictional narrative,
*Euphues* [1578] which introduced it—based on similes drawn from
natural history, intricate balance, antithesis, and repetition of sounds,
words, and ideas)   401 **so** (some editors emend to "yet," but the
imperfect logical correspondence of "though . . . so" may be part
of Falstaff's mockery)   404 **trick** mannerism (possibly a twitch)
408–09 **prove . . . blackberries** be a truant from duty and go black-
berrying   409 **son** (with pun on "sun," the royal symbol)

*Prince.* What manner of man, and it like your Majesty?   *420*

*Falstaff.* A goodly portly° man, i' faith, and a corpulent;° of a cheerful look, a pleasing eye, and a most
noble carriage; and, as I think, his age some fifty,
or, by'r Lady, inclining to threescore; and now I remember me, his name is Falstaff. If that man should   *425*
be lewdly given,° he deceiveth me; for, Harry, I see
virtue in his looks. If then the tree may be known by
the fruit,° as the fruit by the tree, then, peremptorily°
I speak it, there is virtue in that Falstaff. Him keep
with, the rest banish. And tell me now, thou naughty   *430*
varlet, tell me where hast thou been this month?

*Prince.* Dost thou speak like a king? Do thou stand for
me, and I'll play my father.

*Falstaff.* Depose me? If thou dost it half so gravely, so
majestically, both in word and matter, hang me up   *435*
by the heels for a rabbit-sucker° or a poulter's hare.

*Prince.* Well, here I am set.

*Falstaff.* And here I stand. Judge, my masters.

*Prince.* Now, Harry, whence come you?

*Falstaff.* My noble lord, from Eastcheap.   *440*

*Prince.* The complaints I hear of thee are grievous.

*Falstaff.* 'Sblood, my lord, they are false! Nay, I'll tickle
ye for a young prince,° i' faith.

*Prince.* Swearest thou, ungracious boy? Henceforth
ne'er look on me. Thou art violently carried away   *445*
from grace. There is a devil haunts thee in the likeness of an old fat man; a tun° of man is thy companion. Why dost thou converse with that trunk of

---

421 **portly** stately   421-22 **corpulent** well filled out   426 **lewdly
given** inclined to evil-doing   427-28 **If . . . fruit** cf. Matthew 12:33:
"The tree is known by his fruit"   428 **peremptorily** decisively   436
**rabbit-sucker** suckling rabbit   442-43 **I'll . . . prince** I'll act a prince
that will amuse you   447 **tun** hogshead

humors,° that bolting-hutch° of beastliness, that
450   swoll'n parcel of dropsies,° that huge bombard° of
sack, that stuffed cloakbag of guts, that roasted
Manningtree° ox with the pudding in his belly, that
reverend vice,° that gray iniquity,° that father
ruffian,° that vanity° in years? Wherein is he good,
455   but to taste sack and drink it? Wherein neat and
cleanly, but to carve a capon and eat it? Wherein
cunning, but in craft?° Wherein crafty, but in
villainy? Wherein villainous, but in all things?
Wherein worthy, but in nothing?

460   *Falstaff.* I would your Grace would take me with you.°
Whom means your Grace?

*Prince.* That villainous abominable misleader of youth,
Falstaff, that old white-bearded Satan.

*Falstaff.* My lord, the man I know.

465   *Prince.* I know thou dost.

*Falstaff.* But to say I know more harm in him than in
myself were to say more than I know. That he is old,
the more the pity, his white hairs do witness it; but
that he is, saving your reverence, a whoremaster,
470   that I utterly deny. If sack and sugar be a fault, God
help the wicked! If to be old and merry be a sin,
then many an old host that I know is damned. If to
be fat be to be hated, then Pharaoh's lean kine° are
to be loved. No, my good lord: banish Peto, banish
475   Bardolph, banish Poins; but for sweet Jack Falstaff,
kind Jack Falstaff, true Jack Falstaff, valiant Jack

---

448–49 **trunk of humors** receptacle of body fluids (with allusion
to the diseases that were thought to be the product of these fluids)
449 **bolting-hutch** sifting-bin (where impurities collect)   450 **dropsies** internal fluids   450 **bombard** leather wine vessel   452 **Manningtree** town in Essex (where at annual fairs plays were acted and,
evidently, great oxen were stuffed and barbecued)   453–54 **vice,
iniquity, vanity** (names intended to associate Falstaff with
characters of the old morality plays, all of whom were corrupters
of virtue. But unlike Falstaff, who ought to know better, *they* were
young)   456–57 **Wherein cunning but in craft** i.e., wherein skillful
but in underhanded skills   460 **take me with you** let me follow your
meaning   473 **kine** cows (cf. Genesis 41:19–21)

Falstaff, and therefore more valiant being, as he is,
old Jack Falstaff, banish not him thy Harry's company, banish not him thy Harry's company, banish
plump Jack, and banish all the world!        480

*Prince.* I do, I will.                    [*A knocking heard.
        Exeunt Hostess, Francis, and Bardolph.*]

        *Enter Bardolph, running.*

*Bardolph.* O, my lord, my lord! The sheriff with a most
monstrous watch° is at the door.

*Falstaff.* Out, ye rogue! Play out the play, I have much
to say in the behalf of that Falstaff.        485

        *Enter the Hostess.*

*Hostess.* O Jesu, my lord, my lord!

*Prince.* Heigh, heigh, the devil rides upon a fiddlestick!
What's the matter?

*Hostess.* The sheriff and all the watch are at the door.
They are come to search the house. Shall I let        490
them in?

*Falstaff.* Dost thou hear, Hal? Never call a true piece
of gold a counterfeit. Thou art essentially made without seeming so.°

*Prince.* And thou a natural coward without instinct.        495

*Falstaff.* I deny your major.° If you will deny the sheriff,
so; if not, let him enter. If I become not a cart° as
well as another man, a plague on my bringing up!
I hope I shall as soon be strangled with a halter as
another.        500

*Prince.* Go hide thee behind the arras.° The rest walk
up above. Now, my masters, for a true face and good
conscience.

---

483 **watch** group of constables    492–94 **Never . . . so** (a difficult
passage, perhaps meaning that Falstaff, as a true piece of gold
despite appearances, should not be turned over to the sheriff by a
royal friend who is also true gold despite appearances)    496 **major**
i.e., major premise, with pun on "mayor"    497 **cart** hangman's cart
501 **arras** wall-hanging

*Falstaff.* Both which I have had; but their date is out,
505   and therefore I'll hide me.              *Exit.*

*Prince.* Call in the sheriff.
                 *[Exeunt all but the Prince and Peto.]*

        *Enter Sheriff and the Carrier.*

Now, master sheriff, what is your will with me?

*Sheriff.* First, pardon me, my lord. A hue and cry
Hath followed certain men unto this house.

510 *Prince.* What men?

*Sheriff.* One of them is well known, my gracious lord—
  A gross fat man.

*Carrier.*           As fat as butter.

*Prince.* The man, I do assure you, is not here,
  For I myself at this time have employed him.°
515 And, sheriff, I will engage my word to thee
  That I will by tomorrow dinner time
  Send him to answer thee, or any man,
  For anything he shall be charged withal;
  And so let me entreat you leave the house.

520 *Sheriff.* I will, my lord. There are two gentlemen
  Have in this robbery lost three hundred marks.

*Prince.* It may be so. If he have robbed these men,
  He shall be answerable; and so farewell.

*Sheriff.* Good night, my noble lord.

525 *Prince.* I think it is good morrow, is it not?

*Sheriff.* Indeed, my lord, I think it be two o'clock.
               *Exit [with Carrier].*

*Prince.* This oily rascal is known as well as Paul's. Go
  call him forth.

---

513-14 **The man . . . him** (Hal's reply is equivocal: Falstaff is not
"here," in the heir-apparent's presence, but "employed" behind the
arras)

*Peto.* Falstaff! Fast asleep behind the arras, and snort-
  ing° like a horse.                                        530

*Prince.* Hark how hard he fetches breath. Search his
  pockets.
    *He searcheth his pocket and findeth certain papers.*
  What hast thou found?

*Peto.* Nothing but papers, my lord.

*Prince.* Let's see what they be. Read them.               535

[*Peto reads*] "Item, A capon  .  .  .  .   2s. 2d.
              Item, Sauce  .  .  .  .  .       4d.
              Item, Sack two gallons  .  .  5s. 8d.
              Item, Anchovies and sack
                  after supper  .  .  .   2s. 6d.          540
              Item, Bread  .  .  .  .  .       ob."°

*Prince.* O monstrous! But one halfpennyworth of bread
  to this intolerable deal° of sack! What there is else,
  keep close; we'll read it at more advantage. There
  let him sleep till day. I'll to the court in the morn-  545
  ing. We must all to the wars, and thy place shall be
  honorable. I'll procure this fat rogue a charge of
  foot,° and I know his death will be a march of twelve
  score.° The money shall be paid back again with
  advantage.° Be with me betimes° in the morning,        550
  and so good morrow, Peto.

*Peto.* Good morrow, good my lord.                  *Exeunt.*

529–30 snorting snoring   541 ob. obolus, halfpenny   543 deal lot
547–48 charge of foot company of infantry   548–49 twelve score
twelve score paces   550 advantage interest   550 betimes early

# [ACT III

### Scene I. *Wales. A room.*]

*Enter Hotspur, Worcester, Lord Mortimer, Owen
Glendower.*

*Mortimer.* These promises are fair, the parties sure,
And our induction° full of prosperous hope.

*Hotspur.* Lord Mortimer, and cousin Glendower, will
you sit down? And uncle Worcester. A plague upon
5    it! I have forgot the map.

*Glendower.* No, here it is. Sit, cousin Percy, sit, good
cousin Hotspur, for by that name as oft as Lancaster
doth speak of you, his cheek looks pale, and with
a rising sigh he wisheth you in heaven.

10  *Hotspur.* And you in hell, as oft as he hears Owen
Glendower spoke of.°

*Glendower.* I cannot blame him. At my nativity
The front of heaven was full of fiery shapes
Of burning cressets,° and at my birth
15  The frame and huge foundation of the earth
Shakèd like a coward.

III.i.2 **induction** beginning   **3–11 Lord . . . spoke of** (many editors
revise to read as verse, with line breaks after "down/it/is/Hotspur/
you/sigh/hell/of"; or, leaving Hotspur's lines as prose, revise Glendower's speech to read as verse with breaks after "Percy/name/you
sigh/heaven")  **14 cressets** beacons

96

*Hotspur.* Why, so it would have done at the same season
    if your mother's cat had but kittened, though your-
    self had never been born.

*Glendower.* I say the earth did shake when I was born.   *20*

*Hotspur.* And I say the earth was not of my mind,
    If you suppose as fearing you it shook.

*Glendower.* The heavens were all on fire, the earth did
    tremble.

*Hotspur.* O, then the earth shook to see the heavens on
    fire,
    And not in fear of your nativity.   *25*
    Diseasèd nature oftentimes breaks forth
    In strange eruptions; oft the teeming earth
    Is with a kind of colic pinched and vexed
    By the imprisoning of unruly wind
    Within her womb, which, for enlargement striving,   *30*
    Shakes the old beldame° earth and topples down
    Steeples and mossgrown towers. At your birth
    Our grandam earth, having this distemp'rature,°
    In passion° shook.

*Glendower.*             Cousin, of many men
    I do not bear these crossings. Give me leave   *35*
    To tell you once again that at my birth
    The front of heaven was full of fiery shapes,
    The goats ran from the mountains, and the herds
    Were strangely clamorous to the frighted fields.
    These signs have marked me extraordinary,   *40*
    And all the courses of my life do show
    I am not in the roll of common men.
    Where is he living, clipped in with° the sea
    That chides the banks of England, Scotland, Wales,
    Which calls me pupil or hath read to° me?   *45*
    And bring him out that is but woman's son
    Can trace° me in the tedious ways of art°
    And hold me pace in deep experiments.

31 beldame grandmother (cf. "grandam," line 33)  33 distemp'rature physical disorder  34 passion pain  43 clipped in with em-
braced by  45 read to tutored  47 trace follow  47 art magic

*Hotspur.* I think there's no man speaks better Welsh.°
50    I'll to dinner.

*Mortimer.* Peace, cousin Percy; you will make him
    mad.

*Glendower.* I can call spirits from the vasty deep.

*Hotspur.* Why, so can I, or so can any man;
    But will they come when you do call for them?

55  *Glendower.* Why, I can teach you, cousin, to command
    the devil.

*Hotspur.* And I can teach thee, coz, to shame the
    devil—
    By telling truth. Tell truth and shame the devil.
    If thou have power to raise him, bring him hither,
60    And I'll be sworn I have power to shame him hence.
    O, while you live, tell truth and shame the devil!

*Mortimer.* Come, come, no more of this unprofitable
    chat.

*Glendower.* Three times hath Henry Bolingbroke made
    head
    Against my power; thrice from the banks of Wye
65    And sandy-bottomed Severn have I sent him
    Booteless° home and weather-beaten back.

*Hotspur.* Home without boots, and in foul weather too?
    How scapes he agues,° in the devil's name?

*Glendower.* Come, here is the map. Shall we divide our
    right°
70    According to our threefold order ta'en?

*Mortimer.* The Archdeacon hath divided it
    Into three limits° very equally.
    England, from Trent and Severn hitherto,
    By south and east is to my part assigned;

49 **speaks better Welsh** (1) brags better (2) talks more unintelligibly
66 **Booteless** profitless (probably trisyllabic)   68 **agues** i.e., catching cold   69 **our right** i.e., the kingdom they hope to win   72 **limits**
regions

All westward, Wales beyond the Severn shore,        75
And all the fertile land within that bound,
To Owen Glendower; and, dear coz, to you
The remnant northward lying off from Trent.
And our indentures tripartite° are drawn,
Which being sealèd interchangeably°        80
(A business that this night may execute),
Tomorrow, cousin Percy, you and I
And my good Lord of Worcester will set forth
To meet your father and the Scottish power,
As is appointed us, at Shrewsbury.        85
My father Glendower is not ready yet,
Nor shall we need his help these fourteen days.
[*To Glendower*] Within that space you may have
    drawn together
Your tenants, friends, and neighboring gentlemen.

*Glendower*. A shorter time shall send me to you, lords;        90
And in my conduct shall your ladies come,
From whom you now must steal and take no leave,
For there will be a world of water shed
Upon the parting of your wives and you.

*Hotspur*. Methinks my moiety,° north from Burton
    here,        95
In quantity equals not one of yours.
See how this river comes me cranking° in
And cuts me from the best of all my land
A huge half-moon, a monstrous cantle° out.
I'll have the current in this place dammed up,        100
And here the smug° and silver Trent shall run
In a new channel fair and evenly.
It shall not wind with such a deep indent
To rob me of so rich a bottom° here.

*Glendower*. Not wind? It shall, it must! You see it doth.        105

*Mortimer*. Yea, but mark how he bears his course, and

---

79 **indentures tripartite** three-way agreements   80 **interchangeably**
i.e., by all three parties   95 **moiety** share   97 **cranking** winding
99 **cantle** piece   101 **smug** smooth   104 **bottom** valley

runs me up with like advantage° on the other side,
gelding the opposèd continent° as much as on the
other side it takes from you.°

*Worcester.* Yea, but a little charge° will trench° him
110       here
And on this north side win this cape of land;
And then he runs straight and even.

*Hotspur.* I'll have it so, a little charge will do it.

*Glendower.* I'll not have it alt'red.

115 *Hotspur.* Will not you?

*Glendower.* No, nor you shall not.

*Hotspur.* Who shall say me nay?

*Glendower.* Why, that will I.

*Hotspur.* Let me not understand you then; speak it in
120       Welsh.

*Glendower.* I can speak English, lord, as well as you;
For I was trained up in the English court,
Where, being but young, I framèd to the harp
Many an English ditty lovely well,
125       And gave the tongue a helpful ornament°—
A virtue that was never seen in you.

*Hotspur.* Marry, and I am glad of it with all my heart!
I had rather be a kitten and cry mew
Than one of these same meter ballad-mongers.°
130       I had rather hear a brazen canstick turned°
Or a dry wheel grate on the axletree,
And that would set my teeth nothing on edge,
Nothing so much as mincing° poetry.

---

107 **advantage** i.e., disadvantage    108 **gelding the opposèd continent**
cutting out of the opposite bank    106–09 **Yea . . . you** (revised by
most editors to four or five lines of verse, with little agreement about
lineation)    110 **charge** cost    110 **trench** make a new course for
125 **gave . . . ornament** (1) ornamented the words with music? (2)
benefited the English language by my poems?    129 **meter ballad-
mongers** singers of doggerel ballads    130 **canstick turned** i.e., can-
dlestick in process of being burnished (and therefore raucously
scraped)    133 **mincing** affected

'Tis like the forced gait of a shuffling nag.

*Glendower*. Come, you shall have Trent turned.    *135*

*Hotspur*. I do not care. I'll give thrice so much land
To any well-deserving friend;
But in the way of bargain, mark ye me,
I'll cavil on the ninth part of a hair.
Are the indentures drawn? Shall we be gone?    *140*

*Glendower*. The moon shines fair; you may away by
night.
I'll haste the writer, and withal
Break with° your wives of your departure hence.
I am afraid my daughter will run mad,
So much she doteth on her Mortimer.    *Exit. 145*

*Mortimer*. Fie, cousin Percy, how you cross my father!

*Hotspur*. I cannot choose. Sometime he angers me
With telling me of the moldwarp° and the ant,
Of the dreamer Merlin and his prophecies,
And of a dragon and a finless fish,    *150*
A clip-winged griffin and a moulten raven,
A couching° lion and a ramping° cat,
And such a deal of skimble-skamble° stuff
As puts me from my faith. I tell you what—
He held me last night at least nine hours    *155*
In reckoning up the several devils' names
That were his lackeys. I cried "hum," and "Well,
go to!"
But marked him not a word. O, he is as tedious
As a tired horse, a railing wife;
Worse than a smoky house. I had rather live    *160*
With cheese and garlic in a windmill far
Than feed on cates° and have him talk to me
In any summer house in Christendom.

---

143 **Break with** inform   148 **moldwarp** mole, i.e., Henry   152
**couching, ramping** (Hotspur ridicules heraldic crouching and rearing
beasts; evidently Glendower talked of ancient prophecies which held
that the kingdom of the mole should be divided by the lion, dragon
and wolf, which were the crests of Percy, Glendower, and Mortimer)
153 **skimble-skamble** meaningless   162 **cates** delicacies

*Mortimer.* In faith, he is a worthy gentleman,
165  Exceedingly well read and profited
     In strange concealments,° valiant as a lion,
     And wondrous affable, and as bountiful
     As mines of India. Shall I tell you, cousin?
     He holds your temper in a high respect
170  And curbs himself even of his natural scope°
     When you come 'cross his humor.° Faith, he does.
     I warrant you that man is not alive
     Might so have tempted him as you have done
     Without the taste of danger and reproof.
175  But do not use it oft, let me entreat you.

*Worcester.* In faith, my lord, you are too willful-blame,°
     And since your coming hither have done enough
     To put him quite besides his patience.
     You must needs learn, lord, to amend this fault.
     Though sometimes it show greatness, courage,
180      blood°—
     And that's the dearest grace it renders you—
     Yet oftentimes it doth present° harsh rage,
     Defect of manners, want of government,°
     Pride, haughtiness, opinion,° and disdain;
185  The least of which haunting a nobleman
     Loseth men's hearts, and leaves behind a stain
     Upon the beauty of all parts besides,
     Beguiling them of commendation.

*Hotspur.* Well, I am schooled. Good manners be your
         speed!°
190  Here come our wives, and let us take our leave.

         *Enter Glendower with the Ladies.*

*Mortimer.* This is the deadly spite° that angers me—
     My wife can speak no English, I no Welsh.

---

165–66 **profited . . . concealments** expert in secret arts   170 **scope**
tendencies   171 **come 'cross his humor** clash with his temperament
176 **too willful-blame** blamable for too much willfulness   180 **blood**
spirit   182 **present** indicate   183 **government** self-control   184 **opinion** arrogance   189 **be your speed** bring you success   191 **spite** misfortune

*Glendower.* My daughter weeps; she'll not part with
    you,
  She'll be a soldier too, she'll to the wars.

*Mortimer.* Good father, tell her that she and my aunt
    Percy        *195*
  Shall follow in your conduct speedily.
    *Glendower speaks to her in Welsh, and she answers*
                      *him in the same.*

*Glendower.* She is desperate here.
  A peevish self-willed harlotry,° one that no persuasion can do good upon.
                   *The Lady speaks in Welsh.*

*Mortimer.* I understand thy looks. That pretty Welsh°  *200*
  Which thou pourest down from these swelling
    heavens°
  I am too perfect in; and, but for shame,
  In such a parley° should I answer thee.
                 *The Lady again in Welsh.*
  I understand thy kisses, and thou mine,
  And that's a feeling disputation.°        *205*
  But I will never be a truant, love,
  Till I have learnt thy language; for thy tongue
  Makes Welsh as sweet as ditties highly penned,°
  Sung by a fair queen in a summer's bow'r,
  With ravishing division,° to her lute.    *210*

*Glendower.* Nay, if you melt, then will she run mad.
          *The Lady speaks again in Welsh.*

*Mortimer.* O, I am ignorance itself in this!

*Glendower.* She bids you on the wanton° rushes lay
    you down
  And rest your gentle head upon her lap,
  And she will sing the song that pleaseth you    *215*

---

198 **harlotry** ninny, fool  200 **That pretty Welsh** i.e., her tears
201 **heavens** i.e., her eyes  203 **parley** meeting (of tears)  205 **feeling disputation** dialogue by (1) touching (2) the feelings  208 **highly
penned** i.e., lofty  210 **division** musical variation  213 **wanton** lux-
urious

And on your eyelids crown the god of sleep,°
Charming your blood with pleasing heaviness,
Making such difference 'twixt wake and sleep
As is the difference betwixt day and night
220 The hour before the heavenly-harnessed team°
Begins his golden progress in the east.

*Mortimer.* With all my heart I'll sit and hear her sing.
By that time will our book,° I think, be drawn.

*Glendower.* Do so, and those musicians that shall play
to you
225 Hang in the air a thousand leagues from hence,
And straight they shall be here: sit, and attend.

*Hotspur.* Come, Kate, thou art perfect in lying down.
Come, quick, quick, that I may lay my head in thy
lap.

230 *Lady Percy.* Go, ye giddy goose.        *The music plays.*

*Hotspur.* Now I perceive the devil understands Welsh,
And 'tis no marvel he is so humorous,°
By'r Lady, he is a good musician.

*Lady Percy.* Then should you be nothing but musical,
235 For you are altogether governed by humors.
Lie still, ye thief, and hear the lady sing in Welsh.

*Hotspur.* I had rather hear Lady, my brach,° howl in
Irish.

*Lady Percy.* Wouldst thou have thy head broken?

240 *Hotspur.* No.

*Lady Percy.* Then be still.

*Hotspur.* Neither! 'Tis a woman's fault.

*Lady Percy.* Now God help thee!

*Hotspur.* To the Welsh lady's bed.

---

216 **crown the god of sleep** i.e., give sleep sovereignty   220 **the heavenly-harnessed team** the horses of the sun   223 **book** agreement
232 **humorous** capricious   237 **brach** bitch-hound

*Lady Percy.* What's that?   245

*Hotspur.* Peace! She sings.

> *Here the Lady sings a Welsh song.*

Come, Kate, I'll have your song too.

*Lady Percy.* Not mine, in good sooth.°

*Hotspur.* Not yours, in good sooth? Heart, you swear
   like a comfit-maker's° wife. "Not you, in good   250
   sooth!" and "as true as I live!" and "as God shall
   mend me!" and "as sure as day!"
And givest such sarcenet surety° for thy oaths
As if thou never walk'st further than Finsbury.°
Swear me, Kate, like a lady as thou art,   255
A good mouth-filling oath, and leave "in sooth"
And such protest of pepper gingerbread°
To velvet guards° and Sunday citizens.
Come, sing.

*Lady Percy.* I will not sing.   260

*Hotspur.* 'Tis the next way to turn tailor° or be red-
   breast-teacher.° And the indentures be drawn, I'll
   away within these two hours; and so come in when
   ye will.   *Exit.*

*Glendower.* Come, come, Lord Mortimer. You are as
   slow   265
As hot Lord Percy is on fire to go.
By this our book is drawn; we'll but seal,
And then to horse immediately.

*Mortimer.*   With all my heart.
   *Exeunt.*

---

248 **sooth** truth   250 **comfit-maker's** confectioner's   253 **sarcenet
surety** flimsy security ("sarcenet"—a thin silk)   254 **Finsbury** favorite resort near London (frequented by the middle-class groups
whom Hotspur satirizes)   257 **pepper gingerbread** i.e., insubstan-
tial, crumbling in the mouth   258 **velvet guards** i.e., shopkeepers,
who favored velvet trimmings for Sunday wear   261 **tailor** (like
weavers, tailors were famed for singing at their work)   261–62 **red-
breast-teacher** singing master to songbirds

[Scene II. *London. The palace.*]


*Enter the King, Prince of Wales, and others.*


*King.* Lords, give us leave: the Prince of Wales and I
    Must have some private conference; but be near at
      hand,
    For we shall presently have need of you.
                             *Exeunt Lords.*
    I know not whether God will have it so
5    For some displeasing service I have done,
    That, in his secret doom,° out of my blood°
    He'll breed revengement and a scourge for me;
    But thou dost in thy passages° of life
    Make me believe that thou art only marked
10   For the hot vengeance and the rod of heaven
    To punish my mistreadings.° Tell me else,
    Could such inordinate° and low desires,
    Such poor, such bare, such lewd, such mean at-
      tempts,
    Such barren pleasures, rude society,
15   As thou art matched withal° and grafted to,
    Accompany the greatness of thy blood
    And hold their level with thy princely heart?


*Prince.* So please your Majesty, I would I could
    Quit° all offenses with as clear excuse
20   As well° as I am doubtless I can purge
    Myself of many I am charged withal.
    Yet such extenuation let me beg


---

III.ii.6 **doom** judgment    6 **blood** i.e., heirs    8 **passages** courses
9–11 **thou . . . mistreadings** i.e., (1) heaven is punishing me through
you (2) heaven will punish you to punish me    12 **inordinate** i.e.,
out of order (for one of your rank)    15 **withal** with    19 **Quit** clear
myself of    20 **As well** and as well

As, in reproof of many tales devised,
Which oft the ear of greatness needs must hear
By smiling pickthanks and base newsmongers,                  25
I may, for some things true wherein my youth
Hath faulty wand'red and irregular,
Find pardon on my true submission.°


*King.* God pardon thee! Yet let me wonder, Harry,
At thy affections,° which do hold a wing                     30
Quite from the flight of all thy ancestors.
Thy place in council thou hast rudely lost,
Which by thy younger brother is supplied,
And art almost an alien to the hearts
Of all the court and princes of my blood.                    35
The hope and expectation of thy time°
Is ruined, and the soul of every man
Prophetically do forethink thy fall.
Had I so lavish of my presence been,
So common-hackneyed in the eyes of men,                      40
So stale and cheap to vulgar company,
Opinion,° that did help me to the crown,
Had still kept loyal to possession°
And left me in reputeless banishment,
A fellow of no mark nor likelihood.                          45
By being seldom seen, I could not stir
But, like a comet, I was wond'red at;
That men would tell their children, "This is he!"
Others would say, "Where? Which is Bolingbroke?"
And then I stole all courtesy from heaven,°                  50
And dressed myself in such humility
That I did pluck allegiance from men's hearts,
Loud shouts and salutations from their mouths
Even in the presence of the crownèd King.

22–28 **Yet . . . submission** yet let me beg such extenuation that when
I have confuted many manufactured charges (which the ear of
greatness is bound to hear from informers and tattletales) I may
be pardoned for some true faults of which my youth has been
guilty    30 **affections** tastes    36 **time** reign    42 **Opinion** public opinion    43 **possession** i.e., Richard II    50 **I . . . heaven** I took a godlike
graciousness on myself

55    Thus did I keep my person fresh and new,
 My presence, like a robe pontifical,
 Ne'er seen but wond'red at; and so my state,
 Seldom but sumptuous, showed like a feast
 And won by rareness such solemnity.

60    The skipping King, he ambled up and down
 With shallow jesters and rash bavin° wits,
 Soon kindled and soon burnt; carded° his state;
 Mingled his royalty with cap'ring fools;
 Had his great name profanèd with their scorns

65    And gave his countenance, against his name,°
 To laugh at gibing boys and stand the push°
 Of every beardless vain comparative;°
 Grew a companion to the common streets,
 Enfeoffed himself to popularity;°

70    That, being daily swallowed by men's eyes,
 They surfeited with honey and began
 To loathe the taste of sweetness, whereof a little
 More than a little is by much too much.
 So, when he had occasion to be seen,

75    He was but as the cuckoo is in June,
 Heard, not regarded—seen, but with such eyes
 As, sick and blunted with community,°
 Afford no extraordinary gaze,
 Such as is bent on sunlike majesty

80    When it shines seldom in admiring eyes;
 But rather drowsed and hung their eyelids down,
 Slept in his face, and rend'red such aspect
 As cloudy° men use to their adversaries,
 Being with his presence glutted, gorged, and full.

85    And in that very line, Harry, standest thou;
 For thou hast lost thy princely privilege
 With vile participation.° Not an eye
 But is aweary of thy common sight,

---

**61 bavin** brushwood (which flares and burns out)    **62 carded** debased    **65 his name** i.e., (1) his kingly title (2) his kingly authority    **66 stand the push** put up with the impudence    **67 comparative** deviser of insulting comparisons    **69 Enfeoffed . . . popularity** bound himself to low company    **77 with community** by familiarity (with the king)    **83 cloudy** sullen (but also with reference to "clouds" obscuring the royal "sun")    **87 participation** companionship

Save mine, which hath desired to see thee more;
Which now doth that I would not have it do—        *90*
Make blind itself with foolish tenderness.°

*Prince.* I shall hereafter, my thrice-gracious lord,
Be more myself.

*King.*                For all the world,
As thou art to this hour was Richard then
When I from France set foot at Ravenspurgh;        *95*
And even as I was then is Percy now.
Now, by my scepter, and my soul to boot,
He hath more worthy interest° to the state
Than thou the shadow of succession;
For of no right, nor color° like to right,        *100*
He doth fill fields with harness° in the realm,
Turns head against the lion's armèd jaws,
And, being no more in debt to years than thou,
Leads ancient lords and reverend bishops on
To bloody battles and to bruising arms.        *105*
What never-dying honor hath he got
Against renownèd Douglas! whose high deeds,
Whose hot incursions and great name in arms
Holds from all soldiers chief majority°
And military title capital°        *110*
Through all the kingdoms that acknowledge Christ.
Thrice hath this Hotspur, Mars in swathling clothes,
This infant warrior, in his enterprises
Discomfited great Douglas; ta'en him once,
Enlargèd him, and made a friend of him,        *115*
To fill the mouth of deep defiance up°
And shake the peace and safety of our throne.
And what say you to this? Percy, Northumberland,
The Archbishop's grace of York, Douglas, Mortimer
Capitulate° against us and are up.°        *120*
But wherefore do I tell these news to thee?

91 **tenderness** i.e., tears   98 **worthy interest** claim based on worth (as
compared with a "shadow" claim by inheritance)   100 **color** pretense   101 **harness** armor   109 **majority** preeminence   110 **capital**
topmost   116 **To fill . . . up** to deepen the noise of defiance   120
**Capitulate** (1) make a "head" or armed force? (2) draw up "heads"
of an argument?   120 **up** in arms

Why, Harry, do I tell thee of my foes,
Which art my nearest and dearest° enemy?
Thou that art like enough, through vassal fear,
125   Base inclination, and the start of spleen,
To fight against me under Percy's pay,
To dog his heels and curtsy at his frowns,
To show how much thou art degenerate.

*Prince.* Do not think so, you shall not find it so.
130   And God forgive them that so much have swayed
Your Majesty's good thoughts away from me.
I will redeem all this on Percy's head
And, in the closing of some glorious day,
Be bold to tell you that I am your son,
135   When I will wear a garment all of blood,
And stain my favors° in a bloody mask,
Which, washed away, shall scour my shame with it.
And that shall be the day, whene'er it lights,
That this same child of honor and renown,
140   This gallant Hotspur, this all-praisèd knight,
And your unthought-of Harry chance to meet.
For every honor sitting on his helm,
Would they were multitudes, and on my head
My shames redoubled! For the time will come
145   That I shall make this northern youth exchange
His glorious deeds for my indignities.
Percy is but my factor,° good my lord,
To engross° up glorious deeds on my behalf;
And I will call him to so strict account
150   That he shall render every glory up,
Yea, even the slightest worship of his time,°
Or I will tear the reckoning from his heart.
This in the name of God I promise here;
The which if he be pleased I shall perform,
155   I do beseech your Majesty may salve
The long-grown wounds of my intemperance.
If not, the end of life cancels all bands,°

---

123 **dearest** (1) most loved (2) costliest   136 **favors** features
147 **factor** agent   148 **engross** hoard   151 **worship of his time**
honor he has gained in his lifetime   157 **bands** bonds, promises

And I will die a hundred thousand deaths
Ere break the smallest parcel° of this vow.

*King.* A hundred thousand rebels die in this!        160
Thou shalt have charge and sovereign trust herein.

#### *Enter Blunt.*

How now, good Blunt? Thy looks are full of speed.

*Blunt.* So hath the business° that I come to speak of.
Lord Mortimer of Scotland hath sent word
That Douglas and the English rebels met        165
The eleventh of this month at Shrewsbury.
A mighty and a fearful head they are,
If promises be kept on every hand,
As ever off'red foul play in a state.

*King.* The Earl of Westmoreland set forth today;        170
With him my son, Lord John of Lancaster:
For this advertisement is five days old.
On Wednesday next, Harry, you shall set forward;
On Thursday we ourselves will march. Our meeting
Is Bridgenorth; and, Harry, you shall march        175
Through Gloucestershire; by which account,
Our business valuèd,° some twelve days hence
Our general forces at Bridgenorth shall meet.
Our hands are full of business. Let's away:
Advantage feeds him° fat while men delay.  *Exeunt.*   180

[Scene III. *Eastcheap. The tavern.*]

#### *Enter Falstaff and Bardolph.*

*Falstaff.* Bardolph, am I not fall'n away vilely since this
last action? Do I not bate?° Do I not dwindle? Why,

159 **parcel** item   163 **So hath the business** i.e., the business too has
speed (must be dealt with speedily)   177 **Our business valuèd** having sized up what we have to do   180 **him** itself   III.iii.2 **bate** lose
weight

my skin hangs about me like an old lady's loose
gown! I am withered like an old apple-john.° Well,
5  I'll repent, and that suddenly, while I am in some
liking.° I shall be out of heart° shortly, and then I
shall have no strength to repent. And I have not forgotten what the inside of a church is made of, I am
a peppercorn,° a brewer's horse.° The inside of a
10  church! Company, villainous company, hath been
the spoil of me.

Bardolph. Sir John, you are so fretful you cannot live
long.

Falstaff. Why, there is it! Come, sing me a bawdy song,
15  make me merry. I was as virtuously given as a gentleman need to be, virtuous enough: swore little, diced
not above seven times a week, went to a bawdy house
not above once in a quarter of an hour, paid money
that I borrowed three or four times,° lived well, and
20  in good compass;° and now I live out of all order,
out of all compass.

Bardolph. Why, you are so fat, Sir John, that you must
needs be out of all compass—out of all reasonable
compass, Sir John.

25  Falstaff. Do thou amend thy face, and I'll amend my
life. Thou art our admiral,° thou bearest the lantern
in the poop—but 'tis in the nose of thee: thou art
the Knight of the Burning Lamp.

Bardolph. Why, Sir John, my face does you no harm.

30  Falstaff. No, I'll be sworn. I make as good use of it as
many a man doth of a death's-head° or a memento
mori.° I never see thy face but I think upon hellfire

---

4 **old apple-john** apple with shriveled skin   5-6 **am in some liking**
(1) am in the mood (2) still have some flesh left   6 **out of heart** (1)
out of the mood (2) out of shape   9 **peppercorn, brewer's horse**
(Falstaff this time picks objects *not* long and thin, but dry, withered,
decrepit)   16-19 **diced . . . times** (probably spoken with significant
pauses after "diced not," "once," "borrowed")   20 **compass** order
(but Bardolph takes it in the sense of "size")   26 **admiral** flagship
(recognizable by its lantern)   31 **death's-head** ring with a skull
31-32 **memento mori** reminder of death

and Dives° that lived in purple; for there he is in his
robes, burning, burning. If thou wert any way given
to virtue, I would swear by thy face; my oath should       35
be "By this fire, that's God's angel."° But thou art
altogether given over, and wert indeed, but for the
light in thy face, the son of utter darkness. When
thou ran'st up Gad's Hill in the night to catch my
horse, if I did not think thou hadst been an ignis         40
fatuus° or a ball of wildfire,° there's no purchase in
money. O, thou art a perpetual triumph,° an everlasting bonfire-light! Thou hast saved me a thousand
marks in links° and torches, walking with thee in the
night betwixt tavern and tavern; but the sack that         45
thou hast drunk me would have bought me lights as
good cheap° at the dearest chandler's° in Europe.
I have maintained that salamander° of yours with
fire any time this two and thirty years. God reward
me for it!                                                 50

*Bardolph.* 'Sblood, I would my face were in your belly!°

*Falstaff.* God-a-mercy! So should I be sure to be heart-
burned.

*Enter Hostess.*

How now, Dame Partlet° the hen? Have you enquired yet who picked my pocket?                           55

*Hostess.* Why, Sir John, what do you think, Sir John?
Do you think I keep thieves in my house? I have
searched, I have enquired, so has my husband, man
by man, boy by boy, servant by servant. The tithe°
of a hair was never lost in my house before.               60

---

33 **Dives** uncharitable rich man who burns in hell (Luke 16:19–31)
36 **angel** (alluding to the Scriptural accounts of angels manifesting
themselves as fire, or possibly to the seraphs, highest order of angels,
who were fire)    40–41 **ignis fatuus** will-o'-the-wisp    41 **ball of wildfire** firework    42 **triumph** i.e., of the Roman kind, with torches
44 **links** flares    47 **good cheap** cheaply    47 **chandler's** candle mak-
er's    48 **salamander** lizard supposed to live in fire    51 **I . . . belly**
(proverbial retort, to which Falstaff's reply gives new life)    54 **Dame
Partlet** (traditional name for a hen, and well suited to the clucking
Hostess)    59 **tithe** tenth part

*Falstaff.* Ye lie, hostess. Bardolph was shaved and lost
many a hair, and I'll be sworn my pocket was picked.
Go to, you are a woman, go!

*Hostess.* Who, I? No;° I defy thee! God's light, I was
65    never called so in mine own house before!

*Falstaff.* Go to, I know you well enough.

*Hostess.* No, Sir John; you do not know me, Sir John.
I know you, Sir John. You owe me money, Sir John,
and now you pick a quarrel to beguile me of it. I
70    bought you a dozen of shirts to your back.

*Falstaff.* Dowlas,° filthy dowlas! I have given them
away to bakers' wives; they have made bolters° of
them.

*Hostess.* Now, as I am a true woman, holland° of eight
75    shillings an ell.° You owe money here besides, Sir
John, for your diet and by-drinkings,° and money
lent you, four and twenty pound.

*Falstaff.* He had his part of it; let him pay.

*Hostess.* He? Alas, he is poor; he hath nothing.

80 *Falstaff.* How? Poor? Look upon his face. What call
you rich?° Let them coin his nose, let them coin his
cheeks. I'll not pay a denier.° What, will you make
a younker° of me? Shall I not take mine ease in mine
inn but I shall have my pocket picked? I have lost a
85    seal ring of my grandfather's worth forty mark.

*Hostess.* O Jesu, I have heard the Prince tell him, I
know not how oft, that that ring was copper!

*Falstaff.* How? The Prince is a Jack,° a sneak-up.°

<hr/>

64 **No** (the Hostess suspects that any word or phrase of Falstaff's
may contain hidden innuendoes about her moral character; she
sometimes retorts with comments containing amusing innuendoes
about herself that she is too ignorant to understand)  71 **Dowlas**
coarse linen  72 **bolters** sieves  74 **holland** fine linen  75 **ell** one
and a quarter yards  76 **by-drinkings** drinks between meals  81 **rich**
(referring to its red gold-and-copper hues)  82 **denier** tenth of a
penny  83 **younker** greenhorn  88 **Jack** rascal  88 **sneak-up** sneak

'Sblood, and he were here, I would cudgel him like
a dog if he would say so.                                         90

*Enter the Prince [and Poins], marching, and*
*Falstaff meets them, playing upon his truncheon°*
*like a fife.*

How now, lad? Is the wind in that door,° i' faith?
Must we all march?

*Bardolph.* Yea, two and two,° Newgate fashion.

*Hostess.* My lord, I pray you hear me.

*Prince.* What say'st thou, Mistress Quickly? How doth      95
thy husband? I love him well, he is an honest man.

*Hostess.* Good my lord, hear me.

*Falstaff.* Prithee let her alone and list to me.

*Prince.* What say'st thou, Jack?

*Falstaff.* The other night I fell asleep here behind the    100
arras and had my pocket picked. This house is turned
bawdy house; they pick pockets.

*Prince.* What didst thou lose, Jack?

*Falstaff.* Wilt thou believe me, Hal, three or four bonds
of forty pound apiece and a seal ring of my grand-         105
father's.

*Prince.* A trifle, some eightpenny matter.

*Hostess.* So I told him, my lord, and I said I heard your
Grace say so; and, my lord, he speaks most vilely of
you, like a foulmouthed man as he is, and said he         110
would cudgel you.

*Prince.* What! He did not?

*Hostess.* There's neither faith, truth, nor womanhood
in me else.

90s.d. **truncheon** cudgel   91 **Is . . . door** i.e., is that how things are
going   93 **two and two** i.e., bound in pairs like prisoners on the way
to (Newgate) prison

115 *Falstaff.* There's no more faith in thee than in a stewed
prune,° nor no more truth in thee than in a drawn°
fox; and for womanhood, Maid Marian may be the
deputy's wife of the ward to thee.° Go, you thing, go!

*Hostess.* Say, what thing, what thing?

120 *Falstaff.* What thing? Why, a thing to thank God on.

*Hostess.* I am no thing to thank God on, I would thou
shouldst know it! I am an honest man's wife, and,
setting thy knighthood aside, thou art a knave to
call me so.

125 *Falstaff.* Setting thy womanhood aside, thou art a beast
to say otherwise.

*Hostess.* Say, what beast, thou knave, thou?

*Falstaff.* What beast? Why, an otter.

*Prince.* An otter, Sir John? Why an otter?

130 *Falstaff.* Why, she's neither fish nor flesh; a man knows
not where to have her.

*Hostess.* Thou art an unjust man in saying so. Thou
or any man knows where to have me, thou knave,
thou!

135 *Prince.* Thou say'st true, hostess, and he slanders thee
most grossly.

*Hostess.* So he doth you, my lord, and said this other
day you ought° him a thousand pound.

*Prince.* Sirrah, do I owe you a thousand pound?

140 *Falstaff.* A thousand pound, Hal? A million! Thy love
is worth a million, thou owest me thy love.

---

115-16 **stewed prune** (evidently chosen by Falstaff because stewed
prunes were associated with bawdy houses)   116 **drawn** drawn from
his lair and trying every trick to get back to it   117-18 **Maid Marian
. . . thee** a disreputable female in country May games is chaste as the
wife of the ward's most respectable citizen in comparison with you
138 **ought** owed

*Hostess.* Nay, my lord, he called you Jack and said he
would cudgel you.

*Falstaff.* Did I, Bardolph?

*Bardolph.* Indeed, Sir John, you said so.                    *145*

*Falstaff.* Yea, if he said my ring was copper.

*Prince.* I say 'tis copper. Darest thou be as good as thy
word now?

*Falstaff.* Why, Hal, thou knowest, as thou art but man,
I dare; but as thou art Prince, I fear thee as I fear   *150*
the roaring of the lion's whelp.

*Prince.* And why not as the lion?

*Falstaff.* The King himself is to be feared as the lion.
Dost thou think I'll fear thee as I fear thy father?
Nay, and I do, I pray God my girdle break.              *155*

*Prince.* O, if it should, how would thy guts fall about
thy knees! But, sirrah, there's no room for faith,
truth, nor honesty in this bosom of thine. It is all
filled up with guts and midriff. Charge an honest
woman with picking thy pocket? Why, thou whore-         *160*
son, impudent, embossed° rascal,° if there were
anything in thy pocket but tavern reckonings, mem-
orandums of bawdy houses, and one poor pennyworth of sugar candy to make thee long-winded—
if thy pocket were enriched with any other injuries°    *165*
but these, I am a villain. And yet you will stand to
it; you will not pocket up wrong. Art thou not
ashamed?

*Falstaff.* Dost thou hear, Hal? Thou knowest in the
state of innocency Adam fell, and what should poor      *170*
Jack Falstaff do in the days of villainy? Thou seest
I have more flesh than another man, and therefore
more frailty. You confess then, you picked my
pocket?

---

161 **embossed** (1) swollen (2) foaming at the mouth (of a deer)
161 **rascal** (1) rogue (2) lean young deer   165 **injuries** i.e., things
whose loss you call injuries

175 *Prince.* It appears so by the story.

*Falstaff.* Hostess, I forgive thee, go make ready breakfast, love thy husband, look to thy servants, cherish
thy guests. Thou shalt find me tractable to any honest reason. Thou seest I am pacified still. Nay, prithee
180 be gone. *Exit Hostess.*
Now, Hal, to the news at court. For the robbery, lad
—how is that answered?

*Prince.* O my sweet beef, I must still be good angel to
thee. The money is paid back again.

185 *Falstaff.* O, I do not like that paying back! 'Tis a double
labor.

*Prince.* I am good friends with my father, and may do
anything.

*Falstaff.* Rob me the exchequer the first thing thou
190 doest, and do it with unwashed hands° too.

*Bardolph.* Do, my lord.

*Prince.* I have procured thee, Jack, a charge of foot.

*Falstaff.* I would it had been of horse. Where shall I
find one that can steal well? O for a fine thief° of the
195 age of two and twenty or thereabouts! I am heinously
unprovided. Well, God be thanked for these rebels,
they offend none but the virtuous: I laud them, I
praise them.

*Prince.* Bardolph!

200 *Bardolph.* My lord?

*Prince.* Go bear this letter to Lord John of Lancaster,
To my brother John; this to my Lord of Westmore-
land. [*Exit Bardolph.*]
Go, Peto, to horse, to horse; for thou and I
Have thirty miles to ride yet ere dinner time.
[*Exit Peto.*]

190 with unwashed hands with no delay    194 thief i.e., to steal a
horse

Jack, meet me tomorrow in the Temple Hall          205
At two o'clock in the afternoon.
There shalt thou know thy charge, and there receive
Money and order for their furniture.°
The land is burning, Percy stands on high,
And either we or they must lower lie.          [*Exit.*]   210

*Falstaff.* Rare words! Brave world! Hostess, my breakfast, come.
O, I could wish this tavern were my drum!°   [*Exit.*]

# [ACT IV

Scene I. *The rebel camp, near Shrewsbury*.]

*[Enter Hotspur, Worcester, and Douglas.]*

*Hotspur.* Well said, my noble Scot. If speaking truth
In this fine age were not thought flattery,
Such attribution° should the Douglas have
As not a soldier of this season's stamp

5    Should go so general current° through the world.
By God, I cannot flatter, I do defy°
The tongues of soothers!° But a braver place
In my heart's love hath no man than yourself.
Nay, task me° to my word; approve me, lord.

10  *Douglas.* Thou art the king of honor.
No man so potent breathes upon the ground
But I will beard° him.

*Enter one with letters.*

*Hotspur.*                    Do so, and 'tis well.—
What letters hast thou there?—I can but thank you.

*Messenger.* These letters come from your father.

---

IV.i.3 **attribution** recognition   5 **go so general current** be as widely
accepted (the image is of a coin of recent mintage: "this season's
stamp")   6 **defy** despise   7 **soothers** flatterers   9 **task me** try me,
test me   12 **beard** oppose

120

*Hotspur.* Letters from him? Why comes he not himself?    15

*Messenger.* He cannot come, my lord, he is grievous
    sick.

*Hotspur.* Zounds! How has he the leisure to be sick
    In such a justling° time? Who leads his power?
    Under whose government° come they along?

*Messenger.* His letters bears° his mind, not I, my lord.    20

*Worcester.* I prithee tell me, doth he keep his bed?

*Messenger.* He did, my lord, four days ere I set forth,
    And at the time of my departure thence
    He was much feared° by his physicians.

*Worcester.* I would the state of time had first been
    whole    23
    Ere he by sickness had been visited.
    His health was never better worth than now.

*Hotspur.* Sick now? Droop now? This sickness doth
    infect
    The very lifeblood of our enterprise.
    'Tis catching hither, even to our camp.    30
    He writes me here that inward sickness—
    And that his friends by deputation°
    Could not so soon be drawn; nor did he think it meet
    To lay so dangerous and dear a trust
    On any soul removed but on his own.    35
    Yet doth he give us bold advertisement,
    That with our small conjunction° we should on,
    To see how fortune is disposed to us;
    For, as he writes, there is no quailing now,
    Because the King is certainly possessed°    40
    Of all our purposes. What say you to it?

*Worcester.* Your father's sickness is a maim to us.

---

18 **justling** jostling, unquiet  19 **government** command  20 **bears**
(a singular verb with plural subject is not uncommon in Elizabethan
English)  24 **feared** feared for  32 **deputation** a deputy  37 **con-
junction** combination of forces  40 **possessed** informed

*Hotspur.* A perilous gash, a very limb lopped off.
  And yet, in faith, it is not! His present want
45 Seems more than we shall find it. Were it good
  To set° the exact wealth of all our states
  All at one cast? To set so rich a main°
  On the nice° hazard of one doubtful hour?
  It were not good; for therein should we read
50 The very bottom and the soul° of hope,
  The very list,° the very utmost bound
  Of all our fortunes.

*Douglas.*                Faith, and so we should.
  Where now remains a sweet reversion,°
  We may boldly spend upon the hope of what is to
     come in.
55 A comfort of retirement° lives in this.

*Hotspur.* A rendezvous, a home to fly unto,
  If that the devil and mischance look big°
  Upon the maidenhead of our affairs.

*Worcester.* But yet I would your father had been here.
60 The quality and hair° of our attempt
  Brooks° no division. It will be thought
  By some that know not why he is away,
  That wisdom, loyalty, and mere dislike
  Of our proceedings kept the Earl from hence.
65 And think how such an apprehension
  May turn the tide of fearful° faction
  And breed a kind of question in our cause.
  For well you know we of the off'ring side°
  Must keep aloof from strict arbitrament,°
70 And stop all sight-holes, every loop° from whence
  The eye of reason may pry in upon us.
  This absence of your father's draws° a curtain

---

46 **set** risk    47 **main** (1) stake (in gambling) (2) army    48 **nice** precarious    50 **soul** (1) essence (2) sole (cf. "bottom")    51 **list** limit
53 **reversion** inheritance still to be received    55 **A comfort of retirement** a security to fall back on    57 **big** menacingly    60 **hair** nature
61 **Brooks** allows of    66 **fearful** timid    68 **we of the off'ring side** we who take the offensive    69 **arbitrament** evaluation    70 **loop** loophole    72 **draws** draws aside

That shows the ignorant a kind of fear
Before not dreamt of.

*Hotspur.*                You strain too far.
  I rather of his absence make this use:            75
  It lends a luster and more great opinion,°
  A larger dare to our great enterprise,
  Than if the Earl were here; for men must think,
  If we, without his help, can make a head°
  To push against a kingdom, with his help        80
  We shall o'erturn it topsy-turvy down.
  Yet all goes well; yet all our joints are whole.

*Douglas.* As heart can think. There is not such a word
  Spoke of in Scotland as this term of fear.

          *Enter Sir Richard Vernon.*

*Hotspur.* My cousin Vernon, welcome, by my soul.    85

*Vernon.* Pray God my news be worth a welcome, lord.
  The Earl of Westmoreland, seven thousand strong,
  Is marching hitherwards; with him Prince John.

*Hotspur.* No harm. What more?

*Vernon.*                And further, I have learned
  The King himself in person is set forth,          90
  Or hitherwards intended speedily,
  With strong and mighty preparation.

*Hotspur.* He shall be welcome too. Where is his son,
  The nimble-footed madcap Prince of Wales,
  And his comrades, that daffed° the world aside    95
  And bid it pass?

*Vernon.*          All furnished, all in arms;
  All plumed like estridges° that with the wind
  Bated° like eagles having lately bathed;
  Glittering in golden coats like images;
  As full of spirit as the month of May            100
  And gorgeous as the sun at midsummer;

76 opinion prestige   79 a head (1) an army (2) headway   95 daffed
thrust   97 estridges ostriches (ostrich plumes are the emblem of the
Prince of Wales)   98 Bated shook their wings

Wanton° as youthful goats, wild as young bulls.
I saw young Harry with his beaver° on,
His cushes° on his thighs, gallantly armed,
105  Rise from the ground like feathered Mercury,
And vaulted with such ease into his seat
As if an angel dropped down from the clouds
To turn and wind° a fiery Pegasus
And witch the world with noble horsemanship.

*Hotspur.* No more, no more! Worse than the sun in
110     March,
This praise doth nourish agues.° Let them come.
They come like sacrifices in their trim,
And to the fire-eyed maid° of smoky war
All hot and bleeding will we offer them.
115  The mailèd Mars shall on his altars sit
Up to the ears in blood. I am on fire
To hear this rich reprisal° is so nigh,
And yet not ours. Come, let me taste my horse,
Who is to bear me like a thunderbolt
120  Against the bosom of the Prince of Wales.
Harry to Harry shall, hot horse to horse,
Meet, and ne'er part till one drop down a corse.
O that Glendower were come!

*Vernon.*                There is more news.
I learned in Worcester, as I rode along,
125  He cannot draw his power this fourteen days.

*Douglas.* That's the worst tidings that I hear of yet.

*Worcester.* Ay, by my faith, that bears a frosty sound.

*Hotspur.* What may the King's whole battle° reach
unto?

*Vernon.* To thirty thousand.

*Hotspur.*             Forty let it be.
130  My father and Glendower being both away,

102 **Wanton** exuberant    103 **beaver** helmet    104 **cushes** thigh armor    108 **wind** wheel about    111 **agues** chills and fever (the spring
sun was believed to set them going)    113 **maid** Bellona, goddess of
war    117 **reprisal** prize    128 **battle** army

The powers of us may serve so great a day.
Come, let us take a muster speedily.
Doomsday is near. Die all, die merrily.

*Douglas.* Talk not of dying. I am out of fear
Of death or death's hand for this one half year.    *135*
                                        *Exeunt.*


[Scene II. *A road near Coventry.*]


*Enter Falstaff [and] Bardolph.*


*Falstaff.* Bardolph, get thee before to Coventry; fill me
a bottle of sack. Our soldiers shall march through.
We'll to Sutton Co'fil' tonight.

*Bardolph.* Will you give me money, captain?

*Falstaff.* Lay out,° lay out.    *5*

*Bardolph.* This bottle makes an angel.°

*Falstaff.* And if it do, take it for thy labor; and if it
make twenty, take them all; I'll answer the coinage.
Bid my lieutenant Peto meet me at town's end.

*Bardolph.* I will, captain. Farewell.    *Exit.*    *10*

*Falstaff.* If I be not ashamed of my soldiers, I am a
soused gurnet.° I have misused the King's press°
damnably. I have got, in exchange of a hundred and
fifty soldiers, three hundred and odd pounds. I press
me none but good householders, yeomen's sons;° in-    *15*

---

IV.ii.5 **Lay out** i.e., pay out of your own pocket    6 **angel** coin worth,
at various times, six shillings eight pence to ten shillings (Bardolph
means that Falstaff now owes him an angel, but Falstaff jokingly
takes "make" in the literal sense—as if the bottle were minting
angels; he tells Bardolph to take them all and he will guarantee they
are not counterfeit)    12 **soused gurnet** pickled fish    12 **press** power
of conscription    15 **good householders, yeomen's sons** i.e., men of
some means who could pay to be let off

quire me out contracted bachelors, such as had been
asked twice on the banes°—such a commodity of
warm° slaves as had as lief hear the devil as a drum,
such as fear the report of a caliver° worse than a
struck fowl or a hurt wild duck. I pressed me none
but such toasts-and-butter, with hearts in their bellies no bigger than pins' heads, and they have bought
out their services; and now my whole charge consists
of ancients,° corporals, lieutenants, gentlemen of
companies°—slaves as ragged as Lazarus° in the
painted cloth,° where the glutton's dogs licked his
sores; and such as indeed were never soldiers, but
discarded unjust° serving-men, younger sons to
younger brothers, revolted° tapsters, and ostlers
trade-fall'n;° the cankers° of a calm world and a long
peace; ten times more dishonorable ragged than an
old fazed ancient;° and such have I to fill up the
rooms of them as have bought out their services that
you would think that I had a hundred and fifty tattered prodigals lately come from swine-keeping, from
eating draff° and husks. A mad fellow met me on the
way, and told me I had unloaded all the gibbets and
pressed the dead bodies. No eye hath seen such scare-
crows. I'll not march through Coventry with them,
that's flat. Nay, and the villains march wide betwixt
the legs, as if they had gyves° on, for indeed I had
the most of them out of prison. There's not a shirt
and a half in all my company, and the half-shirt is
two napkins tacked together and thrown over the
shoulders like a herald's coat without sleeves; and
the shirt, to say the truth, stol'n from my host at
Saint Albans, or the red-nose innkeeper of Daventry.

17 **asked twice on the banes** i.e., on the verge of marriage (banns
[banes] were announcements of intent to marry, published usually
three times at weekly intervals)    18 **warm** comfortable    19 **caliver**
musket    24 **ancients** ensigns    24–25 **gentlemen of companies** lesser
officers    25 **Lazarus** the beggar in the Dives parable (Luke 16:19–31)
26 **painted cloth** painted wall-hanging    28 **unjust** dishonest    29 **revolted** runaway    30 **trade-fall'n** unemployed    30 **cankers** parasites
32 **fazed ancient** tattered flag    36 **draff** pig-swill (the prodigal son,
in Luke 15:15–16, was so hungry he longed for draff)    41 **gyves** fet-
ters

But that's all one; they'll find linen enough on every hedge.°

*Enter the Prince [and the] Lord of Westmoreland.*

*Prince.* How now, blown° Jack?° How now, quilt?          50

*Falstaff.* What, Hal? How now, mad wag? What a devil dost thou in Warwickshire? My good Lord of Westmoreland, I cry you mercy. I thought your honor had already been at Shrewsbury.

*Westmoreland.* Faith, Sir John, 'tis more than time that          55
I were there, and you too, but my powers are there already. The King, I can tell you, looks for us all, we must away all night.

*Falstaff.* Tut, never fear me: I am as vigilant as a cat to steal cream.          60

*Prince.* I think, to steal cream indeed, for thy theft hath already made thee butter. But tell me, Jack, whose fellows are these that come after?

*Falstaff.* Mine, Hal, mine.

*Prince.* I did never see such pitiful rascals.          65

*Falstaff.* Tut, tut, good enough to toss;° food for powder, food for powder, they'll fill a pit as well as better. Tush, man, mortal men, mortal men.

*Westmoreland.* Ay, but, Sir John, methinks they are exceeding poor and bare, too beggarly.          70

*Falstaff.* Faith, for their poverty, I know not where they had that, and for their bareness, I am sure they never learned that of me.

*Prince.* No, I'll be sworn, unless you call three fingers°
in the ribs bare. But, sirrah, make haste. Percy is          75
already in the field.                    *Exit.*

---

49 **hedge** i.e., where linen was put out to dry   50 **blown** (1) swelled
(2) short of wind   50 **Jack** (1) Falstaff's name (2) soldier's quilted
jacket   66 **toss** i.e., on the end of a pike   74 **three fingers** i.e., of fat

*Falstaff.* What, is the King encamped?

*Westmoreland.* He is, Sir John. I fear we shall stay too
  long.

80  *Falstaff.* Well, to the latter end of a fray and the beginning of a feast fits a dull fighter and a keen guest.

*Exeunt.°*


[Scene III. *The rebel camp, near Shrewsbury.*]


*Enter Hotspur, Worcester, Douglas, Vernon.*

*Hotspur.* We'll fight with him tonight.

*Worcester.*                          It may not be.

*Douglas.* You give him then advantage.

*Vernon.*                          Not a whit.

*Hotspur.* Why say you so? Looks he not for supply?°

*Vernon.* So do we.

*Hotspur.*          His is certain, ours is doubtful.

3  *Worcester.* Good cousin, be advised; stir not tonight.

*Vernon.* Do not, my lord.

*Douglas.*                    You do not counsel well.
  You speak it out of fear and cold heart.

*Vernon.* Do me no slander, Douglas. By my life—
  And I dare well maintain it with my life—
10  If well-respected° honor bid me on,
  I hold as little counsel with weak fear

---

81 s.d. **Exeunt** (the quarto's "Exeunt," implying that Westmoreland
goes off with Falstaff, may be wrong. Falstaff's last speech sounds
as if Westmoreland had departed, and Falstaff winks at the audience)
IV.iii.3 **supply** reinforcement   10 **well-respected** well-considered

As you, my lord, or any Scot that this day lives.
Let it be seen tomorrow in the battle
Which of us fears.

*Douglas.*          Yea, or tonight.

*Vernon.*                    Content.

*Hotspur.* Tonight, say I.                                  15

*Vernon.* Come, come, it may not be.
I wonder much, being men of such great leading° as
    you are,
That you foresee not what impediments
Drag back our expedition.° Certain horse
Of my cousin Vernon's are not yet come up.         20
Your uncle Worcester's horse came but today;
And now their pride and mettle is asleep,
Their courage with hard labor tame and dull,
That not a horse is half the half of himself.

*Hotspur.* So are the horses of the enemy            25
In general journey-bated° and brought low.
The better part of ours are full of rest.

*Worcester.* The number of the King exceedeth ours.
For God's sake, cousin, stay till all come in.
                    *The trumpet sounds a parley.*

                *Enter Sir Walter Blunt.*

*Blunt.* I come with gracious offers from the King,   30
If you vouchsafe me hearing and respect.

*Hotspur.* Welcome, Sir Walter Blunt, and would to God
You were of our determination.°
Some of us love you well; and even those some
Envy your great deservings and good name,         35
Because you are not of our quality,°
But stand against us like an enemy.

---

17 **leading** generalship   19 **expedition** i.e., hastening into battle
26 **journey-bated** travel-weakened   33 **determination** party   36 **quality** company

*Blunt.* And God defend° but still I should stand so,
So long as out of limit° and true rule
40You stand against anointed majesty.
But to my charge.° The King hath sent to know
The nature of your griefs, and whereupon
You conjure from the breast of civil peace
Such bold hostility, teaching his duteous land
45Audacious cruelty. If that the King
Have any way your good deserts forgot,
Which he confesseth to be manifold,
He bids you name your griefs, and with all speed
You shall have your desires with interest,
50And pardon absolute for yourself and these
Herein misled by your suggestion.°

*Hotspur.* The King is kind, and well we know the King
Knows at what time to promise, when to pay.
My father and my uncle and myself
55Did give him that same royalty he wears;
And when he was not six and twenty strong,
Sick in the world's regard, wretched and low,
A poor unminded outlaw sneaking home,
My father gave him welcome to the shore;
60And when he heard him swear and vow to God
He came but to be Duke of Lancaster,
To sue his livery and beg his peace,°
With tears of innocency and terms of zeal,
My father, in kind heart and pity moved,
65Swore him assistance, and performed it too.
Now when the lords and barons of the realm
Perceived Northumberland did lean to him,
The more and less came in with cap and knee;°
Met him in boroughs, cities, villages,
70Attended him on bridges, stood in lanes,°

38 **defend** forbid    39 **limit** i.e., a subject's proper limits    41 **charge**
message    51 **suggestion** instigation    62 **sue . . . peace** sue for the
delivery of his lands (which Richard II had arrogated to the crown)
and make his peace with the king    68 **with cap and knee** i.e., with
cap off and bended knee (in token of allegiance)    70 **lanes** facing
rows

Laid gifts before him, proffered him their oaths,
Gave him their heirs as pages, followed him
Even at the heels in golden multitudes.
He presently, as greatness knows itself,°
Steps me a little higher than his vow                    75
Made to my father, while his blood was poor,
Upon the naked shore at Ravenspurgh;
And now, forsooth, takes on him to reform
Some certain edicts and some strait° decrees
That lie too heavy on the commonwealth;                   80
Cries out upon abuses, seems to weep
Over his country's wrongs; and by this face,
This seeming brow of justice, did he win
The hearts of all that he did angle for;
Proceeded further—cut me off the heads                    85
Of all the favorites that the absent king
In deputation° left behind him here
When he was personal° in the Irish war.

*Blunt.* Tut! I came not to hear this.

*Hotspur.*                              Then to the point.
In short time after, he deposed the King;                 90
Soon after that deprived him of his life;
And in the neck of that° tasked° the whole state;
To make that worse, suff'red his kinsman March
(Who is, if every owner were well placed,
Indeed his king) to be engaged in Wales,                  95
There without ransom to lie forfeited;
Disgraced me in my happy victories,
Sought to entrap me by intelligence;°
Rated° mine uncle from the council board;
In rage dismissed my father from the court;             100
Broke oath on oath, committed wrong on wrong;
And in conclusion drove us to seek out
This head° of safety, and withal to pry

**74 as greatness knows itself** as greatness begins to feel its strength
**79 strait** strict  **87 In deputation** as deputies  **88 personal** personally engaged  **92 in the neck of that** i.e., next  **92 tasked** taxed
**98 intelligence** spies  **99 Rated** scolded (cf. I.iii.14–20)  **103 head**
army

Into his title, the which we find
105 Too indirect° for long continuance.

*Blunt.* Shall I return this answer to the King?

*Hotspur.* Not so, Sir Walter. We'll withdraw awhile.
Go to the King; and let there be impawned
Some surety for a safe return again,
110 And in the morning early shall mine uncle
Bring him our purposes; and so farewell.

*Blunt.* I would you would accept of grace and love.

*Hotspur.* And may be so we shall.

*Blunt.*                              Pray God you do. [*Exeunt.*]


[Scene IV. *York. The Archbishop's palace.*]


*Enter [the] Archbishop of York [and] Sir Michael.*

*Archbishop.* Hie, good Sir Michael; bear this sealèd
brief°
With wingèd haste to the Lord Marshal;
This to my cousin Scroop; and all the rest
To whom they are directed. If you knew
5 How much they do import, you would make haste.

*Sir Michael.* My good lord, I guess their tenor.

*Archbishop.* Like enough you do.
Tomorrow, good Sir Michael, is a day
Wherein the fortune of ten thousand men
10 Must bide the touch;° for, sir, at Shrewsbury,
As I am truly given to understand,
The King with mighty and quick-raisèd power
Meets with Lord Harry; and I fear, Sir Michael,

---

105 **indirect** (1) not in the direct line (from Richard) (2) morally
oblique   IV.iv.1 **brief** message   10 **bide the touch** stand the test (as
metal is tested by the touchstone to know if it is gold)

What with the sickness of Northumberland,
Whose power was in the first proportion,°                    15
And what with Owen Glendower's absence thence,
Who with them was a rated sinew° too
And comes not in, overruled by prophecies—
I fear the power of Percy is too weak
To wage an instant trial with the King.                    20

*Sir Michael*. Why, my good lord, you need not fear;
    There is Douglas and Lord Mortimer.

*Archbishop*. No, Mortimer is not there.

*Sir Michael*. But there is Mordake, Vernon, Lord Harry
        Percy,
    And there is my Lord of Worcester, and a head      25
    Of gallant warriors, noble gentlemen.

*Archbishop*. And so there is; but yet the King hath
        drawn
    The special head° of all the land together—
    The Prince of Wales, Lord John of Lancaster,
    The noble Westmoreland and warlike Blunt,          30
    And many moe corrivals° and dear° men
    Of estimation and command in arms.

*Sir Michael*. Doubt not, my lord, they shall be well op-
        posed.

*Archbishop*. I hope no less, yet needful 'tis to fear;
    And, to prevent the worst, Sir Michael, speed.      35
    For if Lord Percy thrive not, ere the King
    Dismiss his power, he means to visit us,
    For he hath heard of our confederacy,
    And 'tis but wisdom to make strong against him.
    Therefore make haste. I must go write again         40
    To other friends; and so farewell, Sir Michael.
                                    *Exeunt.*

---

15 proportion magnitude   17 rated sinew highly valued strength
28 head army   31 moe corrivals more associates   31 dear important

# [ACT V

Scene I. *The King's camp, near Shrewsbury.*]

*Enter the King, Prince of Wales, Lord John of
Lancaster, Earl of Westmoreland,° Sir Walter
Blunt, Falstaff.*

*King.* How bloodily the sun begins to peer
   Above yon bulky hill! The day looks pale
   At his distemp'rature.°

*Prince.*                    The southern wind
   Doth play the trumpet° to his° purposes
5  And by his hollow whistling in the leaves
   Foretells a tempest and a blust'ring day.

*King.* Then with the losers let it sympathize,
   For nothing can seem foul to those that win.

*The trumpet sounds. Enter Worcester [and Vernon].*

   How now, my Lord of Worcester? 'Tis not well
10 That you and I should meet upon such terms

---

V.i.s.d. **Earl of Westmoreland** (in V.ii.28 we learn that Westmoreland has been held as the "surety" of IV.iii.109, but at this point
Shakespeare apparently had not decided who was the hostage)
3 **his distemp'rature** the sun's apparent ailment   4 **play the trumpet**
(1) act the announcer (2) blow as if playing a trumpet   4 **his** the
sun's

As now we meet. You have deceived our trust
And made us doff our easy robes of peace
To crush our old limbs in ungentle steel.
This is not well, my lord; this is not well.
What say you to it? Will you again unknit                    *15*
This churlish knot of all-abhorrèd war,
And move in that obedient orb° again
Where you did give a fair and natural light,
And be no more an exhaled meteor,°
A prodigy of fear, and a portent                             *20*
Of broachèd° mischief to the unborn times?

*Worcester.* Hear me, my liege.
For mine own part, I could be well content
To entertain the lag-end of my life
With quiet hours, for I protest                              *25*
I have not sought the day of this dislike.

*King.* You have not sought it! How comes it then?

*Falstaff.* Rebellion lay in his way, and he found it.

*Prince.* Peace, chewet,° peace!

*Worcester.* It pleased your Majesty to turn your looks       *30*
Of favor from myself and all our house;
And yet I must remember° you, my lord,
We were the first and dearest of your friends.
For you my staff of office did I break
In Richard's time, and posted day and night                 *35*
To meet you on the way and kiss your hand
When yet you were in place and in account
Nothing so strong and fortunate as I.
It was myself, my brother, and his son
That brought you home and boldly did outdare                *40*
The dangers of the time. You swore to us,
And you did swear that oath at Doncaster,
That you did nothing purpose 'gainst the state,

---

**17 obedient orb** orbit of obedience   **19 exhaled meteor** wandering
body (not subject to orbit, and thought an omen or "prodigy")
**21 broachèd** opened   **29 chewet** (1) jackdaw, i.e., chatterer (2) meat
pie   **32 remember** remind

Nor claim no further than your new-fall'n° right,
<sub>45</sub> The seat of Gaunt, dukedom of Lancaster.
To this we swore our aid. But in short space
It rained down fortune show'ring on your head,
And such a flood of greatness fell on you—
What with our help, what with the absent King,
<sub>50</sub> What with the injuries of a wanton time,
The seeming sufferances that you had borne,
And the contrarious winds that held the King
So long in his unlucky Irish wars
That all in England did repute him dead—
<sub>55</sub> And from this swarm of fair advantages
You took occasion to be quickly wooed
To gripe° the general sway into your hand;
Forgot your oath to us at Doncaster;
And, being fed by us, you used us so
<sub>60</sub> As that ungentle gull,° the cuckoo's bird,°
Useth the sparrow—did oppress our nest,
Grew by our feeding to so great a bulk
That even our love durst not come near your sight
For fear of swallowing; but with nimble wing
<sub>65</sub> We were enforced for safety sake to fly
Out of your sight and raise this present head;
Whereby we stand opposèd by such means
As you yourself have forged against yourself
By unkind usage, dangerous° countenance,
<sub>70</sub> And violation of all faith and troth
Sworn to us in your younger enterprise.

*King.* These things, indeed, you have articulate,°
Proclaimed at market crosses, read in churches,
To face° the garment of rebellion
<sub>75</sub> With some fine color° that may please the eye
Of fickle changelings and poor discontents,

---

44 **new-fall'n** i.e., by the death of his father, John of Gaunt    57 **gripe**
grab    60 **gull, bird** nestling (the cuckoo lays its eggs in other birds'
nests, and the young cuckoos when hatched speedily destroy the
other nestlings)    69 **dangerous** menacing    72 **articulate** spelled out
74 **face** trim    75 **color** (1) hue (2) rhetorical coloring (hence, pretext)

Which gape and rub the elbow° at the news
Of hurlyburly innovation.°
And never yet did insurrection want
Such water colors to impaint his cause,                    80
Nor moody beggars, starving for a time
Of pell-mell havoc and confusion.

*Prince.* In both your armies there is many a soul
Shall pay full dearly for this encounter,
If once they join in trial. Tell your nephew          85
The Prince of Wales doth join with all the world
In praise of Henry Percy. By my hopes,
This present enterprise set off his head,°
I do not think a braver gentleman,
More active-valiant or more valiant-young,            90
More daring or more bold, is now alive
To grace this latter age with noble deeds.
For my part, I may speak it to my shame,
I have a truant been to chivalry;
And so I hear he doth account me too.                 95
Yet this before° my father's majesty—
I am content that he shall take the odds
Of his great name and estimation,
And will, to save the blood on either side,
Try fortune with him in a single fight.               100

*King.* And, Prince of Wales, so dare we venture thee;
Albeit,° considerations infinite
Do make against it. No, good Worcester, no!
We love our people well; even those we love
That are misled upon your cousin's part;              105
And, will they take the offer of our grace,°
Both he, and they, and you, yea, every man
Shall be my friend again, and I'll be his.
So tell your cousin, and bring me word
What he will do. But if he will not yield,            110
Rebuke and dread correction wait on us,°

---

77 **rub the elbow** i.e., hug themselves with delight    78 **innovation**
revolution   88 **set off his head** removed from his record   96 **this
before** let me say this in the presence of    102 **Albeit** on the other
hand   106 **grace** pardon   111 **wait on us** are in our service

And they shall do their office.° So be gone.
We will not now be troubled with reply.
We offer fair; take it advisedly.

*Exit Worcester [with Vernon].*

115 *Prince.* It will not be accepted, on my life.
The Douglas and the Hotspur both together
Are confident against the world in arms.

*King.* Hence, therefore, every leader to his charge;
For, on their answer, will we set on them,
120   And God befriend us as our cause is just!

*Exeunt. Manent° Prince [and] Falstaff.*

*Falstaff.* Hal, if thou see me down in the battle and
bestride me, so!° 'Tis a point of friendship.

*Prince.* Nothing but a colossus can do thee that friendship. Say thy prayers, and farewell.

123 *Falstaff.* I would 'twere bedtime, Hal, and all well.

*Prince.* Why, thou owest God a death.°          [*Exit.*]

*Falstaff.* 'Tis not due yet: I would be loath to pay him
before his day. What need I be so forward with him
that calls not on me? Well, 'tis no matter; honor
130   pricks° me on. Yea, but how if honor prick° me off
when I come on? How then? Can honor set to a leg?
No. Or an arm? No. Or take away the grief of a
wound? No. Honor hath no skill in surgery then?
No. What is honor? A word. What is in that word
135   honor? What is that honor? Air—a trim° reckoning! Who hath it? He that died a Wednesday. Doth
he feel it? No. Doth he hear it? No. 'Tis insensible
then? Yea, to the dead. But will it not live with the
living? No. Why? Detraction° will not suffer it.
140   Therefore I'll none of it. Honor is a mere scutch-
eon°—and so ends my catechism.          *Exit.*

112 **office** duty   120 s.d. **Manent** remain (Latin)   122 **so** i.e., I
shan't object   126 **death** (pronounced like "debt," in which sense
Falstaff takes it)   130 **pricks** spurs   130 **prick** check (as a casualty)
135 **trim** fine (spoken ironically)   139 **Detraction** slander   140–41
**scutcheon** painted shield with coat of arms identifying a dead nobleman

[Scene II. *The rebel camp, near Shrewsbury.*]

*Enter Worcester* [*and*] *Sir Richard Vernon.*

*Worcester.* O no, my nephew must not know, Sir
   Richard,
  The liberal and kind offer of the King.

*Vernon.* 'Twere best he did.

*Worcester.*               Then are we all undone.
  It is not possible, it cannot be,
  The King should keep his word in loving us.       *5*
  He will suspect us still and find a time
  To punish this offense in other faults.
  Supposition all our lives shall be stuck full of eyes;°
  For treason is but trusted like the fox,
  Who, never so tame, so cherished and locked up,  *10*
  Will have a wild trick° of his ancestors.
  Look how we can, or sad or° merrily,
  Interpretation will misquote our looks,
  And we shall feed like oxen at a stall,
  The better cherished still the nearer death.    *15*
  My nephew's trespass may be well forgot;
  It hath the excuse of youth and heat of blood,
  And an adopted name of privilege°—
  A hare-brained Hotspur, governed by a spleen.
  All his offenses live upon my head       *20*
  And on his father's. We did train° him on;
  And, his corruption being ta'en° from us,
  We, as the spring of all, shall pay for all.
  Therefore, good cousin, let not Harry know,
  In any case, the offer of the King.        *25*

---

V.ii.8 **Supposition . . . eyes** suspicion will always be spying on us
11 **trick** (1) trait (2) wile   12 **or sad or** either sad or   18 **an . . . privilege** a nickname which carries a privilege (to be impulsive) with it
21 **train** (1) draw (2) aim   22 **ta'en** taken (like an infection)

*Enter Hotspur [and Douglas].*

*Vernon.* Deliver° what you will, I'll say 'tis so.
Here comes your cousin.

*Hotspur.*                         My uncle is returned.
Deliver up my Lord of Westmoreland.°
Uncle, what news?

30 *Worcester.* The King will bid you battle presently.

*Douglas.* Defy him by the Lord of Westmoreland.

*Hotspur.* Lord Douglas, go you and tell him so.

*Douglas.* Marry, and shall, and very willingly.      *Exit.*

*Worcester.* There is no seeming mercy in the King.

35 *Hotspur.* Did you beg any? God forbid!

*Worcester.* I told him gently of our grievances,
Of his oath-breaking, which he mended thus,
By now forswearing that he is forsworn.
He calls us rebels, traitors, and will scourge
40 With haughty arms this hateful name in us.

*Enter Douglas.*

*Douglas.* Arm, gentlemen, to arms, for I have thrown
A brave defiance in King Henry's teeth,
And Westmoreland, that was engaged,° did bear it;
Which cannot choose but bring him quickly on.

*Worcester.* The Prince of Wales stepped forth before
45     the King
And, nephew, challenged you to single fight.

*Hotspur.* O, would the quarrel lay upon our heads,
And that no man might draw short breath today
But I and Harry Monmouth! Tell me, tell me,
50 How showed his tasking?° Seemed it in contempt?

---

26 **Deliver** report    28 **Westmoreland** (who has been hostage for the
safe return of Worcester and Vernon)    43 **engaged** held as hostage
50 **tasking** challenging

*Vernon.* No, by my soul. I never in my life
  Did hear a challenge urged more modestly,
  Unless a brother should a brother dare
  To gentle exercise and proof of arms.
  He gave you all the duties of a man;°                    55
  Trimmed up your praises with a princely tongue;
  Spoke your deservings like a chronicle;°
  Making you ever better than his praise
  By still dispraising praise valued with you;°
  And, which became him like a prince indeed,             60
  He made a blushing cital of° himself,
  And chid his truant youth with such a grace
  As if he mast'red there a double spirit
  Of teaching and of learning instantly.°
  There did he pause; but let me tell the world,          65
  If he outlive the envy of this day,
  England did never owe° so sweet a hope,
  So much misconstrued in° his wantonness.

*Hotspur.* Cousin, I think thou art enamorèd
  On his follies. Never did I hear                        70
  Of any prince so wild a liberty.°
  But be he as he will, yet once ere night
  I will embrace him with a soldier's arm,
  That° he shall shrink under my courtesy.
  Arm, arm with speed! And, fellows, soldiers, friends,  75
  Better consider what you have to do
  Than I, that have not well the gift of tongue,
  Can lift your blood up with persuasion.

                   *Enter a Messenger.*

*Messenger.* My lord, here are letters for you.

*Hotspur.* I cannot read them now.——                     80
  O gentlemen, the time of life is short!

---

**55 duties of a man** duties that one man can owe another   **57 like
a chronicle** i.e., with the itemized detail characteristic of a chronicle history   **59 dispraising . . . you** i.e., because it must fall so far
short of your deservings   **61 cital of** reference to   **64 instantly** simultaneously   **67 owe** own   **68 in** with respect to   **71 liberty** reckless freedom   **74 That** so that

To spend that shortness basely were too long
If life did ride upon a dial's point,
Still ending at the arrival of an hour.°
85  And if we live, we live to tread on kings;
If die, brave death, when princes die with us!
Now for our consciences, the arms are fair,
When the intent of bearing them is just.

*Enter another [Messenger].*

*Messenger.* My lord, prepare. The King comes on
apace.

90  *Hotspur.* I thank him that he cuts me from my tale,
For I profess not talking: only this—
Let each man do his best; and here draw I
A sword whose temper I intend to stain
With the best blood that I can meet withal
95  In the adventure of this perilous day.
Now, Esperance! Percy! and set on.
Sound all the lofty instruments of war,
And by that music let us all embrace;
For, heaven to earth,° some of us never shall
100  A second time do such a courtesy.
*Here they embrace. The trumpets sound. [Exeunt.]*


[Scene III. *Shrewsbury. The battlefield.*]


*The King enters with his power. Alarum to the
battle. [Exeunt.] Then enter Douglas, and Sir
Walter Blunt [disguised as the King].*


*Blunt.* What is thy name, that in battle thus thou
crossest me?
What honor dost thou seek upon my head?


82–84 **To . . . hour** if life were measured by a clock's hand, closing
after a single hour, it would still be too long if basely spent
99 **heaven to earth** the odds are as great as heaven to earth

*Douglas.* Know then my name is Douglas,
   And I do haunt thee in the battle thus
   Because some tell me that thou art a king.        *5*

*Blunt.* They tell thee true.

*Douglas.* The Lord of Stafford dear today hath bought
   Thy likeness, for instead of thee, King Harry,
   This sword hath ended him: so shall it thee,
   Unless thou yield thee as my prisoner.        *10*

*Blunt.* I was not born a yielder, thou proud Scot;
   And thou shalt find a king that will revenge
   Lord Stafford's death.

   *They fight. Douglas kills Blunt. Then enter*
                 *Hotspur.*

*Hotspur.* O Douglas, hadst thou fought at Holmedon
     thus,
   I never had triumphed upon a Scot.        *15*

*Douglas.* All's done, all's won: here breathless lies the
     King.

*Hotspur.* Where?

*Douglas.* Here.

*Hotspur.* This, Douglas? No. I know this face full well.
   A gallant knight he was, his name was Blunt;        *20*
   Semblably° furnished like the King himself.

*Douglas.* A fool° go with thy soul, whither it goes!
   A borrowed title hast thou bought too dear:
   Why didst thou tell me that thou wert a king?

*Hotspur.* The King hath many marching in his coats.     *25*

*Douglas.* Now, by my sword, I will kill all his coats;
   I'll murder all his wardrobe, piece by piece,
   Until I meet the King.

---

**V.iii.21 Semblably** similarly    **22 fool** i.e., the title "fool"

*Hotspur.*                    Up and away!
Our soldiers stand full fairly for the day.    [*Exeunt.*]

*Alarum. Enter Falstaff solus.*

30 *Falstaff.* Though I could scape shot-free° at London,
I fear the shot here. Here's no scoring° but upon the
pate. Soft! Who are you? Sir Walter Blunt. There's
honor for you! Here's no vanity!° I am as hot as
molten lead, and as heavy too. God keep lead out of
35 me. I need no more weight than mine own bowels.
I have led my rag-of-muffins where they are peppered.° There's not three of my hundred and fifty
left alive, and they are for the town's end, to beg
during life. But who comes here?

*Enter the Prince.*

*Prince.* What, stands thou idle here? Lend me thy
40    sword.
Many a nobleman lies stark and stiff
Under the hoofs of vaunting enemies, whose deaths
are yet unrevenged. I prithee lend me thy sword.

*Falstaff.* O Hal, I prithee give me leave to breathe
45    awhile. Turk Gregory° never did such deeds in arms
as I have done this day. I have paid° Percy, I have
made him sure.

*Prince.* He is indeed, and living to kill thee.
I prithee lend me thy sword.

50 *Falstaff.* Nay, before God, Hal, if Percy be alive, thou
gets not my sword; but take my pistol if thou wilt.

*Prince.* Give it me. What, is it in the case?

30 **shot-free** without paying the bill    31 **scoring** (1) billing (2) striking    33 **Here's no vanity** (spoken ironically: i.e., here *is* "vanity"—
futility, foolishness. But vanity also implies lightness, which is then
set against the "heaviness" of life: cf. "lead," "heavy," "weight")
36–37 **I . . . peppered** (a common practice of officers, who drew the
dead soldiers' pay)    45 **Turk Gregory** (in Shakespeare's time,
"Turk" was a byword for any ruthless man; "Gregory" may refer to
the irascible Pope Gregory VII, or to Elizabeth's enemy, Pope
Gregory XIII. Pope and Turk were regarded as the two great enemies
of Protestant Christendom)    46 **paid** killed

*Falstaff.* Ay, Hal. 'Tis hot, 'tis hot.° There's that will
sack a city.

>                    *The Prince draws it out and finds*
>                        *it to be a bottle of sack.*

*Prince.* What, is it a time to jest and dally now?              55
>                    *He throws the bottle at him. Exit.*

*Falstaff.* Well, if Percy be alive, I'll pierce° him. If he
do come in my way, so; if he do not, if I come in his
willingly, let him make a carbonado° of me. I like
not such grinning honor as Sir Walter hath. Give
me life; which if I can save, so; if not, honor comes       60
unlooked for, and there's an end.                    [*Exit.*]


[Scene IV. *Shrewsbury. The battlefield.*]


*Alarum. Excursions.° Enter the King, the Prince,*
*Lord John of Lancaster, Earl of Westmoreland.*

*King.* I prithee, Harry, withdraw thyself, thou bleedest
too much.
Lord John of Lancaster, go you with him.

*John.* Not I, my lord, unless I did bleed too.

*Prince.* I beseech your Majesty make up,°
Lest your retirement do amaze° your friends.               3

*King.* I will do so. My Lord of Westmoreland, lead
him to his tent.

*Westmoreland.* Come, my lord, I'll lead you to your
tent.

*Prince.* Lead me, my lord? I do not need your help;
And God forbid a shallow scratch should drive            10

---

53 **hot** i.e., he has fired it so often he has had to put it away to cool
56 **pierce** (pronounced "perse")  58 **carbonado** meat slashed open
for broiling   V.iv.s.d. **Excursions** sorties   4 **make up** move forward   5 **amaze** dismay

The Prince of Wales from such a field as this,
Where stained nobility lies trodden on,
And rebels' arms triumph in massacres!

*John.* We breathe° too long. Come, cousin Westmore-
        land,
15      Our duty this way lies. For God's sake, come.
                [*Exeunt Lancaster and Westmoreland.*]

*Prince.* By God, thou hast deceived me, Lancaster!
        I did not think thee lord of such a spirit.
        Before, I loved thee as a brother, John,
        But now I do respect thee as my soul.

20  *King.* I saw him hold Lord Percy at the point
        With lustier maintenance than I did look for
        Of such an ungrown warrior.

*Prince.* O, this boy lends mettle to us all!        *Exit.*

                [*Enter Douglas.*]

*Douglas.* Another king? They grow like Hydra's°
        heads.
25      I am the Douglas, fatal to all those
        That wear those colors on them. What art thou
        That counterfeit'st the person of a king?

*King.* The King himself, who, Douglas, grieves at heart
        So many of his shadows thou hast met,
30      And not the very King. I have two boys
        Seek Percy and thyself about the field;
        But, seeing thou fall'st on me so luckily,
        I will assay thee, and defend thyself.

*Douglas.* I fear thou art another counterfeit;
35      And yet, in faith, thou bearest thee like a king.
        But mine I am sure thou art, whoe'er thou be,
        And thus I win thee.

        *They fight, the King being in danger. Enter Prince
                of Wales.*

14 breathe pause   24 Hydra a many-headed monster which grew
two heads for each one destroyed

*Prince.* Hold up thy head, vile Scot, or thou art like
　　Never to hold it up again. The spirits
　　Of valiant Shirley, Stafford, Blunt° are in my arms.     *40*
　　It is the Prince of Wales that threatens thee,
　　Who never promiseth but he means to pay.
　　　　　　　　　　　*They fight: Douglas flieth.*
　　Cheerly, my lord. How fares your Grace?
　　Sir Nicholas Gawsey hath for succor sent,
　　And so hath Clifton. I'll to Clifton straight.     *45*

*King.* Stay and breathe awhile.
　　Thou hast redeemed thy lost opinion,°
　　And showed thou mak'st some tender° of my life,
　　In this fair rescue thou hast brought to me.

*Prince.* O God, they did me too much injury     *50*
　　That ever said I heark'ned for your death.
　　If it were so, I might have let alone
　　The insulting hand of Douglas over you,
　　Which would have been as speedy in your end
　　As all the poisonous potions in the world,     *55*
　　And saved the treacherous labor of your son.

*King.* Make up to Clifton; I'll to Sir Nicholas Gawsey.
　　　　　　　　　　　　　　　*Exit.*

　　　　　　　*Enter Hotspur.*

*Hotspur.* If I mistake not, thou art Harry Monmouth.

*Prince.* Thou speak'st as if I would deny my name.

*Hotspur.* My name is Harry Percy.     *60*

*Prince.* Why, then I see a very valiant rebel of the name.
　　I am the Prince of Wales, and think not, Percy,
　　To share with me in glory any more.
　　Two stars keep not their motion in one sphere,°
　　Nor can one England brook° a double reign     *65*
　　Of Harry Percy and the Prince of Wales.

40 **Shirley, Stafford, Blunt** (those whom Douglas has killed wearing
the King's coats)　47 **opinion** reputation　48 **tender** value　64 **sphere**
orbit　65 **brook** put up with

*Hotspur.* Nor shall it, Harry, for the hour is come
    To end the one of us; and would to God
    Thy name in arms were now as great as mine!

70 *Prince.* I'll make it greater ere I part from thee,
    And all the budding honors on thy crest
    I'll crop to make a garland for my head.

*Hotspur.* I can no longer brook thy vanities. *They fight.*

              *Enter Falstaff.*

*Falstaff.* Well said, Hal! To it, Hal! Nay, you shall find
75 no boy's play here, I can tell you.

    *Enter Douglas. He fighteth with Falstaff, [who]*
    *falls down as if he were dead. [Exit Douglas.]*
        *The Prince killeth Percy.*

*Hotspur.* O Harry, thou hast robbed me of my youth!
    I better brook the loss of brittle life
    Than those proud titles thou hast won of me.
    They wound my thoughts worse than thy sword my
      flesh.
80 But thoughts, the slaves of life, and life, time's fool,°
    And time, that takes survey of all the world,
    Must have a stop. O, I could prophesy,
    But that the earthy and cold hand of death
    Lies on my tongue. No, Percy, thou art dust,
85 And food for—                  *[Dies.]*

*Prince.* For worms, brave Percy. Fare thee well, great
      heart.
    Ill-weaved ambition, how much art thou shrunk!
    When that this body did contain a spirit,
    A kingdom for it was too small a bound;
90 But now two paces of the vilest earth
    Is room enough. This earth that bears thee dead
    Bears not alive so stout° a gentleman.
    If thou wert sensible of courtesy,
    I should not make so dear° a show of zeal.

80 **slaves . . . fool** i.e., because thoughts are dependent on life and
because life is subservient to time    92 **stout** valiant    94 **dear** heart-
felt

But let my favors° hide thy mangled face;                    95
And, even in thy behalf, I'll thank myself
For doing these fair rites of tenderness.
Adieu, and take thy praise with thee to heaven.
Thy ignominy sleep with thee in the grave,
But not rememb'red in thy epitaph.                          100

        *He spieth Falstaff on the ground.*

What, old acquaintance? Could not all this flesh
Keep in a little life? Poor Jack, farewell!
I could have better spared a better man.
O, I should have a heavy miss° of thee
If I were much in love with vanity.°                        105
Death hath not struck so fat a deer° today,
Though many dearer,° in this bloody fray.
Emboweled° will I see thee by-and-by;
Till then in blood by noble Percy lie.          *Exit.*

        *Falstaff riseth up.*

*Falstaff.* Emboweled? If thou embowel me today, I'll    110
give you leave to powder° me and eat me too tomorrow. 'Sblood, 'twas time to counterfeit, or that
hot termagant° Scot had paid me scot and lot° too.
Counterfeit? I lie; I am no counterfeit. To die is to
be a counterfeit, for he is but the counterfeit of a    115
man who hath not the life of a man; but to counterfeit dying when a man thereby liveth, is to be no
counterfeit, but the true and perfect image of life
indeed. The better part of valor is discretion,° in the
which better part I have saved my life. Zounds, I am    120
afraid of this gunpowder Percy, though he be dead.
How if he should counterfeit too, and rise? By my
faith, I am afraid he would prove the better counterfeit. Therefore I'll make him sure; yea, and I'll swear

95 **favors** (probably Hal's ostrich plumes, his emblem as Prince of
Wales)   104 **heavy miss** "heavy" loss (in two senses)   105 **vanity**
frivolity (and lightness)   106 **deer** (with pun on "dear")   107 **dearer**
nobler, more valuable   108 **Emboweled** disemboweled (for embalm-
ing)   111 **powder** salt   113 **termagant** bloodthirsty   113 **paid me
scot and lot** killed me (literally, paid me in full; "scot" and "lot"
were parish taxes)   119 **The . . . discretion** (Falstaff willfully misin-
terprets the maxim that valor is the better for being accompanied by
discretion)

<sub>125</sub>   I killed him. Why may not he rise as well as I? Nothing confutes me but eyes, and nobody sees me.
Therefore, sirrah [*stabs him*], with a new wound in
your thigh, come you along with me.

*He takes up Hotspur on his back. Enter Prince
[and] John of Lancaster.*

*Prince.* Come, brother John; full bravely hast thou
fleshed
Thy maiden sword.

<sub>130</sub> *John.*                    But, soft! whom have we here?
Did you not tell me this fat man was dead?

*Prince.* I did; I saw him dead,
Breathless and bleeding on the ground. Art thou
alive,
Or is it fantasy that plays upon our eyesight?
<sub>135</sub>   I prithee speak. We will not trust our eyes
Without our ears. Thou art not what thou seem'st.

*Falstaff.* No, that's certain, I am not a double man;°
but if I be not Jack Falstaff, then am I a Jack.° There
is Percy. If your father will do me any honor, so; if
<sub>140</sub> not, let him kill the next Percy himself. I look to be
either earl or duke, I can assure you.

*Prince.* Why, Percy I killed myself, and saw thee dead!

*Falstaff.* Didst thou? Lord, Lord, how this world is
given to lying. I grant you I was down, and out of
<sub>145</sub> breath, and so was he; but we rose both at an instant
and fought a long hour by Shrewsbury clock. If I
may be believed, so; if not, let them that should reward valor bear the sin upon their own heads. I'll
take it upon my death, I gave him this wound in the
<sub>150</sub> thigh. If the man were alive and would deny it,
zounds! I would make him eat a piece of my sword.

*John.* This is the strangest tale that ever I heard.

*Prince.* This is the strangest fellow, brother John.

**137 double man** (1) wraith (2) twofold man    **138 Jack** rascal

Come, bring your luggage nobly on your back.
For my part, if a lie may do thee grace,　　155
I'll gild it with the happiest terms I have.
　　　　　　　　　　　　*A retreat is sounded.*
The trumpet sounds retreat; the day is ours.
Come, brother, let us to the highest of the field,
To see what friends are living, who are dead.
　　　　　*Exeunt [Prince Henry and Prince John].*

*Falstaff.* I'll follow,° as they say, for reward. He that　160
　rewards me, God reward him. If I do grow great,
　I'll grow less; for I'll purge,° and leave sack, and
　live cleanly, as a nobleman should do.
　　　　　　　　　　*Exit [bearing off the body].*


　　　　[Scene V. *Shrewsbury. The battlefield.*]


*The trumpets sound. Enter the King, Prince of
Wales, Lord John of Lancaster, Earl of Westmoreland, with Worcester and Vernon prisoners.*

*King.* Thus ever did rebellion find rebuke.
　Ill-spirited Worcester, did not we send grace,
　Pardon, and terms of love to all of you?
　And wouldst thou turn our offers contrary?
　Misuse the tenor of thy kinsman's trust?　　5
　Three knights upon our party slain today,
　A noble earl, and many a creature else
　Had been alive this hour,
　If like a Christian thou hadst truly borne
　Betwixt our armies true intelligence.°　　10

*Worcester.* What I have done my safety urged me to;
　And I embrace this fortune patiently,
　Since not to be avoided it falls on me.

---

160 **follow** i.e., as hounds do when the quarry is killed, to receive
their reward　162 **purge** repent　V.v.10 **intelligence** information

*King.* Bear Worcester to the death, and Vernon too;
15   Other offenders we will pause upon.
             [*Exeunt Worcester and Vernon, guarded*].
  How goes the field?

*Prince.* The noble Scot, Lord Douglas, when he saw
  The fortune of the day quite turned from him,
  The noble Percy slain, and all his men
20   Upon the foot of fear, fled with the rest;
  And falling from a hill, he was so bruised
  That the pursuers took him. At my tent
  The Douglas is, and I beseech your Grace
  I may dispose of him.

*King.*                 With all my heart.

25 *Prince.* Then, brother John of Lancaster, to you
  This honorable bounty shall belong.
  Go to the Douglas and deliver him
  Up to his pleasure, ransomless and free.
  His valors shown upon our crests today
30   Have taught us how to cherish such high deeds,
  Even in the bosom of our adversaries.

*John.* I thank your Grace for this high courtesy,
  Which I shall give away immediately.

*King.* Then this remains, that we divide our power.
35   You, son John, and my cousin Westmoreland,
  Towards York shall bend you with your dearest
    speed
  To meet Northumberland and the prelate Scroop,
  Who, as we hear, are busily in arms.
  Myself and you, son Harry, will towards Wales
40   To fight with Glendower and the Earl of March.
  Rebellion in this land shall lose his sway,
  Meeting the check of such another day;
  And since this business° so fair is done,
  Let us not leave till all our own be won.      *Exeunt.*

FINIS

43 **business** (trisyllabic)

# Textual Note

The text for the present edition as a whole is the first quarto of 1598. This is generally believed to have been set from an earlier edition of the same year (Qo), of which today only four leaves are known—containing the text of the play from I.iii.199 to II.ii.112. Qo, so far as we have it, shows characteristics which relate it closely to an authorial manuscript, probably a corrected working manuscript rather than a fair copy. Q1 may therefore be regarded as still reasonably faithful to what Shakespeare wrote. The later quartos (Q2, 1599; Q3, 1604; Q4, 1608; Q5, 1613), each set from the one preceding, and the Folio (1623), set from Q5, have increasingly less authority.

Apart from spelling and punctuation, which are modernized in this edition, and regularization of speech prefixes, I have followed Q1, and, where it exists, Qo. With one exception (IV.i.12–13), I preserve the lineation of these editions, printing therefore as prose a number of passages so printed in Q1 but now almost invariably divided into lines of verse. It is possible, even probable, that some of these passages were intended to be verse; but the wide differences exhibited by editors in lineating them persuade me to reserve this entertainment for readers who wish to engage in it. I have usually indicated in the footnotes one or more of the traditional patterns of lineation for each passage.

The table below records departures from Qo–Q1. The first reading (*italics*) is that which I have adopted in the text; the second is that of Q1. Almost all of the emendations were made in the quartos or in the First Folio, indicating that in Shakespeare's own day the passages in question were suspect; but because these early texts have no authority, they are not cited as sources.

Division into acts and scenes is here that of the Folio, save that I follow Capell and most other editors (including those of the Globe edition) in dividing the Folio's V.ii into V.ii and V.iii and renumbering the subsequent scenes. In the quartos there is no indication of acts or scenes.

I.i.62 *a dear* deere    69 *blood did* bloud. Did    76 *In faith it is* [the quartos and folios give to the King]

I.ii.82 *similes* smiles    166 *Bardolph, Peto* Haruey, Rossill [these are names that Shakespeare evidently meant originally to assign to Falstaff's associates: see below, II.iv.173–76, 180–81]

I.iii.199–206 [Q0-Q4 do not assign to Hotspur, but give as part of Northumberland's speech]

II.ii.16 *two and twenty* xxii

II.iii.4 *respect* the respect    70 *A roan* Roane

II.iv.34 *precedent* present    37 [assigned to Prince]    173–76 [assigned to Gadshill, Ross (=Russell: see above, I.ii.166), Falstaff, Ross]    180–81 [assigned to Ross]    244 *eel-skin* elsskin    341 *Owen* O    393 *tristful* trustfull

III.i.99 *cantle* scantle    132 *on* an

III.ii.115 *Enlargèd* Enlargd

III.iii.36 *that's* that    59 *tithe* tight    90s.d. *them* him    178 *guests* ghesse    206 *o'* of

IV.i.20 *I, my lord* I my mind    54 *is* tis    107 *dropped* drop    125 *cannot* can    126 *yet* it

IV.iii.21 *horse* horses    28 *ours* our    82 *country's* Countrey

V.i.138 *will it* wil

V.ii.3 *undone* vnder one    25s.d. *Hotspur* Percy

V.iii.22 *A* Ah

V.iv.67 *Nor* Now    75s.d. *who* he    157 *ours* our

# The Sources of Henry IV [Part One]

So far as we know, the sources on which Shakespeare chiefly drew in writing *Henry IV* [*Part One*] were the following: (1) the pages on Henry's reign in Volume III of Raphael Holinshed's compilation of British history, *Chronicles of England, Scotland, and Ireland,* first published in 1577 but later reissued (1586–87) in an enlarged edition, which seems to have been the text actually consulted by Shakespeare; (2) the relevant stanzas in Book III of Samuel Daniel's long poem, *The First Four Books of the Civil Wars between the Two Houses of Lancaster and York* (1595); and (3) *The Famous Victories of Henry the Fifth, Containing the Honorable Battle of Agincourt*—an anonymous play of uncertain date, first printed in 1598, today extant in only one known copy. This has been called in recent years both "a decrepit potboiler"[1] and a work of "extraordinary power of expression," probably an apprentice-piece by Shakespeare.[2]

The relevant parts of Daniel and Holinshed are printed in the following section, together with the whole of the *Famous Victories,* so that every reader may watch for himself the workings of a first-rate dramatic imagination. There are brief comments on this process in the Introduction, but the reader who would understand in practical terms what is meant by "art" in phrases like "the art of

[1] Bullough, Geoffrey. *Narrative and Dramatic Sources of Shakespeare,* vol. 4. New York: Columbia University Press, 1962, p. 168.
[2] Pitcher, S. M. *The Case for Shakespeare's Authorship of the Famous Victories.* New York: University Publishers, 1961, p. 5.

playwriting" will want to compare minutely at least one act of *1 Henry IV* with the materials out of which it was made. In the case of the *Famous Victories,* comparisons with appropriate parts of *2 Henry IV* and *Henry V* will also be illuminating. Spelling and punctuation have been modernized in reprinting these selections, some emendations have been silently made, and the text of the *Famous Victories,* following the lead of J. Q. Adams and S. M. Pitcher, is set as prose.

### RAPHAEL HOLINSHED

## from *Chronicles of England, Scotland, and Ireland* [1587 Edition]

### [Uneasy Lies the Head that Wears a Crown]

... One night, as the King was going to bed, he was in danger to have been destroyed; for some naughty traitorous persons had conveyed into his bed a certain iron made with smith's craft, like a caltrop, with three long pricks, sharp and small, standing upright in such sort that when he had laid him down and that the weight of his body should come upon the bed, he should have been thrust in with those pricks and peradventure slain; but as God would, the King, not thinking of any such thing, chanced yet to feel and perceive the instrument before he laid him down and so escaped the danger. Howbeit, he was not so soon delivered from fear; for he might well have his life in suspicion and provide for the preservation of the same, sith perils of death crept into his secret chamber and lay lurking in the bed of down where his body was to be reposed and to take rest. Oh what a suspected state therefore is that of a king holding his regiment with the hatred of his people, the heartgrudgings of his courtiers, and the peremptory practices of both together! Could he confidently compose or settle himself to sleep for fear of strangling? Durst he boldly eat and drink without dread of poisoning? Might he adventure to show himself in great meetings or solemn assemblies without mistrust of mischief against his person intended? What pleasure or what felicity could he take in his princely pomp, which he knew by manifest and fearful experience to be envied and maligned to the very death? ...

[Trouble in Wales and Scotland]

. . . Owen Glendower, according to his accustomed manner, robbing and spoiling within the English borders, caused all the forces of the shire of Hereford to assemble together against them, under the conduct of Edmund Mortimer, Earl of March. But coming to try the matter by battle, whether by treason or otherwise, so it fortuned that the English power was discomfited, the Earl taken prisoner, and above a thousand of his people slain in the place. The shameful villainy used by the Welshwomen towards the dead carcasses was such as honest ears would be ashamed to hear and continent tongues to speak thereof. The dead bodies might not be buried without great sums of money given for liberty to convey them away.

The King was not hasty to purchase the deliverance of the Earl of March, because his title to the crown was well-enough known, and therefore suffered him to remain in miserable prison, wishing both the said Earl and all other of his lineage out of this life, with God and his saints in heaven so they had been out of the way, for then all had been well enough as he thought. But to let these things pass, the King this year sent his eldest daughter Blanch, accompanied with the Earl of Somerset, the Bishop of Worcester, the Lord Clifford, and others, into Almanie [i.e., Germany], which brought her to Colin [i.e., Cologne], and there with great triumph she was married to William, Duke of Bavier [i.e., Bavaria], son and heir to Lewis, the Emperor. About mid of August, the King, to chastise the presumptuous attempts of the Welshmen, went with a great power of men into Wales to pursue the captain of the Welsh rebel Owen Glendower, but in effect he lost his labor; for Owen conveyed himself out of the way into his known lurking places, and (as was thought) through art magic[al], he caused such foul weather of winds, tempest, rain, snow, and hail to be raised for the annoyance of the King's army that the like had not been heard of; in such sort, that the King was constrained to return home, having caused his people yet to spoil and burn first a great part of the country. The same time, the Lord Edmund of

Langley, Duke of York, departed this life and was buried at Langley with his brethren.

The Scots, under the leading of Patric Hepborne of the Hales, the younger, entering into England was overthrown at Nesbit in the marches, as in the Scottish chronicle ye may find more at large. This battle was fought the two and twentieth of June, in this year of our Lord, 1402.

Archibald, Earl Douglas, sore displeased in his mind for this overthrow, procured a commission to invade England, and that to his cost, as ye may likewise read in the Scottish histories. For at a place called Homeldon, they were so fiercely assailed by the Englishmen, under the leading of the Lord Percy, surnamed Henry Hotspur, and George, Earl of March, that with violence of the English shot they were quite vanquished and put to flight, on the Rood Day in harvest, with a great slaughter made by the Englishmen. . . . There were slain of men of estimation: Sir John Swinton, Sir Adam Gordon, Sir John Leviston, Sir Alexander Ramsey of Dalhousie, and three and twenty knights, besides ten thousand of the commons; and of prisoners among others were these: Mordake, Earl of Fife, son to the Governor; Archibald, Earl Douglas, which in the fight lost one of his eyes; Thomas, Earl of Murray; Robert, Earl of Angus; (and as some writers have) the Earls of Athol and Menteith, with five hundred other of meaner degrees. . . .

Edmund Mortimer, Earl of March, prisoner with Owen Glendower, whether for irksomeness of cruel captivity or fear of death or for what other cause, it is uncertain, agreed to take part with Owen against the King of England and took to wife the daughter of the said Owen.

Strange wonders happened (as men reported) at the nativity of this man, for the same night he was born, all his father's horses in the stable were found to stand in blood up to the bellies.

### [The Percys' Rebellion]

Henry, Earl of Northumberland, with his brother Thomas, Earl of Worcester, and his son, the Lord Henry Percy, surnamed Hotspur, which were to King Henry in the beginning of his reign both faithful friends and earnest aiders, began now to envy his wealth and felicity; and especially they were grieved because the King demanded of the Earl and his son such Scottish prisoners as were taken at Homeldon and Nesbit: for of all the captives which were taken in the conflicts fought in those two places, there were delivered to the King's possession only Mordake, Earl of Fife, the Duke of Albany's son, though the King did divers and sundry times require deliverance of the residue, and that with great threatenings; wherewith the Percys, being sore offended, for that they claimed them as their own proper prisoners and their peculiar prize, by the counsel of the Lord Thomas Percy, Earl of Worcester, whose study was ever (as some write) to procure malice and set things in a broil, came to the King unto Windsor (upon a purpose to prove him) and there required of him that, either by ransom or otherwise, he would cause to be delivered out of prison Edmund Mortimer, Earl of March, their cousin german, whom (as they reported) Owen Glendower kept in filthy prison, shackled with irons, only for that he took his part and was to him faithful and true.

The King began not a little to muse at this request and not without cause; for indeed it touched him somewhat near, sith this Edmund was son to Roger, Earl of March, son to the Lady Philip, daughter of Lionel, Duke of Clarence, the third son of King Edward the Third; which Edmund, at King Richard's going into Ireland, was proclaimed heir apparent to the crown and realm; whose aunt called Eleanor, the Lord Henry Percy had married; and therefore King Henry could not well hear that any man should be earnest about the advancement of that lineage. The King, when he had studied on the matter, made answer that the Earl of March was not taken prisoner for his cause nor in his service but willingly suffered himself to be taken, because he would not withstand the attempts of Owen Glendower and his [ac]complices, and therefore he would neither ransom him nor relieve him.

The Percys with this answer and fraudulent excuse were not a little fumed, insomuch that Henry Hotspur said openly: "Behold, the heir of the realm is robbed of his right, and yet the robber with his own will not redeem him." So in this fury the Percys departed, minding nothing more than to depose King Henry from the high type of his royalty and to place in his seat their cousin Edmund, Earl of March, whom they did not only deliver out of captivity but also (to the high displeasure of King Henry) entered in league with the foresaid Owen Glendower. Herewith they, by their deputies in the house of the Archdeacon of Bangor, divided the realm amongst them, causing a tripartite indenture to be made and sealed with their seals, by the covenants whereof: all England from Severn and Trent south and eastward was assigned to the Earl of March; all Wales and the lands beyond Severn westward were appointed to Owen Glendower; and all the remnant from Trent northward to the Lord Percy.

This was done (as some have said) through a foolish credit given to a vain prophecy, as though King Henry was the moldwarp, cursed of God's own mouth, and they three were the dragon, the lion, and the wolf, which should divide this realm between them. Such is the deviation (saith Hall [an earlier chronicler]) and not divination of those blind and fantastical dreams of the Welsh prophesiers. King Henry, not knowing of this new confederacy, and nothing less minding than that which after happened, gathered a great army to go again into Wales, whereof the Earl of Northumberland and his son were advertised by the Earl of Worcester, and with all diligence raised all the power they could make, and sent to the Scots which before were taken prisoners at Homeldon for aid of men, promising to the Earl of Douglas the town of Berwick and a part of Northumberland, and to other Scottish lords great lordships and seignories, if they obtained the upper hand. The Scots, in hope of gain and desirous to be revenged of their old griefs, came to the Earl with a great company well appointed.

The Percys, to make their part seem good, devised certain articles by the advice of Richard Scroop, Archbishop of York, brother to the Lord Scroop, whom King Henry had caused to be beheaded at Bristol. These articles being shown to diverse noblemen and other states of the realm,

moved them to favor their purpose, insomuch that many
of them did not only promise to the Percys aid and succor
by words, but also by their writings and seals confirmed
the same. Howbeit, when the matter came to trial, the most
part of the confederates abandoned them and at the day
of the conflict left them alone. Thus after that the con-
spirators had discovered themselves, the Lord Henry
Percy, desirous to proceed in the enterprise, upon trust to
be assisted by Owen Glendower, the Earl of March, and
others, assembled an army of men-of-arms and archers
forth of Cheshire and Wales. Incontinently, his uncle
Thomas Percy, Earl of Worcester, that had the government of the Prince of Wales, who as then lay at London
in secret manner, conveyed himself out of the Prince's
house, and coming to Stafford (where he met his nephew),
they increased their power by all ways and means they
could devise. The Earl of Northumberland himself was not
with them but, being sick, had promised upon his amendment to repair unto them (as some write) with all convenient speed.

These noblemen, to make their conspiracy to seem ex-
cusable, besides the articles above mentioned sent letters
abroad, wherein was contained that their gathering of an
army tended to none other end but only for the safeguard
of their own persons and to put some better government
in the commonwealth. For whereas taxes and taillages
[i.e., imposts] were daily levied under pretense to be employed in defense of the realm, the same were vainly
wasted and unprofitably consumed; and where through the
slanderous reports of their enemies the King had taken a
grievous displeasure with them, they durst not appear personally in the King's presence, until the prelates and barons
of the realm had obtained of the King license for them to
come and purge themselves before him, by lawful trial of
their peers, whose judgment (as they pretended) they
would in no wise refuse. Many that saw and heard these
letters did commend their diligence and highly praised their
assured fidelity and trustiness towards the commonwealth.

But the King, understanding their cloaked drift, devised
(by what means he might) to quiet and appease the commons and deface their contrived forgeries; and therefore

he wrote an answer to their libels that he marveled much, sith the Earl of Northumberland and the Lord Henry Percy, his son, had received the most part of the sums of money granted to him by the clergy and commonalty for defense of the marches, as he could evidently prove what should move them to complain and raise such manifest slanders. And whereas he understood that the Earls of Northumberland and Worcester and the Lord Percy had by their letters signified to their friends abroad that, by reason of the slanderous reports of their enemies, they durst not appear in his presence without the mediation of the prelates and nobles of the realm, so as they required pledges whereby they might safely come afore him to declare and allege what they had to say in proof of their innocency, he protested by letters sent forth under his seal that they might safely come and go, without all danger or any manner of endamagement to be offered to their persons.

But this could not satisfy those men but that, resolved to go forwards with their enterprise, they marched towards Shrewsbury upon hope to be aided (as men thought) by Owen Glendower and his Welshmen, publishing abroad throughout the countries on each side that King Richard was alive, whom if they wished to see, they willed them to repair in armor unto the castle of Chester, where (without all doubt) he was at that present and ready to come forward. This tale being raised, though it were most untrue, yet it bred variable motions in men's minds, causing them to waver so as they knew not to which part they should stick; and verily divers were well affected towards King Richard, specially such as had tasted of his princely bountifulness, of which there was no small number. And to speak a truth, no marvel it was if many envied the prosperous state of King Henry, sith it was evident enough to the world that he had with wrong usurped the crown, and not only violently deposed King Richard but also cruelly procured his death; for the which, undoubtedly, both he and his posterity tasted such troubles as put them still in danger of their states, till their direct succeeding line was quite rooted out by the contrary faction, as in Henry the Sixth and Edward the Fourth it may appear.

But now to return where we left. King Henry, adver-

tised of the proceedings of the Percys, forthwith gathered
about him such power as he might make, and being earnestly called upon by the Scot, the Earl of March [not Mortimer, but George Dunbar, Earl of March of Scotland], to
make haste and give battle to his enemies, before their
power by delaying of time should still too much increase,
he passed forward with such speed that he was in sight of
his enemies, lying in camp near to Shrewsbury, before they
were in doubt of any such thing; for the Percys thought
that he would have stayed at Burton-upon-Trent till his
council had come thither to him to give their advice what
he were best to do. But herein the enemy was deceived of
his expectation, sith the King had great regard of expedition and making speed for the safety of his own person
whereunto the Earl of March incited him, considering that
in delay is danger and loss in lingering, as the poet in the
like case saith:

> *Tolle moras, nocuit semper differre paratis,*
> *Dum trepidant nullo firmatae robore partes.*

By reason of the King's sudden coming in this sort, they
stayed from assaulting the town of Shrewsbury, which enterprise they were ready at that instant to have taken in
hand, and forthwith the Lord Percy (as a captain of high
courage) began to exhort the captains and soldiers to prepare themselves to battle, sith the matter was grown to
that point that by no means it could be avoided, so that
(said he): "This day shall either bring us all to advancement and honor or else, if it shall chance us to be overcome, shall deliver us from the King's spiteful malice and
cruel disdain; for playing the men (as we ought to do),
better it is to die in battle for the commonwealth's cause
than through cowardlike fear to prolong life, which after
shall be taken from us by sentence of the enemy."

Hereupon the whole army, being in number about fourteen thousand chosen men, promised to stand with him
so long as life lasted. There were with the Percys as chief-
tains of this army: the Earl of Douglas, a Scottish man;
the Baron of Kinderton; Sir Hugh Browne and Sir Richard
Vernon, knights; with diverse other stout and right valiant

captains. Now when the two armies were encamped, the one against the other, the Earl of Worcester and the Lord Percy with their [ac]complices sent the articles (whereof I spake before) by Thomas Caiton and Thomas Salvain, esquiers to King Henry, under their hands and seals, which articles in effect charged him with manifest perjury, in that (contrary to his oath received upon the evangelists at Doncaster, when he first entered the realm after his exile) he had taken upon him the crown and royal dignity, imprisoned King Richard, caused him to resign his title and, finally, to be murdered. Diverse other matters they laid to his charge: as levying of taxes and taillages, contrary to his promise; infringing of laws and customs of the realm; and suffering the Earl of March to remain in prison without travailing to have him delivered. All which things they, as procurers and protectors of the commonwealth, took upon them to prove against him, as they protested unto the whole world.

King Henry, after he had read their articles, with the defiance which they annexed to the same, answered the esquiers that he was ready with dint of sword and fierce battle to prove their quarrel false and nothing else than a forged matter, not doubting but that God would aid and assist him in his righteous cause against the disloyal and false forsworn traitors. The next day in the morning early, being the even of Mary Magdalen, they set their battles in order on both sides, and now, whilest the warriors looked when the token of battle should be given, the Abbot of Shrewsbury and one of the clerks of the privy seal were sent from the King unto the Percys to offer them pardon if they would come to any reasonable agreement. By their persuasions, the Lord Henry Percy began to give ear unto the King's offer and so sent with them his uncle, the Earl of Worcester, to declare unto the King the causes of those troubles and to require some effectual reformation in the same.

[The Battle of Shrewsbury, July 21, 1403]

It was reported for a truth that now, when the King had condescended unto all that was reasonable at his hands to be required and seemed to humble himself more than was meet for his estate, the Earl of Worcester (upon his return to his nephew) made relation clean contrary to that the King had said, in such sort that he set his nephew's heart more in displeasure towards the King than ever it was before, driving him by that means to fight whether he would or not; then suddenly [he] blew the trumpets, the King's part crying S[aint] George upon them, the adversaries cried "Esperance Percy," and so the two armies furiously joined. The archers on both sides shot for the best game, laying on such load with arrows that many died and were driven down that never rose again.

The Scots (as some write), which had the fore ward on the Percys' side, intending to be revenged of their old displeasures done to them by the English nation, set so fiercely on the King's fore ward, led by the Earl of Stafford, that they made the same draw back, and had almost broken their adversaries' array. The Welshmen also, which before had lain lurking in the woods, mountains, and marshes, hearing of this battle toward, came to the aid of the Percys and refreshed the wearied people with new succors. The King, perceiving that his men were thus put to distress, what with the violent impression of the Scots and the tempestuous storms of arrows that his adversaries discharged freely against him and his people, it was no need to will him to stir; for suddenly, with his fresh battle, he approached and relieved his men, so that the battle began more fierce than before. Here the Lord Henry Percy and the Earl Douglas, a right stout and hardy captain, not regarding the shot of the King's battle nor the close order of the ranks, pressing forward together bent their whole forces towards the King's person, coming upon him with spears and swords so fiercely that the Earl of March the Scot [again George Dunbar], perceiving their purpose, withdrew the King from that side of the field (as some write) for his great benefit and safeguard (as it appeared), for they gave such a violent onset upon them that stood about the King's standard that, slaying his standard-bearer, Sir Walter Blunt, and overthrowing the standard, they made slaughter of all those that stood about it, as the Earl of

Stafford, that day made by the King Constable of the realm, and diverse other.

The Prince that day holp his father like a lusty young gentleman; for although he was hurt in the face with an arrow, so that diverse noblemen that were about him would have conveyed him forth of the field, yet he would not suffer them so to do, lest his departure from amongst his men might haply have stricken some fear into their hearts; and so, without regard of his hurt, he continued with his men and never ceased either to fight where the battle was most hot or to encourage his men where it seemed most need. This battle lasted three long hours with indifferent fortune on both parts, till at length the King, crying Saint George victory, brake the array of his enemies and adventured so far that (as some write) the Earl Douglas strake him down and at that instant slew Sir Walter Blunt and three others appareled in the King's suit and clothing, saying: "I marvel to see so many kings thus suddenly arise one in the neck of another." The King indeed was raised and did that day many a noble feat of arms, for as it is written, he slew that day with his own hands six and thirty persons of his enemies. The other on his part, encouraged by his doings, fought valiantly and slew the Lord Percy, called Sir Henry Hotspur. To conclude, the King's enemies were vanquished and put to flight, in which flight the Earl of Douglas, for haste, falling from the crag of a high mountain, brake one of his cullions and was taken, and for his valiantness, of the King frankly and freely delivered.

There was also taken the Earl of Worcester, the procurer and setter forth of all this mischief, Sir Richard Vernon, and the Baron of Kinderton, with diverse other. There were slain upon the King's part, besides the Earl of Stafford, to the number of ten knights: Sir Hugh Shirley, Sir John Clifton, Sir John Cokaine, Sir Nicholas Gawsey, Sir Walter Blunt, Sir John Claverley, Sir John Macy of Podington, Sir Hugh Mortimer, and Sir Robert Gawsey, all the which received the same morning the order of knighthood; Sir Thomas Wendesley was wounded to death and so passed out of this life shortly after. There died in all upon the King's side sixteen hundred, and four thousand were griev-

ously wounded. On the contrary side were slain, besides
the Lord Percy, the most part of the knights and esquiers
of the county of Chester, to the number of two hundred,
besides yeomen and footmen; in all there died of those that
fought on the Percys' side about five thousand. This battle
was fought on Mary Magdalen Even, being Saturday. Upon
the Monday following, the Earl of Worcester, the Baron
of Kinderton, and Sir Richard Vernon, knights, were con-
demned and beheaded. The Earl's head was sent to London, there to be set on the bridge.

## [Reconciliation of Prince and King, 1411]

. . . The Lord Henry, Prince of Wales, eldest son to King
Henry, got knowledge that certain of his father's servants
were busy to give informations against him, whereby discord might arise betwixt him and his father; for they put
into the King's head not only what evil rule (according to
the course of youth) the Prince kept, to the offense of
many, but also what great resort of people came to his
house, so that the court was nothing furnished with such
a train as daily followed the Prince. These tales brought no
small suspicion into the King's head, lest his son would
presume to usurp the Crown, he being yet alive, through
which suspicious jealousy it was perceived that he favored
not his son, as in times past he had done.

The Prince, sore offended with such persons as, by slanderous reports, sought not only to spot his good name
abroad in the realm but to sow discord also betwixt him
and his father, wrote his letters into every part of the realm
to reprove all such slanderous devices of those that sought
his discredit. And to clear himself the better, that the world
might understand what wrong he had to be slandered in
such wise, about the feast of Peter and Paul, to wit, the
nine and twentieth day of June, he came to the court with
such a number of noblemen and other his friends that
wished him well, as the like train had been seldom seen re-
pairing to the court at any one time in those days. He was
appareled in a gown of blue satin full of small eyelet holes,
at every hole the needle hanging by a silk thread with which

it was sewed. About his arm he wore a hound's collar set full of SS of gold, and the tirets likewise being of the same metal.

The court was then at Westminster where, he being entered into the hall, not one of his company durst once advance himself further than the fire in the same hall, notwithstanding they were earnestly requested by the lords to come higher; but they, regarding what they had in commandment of the Prince, would not presume to do in any thing contrary thereunto. He himself, only accompanied with those of the King's house, was straight admitted to the presence of the King his father, who being at that time grievously diseased, yet caused himself in his chair to be borne into his privy chamber, where in the presence of three or four persons in whom he had confidence, he commanded the Prince to show what he had to say concerning the cause of his coming.

The Prince, kneeling down before his father, said: "Most redoubted and sovereign lord and father, I am at this time come to your presence as your liege man and as your natural son, in all things to be at your commandment. And where I understand you have in suspicion my demeanor against your Grace, you know very well that if I knew any man within this realm of whom you should stand in fear, my duty were to punish that person, thereby to remove that grief from your heart. Then how much more ought I to suffer death, to ease your Grace of that grief which you have of me, being your natural son and liege man; and to that end I have this day made myself ready by confession and receiving of the sacrament. And therefore I beseech you, most redoubted lord and dear father, for the honor of God, to ease your heart of all such suspicion as you have of me and to dispatch me here before your knees with this same dagger," and withal he delivered unto the King his dagger, in all humble reverence, adding further that his life was not so dear to him that he wished to live one day with his displeasure, "and therefore in thus ridding me out of life and yourself from all suspicion, here in presence of these lords and before God at the day of the general judgment, I faithfully protest clearly to forgive you."

The King, moved herewith, cast from him the dagger and, embracing the Prince, kissed him and with shedding tears confessed that indeed he had him partly in suspicion, though now (as he perceived) not with just cause, and therefore, from thenceforth no misreport should cause him to have him in mistrust, and this he promised of his honor. So by his great wisdom was the wrongful suspicion which his father had conceived against him removed and he restored to his favor. And further, where he could not but grievously complain of them that had slandered him so greatly, to the defacing not only of his honor but also putting him in danger of his life, he humbly besought the King that they might answer their unjust accusation; and in case they were found to have forged such matters upon a malicious purpose, that then they might suffer some punishment for their faults, though not to the full of that they had deserved. The King, seeming to grant his reasonable desire, yet told him that he must tarry a parliament that such offenders might be punished by judgment of their peers; and so for that time he was dismissed, with great love and signs of fatherly affection.

Thus were the father and the son reconciled, betwixt whom the said pickthanks had sown division, insomuch that the son, upon a vehement conceit of unkindness sprung in the father, was in the way to be worn out of favor. Which was the more likely to come to pass by their informations that privily charged him with riot and other uncivil demeanor unseemly for a prince. Indeed, he was youthfully given, grown to audacity, and had chosen him companions agreeable to his age, with whom he spent the time in such recreations, exercises, and delights as he fancied. But yet (it should seem by the report of some writers) that his behavior was not offensive or at least tending to the damage of anybody, sith he had a care to avoid doing of wrong and to tender his affections within the tract of virtue, whereby he opened unto himself a ready passage of good liking among the prudent sort and was beloved of such as could discern his disposition, which was in no degree so excessive as that he deserved in such vehement manner to be suspected. In whose dispraise I find little but to his praise very much. . . .

SAMUEL DANIEL

## from *The First Four Books of the Civil Wars between the Two Houses of Lancaster and York* [1595]

[Bolingbroke, having become Henry IV, has military difficulties.]

### 86

And yet new Hydras lo, new heads appear
T'afflict that peace reputed then so sure,
And gave him much to do, and much to fear,
And long and dangerous tumults did procure,
And those even of his chiefest followers were
Of whom he might presume him most secure,
Who whether not so graced or so preferred
As they expected, these new factions stirred.

### 87

The Percys were the men, men of great might,
Strong in alliance, and in courage strong
That thus conspire, under pretense to right
The crookèd courses they had suffered long:
Whether their conscience urged them or despite,
Or that they saw the part they took was wrong,
Or that ambition hereto did them call,
Or others envied grace, or rather all.

### 88

What cause soever were, strong was their plot,
Their parties great, means good, th' occasion fit:
Their practice close, their faith suspected not,
Their states far off and they of wary wit:
Who with large promises draw in the Scot
To aid their cause—he likes, and yields to it,
Not for the love of them or for their good,
But glad hereby of means to shed our blood.

### 89

Then join they with the Welsh, who fitly trained
And all in arms under a mighty head
Great Glendow'r, who long warred, and much attained,
Sharp conflicts made, and many vanquishèd:
With whom was Edmund Earl of March retained
Being first his prisoner, now confederèd,
A man the King much feared, and well he might
Lest he should look whether his crown stood right.

### 90

For Richard, for the quiet of the state,
Before he took those Irish wars in hand
About succession doth deliberate,
And finding how the certain right did stand,
With full consent this man did ordinate
The heir apparent in the Crown and land:
Then judge if this the King might nearly touch,
Although his might were small, his right being much.

### 91

With these the Percys them confederate,
And as three heads they league in one intent,
And instituting a triumvirate
Do part the land in triple government:
Dividing thus among themselves the state,
The Percys should rule all the North from Trent
And Glendow'r Wales: the Earl of March should be
Lord of the South from Trent; and thus they 'gree.

### 92

Then those two helps which still such actors find—
Pretense of common good, the King's disgrace—
Doth fit their course, and draw the vulgar mind
To further them and aid them in this case:
The King they accused for cruel, and unkind
That did the state, and Crown, and all deface;
A perjured man that held all faith in scorn,
Whose trusted oaths had others made forsworn.

### 93

Besides the odious detestable act
Of that late murdered king they aggravate,
Making it his that so had willed the fact
That he the doers did remunerate:
And then such taxes daily doth exact
That were against the orders of the state,
And with all these or worse they him assailed
Who late of others with the like prevailed.

### 94

Thus doth contentious proud mortality
Afflict each other and itself torment:
And thus O thou, mind-tort'ring misery,
Restless ambition, born in discontent,
Turn'st and retossest with iniquity
The unconstant courses frailty did invent:
And foul'st fair order and defil'st the earth
Fost'ring up war, father of blood and dearth.

### 95

Great seemed the cause, and greatly, too, did add
The peoples' love thereto, these crimes rehearsed,
That many gathered to the troops they had
And many more do flock from coasts dispersed:
But when the King had heard these news so bad,
Th' unlookt for dangerous toil more nearly pierced;
For bent t'wards Wales t'appease those tumults there,
H' is forced divert his course, and them forbear.

### 96

Not to give time unto th' increasing rage
And gathering fury, forth he hastes with speed,
Lest more delay or giving longer age
To th' evil grown, it might the cure exceed:
All his best men at arms, and leaders sage
All he prepared he could, and all did need;
For to a mighty work thou goest O King,
To such a field that power to power shall bring.

### 97

There shall young Hotspur with a fury led
Meet with thy forward son as fierce as he:
There warlike Worcester long experiencèd
In foreign arms, shall come t' encounter thee:
There Douglas to thy Stafford shall make head:
There Vernon for thy valiant Blunt shall be:
There shalt thou find a doubtful bloody day,
Though sickness keep Northumberland away.

### 98

Who yet reserved, though after quit for this,
Another tempest on thy head to raise
As if still-wrong revenging *Nemesis*
Did mean t' afflict all thy continual days:
And yet this field he happily might miss
For thy great good, and therefore well he stays:
What might his force have done being joined thereto
When that already gave so much to do?

### 99

The swift approach and unexpected speed
The King had made upon this new-raised force
In th' unconfirmèd troops much fear did breed,
Untimely hind'ring their intended course;
The joining with the Welsh they had decreed
Was hereby stopped which made their part the worse,
Northumberland with forces from the North
Expected to be there, was not set forth.

### 100

And yet undaunted Hotspur seeing the King
So near approached leaving the work in hand
With forward speed his forces marshaling,
Sets forth his farther coming to withstand:
And with a cheerful voice encouraging
By his great spirit his well emboldened band,
Brings a strong host of firm resolvèd might,
And placed his troops before the King in sight.

### 101

This day (saith he) O faithful valiant friends,
Whatever it doth give, shall glory give:
This day with honor frees our state, or ends
Our misery with fame, that still shall live,
And do but think how well this day he spends
That spends his blood his country to relieve:
Our holy cause, our freedom, and our right,
Sufficient are to move good minds to fight.

### 102

Besides th' assurèd hope of victory
That we may even promise on our side
Against this weak-constrainèd company,
Whom force and fear, not will and love doth guide
Against a prince whose foul impiety
The heavens do hate, the earth cannot abide,
Our number being no less, our courage more,
What need we doubt if we but work therefor.

### 103

This said, and thus resolved even bent to charge
Upon the King, who well their order viewed
And careful noted all the form at large
Of their proceeding, and their multitude:
And deeming better if he could discharge
The day with safety, and some peace conclude,
Great proffers sends of pardon, and of grace
If they would yield, and quietness embrace.

## 104

But this refused, the King with wrath incensed
Rage against fury doth with speed prepare:
And O, saith he, though I could have dispensed
With this day's blood, which I have sought to spare
That greater glory might have recompensed
The forward worth of these that so much dare,
That we might honor had by th' overthrown,
That th' wounds we make, might not have been our own.

## 105

Yet since that other men's iniquity
Calls on the sword of wrath against my will,
And that themselves exact this cruelty,
And I constrainèd am this blood to spill:
Then on my masters, on courageously
True-hearted subjects against traitors ill,
And spare them not who seek to spoil us all,
Whose foul confusèd end soon see you shall.

## 106

Straight moves with equal motion equal rage
The like incensèd armies unto blood,
One to defend, another side to wage
Foul civil war, both vows their quarrel good:
Ah too much heat to blood doth now enrage
Both who the deed provokes and who withstood,
That valor here is vice, here manhood sin,
The forward'st hands doth O least honor win.

## 107

But now begin these fury-moving sounds
The notes of wrath that music brought from hell,
The rattling drums which trumpets voice confounds,
The cries, th' encouragements, the shouting shrill;
That all about the beaten air rebounds,
Thund'ring confusèd, murmurs horrible,
To rob all sense except the sense to fight:
Well hands may work, the mind hath lost his sight.

## 108

O war! begot in pride and luxury,
The child of wrath and of dissension,
Horrible good; mischief necessary,
The foul reformer of confusion,
Unjust-just scourge of our iniquity,
Cruel recurrer of corruption:
O that these sin-sick states in need should stand
To be let blood with such a boist'rous hand!

## 109

And O how well thou hadst been spared this day
Had not wrong-counseled Percy been perverse,
Whose young undangered hand now rash makes way
Upon the sharpest fronts of the most fierce:
Where now an equal fury thrusts to stay
And rebeat-back that force and his disperse,
Then these assail, then those chase back again,
Till stayed with new-made hills of bodies slain.

## 110

There lo that new-appearing glorious star
Wonder of Arms, the terror of the field,
Young Henry, laboring where the stoutest are,
And even the stoutest forces back to yield,
There is that hand bold'ned to blood and war
That must the sword in woundrous° actions wield:
But better hadst thou learned with others blood
A less expense to us, to thee more good.

## 111

Hadst thou not there lent present speedy aid
To thy endangered father nearly tired,
Whom fierce encountring Douglas overlaid,
That day had there his troublous life expired:
Heroical courageous Blunt arrayed
In habit like as was the King attired

---

° **woundrous** (Daniel's pun on "wound" and "wondress")

And deemed for him, excused that fate with his,
For he had what his lord did hardly miss.

### 112

For thought a king he would not now disgrace
The person then supposed, but princelike shows
Glorious effects of worth that fit his place,
And fighting dies, and dying overthrows:
Another of that forward name and race
In that hot work his valiant life bestows,
Who bare the standard of the King that day,
Whose colors overthrown did much dismay.

### 113

And dear it cost, and O much blood is shed
To purchase thee this losing victory
O travailed King: yet hast thou conquerèd
A doubtful day, a mighty enemy:
But O what wounds, what famous worth lies dead!
That makes the winner look with sorrowing eye,
Magnanimous Stafford lost that much had wrought,
And valiant Shirley who great glory got.

### 114

Such wreck of others' blood thou didst behold,
O furious Hotspur, ere thou lost thine own!
Which now once lost that heat in thine waxed cold,
And soon became thy army overthrown;
And O that this great spirit, this courage bold,
Had in some good cause been rightly shown!
So had not we thus violently then
Have termed that rage, which valor should have been.

ANONYMOUS

## The Famous Victories of Henry the Fifth

[Dramatis Personae

King Henry IV
Prince Henry of Monmouth, his son (later
    King Henry V)
Duke of York ⎰
Duke of Exeter ⎱ brothers of Henry IV
Earl of Oxford
Archbishop of Canterbury
The Lord Chief Justice
The Lord Mayor of London
The Sheriff
Ned
Tom                                              ⎱ friends to Prince Henry
Sir John Oldcastle, alias Jockey ⎰
English Captain
English Soldier
Two Receivers
Clerk of the King's Bench
The Jailer
The Thief, Cutbert Cutter, alias Gad's Hill
Derick, a poor carrier

John Cobbler  
Robin Pewterer  } the Watch  
Lawrence Costermonger )  
The Vintner's Boy, Robin  
The Porter  
King Charles VI, of France  
The Dolphin, his son  
Duke of Burgundy  
Archbishop of Bourges  
The Constable  
A Herald  
A Messenger  
A French Captain  
Jack Drummer  
French Soldiers  
A Frenchman  

Princess Katherine, daughter of Charles VI  
Mistress Cobbler  

Lords, Ladies, Attendants  

*Scene:* England and France]

# The Famous Victories of Henry the Fifth
## Containing the
### Honorable Battle of Agincourt

[*Scene I*]

*Enter the young Prince, Ned, and Tom.*

*Prince.* Come away, Ned and Tom.

*Both.* Here, my lord.

*Prince.* Come away, my lads. Tell me, sirs, how much gold have you got?

*Ned.* Faith, my lord, I have got five hundred pound.　　5

*Prince.* But tell me, Tom, how much hast thou got?

*Tom.* Faith, my lord, some four hundred pound.

*Prince.* Four hundred pounds! Bravely spoken, lads! But tell me, sirs, think you not that it was a villainous part of me to rob my father's receivers?　　10

*Ned.* Why, no, my lord; it was but a trick of youth.

*Prince.* Faith, Ned, thou sayest true. But tell me, sirs, whereabouts are we?

*Tom.* My lord, we are now about a mile off London.

*Prince.* But, sirs, I marvel that Sir John Oldcastle comes　　15
not away. Zounds, see where he comes.

*Enter Jockey [i.e., John Oldcastle].*

How now, Jockey, what news with thee?

*John Oldcastle.* Faith, my lord, such news as passeth!
For the town of Deptford is risen with hue and cry
20    after your man, which parted from us the last night
and has set upon and hath robbed a poor carrier.

*Prince.* Zounds, the villain that was wont to spy out our
booties?

*John Oldcastle.* Ay, my lord, even the very same.

25  *Prince.* Now base-minded rascal to rob a poor carrier!
Well, it skills not; I'll save the base villain's life, ay,
I may. But tell me, Jockey, whereabouts be the re-
ceivers?

*John Oldcastle.* Faith, my lord, they are hard by; but
30    the best is we are ahorseback and they be afoot, so
we may escape them.

*Prince.* Well, if the villains come, let me alone with
them! But tell me, Jockey, how much gotst thou from
the knaves? For I am sure I got something, for one
33   of the villains so belammed me about the shoulders
as I shall feel it this month.

*John Oldcastle.* Faith, my lord, I have got a hundred
pound.

*Prince.* A hundred pound! Now bravely spoken,
40  Jockey. But come, sirs, lay all your money before
me. Now, by heaven, here is a brave show! But, as
I am true gentleman, I will have the half of this spent
tonight! But, sirs, take up your bags; here comes the
receivers. Let me alone.

*Enters two Receivers.*°

45  *First Receiver.* Alas, good fellow, what shall we do? I
dare never go home to the court, for I shall be
hanged. But look, here is the young Prince. What
shall we do?

*Prince.* How now, you villains! What are you?

44 s.d. Receivers i.e., of taxes

*First Receiver.* Speak you to him.                              50

*Second Receiver.* No, I pray, speak you to him.

*Prince.* Why, how now, you rascals! Why speak you not?

*First Receiver.* Forsooth, we be—pray speak you to him.                                                          55

*Prince.* Zounds, villains, speak, or I'll cut off your heads!

*Second Receiver.* Forsooth, he can tell the tale better than I.

*First Receiver.* Forsooth, we be your father's receivers.     60

*Prince.* Are you my father's receivers? Then I hope ye have brought me some money.

*First Receiver.* Money? Alas, sir, we be robbed!

*Prince.* Robbed! How many were there of them?

*First Receiver.* Marry, sir, there were four of them;         65
and one of them had Sir John Oldcastle's bay hobby, and your black nag.

*Prince.* Gog's wounds! How like you this, Jockey? Blood, you villains! My father robbed of his money abroad, and we robbed in our stables! But tell me,   70
how many were of them?

*First Receiver.* If it please you, there were four of them; and there was one about the bigness of you—but I am sure I so belammed him about the shoulders that he will feel it this month.                              75

*Prince.* Gog's wounds! You lammed them fairly—so that they have carried away your money. But come, sirs, what shall we do with the villains?

*Both Receivers.* I beseech your Grace, be good to us.

*Ned.* I pray you, my lord, forgive them this once.            80

[*Prince.*] Well, stand up, and get you gone. And look

that you speak not a word of it—for, if there be—
zounds! I'll hang you and all your kin!

*Exit [Receivers].*

*Prince.* Now, sirs, how like you this? Was not this
85     bravely done? For now the villains dare not speak a
word of it, I have so feared them with words. Now,
whither shall we go?

*All.* Why, my lord, you know our old host's at Faversham.

90  *Prince.* Our host's at Faversham! Blood, what shall we
do there? We have a thousand pound about us, and
we shall go to a petty ale-house? No, no! You know
the old tavern in Eastcheap; there is good wine—
besides, there is a pretty wench that can talk well;
95     for I delight as much in their tongues as any part
about them.

*All.* We are ready to wait upon your Grace.

*Prince.* Gog's wounds! "Wait"? We will go altogether;
we are all fellows. I tell you, sirs, and the King my
100    father were dead, we would be all kings. Therefore,
come away!

*Ned.* Gog's wounds, bravely spoken, Harry!

*[Exeunt omnes.]*


[Scene II]


*Enter John Cobbler, Robin Pewterer,
Lawrence Costermonger.*

*John.* All is well here; all is well, masters.

*Lawrence.* How say you, neighbor John Cobbler? I
think it best that my neighbor, Robin Pewterer, went
to Pudding Lane End, and we will watch here at
5     Billingsgate Ward. How say you, neighbor Robin?
How like you this?

*Robin.* Marry, well, neighbors; I care not much if I go
to Pudding Lane's End. But, neighbors, if you hear
any ado about me, make haste; and if I hear any ado
about you, I will come to you.          *Exit Robin.*   10

*Lawrence.* Neighbor, what news hear you of the young
Prince?

*John.* Marry, neighbor, I hear say he is a toward young
prince; for, if he meet any by the highway, he will
not let° to—talk with him. I dare not call him thief,   15
but sure he is one of these taking fellows.

*Lawrence.* Indeed, neighbor, I hear say he is as lively
a young prince as ever was.

*John.* Ay, and I hear say if he use it long, his father will
cut him off from the Crown. But, neighbor, say noth-   20
ing of that!

*Lawrence.* No, no, neighbor, I warrant you!

*John.* Neighbor, methinks you begin to sleep. If you
will, we will sit down; for I think it is about midnight.

*Lawrence.* Marry, content, neighbor; let us sleep.   25

*Enter Derick, roving.*

*Derick.* Who! Who there, who there!          *Exit Derick.*

*Enter Robin.*

*Robin.* Oh, neighbors, what mean you to sleep, and
such ado in the streets?

*Both.* How now, neighbor, what's the matter?

*Enter Derick again.*

*Derick.* Who there! Who there! Who there!   30

*John.* Why, what ailst thou? Here is no horses.

*Derick.* O alas, man, I am robbed! Who there! Who
there!

---

15 let hesitate (the speaker is about to add "rob", then thinks better
of it)

*Robin.* Hold him, neighbor Cobbler. Why, I see thou
35    art a plain clown.°

*Derick.* Am I a clown? Zounds, masters, do clowns go
in silk apparel? I am sure all we gentlemen-clowns in
Kent scant go so well. Zounds, you know clowns very
well! Hear you, are you Master Constable? And you
40    be, speak, for I will not take it at his hands.

*John.* Faith, I am not Master Constable; but I am one
of his bad° officers, for he is not here.

*Derick.* Is not Master Constable here? Well, it is no matter. I'll have the law at his hands.

45  *John.* Nay, I pray you, do not take the law of us.

*Derick.* Well, you are one of his beastly officers.

*John.* I am one of his bad° officers.

*Derick.* Why, then, I charge thee, look to him!

*John.* Nay, but hear you, sir; you seem to be an honest
50    fellow, and we are poor men; and now 'tis night, and
we would be loath to have anything ado; therefore,
I pray thee, put it up.

*Derick.* First, thou sayest true; I am an honest fellow
—and a proper, handsome fellow, too! And you
55    seem to be poor men; therefore I care not greatly.
Nay, I am quickly pacified. But, and you chance to
spy the thief, I pray you lay hold on him.

*Robin.* Yes, that we will, I warrant you.

*Derick.* 'Tis a wonderful thing to see how glad the knave
60    is, now I have forgiven him.

*John.* Neighbors, do you look about you. How now,
who's there?

### *Enter the Thief.*

*Thief.* Here is a good fellow. I pray you, which is the
way to the old tavern in Eastcheap?

35 **clown** rustic    42, 47 **bad** regularly installed (i.e., "bade")

*Derick.* Whoop halloo! Now, Gad's Hill, knowest  65
thou me?

*Thief.* I know thee for an ass.

*Derick.* And I know thee for a taking fellow upon
Gad's Hill in Kent. A bots light upon ye.

*Thief.* The whoreson villain would be knocked.  70

*Derick.* Masters, villain, and ye be men, stand to him,
and take his weapon from him. Let him not pass you!

*John.* My friend, what make you abroad now? It is too
late to walk now.

*Thief.* It is not too late for true men to walk.  75

*Lawrence.* We know thee not to be a true man.

[*They seize the Thief.*]

*Thief.* Why, what do you mean to do with me? Zounds!
I am one of the King's liege people.

*Derick.* Hear you, sir, are you one of the King's liege
people?  80

*Thief.* Ay, marry am I, sir! What say you to it?

*Derick.* Marry, sir, I say you are one of the King's
filching people.

*John.* Come, come. let's have him away.

*Thief.* Why, what have I done?  85

*Robin.* Thou hast robbed a poor fellow, and taken
away his goods from him.

*Thief.* I never saw him before.

*Derick.* Masters, who comes here?

*Enter the Vintner's Boy.*

*Boy.* How now, goodman Cobbler.  90

*John.* How now, Robin, what makes thou abroad at
this time of night?

*Boy.* Marry, I have been at the Counter;° I can tell
such news as never you have heard the like!

95  *John.* What is that, Robin? What is the matter?

*Boy.* Why, this night, about two hours ago, there came
the young Prince, and three or four more of his companions, and called for wine good store; and then
they sent for a noise of musicians, and were very
100  merry for the space of an hour; then, whether their
music liked them not, or whether they had drunk
too much wine or no, I cannot tell, but our pots flew
against the walls; and then they drew their swords
and went into the street and fought, and some took
105  one part and some took another; but for the space
of half an hour there was such a bloody fray as
passeth! And none could part them until such time
as the Mayor and Sheriff were sent for; and then, at
the last, with much ado, they took them; and so the
110  young Prince was carried to the Counter; and then,
about one hour after, there came a messenger from
the Court in all haste from the King for my Lord
Mayor and the Sheriff—but for what cause I know
not.

115  *John.* Here is news, indeed, Robert!

*Lawrence.* Marry, neighbor, this news is strange, indeed! I think it best, neighbor, to rid our hands of
this fellow first.

*Thief.* What mean you to do with me?

120  *John.* We mean to carry you to the prison, and there
to remain till the sessions day.

*Thief.* Then, I pray you, let me go to the prison where
my master is.

*John.* Nay, thou must go to the country prison, to New-
125  gate. Therefore, come away.

*Thief.* [*To Derick*] I prithee, be good to me, honest
fellow.

93 **Counter** London prison under jurisdiction of the Lord Mayor

*Derick*. Ay, marry, will I; I'll be very charitable to
thee, for I will never leave thee—till I see thee on
the gallows.                                                    130

                                              [*Exeunt omnes*.]


[*Scene III*]


*Enter Henry the Fourth [attended], with the
    Earl of Exeter, and the Lord of Oxford.*


*Oxford*. And please your Majesty, here is my Lord
Mayor and the Sheriff of London to speak with your
Majesty.

*King*. Admit them to our presence.

            *Enter the Mayor and the Sheriff.*

*King*. Now, my good Lord Mayor of London, the      5
cause of my sending for you at this time is to tell
you of a matter which I have learned of my council.
Herein I understand that you have committed my
son to prison without our leave and license. What!
Although he be a rude youth, and likely to give occa-   10
sion, yet you might have considered that he is a
prince, and my son, and not to be haled to prison by
every subject.

*Mayor*. May it please your Majesty to give us leave to
tell our tale?                                                  15

*King*. Or else God forbid! Otherwise, you might think
me an unequal judge, having more affection to my
son than to any rightful judgment.

*Mayor*. Then I do not doubt but we shall rather deserve commendations at your Majesty's hands than      20
any anger.

*King*. Go to, say on.

*Mayor*. Then, if it please your Majesty, this night be-

twixt two and three of the clock in the morning my
25   lord the young Prince, with a very disordered company, came to the old tavern in Eastcheap; and
whether it was that their music liked them not, or
whether they were overcome with wine, I know not,
but they drew their swords, and into the street they
30   went; and some took my lord the young Prince's
part, and some took the other; but betwixt them
there was such a bloody fray for the space of half
an hour that neither watchmen nor any other could
stay them; till my brother, the Sheriff of London,
35   and I were sent for; and, at the last, with much ado,
we stayed them. But it was long first, which was a
great disquieting to all your loving subjects thereabouts. And then, my good lord, we knew not
whether your Grace had sent them to try us whether
40   we would do justice, or whether it were of their own
voluntary will or not, we cannot tell. And, therefore,
in such a case, we knew not what to do; but, for our
own safeguard, we sent him to ward; where he
wanteth nothing that is fit for his Grace and your
45   Majesty's son. And thus, most humbly beseeching
your Majesty to think of our answer—

*King.* Stand aside until we have further deliberated on
your answer.

*Exit Mayor [with Sheriff].*
Ah, Harry, Harry, now thrice-accursed Harry, that
50   hath gotten a son which with grief will end his
father's days! Oh, my son, a prince thou art, ay, a
prince indeed—and to deserve imprisonment! And
well have they done, and like faithful subjects. [*To
his Attendants*] Discharge them, and let them go.

55   *Exeter.* I beseech your Grace, be good to my lord the
young Prince.

*King.* Nay, nay, 'tis no matter; let him alone.

*Oxford.* Perchance the Mayor and the Sheriff have been
too precise in this matter.

*King.* No, they have done like faithful subjects. I will go  *60*
myself to discharge them and let them go.

        *Exit omnes.*


### [Scene IV]


*Enter Lord Chief Justice, Clerk of the Office,
Jailer, John Cobbler, Derick, and the Thief.*

*Judge.* Jailer, bring the prisoner to the bar.

*Derick.* Hear you, my lord; I pray you, bring the bar
to the prisoner.

*Judge.* Hold thy hand up at the bar.

*Thief.* Here it is, my lord.       *5*

*Judge.* Clerk of the Office, read his indictment.

*Clerk.* What is thy name?

*Thief.* My name was known before I came here, and
shall be when I am gone, I warrant you.

*Judge.* Ay, I think so; but we will know it better be-  *10*
fore thou go.

*Derick.* Zounds, and you do but send to the next jail,
we are sure to know his name; for this is not the first
prison he hath been in, I'll warrant you.

*Clerk.* What is thy name?      *15*

*Thief.* What need you to ask, and have it in writing?

*Clerk.* Is not thy name Cutbert Cutter?

*Thief.* What the devil need you ask, and know it so
well?

*Clerk.* Why then, Cutbert Cutter, I indict thee, by the  *20*
name of Cutbert Cutter, for robbing a poor carrier
the 20th day of May last past, in the fourteenth year

of the reign of our sovereign lord King Henry the
Fourth, for setting upon a poor carrier upon Gad's
25  Hill, in Kent, and having beaten and wounded the
said carrier, and taken his goods from him—

*Derick.* Oh, masters, stay there! Nay, let's never belie
the man, for he hath not beaten and wounded me
also, but he hath beaten and wounded my pack, and
30  hath taken the great raze° of ginger that Bouncing
Bess with the jolly buttocks should have had. That
grieves me most.

*Judge.* Well, what sayest thou? Art thou guilty, or not
guilty?

35  *Thief.* Not guilty, my lord.

*Judge.* By whom wilt thou be tried?

*Thief.* By my lord the young Prince, or by myself,
whether you will.

*Enter the young Prince, with Ned and Tom.*

*Prince.* Come away, my lads. Gog's wounds, ye villain,
40  what make you here? I must go about my business
myself and you must stand loitering here?

*Thief.* Why, my lord, they have bound me, and will not
let me go.

*Prince.* Have they bound thee, villain? Why, how now,
45  my lord?

*Judge.* I am glad to see your Grace in good health.

*Prince.* Why, my lord, this is my man. 'Tis marvel you
knew him not long before this. I tell you, he is a
man of his hands.

50  *Thief.* Ay, Gog's wounds, that I am! Try me, who dare.

*Judge.* Your Grace shall find small credit by acknowl-
edging him to be your man.

*Prince.* Why, my lord, what hath he done?

30 **raze** root

*Judge.* And it please your Majesty, he hath robbed a
poor carrier.                                              55

*Derick.* Hear you, sir; marry, it was one Derick, goodman Hobling's man, of Kent.

*Prince.* What! Was't you, buttonbreech? Of my word,
my lord, he did it but in jest.

*Derick.* Hear you, sir, is it your man's quality to rob    60
folks in jest? In faith, he shall be hanged in earnest.

*Prince.* Well, my lord, what do you mean to do with
my man?

*Judge.* And please your Grace, the law must pass on
him according to justice; then he must be executed.        65

*Prince.* Why, then, belike you mean to hang my man?

*Judge.* I am sorry that it falls out so.

*Prince.* Why, my lord, I pray you, who am I?

*Judge.* And it please your Grace, you are my lord the
young Prince, our king that shall be after the decease      70
of our sovereign lord King Henry the Fourth, whom
God grant long to reign!

*Prince.* You say true, my lord. And you will hang my
man?

*Judge.* And it like your Grace, I must needs do justice.   75

*Prince.* Tell me, my lord, shall I have my man?

*Judge.* I cannot, my lord.

*Prince.* But will you not let him go?

*Judge.* I am sorry that his case is so ill.

*Prince.* Tush, case me no casings! Shall I have my man?   80

*Judge.* I cannot, nor I may not, my lord.

*Prince.* Nay, and "I shall not," say—and then I am
answered?

*Judge.* No.

**83**  *Prince.* No! Then I will have him.

> *He giveth him a box on the ear.*

*Ned.* Gog's wounds, my lord, shall I cut off his head?

*Prince.* No. I charge you, draw not your swords. But get you hence. Provide a noise of musicians. Away, begone!

> *Exeunt Ned and Tom.*

**90**  *Judge.* Well, my lord, I am content to take it at your hands.

*Prince.* Nay, and you be not, you shall have more!

*Judge.* Why, I pray you, my lord, who am I?

*Prince.* You, who knows not you? Why, man, you are
**95**  Lord Chief Justice of England.

*Judge.* Your Grace hath said truth; therefore, in strik- ing me in this place you greatly abuse me; and not me only but also your father, whose lively person here in this place I do represent. And therefore to
**100**  teach you what prerogatives mean, I commit you to the Fleet until we have spoken with your father.

*Prince.* Why, then, belike you mean to send me to the Fleet!

*Judge.* Ay, indeed; and therefore, carry him away.

> *Exeunt Henry V with the Officers.*

**105**  Jailer, carry the prisoner to Newgate again until the next 'sizes.

*Jailer.* At your commandment, my lord, it shall be done.

> *[Exeunt all except] Derick and John Cobbler.*

### [Scene V]

*Derick.* Zounds, masters, here's ado when princes must go to prison! Why, John, didst ever see the like?

*John.* O Derick, trust me, I never saw the like!

*Derick.* Why, John, thou mayst see what princes be in
   choler. A judge a box on the ear! I'll tell thee, John,   *5*
   O John, I would not have done it for twenty shillings.

*John.* No, nor I. There had been no way but one with
   us—we should have been hanged.

*Derick.* Faith, John, I'll tell thee what; thou shalt be
   my Lord Chief Justice, and thou shalt sit in the chair;   *10*
   and I'll be the young Prince, and hit thee a box on
   the ear; and then thou shalt say, "To teach you what
   prerogatives mean, I commit you to the Fleet."

*John.* Come on; I'll be your judge! But thou shalt not
   hit me hard?   *15*

*Derick.* No, no.
                    [*John Cobbler takes the Judge's seat.*]

*John.* What hath he done?

*Derick.* Marry, he hath robbed Derick.

*John.* Why, then, I cannot let him go.

*Derick.* I must needs have my man.   *20*

*John.* You shall not have him!

*Derick.* Shall I not have my man? Say No, and you
   dare! How say you? Shall I not have my man?

*John.* No, marry, shall you not!

*Derick.* Shall I not, John?   *25*

*John.* No, Derick.

*Derick.* Why, then, take you that [*boxing his ear*] till
   more come! Zounds, shall I not have him?

*John.* Well, I am content to take this at your hand.
   But, I pray you, who am I?   *30*

*Derick.* Who art thou? Zounds, dost not know thyself?

*John.* No.

*Derick.* Now away, simple fellow. Why, man, thou art
     John the Cobbler.

35 *John.* No, I am my Lord Chief Justice of England.

*Derick.* Oh, John, mass, thou sayst true, thou art in-
     deed.

*John.* Why, then, to teach you what prerogatives mean,
     I commit you to the Fleet.

40 *Derick.* Well, I will go; but, i'faith, you gray-beard
     knave, I'll course° you.
                              *Exit. And straight enters again.*
     Oh, John, come, come out of thy chair. Why, what
     a clown wert thou to let me hit thee a box on the ear!
     And now thou seest they will not take me to the Fleet.
45     I think that thou art one of these Worenday° clowns.

*John.* But I marvel what will become of thee.

*Derick.* Faith, I'll be no more a carrier.

*John.* What wilt thou do, then?

*Derick.* I'll dwell with thee, and be a cobbler.

50 *John.* With me? Alas, I am not able to keep thee. Why,
     thou wilt eat me out of doors.

*Derick.* Oh, John! No, John; I am none of these great
     slouching fellows that devour these great pieces of
     beef and brews.° Alas, a trifle serves me—a wood-
55     cock, a chicken, or a capon's leg, or any such little
     thing serves me.

*John.* A capon! Why, man, I cannot get a capon once
     a year—except it be at Christmas, at some other
     man's house; for we cobblers be glad of a dish of
60     roots.

*Derick.* Roots, why, are you so good at rooting? Nay,
     cobbler, we'll have you ringed.°

*John.* But, Derick,

41 **course** keep pace with   45 **Worenday** workaday (?)   54 **brews**
beef broth   62 **ringed** i.e., in the nose, like a pig

Though we be so poor,
Yet will we have in store                    65
A crab in the fire,
With nut-brown ale
That is full stale,°
Which will a man quail
And lay in the mire.                          70

*Derick.* A bots on you! And be but for your ale, I'll
dwell with you. Come, let's away as fast as we can.
*Exeunt.*


[*Scene VI*]


*Enter the young Prince, with Ned and Tom.*

*Prince.* Come away, sirs. Gog's wounds, Ned, didst
thou not see what a box on the ear I took my Lord
Chief Justice?

*Tom.* By Gog's blood, it did me good to see it. It made
his teeth jar in his head!                           5

*Enter Sir John Oldcastle.*

*Prince.* How now, Sir John Oldcastle, what news with
you?

*John Oldcastle.* I am glad to see your Grace at liberty.
I was come, I, to visit you in prison.

*Prince.* To visit me! Didst thou not know that I am a    10
prince's son? Why, 'tis enough for me to look into
a prison, though I come not in myself. But here's
such ado nowadays—here's prisoning, here's hanging, whipping, and the devil and all. But I tell you,
sirs, when I am King we will have no such things.     15
But, my lads, if the old King, my father, were dead,
we would be all kings.

68 stale strong

*John Oldcastle.* He is a good old man; God take him
to his mercy the sooner!

20  *Prince.* But, Ned, so soon as I am King, the first thing
I will do shall be to put my Lord Chief Justice out
of office, and thou shalt be my Lord Chief Justice
of England.

*Ned.* Shall I be Lord Chief Justice? By Gog's wounds,
25  I'll be the bravest Lord Chief Justice that ever was
in England!

*Prince.* Then, Ned, I'll turn all these prisons into fence-
schools, and I will endue thee with them, with lands
to maintain them withal. Then I will have a bout
30  with my Lord Chief Justice. Thou shalt hang none
but pick-purses, and horse-stealers, and such base-
minded villains; but that fellow that will stand by
the highway side courageously with his sword and
buckler and take a purse—that fellow, give him
35  commendations! Beside that, send him to me, and
I will give him an annual pension out of my exchequer to maintain him all the days of his life.

*John Oldcastle.* Nobly spoken, Harry! We shall never
have a merry world till the old King be dead.

40  *Ned.* But whither are you going now?

*Prince.* To the court; for I hear say my father lies very
sick.

*Tom.* But I doubt he will not die.

*Prince.* Yet will I go thither; for the breath shall be no
45  sooner out of his mouth but I will clap the crown
on my head.

*John Oldcastle.* Will you go to the court with that cloak
so full of needles?

*Prince.* Cloak, eyelet-holes, needles, and all was of
50  mine own devising; and therefore I will wear it.

*Tom.* I pray you, my lord, what may be the meaning
thereof?

*Prince.* Why, man, 'tis a sign that I stand upon thorns
   till the crown be on my head.

*John Oldcastle.* Or that every needle might be a prick   55
   to their hearts that repine at your doings?

*Prince.* Thou sayst true, Jockey. But there's some will
   say the young Prince will be "a well toward young
   man"—and all this gear,° that I had as leave they
   would break my head with a pot as to say any such   60
   thing. But we stand prating here too long; I must
   needs speak with my father. Therefore, come away!
                [*They cross the stage, and rap.*]

                [*Enter a Porter.*]

*Porter.* What a rapping keep you at the King's court-
   gate?

*Prince.* Here's one that must speak with the King.   65

*Porter.* The King is very sick, and none must speak
   with him.

*Prince.* No? You rascal, do you not know me?

*Porter.* You are my lord, the young Prince.

*Prince.* Then go and tell my father that I must, and will,   70
   speak with him.

*Ned.* Shall I cut off his head?

*Prince.* No, no. Though I would help you in other
   places, yet I have nothing to do here. What, you are
   in my father's court.   75

*Ned.* I will write him in my tables; for so soon as I am
   made Lord Chief Justice I will put him out of his
   office.                          *The trumpet sounds.*

*Prince.* Gog's wounds, sirs, the King comes. Let's all
   stand aside.   80

        *Enter the King, with the Lord of Exeter.*

*King.* And is it true, my lord, that my son is already
   sent to the Fleet? Now, truly, that man is more fitter

59 **gear** nonsense

to rule the realm than I; for by no means could I
rule my son, and he, by one word, hath caused him
85 to be ruled. Oh, my son, my son, no sooner out of
one prison but into another? I had thought once
whiles I had lived to have seen this noble realm of
England flourish by thee, my son; but now I see it
goes to ruin and decay. *He weepeth.*

*Enters Lord of Oxford.*

90 *Oxford.* And please your Grace, here is my lord your
son that cometh to speak with you. He saith he must,
and will, speak with you.

*King.* Who? My son Harry?

*Oxford.* Ay, and please your Majesty.

95 *King.* I know wherefore he cometh. But look that none
come with him.

*Oxford.* A very disordered company, and such as make
very ill rule in your Majesty's house.

*King.* Well, let him come; but look that none come
100 with him. *He goeth.*

*Oxford.* And please your Grace, my lord the King
sends for you.

*Prince.* Come away, sirs, let's go all together.

*Oxford.* And please your Grace, none must go with
105 you.

*Prince.* Why, I must needs have them with me; otherwise I can do my father no countenance: therefore,
come away.

*Oxford.* The King your father commands there should
110 none come.

*Prince.* Well, sirs, then be gone—and provide me three
noise of musicians. *Exeunt Knights.*

*Enters the Prince, with a dagger in his hand,
[to the King, attended].*

*King.* Come, my son; come on, a God's name! I know
　wherefore thy coming is. Oh, my son, my son, what
　cause hath ever been that thou shouldst forsake me,   *115*
　and follow this vile and reprobate company, which
　abuseth youth so manifestly? Oh, my son, thou
　knowest that these thy doings will end thy father's
　days.                                  *He weeps.*
　Ay, so, so, my son, thou fearest not to approach the   *120*
　presence of thy sick father in that disguised sort. I
　tell thee, my son, that there is never a needle in thy
　cloak but it is a prick to my heart, and never an
　eyelet-hole but it is a hole to my soul; and wherefore
　thou bringest that dagger in thy hand I know not, but   *125*
　by conjecture.                          *He weeps.*

*Prince.* My conscience accuseth me. Most sovereign
　lord, and well-beloved father, to answer first to the
　last point, that is, whereas you conjecture that this
　hand and this dagger shall be armed against your   *130*
　life, no! Know, my beloved father, far be the
　thoughts of your son—"son," said I? an unworthy
　son for so good a father!—but far be the thoughts
　of any such pretended mischief. And I most humbly
　render it [*giving him the dagger*] to your Majesty's   *135*
　hand. And live, my lord and sovereign, forever! And
　with your dagger-arm show like vengeance upon the
　body of—"that, your son," I was about to say, and
　dare not; ah, woe is me therefore!—that, your wild°
　slave. 'Tis not the crown that I come for, sweet   *140*
　father, because I am unworthy. And those vile and
　reprobate companions—I abandon and utterly abol-
　ish their company forever! Pardon, sweet father,
　pardon, the least thing and most desire. And this
　ruffianly cloak I here tear from my back, and sacri-   *145*
　fice it to the devil, which is master of all mischief.
　Pardon me, sweet father, pardon me! Good my
　Lord of Exeter, speak for me. Pardon me, pardon,
　good father! Not a word? Ah, he will not speak one
　word! Ah, Harry, now thrice-unhappy Harry! But   *150*
　what shall I do? I will go take me into some solitary

139 **wild** (the quarto has *wilde* = vilde = vile? cf. the King's previous speech)

place, and there lament my sinful life; and, when I
have done, I will lay me down and die.        *Exit.*

*King.* Call him again! Call my son again!

[*Enter the Prince.*]

155 *Prince.* And doth my father call me again? Now,
Harry, happy be the time that thy father calleth thee
again! [*He kneels.*]

*King.* Stand up, my son; and do not think thy father
but at the request of thee, my son, I will pardon thee.
160        And God bless thee, and make thee his servant.

*Prince.* Thanks, good my lord. And no doubt but this
day, even this day, I am born new again.
*King.* Come, my son and lords, take me by the hands.
        *Exeunt omnes.*

[*Scene VII*]

*Enter Derick* [*shouting at Mistress Cobbler
within*].

*Derick.* Thou art a stinking whore, and a whoreson
stinking whore! Dost think I'll take it at thy hands?

*Enter John Cobbler, running.*

*John.* Derick, Derick, Derick, hearest 'a? Do, Derick,
never while thou livest use that! Why, what will my
5        neighbors say and thou go away so?

*Derick.* She's an arrant whore; and I'll have the law on
you, John.

*John.* Why, what hath she done?

*Derick.* Marry, mark thou, John. I will prove it, that
10        I will!

*John.* What wilt thou prove?

*Derick.* That she called me in to dinner—John, mark
the tale well, John—and when I was set, she brought
me a dish of roots and a piece of barrel-butter°
therein! And she is a very knave, and thou a drab    15
if thou take her part.

*John.* Hearest 'a, Derick? Is this the matter? Nay, if
it be no worse we will go home again, and all shall
be amended.

*Derick.* Oh, John, hearest 'a, John? Is all well?    20

*John.* Ay, all is well.

*Derick.* Then I'll go home before, and break all the
glass windows.              [*Exeunt Derick and John.*]


### [Scene *VIII*]


*Enter the King with his Lords.*

*King.* Come, my lords. I see it boots me not to take
any physic, for all the physicians in the world cannot cure me; no, not one. But, good my lords, remember my last will and testament concerning my
son; for truly, my lords, I do not think but he will    5
prove as valiant and victorious a king as ever reigned
in England.

*Both.* Let heaven and earth be witness between us if we
accomplish not thy will to the uttermost.

*King.* I give you most unfeigned thanks, good my lords.    10
Draw the curtains, and depart my chamber awhile;
and cause some music to rock me asleep.
                    *He sleepeth. Exeunt Lords.*
            *Enter the Prince.*

*Prince.* Ah, Harry, thrice-unhappy, that hath neglect
so long from visiting of thy sick father! I will go.

**14 barrel-butter** butter heavily salted (to preserve it)

15  Nay, but why do I not go to the chamber of my sick
father to comfort the melancholy soul of his body?
His soul, said I? Here is his body, indeed, but his
soul is whereas it needs no body. Now, thrice-
accursed Harry, that hath offended thy father so
20  much! And could not I crave pardon for all? O my
dying father! Cursed be the day wherein I was born,
and accursed be the hour wherein I was begotten!
But what shall I do? If weeping tears, which come
too late, may suffice the negligence neglected to
25  some,° I will weep day and night until the fountain
be dry with weeping.          *Exit [taking the crown.]*

*Enter Lord[s] of Exeter and Oxford.*

*Exeter.* Come easily, my lord, for waking of the King.

*King.* [*Waking*] Now, my lords?

*Oxford.* How doth your Grace feel yourself?

30  *King.* Somewhat better after my sleep. But, good my
lords, take off my crown. Remove my chair a little
back, and set me right.

*Both.* And please your Grace, the crown is taken away.

*King.* The crown taken away! Good my Lord of
35  Oxford, go see who hath done this deed.
                              [*Exit Oxford.*]
No doubt 'tis some vile traitor that hath done it to
deprive my son. They that would do it now would
seek to scrape and scrawl for it after my death.

*Enter Lord of Oxford with the Prince.*

*Oxford.* Here, and please your Grace, is my lord the
40  young Prince with the crown.

*King.* Why, how now, my son? I had thought the last
time I had you in schooling I had given you a lesson
for all; and do you now begin again? Why, tell me,
my son, dost thou think the time so long that thou

24–25 **suffice . . . some** atone for my neglect toward some (but "too
some" may be an error for "too soon," intended to match "too late"
in line 24)

wouldst have it before the breath be out of my        45
mouth?

*Prince.* Most sovereign lord and well-beloved father, I
came into your chamber to comfort the melancholy
soul of your body; and finding you at that time past
all recovery, and dead, to my thinking—God is my        50
witness—and what should I do, but with weeping
tears lament the death of you, my father? And after
that, seeing the crown, I took it. And tell me, my
father, who might better take it than I, after your
death? But, seeing you live, I most humbly render        55
it into your Majesty's hands; and the happiest man
alive that my father live. And live, my lord and
father, forever!

*King.* Stand up, my son. Thine answer hath sounded
well in mine ears; for I must need confess that I was        60
in a very sound sleep, and altogether unmindful of
thy coming. But come near, my son, and let me put
thee in possession whilst I live, that none deprive
thee of it after my death.

*Prince.* Well may I take it at your Majesty's hands; but        65
it shall never touch my head so long as my father
lives.                                *He taketh the crown.*

*King.* God give thee joy, my son. God bless thee, and
make thee his servant, and send thee a prosperous
reign! For God knows, my son, how hardly I came        70
by it, and how hardly I have maintained it.

*Prince.* Howsoever you came by it I know not; but now
I have it from you, and from you I will keep it. And
he that seeks to take the crown from my head, let
him look that his armor be thicker than mine, or I        75
will pierce him to the heart, were it harder than brass
or bullion.

*King.* Nobly spoken, and like a king! Now trust me, my
lords, I fear not but my son will be as warlike and
victorious a prince as ever reigned in England.        80

*Both Lords.* His former life shows no less.

*King.* Well, my lords, I know not whether it be for
sleep, or drawing near of drowsy summer of death,
but I am very much given to sleep. Therefore, good
85    my lords, and my son, draw the curtains; depart my
chamber; and cause some music to rock me asleep.

           *Exeunt omnes. The King dieth.*


### [Scene IX]


*Enter the Thief.*

*Thief.* Ah, God, I am now much like to a bird which
hath escaped out of the cage; for so soon as my Lord
Chief Justice heard that the old King was dead he
was glad to let me go for fear of my lord the young
5    Prince. But here come some of his companions. I
will see if I can get anything of them for old acquaintance.

*Enter Knights, ranging.*

*Tom.* Gog's wounds, the King is dead!

*John Oldcastle.* Dead! Then, Gog's blood, we shall be
10    all kings!

*Ned.* Gog's wounds, I shall be Lord Chief Justice of
England.

*Tom.* [*To the Thief*] Why, how! Are you broken out
of prison?

15  *Ned.* Gog's wounds, how the villain stinks!

*John Oldcastle.* Why, what will become of thee now?
Fie upon him, how the rascal stinks!

*Thief.* Marry, I will go and serve my master again.

*Tom.* Gog's blood, dost think that he will have any
20    such scabbed knave as thou art? What, man, he is
a king now.

*Ned.* [*Giving him money*] Hold thee. Here's a couple of angels for thee. And get thee gone, for the King will not be long before he come this way. And hereafter I will tell the King of thee.          *Exit Thief.*    25

*John Oldcastle.* Oh, how it did me good to see the King when he was crowned! Methought his seat was like the figure of heaven, and his person was like unto a god.

*Ned.* But who would have thought that the King would    30 have changed his countenance so?

*John Oldcastle.* Did you not see with what grace he sent his embassage into France to tell the French King that Harry of England hath sent for the crown, and Harry of England will have it?          35

*Tom.* But 'twas but a little to make the people believe that he was sorry for his father's death.

                    *The trumpet sounds.*

*Ned.* Gog's wounds, the King comes! Let's all stand aside.

*Enter the King with the Archbishop [of Canterbury], and the Lord of Oxford.*

*John Oldcastle.* How do you, my lord?          40

*Ned.* How now, Harry? Tut, my lord, put away these dumps. You are a king, and all the realm is yours. What, man, do you not remember the old sayings? You know I must be Lord Chief Justice of England. Trust me, my lord, methinks you are very much    45 changed. And 'tis but with a little sorrowing, to make folks believe the death of your father grieves you—and 'tis nothing so.

*King.* I prithee, Ned, mend thy manners, and be more modester in thy terms; for my unfeigned grief is not    50 to be ruled by thy flattering and dissembling talk. Thou sayst I am changed; so I am, indeed; and so must thou be, and that quickly, or else I must cause thee to be changed.

53 *John Oldcastle.* Gog's wounds, how like you this? Zounds, 'tis not so sweet as music.

*Tom.* I trust we have not offended your Grace no way.

*King.* Ah, Tom, your former life grieves me, and makes me to abandon and abolish your company forever.
60 And therefore, not upon pain of death to approach my presence by ten miles space. Then, if I hear well of you, it may be I will do somewhat for you; otherwise, look for no more favor at my hands than at any other man's. And, therefore, begone! We have
65 other matters to talk on. *Exeunt Knights.*

Now, my good Lord Archbishop of Canterbury, what say you to our embassage into France?

*Archbishop.* Your right to the French crown of France came by your great grandmother Isabel, wife to King
70 Edward the Third, and sister to Charles, the French king. Now, if the French king deny it, as likely enough he will, then must you take your sword in hand and conquer the right. Let the usurped Frenchman know, although your predecessors have let it
75 pass, you will not; for your countrymen are willing with purse and men to aid you. Then, my good lord, as it hath been always known that Scotland hath been in league with France by a sort of pensions which yearly come from thence, I think it therefore best to
80 conquer Scotland; and then I think that you may go more easily into France. And this is all that I can say, my good lord.

*King.* I thank you, my good Lord Archbishop of Canterbury. What say you, my good Lord of Oxford?

85 *Oxford.* And please your Majesty, I agree to my Lord Archbishop, saving in this: "He that will Scotland win must first with France begin," according to the old saying. Therefore, my good lord, I think it best first to invade France; for in conquering Scotland
90 you conquer but one; and conquer France and conquer both.

*Enter Lord of Exeter.*

**Exeter.** And please your Majesty, my Lord Ambassador is come out of France.

**King.** Now trust me, my lord, he was the last man that we talked of. I am glad that he is come to resolve   95
us of our answer. Commit him to our presence.

*Enter Duke of York.*

**York.** God save the life of my sovereign lord the King!

**King.** Now, my good lord the Duke of York, what news from our brother, the French king?

**York.** And please your Majesty, I delivered him my   100
embassage, whereof I took some deliberation. But for the answer, he hath sent my Lord Ambassador of Bourges, the Duke of Burgundy, Monsieur le Cole, with two hundred and fifty horsemen to bring the embassage.   105

**King.** Commit my Lord Archbishop of Bourges into our presence.

*Enter Archbishop of Bourges.*

**King.** Now, my Lord Archbishop of Bourges, we do learn by our Lord Ambassador that you have our message to do from our brother, the French king.   110
Here, my good lord, according to our accustomed order, we give you free liberty and license to speak with good audience.

**Archbishop.** God save the mighty King of England! My lord and master, the most Christian king, Charles   115
the Seventh, the great and mighty King of France, as a most noble and Christian king not minding to shed innocent blood, is rather content to yield somewhat to your unreasonable demands—that, if fifty thousand crowns a year, with his daughter, the said   120
Lady Katherine, in marriage, and some crowns which he may well spare not hurting of his king-

dom, he is content to yield so far to your unreasonable desire.

125 *King.* Why, then, belike your lord and master thinks to
puff me up with fifty thousands crowns a year? No!
Tell thy lord and master that all the crowns in France
shall not serve me, except the crown and kingdom
itself! And perchance hereafter I will have his daugh-
130 ter.

*Archbishop.* If it please your Majesty, my Lord Prince
Dolphin greets you well with this present.
*He delivereth a tun of tennis balls.*

*King.* What, a gilded tun! I pray you, my Lord of
York, look what is in it.

135 *York.* And it please your Grace, here is a carpet, and a
tun of tennis balls.

*King.* A tun of tennis balls! I pray you, good my Lord
Archbishop, what might the meaning thereof be?

*Archbishop.* And it please you, my lord, a messenger,
140 you know, ought to keep close his message—and
specially an ambassador.

*King.* But I know that you may declare your message
to a king; the Law of Arms allows no less.

*Archbishop.* My lord, hearing of your wildness before
145 your father's death, sent you this, my good lord,
meaning that you are more fitter for a tennis court
than a field, and more fitter for a carpet than the
camp.

*King.* My Lord Prince Dolphin is very pleasant with
150 me! But tell him that instead of balls of leather we
will toss him balls of brass and iron—yea, such balls
as never were tossed in France. The proudest tennis
court shall rue it! Ay, and thou, Prince of Bourges,
shalt rue it! Therefore, get thee hence; and tell him
155 thy message quickly, lest I be there before thee.
Away, priest! Begone!

*Archbishop.* I beseech your Grace to deliver me your
safe conduct under your broad seal manual.°

*King.* Priest of Bourges, know that the hand and seal
of a king, and his word, is all one. And instead of my    *160*
hand and seal I will bring him my hand and sword.
And tell thy lord and master that I, Harry of England, said it; and I, Harry of England, will perform
it! My Lord of York, deliver him our safe conduct
under our broad seal manual.    *165*

   *Exeunt Archbishop and the Duke of York.*

Now, my lords, to arms, to arms! For I vow by
heaven and earth that the proudest Frenchman in
all France shall rue the time that ever these tennis
balls were sent into England. My lord, I will that
there be provided a great navy of ships with all speed    *170*
at Southampton, for there I mean to ship my men;
for I would be there before him, if it were possible.
Therefore come—but stay! I had almost forgot the
chiefest thing of all with chafing with this French
ambassador. Call in my Lord Chief Justice of Eng-    *175*
land.

   *Enters Lord Chief Justice of England.*

*Exeter.* Here is the King, my lord.

*Justice.* God preserve your Majesty!

*King.* Why, how now, my lord, what is the matter?

*Justice.* I would it were unknown to your Majesty.    *180*

*King.* Why, what ail you?

*Justice.* Your Majesty knoweth my grief well.

*King.* Oh, my lord, you remember you sent me to the
 Fleet, did you not?

*Justice.* I trust your Grace have forgotten that.    *185*

*King.* Ay, truly, my lord; and for revengement I have
 chosen you to be my Protector over my realm, until

158 **manual** inscribed by hand

it shall please God to give me speedy return out of
France.

190 *Justice.* And if it please your Majesty, I am far unworthy of so high dignity.

*King.* Tut, my lord, you are not unworthy, because I
think you worthy; for you that would not spare me,
I think, will not spare another. It must needs be so.
195 And therefore, come, let us be gone, and get our
men in a readiness.                    *Exeunt omnes.*

[*Scene X*]

*Enter a Captain, John Cobbler, and his Wife.*

*Captain.* Come, come; there's no remedy. Thou must
needs serve the King.

*John.* Good master Captain, let me go. I am not able
to go so far.

5 *Wife.* I pray you, good master Captain, be good to my
husband.

*Captain.* Why, I am sure he is not too good to serve the
King.

*John.* Alas, no——but a great deal too bad; therefore, I
10 pray you, let me go.

*Captain.* No, no; thou shalt go.

*John.* Oh, sir, I have a great many shoes at home to
cobble.

*Wife.* I pray you, let him go home again.

15 *Captain.* Tush, I care not. Thou shalt go.

*John.* Oh, wife, and you had been a loving wife to me
this had not been; for I have said many times that I

would go away, and now I must go—against my will.

*He weepeth.*

*Enter Derick [with a pot-lid for a shield].*

*Derick.* How now, ho! *Basillus manus,*° for an old cod-
piece! Master Captain, shall we away? Zounds, how    20
now, John? What, a-crying? What make you and
my dame there? [*To the Wife*] I marvel whose head
you will throw the stools at now we are gone.

*Wife.* I'll tell you! Come, ye cloghead! What do you
with my pot-lid? Here you, will you have it rapped    25
about your pate?    *She beateth him with her pot-lid.*

*Derick.* Oh good dame!          *Here he shakes her.*
And I had my dagger here I would worry you all to
pieces—that I would!

*Wife.* Would you so? I'll try that.     *She beateth him.*    30

*Derick.* Master Captain, will you suffer her? Go to,
dame! I will go back as far as I can; but, and you
come again—I'll clap the law on your back, that's
flat! I'll tell you, Master Captain, what you shall do:
press her for a soldier! I warrant you she will do as    35
much good as her husband and I too.

*Enters the Thief.*

Zounds, who comes yonder?

*Captain.* How now, good fellow; dost thou want a master?

*Thief.* Ay, truly, sir.                                          40

*Captain.* Hold thee, then. I press thee for a soldier to
serve the King in France.

*Derick.* How now, Gads! What, dost know us, thinkest?

*Thief.* Ay, I knew thee long ago.

*Derick.* Hear you, Master Captain.                              45

19 Basillus manus (corruption of *besa las manos* = kiss the hands,
say good-bye)

*Captain.* What sayst thou?

*Derick.* I pray you, let me go home again.

*Captain.* Why, what wouldst thou do at home?

*Derick.* Marry, I have brought two shirts with me, and
50    I would carry one of them home again; for I am sure
he'll steal it from me, he is such a filching fellow.

*Captain.* I warrant thee he will not steal it from thee.
Come, let's away.

*Derick.* Come, Master Captain, let's away. Come, fol-
55    low me.

*John.* Come, wife, let's part lovingly.

*Wife.* Farewell, good husband.

*Derick.* Fie, what a kissing and crying is here! Zounds,
do you think he will never come again? Why, John,
60    come away! Dost think that we are so base-minded
to die among Frenchmen? Zounds, we know not
whether they will lay us in their church or no. Come,
Master Captain, let's away.

*Captain.* I cannot stay no longer; therefore, come away.
                                *Exeunt omnes.*


### [Scene XI]


*Enter the [French] King, Prince Dolphin, and
Lord High Constable of France.*

*King.* Now, my Lord High Constable, what say you to
our embassage into England?

*Constable.* And it please your Majesty, I can say nothing until my lords ambassadors be come home. But
5    yet methinks your Grace hath done well to get your
men in so good a readiness for fear of the worst.

*King.* Ay, my lord, we have some in a readiness; but if
the King of England make against us we must have
thrice so many more.

*Dolphin.* Tut, my lord; although the King of England   *10*
   be young and wild-headed, yet never think he will be
   so unwise to make battle against the mighty King of
   France.

*King.* Oh, my son, although the King of England be
   young and wild-headed, yet never think but he is   *15*
   ruled by his wise councillors.

### Enter Archbishop of Bourges.

*Archbishop.* God save the life of my sovereign lord the
   King!

*King.* Now, my good Lord Archbishop of Bourges,
   what news from our brother, the English king?   *20*

*Archbishop.* And please your Majesty, he is so far from
   your expectation that nothing will serve him but the
   crown and kingdom itself. Besides, he bade me haste
   quickly lest he be there before me. And, so far as I
   hear, he hath kept promise; for they say he is already   *25*
   landed at Kidocks in Normandy upon the River
   Seine, and laid his siege to the garrison-town of Harfleur.

*King.* You have made great haste in the meantime, have
   you not?   *30*

*Dolphin.* I pray you, my lord, how did the King of England take my presents?

*Archbishop.* Truly, my lord, in very ill part. For these
   your balls of leather he will toss you balls of brass
   and iron. Trust me, my lord, I was very afraid of him,   *33*
   he is such a haughty and high-minded prince. He is
   as fierce as a lion.

*Constable.* Tush, we will make him as tame as a lamb,
   I warrant you.

### Enters a Messenger.

*Messenger.* God save the mighty King of France!   *40*

*King.* Now, messenger, what news?

*Messenger.* And it please your Majesty, I come from
your poor distressed town of Harfleur, which is so
beset on every side, if your Majesty do not send pres-
45   ent aid the town will be yielded to the English king.

*King.* Come, my lords, come! Shall we stand still till
our country be spoiled under our noses? My lords,
let the Normans, Brabanters, Picards, and Danes be
sent for with all speed. And you, my Lord High Con-
50   stable, I make General over all my whole army;
Monsieur le Colle, Master of the Bows, Seigneur
Devens, and all the rest, at your appointment.

*Dolphin.* I trust your Majesty will bestow some part of
the battle on me. I hope not to present any otherwise
55   than well.

*King.* I tell thee, my son, although I should get the victory, and thou lose thy life, I should think myself
quite conquered, and the Englishmen to have the victory.

60 *Dolphin.* Why, my lord and father, I would have the
petty king of England to know that I dare encounter
him in any ground of the world.

*King.* I know well, my son; but at this time I will have
it thus. Therefore, come away.     *Exeunt omnes.*

### [Scene XII]

*Enters Henry the Fifth, with his Lords.*

*King.* Come, my lords of England. No doubt this good
luck of winning this town is a sign of an honorable
victory to come! But, good my lord, go and speak
to the captains with all speed, to number the host of
5   the Frenchmen, and by that means we may the better know how to appoint the battle.

*York.* And it please your Majesty, there are many of
your men sick and diseased, and many of them die
for want of victuals.

*King.* And why did you not tell me of it before? If we   *10*
cannot have it for money we will have it by dint of
sword; the Law of Arms allows no less.

*Oxford.* I beseech your Grace to grant me a boon.

*King.* What is that, my good lord?

*Oxford.* That your Grace would give me the vanguard   *15*
in the battle.

*King.* Trust me, my Lord of Oxford, I cannot; for I
have already given it to my uncle, the Duke of York.
Yet I thank you for your good will.

                              *A trumpet sounds.*
How now, what is that?   *20*

*York.* I think it be some herald of arms.

              *Enters a Herald.*

*Herald.* King of England, my Lord High Constable and
others of the noblemen of France sends me to defy
thee as open enemy to God, our country, and us;
and hereupon they presently bid thee battle.   *25*

*King.* Herald, tell them that I defy them as open enemies to God, my country, and me, and as wrongful
usurpers of my right. And whereas thou sayst they
presently bid me battle, tell them, that I think they
know how to please me. But, I pray thee, what place   *30*
hath my lord Prince Dolphin here in battle?

*Herald.* And it please your Grace, my Lord and King,
his father, will not let him come into the field.

*King.* Why, then, he doth me great injury. I thought
that he and I should have played at tennis together;   *35*
therefore I have brought tennis balls for him—but
other manner of ones than he sent me. And, Herald,
tell my Lord Prince Dolphin that I have inured my
hands with other kind of weapons than tennis balls
ere this time of day, and that he shall find it, ere it   *40*
be long. And so, adieu, my friend. And tell my
lord that I am ready when he will.     *Exit Herald.*

Come, my lords. I care not and I go to our captains;
and I'll see the number of the French army myself.
43   Strike up the drum!                    *Exeunt omnes.*


[*Scene XIII*]


*Enter French Soldiers.*

*First Soldier.* Come away, Jack Drummer! Come away
all, and me will tell you what me will do. Me will tro
one chance on the dice who shall have the King of
England and his lords.

5    *Second Soldier.* Come away, Jack Drummer, and tro
your chance; and lay down your drum.

*Enter Drummer.*

*Drummer.* Oh, the brave apparel that the English-mans
hay broth° over! I will tell you what me ha done. Me
ha provided a hundreth trunks, and all to put the
10   fine 'parel of the English-mans in.

*First Soldier.* What do thou mean by "trunks"?

*Second Soldier.* A shest, man, a hundred shests.

*First Soldier.* Awee, awee, awee. Me will tell you what:
me ha put five shildren out of my house, and all too
15   little to put the fine apparel of the English-mans in.

*Drummer.* Oh, the brave, the brave apparel that we
shall have anon! But come, and you shall see what
me will tro at the king's drummer and fife. Ha, me
ha no good luck. Tro you.

20   *Third Soldier.* Faith, me will tro at the Earl of Northumberland, and my Lord o' Willoughby, with his
great horse, snorting, farting—oh brave horse!

*First Soldier.* Ha! By'r Lady, you ha reasonable good
luck. Now I will tro at the King himself. Ha! Me
25   have no good luck.

8 hay broth i.e., have brought

*Enters a Captain.*

*Captain.* How now, what make you here so far from
   the camp?

*Second Soldier.* Shall me tell our captain what we have
   done here?

*Drummer.* Awee, awee.                                    30
                        *Exeunt Drummer and one Soldier.*

*Second Soldier.* I will tell you what we have done. We
   have been troing our chance on the dice; but none
   can win the King.

*Captain.* I think so. Why, he is left behind for me! And
   I have set three or four chair-makers a-work to make   35
   a new disguised chair to set that womanly King of
   England in, that all the people may laugh and scoff
   at him.

*Second Soldier.* Oh brave captain!

*Captain.* I am glad, and yet with a kind of pity, to see   40
   the poor King—why, who ever saw a more flourish-
   ing army in France in one day than here is? Are not
   here all the peers of France? Are not here the Normans, with their fiery handguns and flaunching° curtleaxes?° Are not here the barbarians, with their       45
   bard° horses and launching spears? Are not here the
   Picards, with their cross-bows and piercing darts?
   The Henneys° with their cutting glaives° and sharp
   carbuncles?° Are not here the lance-knights of Burgundy? And, on the other side, a sight of poor Eng-   50
   lish scabs! Why, take an English-man out of his warm
   bed and his stale drink but one month, and, alas,
   what will become of him? But give the Frenchman a

---

44 **flaunching** (a word of uncertain origin and meaning, which is
perhaps here intended to mean "flaming," but has been confused
or conflated with the armorial and heraldic term, "flanch" = any
subdevice borne on an escutcheon)    44–45 **curtleaxes** cutlasses
46 **bard** barded, armed with metal plates    48 **Henneys** men of
Hainault    48 **glaives** broadswords    49 **carbuncles** eight-rayed blazon (escarboucle) on the French shields, which often had a spike
at its center

radish root, and he will live with it all the days of his
life.                                                    *Exit.*

*Second Soldier.* Oh, the brave apparel that we shall
have of the English-mans.                                *Exit.*


## [Scene XIV]


*Enters the King of England and his Lords.*

*King.* Come, my lords and fellows of arms. What company is there of the Frenchmen?

*Oxford.* If it please your Majesty, our captains have
numbered them, and, so near as they can judge, they
are about threescore thousand horsemen and forty
thousand footmen.

*King.* They threescore thousand horsemen, and we but
two thousand! They forty thousand footmen, and we
twelve thousand! They are a hundred thousand, and
we forty thousand! Ten to one! My lords and loving
countrymen, though we be few, and they many, fear
not. Your quarrel is good, and God will defend you.
Pluck up your hearts, for this day we shall either
have a valiant victory, or a honorable death! Now,
my lords, I will that my uncle, the Duke of York,
have the vanguard in the battle; the Earl of Derby,
the Earl of Oxford, the Earl of Kent, the Earl of
Nottingham, the Earl of Huntingdon I will have beside the army, that they may come fresh upon them;
and I myself, with the Duke of Bedford, the Duke of
Clarence, and the Duke of Gloucester will be in the
midst of the battle. Furthermore, I will that my Lord
of Willoughby and the Earl of Northumberland, with
their troops of horsemen, be continually running like
wings on both sides of the army—my Lord of Northumberland on the left wing. Then I will that every
archer provide him a stake of a tree, and sharp it at
both ends; and, at the first encounter of the horse-

men, to pitch their stakes down into the ground before them, that they may gore themselves upon them; 30
and then, to recoil back, and shoot wholly altogether,
and so discomfit them.

*Oxford.* And it please your Majesty, I will take that in
charge, if your Grace be therewith content.

*King.* With all my heart, my good Lord of Oxford. And 35
go and provide quickly.

*Oxford.* I thank your Highness. *Exit.*

*King.* Well, my lords, our battles are ordained, and the
French making of bonfires, and at their banquets.
But let them look, for I mean to set upon them. 40
                        *The trumpet sounds.*
Soft, here comes some other French message.

### Enters Herald.

*Herald.* King of England, my Lord High Constable and
other of my lords, considering the poor estate of thee
and thy poor countrymen, sends me to know what
thou wilt give for thy ransom. Perhaps thou mayst 45
agree better cheap° now than when thou art conquered.

*King.* Why then, belike, your High Constable sends to
know what I will give for my ransom? Now trust me,
Herald, not so much as a tun of tennis balls—no, 50
not so much as one poor tennis ball! Rather shall
my body lie dead in the field to feed crows than ever
England shall pay one penny ransom for my body.

*Herald.* A kingly resolution!

*King.* No, Herald; 'tis a kingly resolution and the reso- 55
lution of a king. Here, take this for thy pains.
                        *Exit Herald.*

*King.* But stay, my lords; what time is it?

*All.* Prime, my lord.

---

46 agree better cheap make a better bargain

*King.* Then is it good time, no doubt, for all England
60       prayeth for us. What, my lords! Methinks you look
cheerfully upon me. Why, then, with one voice, and
like true English hearts, with me throw up your caps,
and for England cry, "Saint George!" And God and
Saint George help us!

*Strike Drummer. Exeunt omnes.*

### [Scene XV]

*The Frenchmen cry within, "Saint Denis! Saint Denis!*
*Mount Joy! Saint Denis!"*

*The battle.*

*Enters King of England and his Lords.*

*King.* Come, my lords, come! By this time our swords
are almost drunk with French blood. But, my lords,
which of you can tell me how many of our army be
slain in the battle?

5    *Oxford.* And it please your Majesty, there are of the
French army slain above ten thousand twenty-six
hundred, whereof are princes and nobles bearing
banners; besides, all the nobility of France are taken
prisoners. Of your Majesty's army are slain none but
10       the good Duke of York, and not above five or six
and twenty common soldiers.

*King.* For the good Duke of York, my uncle, I am
heartily sorry, and greatly lament his misfortune.
Yet the honorable victory which the Lord hath given
15       us doth make me much rejoice. But, stay! Here
comes another French message.       *Sound trumpet.*

*Enters a Herald, and kneeleth.*

*Herald.* God save the life of the most mighty conqueror,
the honorable King of England!

*King.* Now, Herald, methinks the world is changed with

you now. What! I am sure it is a great disgrace for 20
a herald to kneel to the King of England! What is
thy message?

*Herald.* My lord and master, the conquered King of
France, sends thee long health, with hearty greeting.

*King.* Herald, his greetings are welcome; but I thank 25
God for my health. Well, Herald, say on.

*Herald.* He hath sent me to desire your Majesty to give
him leave to go into the field to view his poor countrymen, that they may all be honorably buried.

*King.* Why, Herald, doth thy lord and master send to 30
me to bury the dead? Let him bury them, a God's
name! But, I pray thee, Herald, where is my Lord
High Constable, and those that would have had my
ransom?

*Herald.* And it please your Majesty, he was slain in the 35
battle.

*King.* Why, you may see—you will make yourselves
sure before the victory be won. But, Herald, what
castle is this so near adjoining to our camp?

*Herald.* And it please your Majesty, 'tis called the 40
Castle of Agincourt.

*King.* Well then, my lords of England, for the more
honor of our Englishmen, I will that this be forever
called The Battle of Agincourt.

*Herald.* And it please your Majesty, I have a further 45
message to deliver to your Majesty.

*King.* What is that, Herald? Say on.

*Herald.* And it please your Majesty, my lord and master
craves to parley with your Majesty.

*King.* With a good will—so some of my nobles view the 50
place for fear of treachery and treason.

*Herald.* Your Grace needs not to doubt that.

*King.* Well, tell him, then, I will come.     *Exit Herald.*
    Now, my lords, I will go into the field myself to view
55   my countrymen, and to have them honorably buried;
    for the French king shall never surpass me in cour-
    tesy whiles I am Harry, King of England. Come on,
    my lords.                              *Exeunt omnes.*


### [Scene XVI]


*Enters John Cobbler and Robin Pewterer.*

*Robin.* Now, John Cobbler, didst thou see how the King
    did behave himself?

*John.* But, Robin, didst thou see what a policy the King
    had? To see how the Frenchmen were killed with
5    the stakes of the trees!

*Robin.* Ay, John, there was a brave policy!


*Enters an English Soldier, roaming.*

*Soldier.* What are you, my masters?

*Both.* Why, we be Englishmen.

*Soldier.* Are you Englishmen? Then change your lan-
10   guage, for the King's tents are set afire, and all they
    that speak English will be killed.          *[Exit.]*

*John.* What shall we do, Robin? Faith, I'll shift, for I
    can speak broken French.

*Robin.* Faith, so can I. Let's hear how thou canst speak.

15   *John. Commodevales,°* Monsieur?

*Robin.* That's well. Come, let's be gone.     *[Exeunt.]*


15 **Commodevales** *Comment allez* [*-vous*]? How are you?

### [Scene XVII]

*Drum and trumpet sounds.*

*Enters Derick, roaming. After him a Frenchman,
and takes him prisoner.*

*Derick.* Oh, good *Mounser!°*

*Frenchman.* Come, come, you *villeaco.°*

*Derick.* Oh, I will, sir, I will.

*Frenchman.* Come quickly, you peasant!

*Derick.* I will, sir. What shall I give you?                          5

*Frenchman.* Marry, thou shalt give me one, two, tre,
four hundred crowns.

*Derick.* Nay, sir, I will give you more; I will give you
as many crowns as will lie on your sword.

*Frenchman.* Wilt thou give me as many crowns as will      10
lie on my sword?

*Derick.* Ay, marry, will I. Ay, but you must lay down
your sword, or else they will not lie on your sword.

*Here the Frenchman lays down his sword, and the
Clown [Derick] takes it up, and hurls him down.*

*Derick.* Thou villain! darest thou look up?

*Frenchman.* Oh, good *Monsieur, comparteve!°* Mon-      15
sieur, pardon me!

*Derick.* O you villain! Now you lie at my mercy. Dost
thou remember since thou lammedst me in thy short
ell?° O villain! Now I will strike off thy head.

*Here, whiles he turns his back, the Frenchman runs his
ways.*                                                                 20

*Derick.* What, is he gone? Mass, I am glad of it. For, if
he had stayed, I was afraid he would have stirred

1 **Mounser** *Monsieur*   2 **villeaco** *villanaccio* (?) = rustic   15 **comparteve** *compat[iss]ez vous* (?) = have pity   18-19 **lammedst . . .
ell** gave me a short measure

again, and then I should have been spilt. But I will
away to kill more Frenchmen.                    [*Exit.*]


[*Scene XVIII*]

*Enters King of France, King of England, and
Attendants.*

*King of England.* Now, my good brother of France, my
coming into this land was not to shed blood, but for
the right of my country; which, if you can deny, I
am content peaceably to leave my siege and to depart
5    out of your land.

*King of France.* What is it you demand, my loving
brother of England?

*King of England.* My secretary hath it written. Read it.

*Secretary.* Item, that immediately Henry of England be
10   crowned King of France.

*King of France.* A very hard sentence, my good brother
of England.

*King of England.* No more but right, my good brother
of France!

15  *King of France.* Well, read on.

*Secretary.* Item, that after the death of the said Henry
the crown remain to him and his heirs forever.

*King of France.* Why then, you do not only mean to
dispossess me, but also my son!

20  *King of England.* Why, my good brother of France, you
have had it long enough. And as for Prince Dolphin,
it skills not though he sit beside the saddle. Thus I
have set it down, and thus it shall be!

*King of France.* You are very peremptory, my good
25   brother of England.

*King of England.* And you as perverse, my good brother
of France.

*King of France.* Why then, belike all that I have here
is yours!

*King of England.* Ay, even as far as the kingdom of    30
France reaches.

*King of France.* Ay, for by this hot beginning we shall
scarce bring it to a calm ending.

*King of England.* It is as you please. Here is my resolution.                                                    35

*King of France.* Well, my brother of England, if you
will give me a copy we will meet you again tomorrow.

*King of England.* With a good will, my good brother of
France. Secretary, deliver him a copy.
          *Exit King of France and all their Attendants.*

*King of England.* My lords of England, go before, and    40
I will follow you.                  *Exeunt Lords.*
*Speaks to himself.* Ah, Harry, thrice-unhappy Harry!
Hast thou now conquered the French king, and begins a fresh supply with his daughter? But with what
face canst thou seek to gain her love which hath        45
sought to win her father's crown? Her father's crown,
said I? No, it is mine own.

        Ay, but I love her, and must crave her—
        Nay, I love her, and will have her!

    *Enters Lady Katherine and her Ladies.*

*King of England.* But here she comes. How now, fair    50
Lady Katherine of France, what news?

*Katherine.* And it please your Majesty, my father sent
me to know if you will debate any of these unreasonable demands which you require.

*King of England.* Now trust me, Kate, I commend thy    55
father's wit greatly in this; for none in the world
could sooner have made me debate it, if it were possible. But tell me, sweet Kate, canst thou tell how to
love?

60  *Katherine.* I cannot hate, my good lord; therefore, far
unfit were it for me to love.

*King of England.* Tush, Kate! but tell me in plain terms,
canst thou love the King of England? I cannot do as
these countries do that spend half their time in woo-
65  ing. Tush, wench, I am none such. But, wilt thou go
over to England?

*Katherine.* I would to God that I had your Majesty as
fast in love as you have my father in wars! I would
not vouchsafe so much as one look until you had
70  abated all these unreasonable demands.

*King of England.* Tush, Kate! I know thou wouldst not
use me so hardly. But tell me, canst thou love the
King of England?

*Katherine.* How should I love him that hath dealt so
75  hardly with my father?

*King of England.* But I'll deal as easily with thee as thy
heart can imagine, or tongue can require. How sayst
thou? What! will it be?

*Katherine.* If I were of my own direction I could give
80  you answer; but seeing I stand at my father's direction, I must first know his will.

*King of England.* But shall I have thy good will in the
mean season?

*Katherine.* Whereas I can put your Grace in no assur-
85  ance, I would be loath to put you in any despair.

*King of England.* Now, before God, it is a sweet wench!

*She goes aside, and speaks as followeth.*

*Katherine.* I may think myself the happiest in the world
that is beloved of the mighty King of England!

*King of England.* Well, Kate, are you at host° with me?
90  Sweet Kate, tell thy father from me that none in the

89 at host in accord

world could sooner have persuaded me to it than
thou; and so tell thy father from me.

*Katherine.* God keep your Majesty in good health.
                    *Exit Katherine.*

*King of England.* Farewell, sweet Kate. In faith, it is a
sweet wench! But if I knew I could not have her        95
father's good will, I would so rouse the towers over
his ears that I would make him be glad to bring her
me upon his hands and knees.        *Exit King.*


### [Scene XIX]


*Enters Derick with his girdle full of shoes.*

*Derick.* How, now! Zounds, it did me good to see how
I did triumph over the Frenchmen!

*Enters John Cobbler, roving, with a pack
full of apparel.*

*John.* Whoop, Derick! How dost thou?

*Derick.* What, John! *Comedevales?* Alive yet?

*John.* I promise thee, Derick, I scaped hardly; for I was      5
within half a mile when one was killed!

*Derick.* Were you so?

*John.* Ay, trust me. I had like been slain.

*Derick.* But, once killed—why it—'tis nothing. I was
four or five times slain.        10

*John.* Four or five times slain. Why, how couldst thou
have been alive now?

*Derick.* O John, never say so! For I was called "the
bloody soldier" amongst them all.

*John.* Why, what didst thou?        15

*Derick.* Why, I will tell thee, John. Every day when I
went into the field I would take a straw and thrust

it into my nose and make my nose bleed; and then
I would go into the field. And when the captain saw
20  me, he would say, "Peace, a bloody soldier!" and
bid me stand aside. Whereof I was glad. But mark
the chance, John: I went and stood behind a tree—
but mark, then, John—I thought I had been safe;
but on a sudden there steps to me a lusty, tall
25  Frenchman; now he drew, and I drew; now I lay
here, and he lay there; now I set this leg before, and
turned this backward—and skipped quite over a
hedge; and he saw me no more there that day! And
was not this well done, John?

30  *John.* Mass, Derick, thou hast a witty head.

*Derick.* Ay, John, thou mayst see, if thou hadst taken
my counsel. But what hast thou there? I think thou
hast been robbing the Frenchmen.

*John.* In faith, Derick, I have gotten some reparel to
35  carry home to my wife.

*Derick.* And I have got some shoes; for I'll tell thee
what I did: when they were dead, I would go take
off all their shoes.

*John.* Ay, but Derick, how shall we get home?

40  *Derick.* Nay, zounds, and they take thee they will hang
thee. O, John, never do so! If it be thy fortune to be
hanged, be hanged in thy own language, whatsoever
thou dost!

*John.* Why, Derick, the wars is done; we may go home
45  now.

*Derick.* Ay, but you may not go before you ask the
King leave. But I know a way to go home and ask
the King no leave.

*John.* How is that, Derick?

50  *Derick.* Why, John, thou knowest the Duke of York's
funeral must be carried into England, dost thou not?

*John.* Ay, that I do.

*Derick.* Why, then, thou knowest we'll go with it.

*John.* Ay, but Derick, how shall we do for to meet
   them?                                                    55

*Derick.* Zounds, if I make not shift to meet them, hang
   me! Sirrah, thou knowest that in every town there
   will be ringing, and there will be cakes and drink.
   Now I will go to the clerk and sexton, and keep
   a-talking and say, "Oh, this fellow rings well!" And    60
   thou shalt go and take a piece of cake. Then I'll ring,
   and thou shalt say, "Oh, this fellow keeps a good
   stint!" And then I will go drink to thee all the way.
   But I marvel what my dame will say when we come
   home, because we have not a French word to cast         65
   at a dog by the way.

*John.* Why, what shall we do, Derick?

*Derick.* Why, John, I'll go before and call my dame
   whore; and thou shalt come after and set fire on the
   house. We may do it, John, for I'll prove it—because    70
   we be soldiers.                    *The trumpets sound.*

*John.* Derick, help me to carry my shoes and boots.
                         [*Exeunt Derick and John.*]


[*Scene XX*]

*Enters King of England, Lord of Oxford and*
*Exeter, then the King of France, Prince Dolphin,*
*and the Duke of Burgundy, [Princess Katherine]*
*and Attendants.*


*King of England.* Now, my good brother of France,
   I hope by this time you have deliberated of your
   answer.

*King of France.* Ay, my well-beloved brother of England. We have viewed it over with our learned coun-    5
   cil, but cannot find that you should be crowned
   King of France.

*King of England.* What, not King of France? Then
nothing. I must be King. But, my loving brother of
France, I can hardly forget the late injuries offered
me when I came last to parley; the Frenchmen had
better 'a raked the bowels out of their fathers' carcasses than to have fired my tents. And if I knew thy
son Prince Dolphin, for one, I would so rouse him
as he was never so roused!

*King of France.* I dare swear for my son's innocency in
this matter. But if this please you, that immediately
you be proclaimed and crowned Heir and Regent
of France, not King, because I myself was once
crowned king—

*King of England.* Heir and Regent of France? That is
well. But that is not all that I must have.

*King of France.* The rest my secretary hath in writing.

*Secretary.* [*Reads*] Item, that Henry, King of England,
be crowned Heir and Regent of France during the
life of King Charles; and after his death the crown
with all rights to remain to King Henry of England,
and to his heirs forever.

*King of England.* Well, my good brother of France,
there is one thing I must needs desire.

*King of France.* What is that, my good brother of
England?

*King of England.* That all your nobles must be sworn
to be true to me.

*King of France.* Whereas they have not stuck with
greater matters, I know they will not stick with such
a trifle. Begin you, my Lord Duke of Burgundy.

*King of England.* Come, my Lord of Burgundy; take
your oath upon my sword.

*Burgundy.* I, Philip, Duke of Burgundy, swear to
Henry, King of England, to be true to him, and to
become his liege man; and that if I, Philip, hear of

any foreign power coming to invade the said Henry,
or his heirs, then I, the said Philip, to send him word,
and aid him with all the power I can make. And     45
thereunto I take my oath.     *He kisseth the sword.*

*King of England.* Come, Prince Dolphin, you must
swear, too.                    *He kisseth the sword.*
Well, my brother of France, there is one thing more
I must needs require of you.                        50

*King of France.* Wherein is it that we may satisfy your
Majesty?

*King of England.* A trifle, my good brother of France;
I mean to make your daughter Queen of England, if
she be willing, and you therewith content. How sayst  55
thou, Kate? Canst thou love the King of England?

*Katherine.* How should I love thee, which is my father's
enemy?

*King of England.* Tut, stand not upon these points. 'Tis
you must make us friends. I know, Kate, thou art     60
not a little proud that I love thee. What, wench, the
King of England?

*King of France.* Daughter, let nothing stand betwixt
the King of England and thee. Agree to it.

*Katherine.* [*Aside*] I had best whilst he is willing, lest  65
when I would he will not—I rest at your Majesty's
command.

*King of England.* Welcome, sweet Kate! But, my
brother of France, what say you to it?

*King of France.* With all my heart I like it. But when  70
shall be your wedding day?

*King of England.* The first Sunday of the next month,
God willing.          *Sound trumpets. Exeunt omnes.*

FINIS

# Commentaries

SAMUEL JOHNSON

## from *The Plays of William Shakespeare*

None of Shakespeare's plays are more read than the *First and Second Parts of Henry the Fourth*. Perhaps no author has ever in two plays afforded so much delight. The great events are interesting, for the fate of kingdoms depends upon them; the slighter occurrences are diverting and, except one or two, sufficiently probable; the incidents are multiplied with wonderful fertility of invention, and the characters diversified with the utmost nicety of discernment and the profoundest skill in the nature of man.

The Prince, who is the hero both of the comic and tragic part, is a young man of great abilities and violent passions, whose sentiments are right, though his actions are wrong; whose virtues are obscured by negligence, and whose understanding is dissipated by levity. In his idle hours he is rather loose than wicked; and when the occasion forces out his latent qualities, he is great without effort and brave without tumult. The trifler is roused into a hero, and the hero again reposes in the trifler. This character is great, original, and just.

Percy is a rugged soldier, choleric, and quarrelsome, and has only the soldier's virtues, generosity and courage.

But Falstaff, unimitated, unimitable Falstaff, how shall I describe thee? Thou compound of sense and vice; of sense which may be admired but not esteemed, of vice which may be despised but hardly detested. Falstaff is a character loaded with faults, and with those faults which naturally produce contempt. He is a thief and a glutton, a coward and a boaster, always ready to cheat the weak and prey upon the poor; to terrify the timorous and insult the defenseless. At once obsequious and malignant, he satirizes in their absence those whom he lives by flattering. He is familiar with the Prince only as an agent of vice, but of this familiarity he is so proud as not only to be supercilious and haughty with common men but to think his interest of importance to the Duke of Lancaster. Yet the man thus corrupt, thus despicable, makes himself necessary to the Prince that despises him, by the most pleasing of all qualities, perpetual gaiety, by an unfailing power of exciting laughter, which is the more freely indulged as his wit is not of the splendid or ambitious kind but consists in easy escapes and sallies of levity, which make sport but raise no envy. It must be observed that he is stained with no enormous or sanguinary crimes, so that his licentiousness is not so offensive but that it may be borne for his mirth.

The moral to be drawn from this representation is that no man is more dangerous than he that, with a will to corrupt, hath the power to please; and that neither wit nor honesty ought to think themselves safe with such a companion when they see Henry seduced by Falstaff.    [1765]

# SAMUEL TAYLOR COLERIDGE

## from *H. C. Robinson's Memoranda*

Falstaff Coleridge also considered as an instance of the predominance of intellectual power. He is content to be thought both a liar and a coward in order to obtain influence over the minds of his associates. His aggravated lies about the robbery are conscious and purposed, not inadvertent untruths. On my observing that this account seemed to justify [George Frederick] Cooke's representation, according to which a foreigner imperfectly understanding the character would fancy Falstaff to be the designing knave who actually does outwit the Prince, Coleridge answered that in his *own* estimation Falstaff is the superior who cannot easily be convinced that the Prince has escaped him; but that as in other instances Shakespeare has shown us the defeat of mere intellect by a noble feeling, the Prince being the superior moral character who rises above his insidious companion.

## from *Seven Lectures*

Falstaff was no coward, but pretended to be one merely for the sake of trying experiments on the credulity of mankind: he was a liar with the same object, and not because

Both selections by Coleridge come from *Shakespearean Criticism* by Samuel Taylor Coleridge, 2nd ed., ed. Thomas Middleton Raysor. 2 vols. New York: E. P. Dutton and Company, Inc., 1960; London: J. M. Dent & Sons, Ltd., 1961. The first passage is Robinson's memorandum of one of Coleridge's conversations of 1810; the second passage is J. P. Collier's memorandum of a conversation of 1811. In the first, abbreviations have been expanded.

he loved falsehood for itself. He was a man of such preeminent abilities, as to give him a profound contempt for all those by whom he was usually surrounded, and to lead to a determination on his part, in spite of their fancied superiority, to make them his tools and dupes. He knew, however low he descended, that his own talents would raise him and extricate him from any difficulty. While he was thought to be the greatest rogue, thief, and liar, he still had that about him which could render him not only respectable, but absolutely necessary to his companions. It was in characters of complete moral depravity, but of first-rate wit and talents, that Shakespeare delighted; and Coleridge instanced Richard the Third, Falstaff, and Iago.

# JOHN DOVER WILSON

## from *The Fortunes of Falstaff*

Falstaff may be the most conspicuous, he is certainly the most fascinating, character in *Henry IV*, but all critics are agreed, I believe, that the technical center of the play is not the fat knight but the lean prince. Hal links the low life with the high life, the scenes at Eastcheap with those at Westminster, the tavern with the battlefield; his doings provide most of the material for both Parts, and with him too lies the future, since he is to become Henry V, the ideal king, in the play that bears his name; finally, the mainspring of the dramatic action is the choice I have already spoken of, the choice he is called upon to make between Vanity and Government, taking the latter in its accepted Tudor meaning, which includes Chivalry or prowess in the field, the theme of Part I, and Justice, which is the theme of Part II. Shakespeare, moreover, breathes life into these abstractions by embodying them, or aspects of them, in prominent characters, who stand, as it were, about the Prince, like attendant spirits: Falstaff typifying Vanity in every sense of the word, Hotspur Chivalry, of the old anarchic kind, and the Lord Chief Justice the Rule of Law or the new ideal of service to the state.

Thus considered, Shakespeare's *Henry IV* is a Tudor version of a time-honored theme, already familiar for dec-

From *The Fortunes of Falstaff* by John Dover Wilson. Cambridge: Cambridge University Press, 1943, pp. 17–21.

ades, if not centuries, upon the English stage. Before its
final secularization in the first half of the sixteenth century,
our drama was concerned with one topic, and one only:
human salvation. It was a topic that could be represented
in either of two ways: (i) historically, by means of miracle
plays, which in the Corpus Christi cycles unrolled before
spectators' eyes the whole scheme of salvation from the
Creation to the Last Judgment; or (ii) allegorically, by
means of morality plays, which exhibited the process of
salvation in the individual soul on its road between birth
and death, beset with the snares of the World or the wiles
of the Evil One. In both kinds the forces of iniquity were
allowed full play upon the stage, including a good deal of
horseplay, provided they were brought to nought, or safely
locked up in Hell, at the end. Salvation remains the su-
preme interest, however many capers the Devil and his
Vice may cut on Everyman's way thither, and always the
powers of darkness are withstood, and finally overcome,
by the agents of light. But as time went on the religious
drama tended to grow longer and more elaborate, after the
encyclopedic fashion of the Middle Ages, and such development invited its inevitable reaction. With the advent of
humanism and the early Tudor court, morality plays became tedious and gave place to lighter and much shorter
moral interludes dealing, not with human life as a whole,
but with youth and its besetting sins.

An early specimen, entitled *Youth* and composed about
1520, may be taken as typical of the rest. The plot, if plot
it can be called, is simplicity itself. The little play opens
with a dialogue between Youth and Charity. The young
man, heir to his father's land, gives insolent expression to
his self-confidence, lustihood, and contempt for spiritual
things. Whereupon Charity leaves him, and he is joined
by Riot, that is to say wantonness, who presently intro-
duces him to Pride and Lechery. The dialogue then becomes boisterous, and continues in that vein for some
time, much no doubt to the enjoyment of the audience.
Yet, in the end, Charity reappears with Humility; Youth
repents; and the interlude terminates in the most seemly
fashion imaginable.

No one, I think, reading this lively playlet, no one certainly who has seen it performed, as I have seen it at the Malvern Festival, can have missed the resemblance between Riot and Falstaff. The words he utters, as he bounces onto the stage at his first entry, give us the very note of Falstaff's gaiety:

> Huffa! huffa! who calleth after me?
> I am Riot full of jollity.
> My heart is as light as the wind,
> And all on riot is my mind,
> Wheresoever I go.

And the parallel is even more striking in other respects. Riot, like Falstaff, escapes from tight corners with a quick dexterity; like Falstaff, commits robbery on the highway; like Falstaff, jests immediately afterward with his young friend on the subject of hanging; and like Falstaff, invites him to spend the stolen money at a tavern, where, he promises, "We will drink diuers wine" and "Thou shalt haue a wench to kysse Whansoeuer thou wilte"; allurements which prefigure the Boar's Head and Mistress Doll Tearsheet.

But Youth at the door of opportunity, with Age or Experience, Charity or Good Counsel, offering him the yoke of responsibility, while the World, the Flesh, and the Devil beckon him to follow them on the primrose way to the everlasting bonfire, is older than even the medieval religious play. It is a theme to which every generation gives fresh form, while retaining its eternal substance. Young men are the heroes of the Plautine and Terentian comedy which delighted the Roman world; and these young men, generally under the direction of a clever slave or parasite, disport themselves, and often hoodwink their old fathers, for most of the play, until they too settle down in the end. The same theme appears in a very different story, the parable of the Prodigal Son. And the similarity of the two struck humanist teachers of the early sixteenth century with such force that, finding Terence insufficiently edifying for their pupils to act, they developed a "Christian Terence" by turning the parable into Latin plays, of which many examples by different authors have come down to us. In these plot and structure are much the same. The opening scene shows us Acolastus, the prodigal, demanding his portion, receiving good counsel from his father, and going off into a far country. Then follow three or four acts of entertainment almost purely Terentian in atmosphere, in which he wastes his substance in riotous living and falls at length to feeding with the pigs. Finally, in the last act he returns home, penniless and repentant, to receive his pardon. This ingenious blend of classical comedy and humanistic morality preserves, it will be noted, the traditional ratio between edification and amusement, and distributes them in the traditional manner. So long as the serious note is duly emphasized at the beginning and end of the play, almost any quantity of fun, often of the most unseemly nature, was allowed and expected during the intervening scenes.

All this, and much more of a like character, gave the pattern for Shakespeare's *Henry IV*. Hal associates Falstaff in turn with the Devil of the miracle play, the Vice of the morality, and the Riot of the interlude, when he calls him "that villainous abominable misleader of Youth, that old white-bearded Satan," "that reverend Vice, that gray Iniquity, that father Ruffian, that Vanity in years," and "the tutor and the feeder of my riots." "Riot," again, is the word that comes most readily to King Henry's lips when speaking of his prodigal son's misconduct. And, as heir to the Vice, Falstaff inherits by reversion the functions and attributes of the Lord of Misrule, the Fool, the Buffoon, and the Jester, antic figures the origins of which are lost in the dark backward and abysm of folk custom. We shall find that Falstaff possesses a strain, and more than a strain, of the classical *miles gloriosus* as well. In short, the Falstaff-Hal plot embodies a composite myth which had been centuries amaking, and was for the Elizabethans full of meaning that has largely disappeared since then: which is one reason why we have come so seriously to misunderstand the play.

Nor was Shakespeare the first to see Hal as the prodigal.

The legend of Harry of Monmouth began to grow soon
after his death in 1422; and practically all the chroniclers,
even those writing in the fifteenth century, agree on his
wildness in youth and on the sudden change that came
upon him at his accession to the throne. The essence of
Shakespeare's plot is, indeed, already to be found in the
following passage about King Henry V taken from Fab-
yans' *Chronicle* of 1516:

> This man, before the death of his fader, applyed him
> unto all vyce and insolency, and drewe unto hym all
> ryottours and wylde disposed persones; but after he was
> admytted to the rule of the lande, anone and suddenly he
> became a newe man, and tourned al that rage into sober-
> nesse and wyse sadnesse, and the vyce into constant
> vertue. And for he wolde contynewe the vertue, and not
> to be reduced thereunto by the familiarytie of his olde
> nyse company, he therefore, after rewardes to them
> gyuen, charged theym upon payne of theyr lyues, that
> none of theym were so hardy to come within x. myle of
> such place as he were lodgyd, after a day by him assigned.

There appears to be no historical basis for any of this, and
Kingsford has plausibly suggested that its origin may be
"contemporary scandal which attached to Henry through
his youthful association with the unpopular Lollard leader" Sir John Oldcastle. "It is noteworthy," he points out,
"that Henry's political opponents were Oldcastle's religious persecutors; and also that those writers who charge
Henry with wildness as Prince find his peculiar merit as
King in the maintaining of Holy Church and destroying of
heretics. A supposed change in his attitude on questions of
religion may possibly furnish a partial solution for his
alleged 'change suddenly into a new man.' " The theory is
the more attractive that it would account not only for
Hal's conversion but also for Oldcastle's degradation from
a protestant martyr and distinguished soldier to what
Ainger calls "a broken-down Lollard, a fat old sensualist,
retaining just sufficient recollection of the studies of his
more serious days to be able to point his jokes with them."
Yet when all is said, the main truth seems to be that the

fifteenth and early sixteenth centuries, the age of allegory in poetry and morality in drama, needed a Prodigal Prince, whose miraculous conversion might be held up as an example by those concerned (as what contemporary political writer was not?) with the education of young noblemen and princes. And could any more alluring fruits of repentance be offered such pupils than the prowess and statesmanship of Henry V, the hero of Agincourt, the mirror of English kingship for a hundred years? In his miracle play, *Richard II*, Shakespeare had celebrated the traditional royal martyr; in his morality play, *Henry IV*, he does the like with the traditional royal prodigal.

# DEREK TRAVERSI

## The Battle Scenes

Shakespeare's battle scenes, of which the two following episodes (v.iii and iv) are a fair example, show in their careful parallelisms a deliberate effort to turn the inadequacy of stage convention to dramatic effect. One has only to consider the treatment of material not altogether dissimilar in *Troilus and Cressida* and *Julius Caesar,* both written at dates not so much later, to realize that they turn upon a nice opposition between the conception of military "honor" and a critical presentation of the heroism of war; as such, they offer, moreover, a first faint approximation to the characteristic Shakespearean attitude, involving a fine balance of contraries, to the tragic heroes of the mature masterpieces. Read in this way, the stage representation of the battle of Shrewsbury becomes something more than the rather perfunctory staging of action which we might otherwise be inclined to see in it. A truer estimate demands a certain suspension of judgment, in which neither the heroic nor the satirical element will predominate, but in which each will be seen as correcting its opposite to produce finally an impression where simplicity of evaluation has no place.

The opening presentation of the battle (v.iii) calls for a balanced reading of this kind. Sir Walter Blunt incarnates a simple conception of "honor," ready to assert itself in loyal service of his royal master; but the king for whom he is ready to die, and does so, is willing to use his loyalty

From *Shakespeare from Richard II to Henry V* by Derek Traversi. Stanford, Calif.: Stanford University Press, pp. 100–03. The above title is the general editor's.

for a stratagem which, without overstressing the case, can hardly be admired. Blunt, in fact, like so many others on this field, is something less than a master of his fate. After his death at the hands of Douglas, the double attitude to his sacrifice is brought out in the comments of his victor and of Hotspur. For Hotspur, to whom the simple idea of "honor" has always been a sufficient guide to action, the dead Sir Walter was a "gallant knight"; but his slayer, less committed to the heroic idea, and indeed a character drawn on lines altogether more barbarous, utters his epitaph in savage terms in which frustrated impatience and a certain contempt both play their part:

> A fool go with thy soul, whither it goes!
> A borrowed title hast thou bought too dear.
>
> (v.iii)

Here again, though we need not overstress the casual skepticism implied in "whither it goes," the attitude fits well with the grotesque irony of the following reference to the royal disguises:

> I'll murder all his wardrobes, piece by piece,
> Until I meet the king.

A royalty that needs to disguise itself behind a "wardrobe" is something less than truly royal; and both it and the callous, impatient brutality of this "murderer" of wardrobes throw light on the spirit in which this part of the play is conceived.

As usual, something like the last word is left with Falstaff, whose part in the battle is not circumscribed to the mixture of self-interest and heroic values by which the main political actors are at once moved and limited. His first comment is a confession of fear—"I fear the shot here"—but a confession, as always, which implies a sense of the value of life, a protest—so to call it—against its sacrifice for motives finally obscure. As he glances down on Sir Walter's dead body, his point of view is uttered with greater force: "Sir Walter Blunt: there's honor for you! here's no vanity!" To appreciate the comment we need to sense the touch of morality which here, as so often, underlies it. "Vanity," of course, offers a double sense, that of pride (which ends traditionally in death and is here associated, moreover, with the wearing of borrowed plumes) and that of nothingness, futility, itself related to death and to the sense of empty honor that has brought it upon the victim. To read such an utterance in its full complexity is to appreciate once more the baseless nature of the discussion as to Falstaff's "cowardice" which reflects a fundamental misunderstanding of the dramatic function of the character. When Falstaff says, just below,

> I have led my ragamuffins where they are peppered: there's not three of my hundred and fifty left alive; and they are for the town's end, to beg during life,

the question is not, finally, one of the speaker's bravery or its opposite. That Falstaff "led" his men into battle is no more a proof of courage than his exclamation "God keep lead out of me!" is an indication of its opposite. The essence of Falstaff lies in his standing, alone in this play and until the supremacy of the political theme of kingship finally asserts itself, outside the categories by which those around him are respectively defined and limited. We may agree, if we will, that he *is* a coward; the dramatic tradition (or part of it )behind the character accounts for this, but not for the fact that he can look with detachment on his own cowardice, present it as a normal human reaction, associate it with his clear conception of the nature of the "ragamuffins" whom he shows, with a typical mixture of realistic contempt, and understanding, as having deserted "for the town's end, to beg during life." Falstaff is, let us say, a coward who can contemplate his own cowardice with detachment; and, by so doing, he offers an estimate, not final indeed (for few Shakespearean judgments are final) but relevant, upon the heroic values which are themselves related to a positive interpretation of life, but which need the operation of this objective check to prevent them from degenerating into a verbose pose.

The concluding exchange with the Prince, now entirely dedicated to his political and chivalrous function, confirms this position. Hal, as befits his regenerated state, is concerned with the death of the "noblemen" who lie

> stark and stiff
> Under the hoofs of vaunting enemies;

there is something limiting (which we need not, however, call insincere) about the rhetorical quality of the phrase which Falstaff is perfectly fitted to take up. He does so, indeed, first in his own parody of warlike boasting—"Turk Gregory never did such deeds in arms as I have done this day"—and then by giving Hal his "pistol," which turns out to be a bottle of sack. Once more, it is not cowardice or its opposite that is at stake, but rather the assertion of an independence that refuses to accept verbal values—however respectable and, in their own sphere, necessary they may be—at their own estimate, but plays upon them with a free judgment that expresses itself by converting humor and farce into a distinctive irony. Such is the spirit of the famous final comment on Blunt's sacrifice: "I like not such grinning honor as Sir Walter hath: *give me life*: which if I can save, so; if not, honor comes unlooked for, and there's an end." In the phrase "give me life" may be found the key to this judgment in which once more we may detect, if we will, a foundation of fear, but in which this very "cowardice," if it exists, is transformed by self-awareness into something different; for this is a comment, human and finally dispassionate, on the waste implied (once again, among other things: the judgment is relevant, not final) in a battle so many of whose causes are suspect. Inspired by this spirit, Falstaff moves through the conflict without being subdued to its tone, viewing it, as he views himself, with characteristic frankness, and dominating it, when all the necessary reservations have been made, by the very force of his vitality.

The second and longer battle scene (v.iv) represents simultaneously the culmination of the "honor" theme, as developed in the contrast between Prince Hal and Hot-

spur, and provides, in the customary way, a parallel comment through the fortunes of Falstaff. The earlier part of
the scene, leading to the rescue of the king by his son and
the discomfiture of Douglas, follows a familiar pattern and
is expressed in rhetorical terms which culminate in Henry's
recognition of his son's redemption on the field of battle:

> Thou hast redeemed thy lost opinion,
> And showed thou makest some tender of my life,
> In this fair rescue thou hast brought to me.

In the general conception of the play, this is a central moment. Hal, embarked on the path which will eventually
lead him to the crown and to Agincourt, needed thus to
be reconciled to his father as a result of his assumption of
the values of chivalry. Yet, accepting this, we must also
feel that the reconciliation is conventionally expressed, that
—though it would be wrong to invest it with irony—it
lacks the deeper feeling of other scenes in which the relationship between father and son is more intimately revealed. The Prince's reply is, as we may feel, a little too
ready to take up the point which confirms his own justification:

> O God! they did me too much injury
> That ever said I heark'ned for your death.
> If it were so, I might have let alone
> The insulting hand of Douglas over you,
> Which would have been as speedy in your end
> As all the poisonous potions in the world
> And saved the treacherous labor of your son.
>
>                                          (V.iv)

As a public justification, this is well enough; but as the
attitude of a son to his father, who has just expressed his
recovered faith in him, it is—to say the least—somewhat
frigid. The truth is that King Henry IV and the Prince
alike belong to the public rather than to the private sphere,
and that such efforts as they make to move out of it are
not always dramatically convincing.

# JAMES WINNY

## from *The Player King: A Theme of Shakespeare's Histories*

[Falstaff's] debts are a comic issue of both parts of *Henry IV*. In the third tavern scene of Part I he brings a trumped-up charge against his hostess of harboring pickpockets in the house, with motives which she is quick to recognize:

> You owe me money, Sir John, and now you pick a quarrel
> to beguile me of it.
>
> III.iii. 68–69.

She has a truer intuition than the rebels, who fail to perceive that Bolingbroke deliberately sows discord between himself and them for the same reason. The general parallel becomes suddenly more specific as Quickly mentions some items of Falstaff's debt, "a dozen of shirts to your back," besides twenty-four pounds in ready money. The suggestion of threadbare poverty, relieved only to be scornfully denied—"Dowlas, filthy dowlas"—offers a ludicrous counterpart to Bolingbroke's ingratitude toward the friends who gave him "that same majesty he wears" at a time when he was destitute, "a poor unminded outlaw sneaking home." Falstaff remains brazenly defiant in the face of Quickly's reminder, refusing to pay a denier but at least admitting a past obligation, where Bolingbroke declines to

From *The Player King: A Theme of Shakespeare's Histories* by James Winny. London: Chatto and Windus, 1968, pp. 113–14.

notice the impeachment. Hotspur's bitter comment rebukes his own credulity as much as Bolingbroke's bad faith:

> The King is kind, and well we know the King
> Knows at what time to promise, when to pay.
>
> IV.iii. 52–53.

The remark is halfway to the indirect satire which Falstaff enacts in his own attempt to evade his debt. His impudent retort to his accuser matches the accusation of wrongful proceeding brought by the King's spokesmen, condemning the rebels for faults more glaringly obvious in their master:

> There's no more faith in thee than in a stewed prune, nor no more truth in thee than in a drawn fox—and for womanhood, Maid Marian may be the deputy's wife of the ward to thee.
>
> III.iii. 115–18.

Hal intervenes with a moral rebuke of Falstaff's lying and duplicity which shows his air of personal consequence to be so much worthless stuffing:

> There's no room for faith, truth, nor honesty in this bosom of thine—it is all filled up with guts and midriff ... If there were anything in thy pocket but tavern-reckonings, memorandums of bawdy-houses, and one poor pennyworth of sugar-candy to make thee long-winded ... I am a villain.
>
> Ibid., 157–66.

Falstaff is carrying out his satirical function by behaving in a fashion which encourages the Prince to castigate him in terms appropriate to Bolingbroke. This is not the only occasion, in either part of the play, when Hal seems to be tacitly denouncing his father's viciousness by attacking the same faults in Falstaff. This means of registering moral disapproval of Bolingbroke's crimes indirectly allows the Prince to dissociate himself completely from a lawless régime without overt disloyalty to his father. When we realize that Falstaff is unwittingly standing in for the man whose moral character he shares, we may feel less uneasy about the gratuitousness of Hal's sometimes scathing attacks upon Falstaff, whose company he is not obliged to tolerate. The vehemence of his personal insults—"that bolting-hutch of beastliness, that swollen parcel of dropsies . . . that stuffed cloak-bag of guts"—springs partly from moral disgust, but perhaps more from the frustration of being denied any direct outlet for this revulsion. At such moments Falstaff becomes the scapegoat for Bolingbroke, and the target of a satirical venom whose shafts are often ambiguously appropriate to both. This ambiguousness is particularly evident in Hal's speech from the throne denouncing

> that reverend vice, that gray iniquity, that father ruffian.
> II.iv. 453.

His satirical terms fit Bolingbroke rather better than Falstaff. Sir John may deserve "reverend vice" for his jocular pretense of respectability, but the King—a crowned robber, holding sacred office in defiance of right—has a stronger claim to the description. The second epithet applies to both without distinction; but "that father ruffian" must indicate Bolingbroke rather than Falstaff, if only because "your father" is a common form of reference to the King in the tavern scenes. Falstaff may be a father ruffian in the sense that he embodies riot and misrule, but the description applies to Bolingbroke in a literal as well as a figurative sense, as the speaker has best reason to know. The indictment of Falstaff cannot be transferred entirely to the King, as though he and not Falstaff were being charged, but the terms of Hal's speech are equivocal enough to suggest some merging of their individual identities, allowing one to be seen as a variant form of the other.

## ROBERT ORNSTEIN

## from *A Kingdom for a Stage*

I do not think that it is "sentimental" to enjoy Hotspur's openness and good humor, so long as we recognize the conceit and infatuation with risk that sully his noblest impulse. Hungering for reputation in the way other men hunger for power, he will let another sit on the throne, but he must wear the dignities of great renown "without corrival." Generous in spirit, he would open his veins in a "good cause," but he will not think of the misery of the thousands of other men who will unwillingly bleed because of the rebellion. Too narrow in his devotion to family and too trusting of his kin, he cannot admit the egotism of his motives or realize the contradictions of his outrage. On the one hand, he would see his family as innocent dupes of the vile politician Bolingbroke, who deceived them by pledging that he came back only for his ducal rights. On the other hand, he fumes at the ingratitude of Henry, who reneged on his promises and now orders the Percies about as if he owed them nothing. Thus, Hotspur would be innocent of the "crime" of having aided Henry to the throne even as he is furious that his family was not sufficiently rewarded for their aid to Bolingbroke. In Hotspur's view, the Percies acted as Henry's hangman but did not receive the hangman's perquisite. They helped to kill a king but did not receive the king's clothes, for it is the cankered

From *A Kingdom for a Stage: The Achievement of Shakespeare's History Plays* by Robert Ornstein. Cambridge, Mass.: Harvard University Press, 1972, pp. 134–39.

Bolingbroke who wears the robes of majesty and denies their present suit for Mortimer.

The richness and delight of Hotspur's personality makes one wonder at the desire of some critics to treat him as a clown or as the sullen ground on which Hal's princely brilliance glitters. The actors who play Hotspur will not demean him in this way. They make us aware of his warmth, exuberance, and poetry, qualities somewhat lacking in Hal; and they almost convince us that the rebel is more attractive than the prince. For if Hal's poise accentuates Hotspur's recklessness, Hotspur's frankness calls attention to what is calculating and disingenuous in Hal's relations with others. When Hotspur teases his adoring wife, the humor is tender and intimate; when Hal, slightly bored and drunk, teases Francis, the joke smacks of contempt and casual cruelty.

We can say that Hotspur is the better companion, Hal the better prince. The one is more engaging as a man, the other far better suited to great responsibility. To grant Hal the fullest measure of his princely talents is not, however, to agree that he is Shakespeare's ideal of rule—a character whose personal defects are a part of his princely perfection, whose coldness and calculation are seen by Shakespeare as necessary virtues in a leader. If Shakespeare gave us the Hal of the folk legend, a youth who loved the low company which he ultimately turned away, we might speak of his aloofness in the tavern scenes as a schooling of self for the impersonal demands of office. But what shall we say of the Prince who in his first appearance speaks contemptuously of his tavern companions, whom he intends to use to line his princely enterprise? Just as Falstaff keeps his eye on the main chance and expects to profit in times to come from his friendship with Hal, Hal confesses in soliloquy that he intends to turn a small investment in seeming prodigality into a handsome profit of reputation. Although he obviously enjoys Falstaff's company, Hal tells us that he plays at comradeship as well as at prodigality and not only plans to discard his cronies but even now considers them the base contagion that momentarily obscures his princely radiance.

To be sure, Hal is not, as some have pictured him, a Machiavellian prince who craftily deceives his tavern cronies even as he will later "dupe" his English subjects into supporting his claim to the throne of France. He never pretends deep feeling for Falstaff and Poins, and, if anything, he is more ingenious in his self-justifications than cunning in his dissimulations. He is more candid in his conversations with other men than in his colloquies with himself in which he labors to rationalize his behavior. When Hotspur embroiders the truth about Mortimer's soldiership, his artificiality of manner betrays him; when he tries to argue before Shrewsbury that rashness is caution, his illogic is transparent. More conscious of, and subtle in, his casuistries, Hal is more difficult to "see through." Though we know him better than does Falstaff, who claims to know him "like the Lord that made ye," we cannot say that we fully understand the prince who plays a limited engagement as tavern roisterer and who explains his tavern holiday as a clever public relations stunt. This is a man whose reasons and rationalizations so finely commingle that they cannot be sorted out, but whose bent of mind is consistent in conversation and soliloquy. Shrewd in his appraisals and thoroughly pragmatic, he studies other men so that he may learn to master them; and because his moral attitudes are attuned to those of the practical world, he sees no reason to justify his manipulation of others, though he feels compelled to justify his seeming dissipation. It would not occur to him that drinking sack and sugar may be less of a fault than falsifying men's hopes, and he could not imagine that his tavern holiday might seem to others more attractive than his utilitarian justification of it.[1]

Although we cannot allow one soliloquy to determine our view of a character as fully developed as Hal is in

1 John Palmer shrewdly notes that if Hal "is merely looking for a reason to be merry with his friends, surely he might have found a better one. To plead that he is permitting their base contagious clouds to smother up his beauty in order that he may shine all the more brightly when they have served his turn is not the sort of excuse which would have suggested itself to a really good companion" (*Political Characters*, p. 185).

dialogue and dramatic action, neither can we ignore the
fact that in each play in which Hal appears, he is allowed
only one soliloquy, and in each instance that soliloquy is a
crucial revelation of character and motive.[2] The alterna-
tive to viewing Hal's soliloquy in I.ii as a disclosure of self
is to regard it, as many critics have done, as a choric
device by which Shakespeare communicates essential narrative information to his audience, assuring them that Hal
"will exhibit all the proper regal virtues" when the time
comes.[3] One must wonder, however, why an Elizabethan
audience needed reassurance about the princely character
or destiny of the greatest of England's heroic kings, whose
exploits at Agincourt were celebrated in poems and ballads, in the Chronicles, and in the source play *The Famous
Victories*. If, as Professor Tillyard argues, Shakespeare
was compelled to make Hal a "copybook paragon" in
*Henry V* because his audience knew the legend of Harry's
perfection by heart,[4] surely there was no need to dispel
any doubts about Hal's future greatness in scene ii of
*Henry IV Part I*, especially when, as Tillyard notes, there
is not the slightest intimation that Hal can be seduced by
Falstaff. Describing Hal as "aloof and Olympian from the
start," Tillyard remarks that he "never treats Falstaff any
better than his dog, with whom he condescends once in a
way to have a game."[5]

Even if we grant that Shakespeare may have thought his
audience too gross to see what Tillyard and others do in
the Hal of the first tavern scene, we must still wonder why
he did not just allow the groundlings to enjoy their super-
ficial view of Hal as the prodigal of the legend. Unless

[2] Compare the soliloquy at the end of the first tavern scene with the
one soliloquy which Hal speaks in *Henry IV Part II*, when he takes the
crown from his father's pillow (IV.v.21–47); and with his one soliloquy
in *Henry V*, which occurs after his encounter with his soldiers about
the campfire on the eve of Agincourt (IV.i.247–301).

[3] Tillyard, *History Plays*, p. 300. J. Dover Wilson also insists that the
soliloquy has a conventional function of conveying "information to the
audience about the general drift of the play" (*The Fortunes of Falstaff*
[Cambridge: Cambridge Univ. Press, 1964], p. 41).

[4] *History Plays*, p. 305.

[5] *History Plays*, pp. 271–72.

Shakespeare's audience was made up of prigs and Puritans, they could not really have trembled for Hal's future
because, like thousands of theatergoers, he enjoyed Falstaff. After all, we never see Hal in the throes of debauch-
ery and we find his capacity for holiday reassuring; we like
and trust a man who can drink and joke, unbend and
stoop to the level of our own tastes. To have our confidence and good will, a youthful profligate need not apol-
ogize for his casual "vices." If he appears generous, frank
in his affections, and fundamentally innocent in spirit, we
are perfectly ready to grant that having sowed his wild
oats, he deserves—as do all the youthful profligates of
seventeenth-century comedy—a good wife, a handsome
fortune, and a noble future.[6] In other words, Hal needs
no choric soliloquy to warn us that he is the Cinderella
prince of the legend. He needs the soliloquy to underline
the fact that he is not prodigal in temperament at all, and
certainly not a happy-go-lucky youth indifferent to his
royal future. Rather than a Huck Finn who prefers the
freedom of the tavern to the restrictions imposed by his
noble destiny, he is a Tom Sawyer who enjoys his moment
of raffishness but by inclination is one of the respectable
and perhaps even one of the Elect. Very conscious of the
way that men respond to the image of royalty, and no less
instinctive a politician than his father, Hal is the creator
as well as the creature of political mythology, the author
as well as the hero of his legend.

It seems to me preferable to interpret the soliloquy as
soliloquy rather than to turn Shakespeare into a blunderer
who did not realize the chilling effect of Hal's contemptu-
ous lines about his comrades and who failed to see how
Hal's diction and metaphors associate his calculated redemption with the crassness of commodity and sharp
business practices:

6 The generous rake enjoys a happy career also in Restoration
comedy. Indeed, his type can be seen in any number of Hollywood
movies in which a slightly ribald, reckless, and warmhearted young hero
wins the heroine away from the proper, respectable, young banker
whom the parents prefer.

So, when this loose behavior I throw off
And pay the debt I never promised,
By how much better than my word I am,
By so much shall I falsify men's hopes;
And, like bright metal on a sullen ground,
My reformation, glitt'ring o'er my fault,
Shall show more goodly and attract more eyes
Than that which hath no foil to set it off.
I'll so offend to make offense a skill,
Redeeming time when men think least I will.

(I.ii.212-21)

Like a clever Elizabethan shopkeeper, Hal knows how to display the merchandise of his behavior in such a light that it appears richer than it is. He knows, too, how to play the princely bankrupt—how to conceal his princely assets until they bring a double profit. We may not like this element of calculation in him, but it is one of his fundamental traits. The Hal who will "use" his tavern companions is the same Hal who will make Percy his factor and who promises to tear the reckoning of honor out of Hotspur's heart. He is also the same Hal who in soliloquy in *Part II* will promise to "pay plenteously" with tears for the crown he takes from his father's pillow, and who in soliloquy in *Henry V* will ask what are the "rents" and "comings-in" of Ceremony and promise God to pay more fully the debt of conscience.

Far from being a neutral choric announcement, Hal's soliloquy in the tavern strikes the keynote of his characterization in succeeding plays. For just as he explains to the audience why he wastes his time with low companions in *Part I*, he will explain to Poins in *Part II* why he cannot weep for his dying father, and to the traitors in *Henry V* why he cannot be merciful to them.[7] We can take Hal's part in Hal's casuistic way and explain that it is Francis' fault that Hal plays nasty jokes on him—because the "subhuman" deserve subhuman treatment. Or we can

---

[7] Palmer writes very penetratingly of the need for self-justification which characterizes Harry in each play in which he appears (*Political Characters*, pp. 185-87).

accept Hal for what he is: fascinating but not endearing; not quite the paragon some would have him nor the heartless prig others see. Although quick-witted, he is rarely a match for Falstaff because he cannot anticipate the sudden dazzling reversals and agile leaps of Falstaff's thought and mood. Thus, even though he holds the trump cards after Gadshill, he does not win the game of wits, because Falstaff makes the very questions of cowardice and truth seem ridiculous. In these encounters Hal has a grave disadvantage in that he cannot, like Falstaff, ridicule everything. Although he jokes coarsely about cheapening maidenheads, he will not cheapen courage or princeliness; he will not pretend to be a good fellow at the price of his royal dignity.

The time will come when Henry V will look back with shame on the "riots" of his tavern days. Even now there is a faint tinge of disgust in his reference to the base contagion that smothers up his beauty from the world. He can take Falstaff's bulk as a subject for his wit, but he does not share Falstaff's pleasure in the flesh. When Sir John plays at being king, corpulence is rhapsodized as well as licensed. When Hal becomes the kingly homilist, Falstaff's great belly becomes an emblem of surfeited appetite as well as of festive indulgence:

> Why dost thou converse with that trunk of humors, that bolting hutch of beastliness, that swoll'n parcel of dropsies, that huge bombard of sack, that stuffed cloakbag of guts, that roasted Manningtree ox with the pudding in his belly, that reverend vice, that gray iniquity, that father ruffian, that vanity in years?
>
> (II.iv. 448–54)

For Falstaff the urge to repentance is a fleeting impulse or a comic pose. For Hal the thought of redemption is no laughing matter. Earnest even in holiday, he scrupulously examines his conduct and finds it good; he explains to us and to himself that he labors in the tavern in his vocation as a prince just as Falstaff explains that he labors in his vocation as a highway robber. Knowing how men merchandize their reputations and hope for bargain redemptions, Falstaff jokes about finding a commodity of good names. Hal, on the other hand, seriously intends to gain that commodity even as he seriously intends to reject Falstaff as the "tutor and feeder" of his "riots." After all, it is not Shakespeare who casts Hal as the hero of a Morality drama of temptation and redemption. It is Hal who casts himself in the role even as he casts Falstaff in the role of reverend Vice and gray iniquity. I do not mean to suggest that beneath the loose behavior of the pseudo-libertine is the tight-lipped manner of the Precisian to be. I do suggest that Shakespeare's conception of Harry, as it unfolds in the second tetralogy, is all of one piece, a marvelously unified and sustained study of a personality that develops in Aristotelian fashion from potentiality to essence—from seeming roisterer to devout conqueror. The more we see of Hal in the tavern, the less we fear that he will grow too attached to Falstaff. We wonder, however, whether this poised, ironic, self-absorbed prince will ever be capable of intimacy or of emotional attachment to another person. We sense, even in *Part I,* that Hal needs Falstaff even as he needs ultimately to banish him.

# MICHAEL GOLDMAN

## from *Shakespeare and the Energies of Drama*

Falstaff is always at Hal's mercy, and we love him for the way he stretches the limits of his situation and gets away with it; it is an aspect of his fatness. At the end of the Boar's Head Tavern scene, when it is learned that the Sheriff and his watch are at the door hunting Falstaff, he hides behind the arras while the Prince persuades the Sheriff to leave. The curtain is then drawn back, and Falstaff is revealed, asleep and "snorting like a horse." The Prince goes through his pockets. Falstaff sleeps on for twenty lines as the scene concludes. The episode is memorable, funny, famous even among familiar quotations ("O monstrous! but one half-pennyworth of bread to this intolerable deal of sack!"), and—perhaps because Falstaff cannot speak—suggests with a fascinating strength the intensity and complexity of our attachment to him. Falstaff asleep is the man we have seen wildly and ingeniously awake moments before, and we look forward to the moment he will rise again. His belches and snorts undoubtedly have more life in them than an army of tapsters. Francis's actions belong to the comedy of mechanism; he has responded to the Prince's commands like an automaton. Falstaff's, even asleep, belong to the comedy of irrepressibility; he is doing what he wants in the most unlikely of circumstances. And yet perhaps because he is asleep, certain other strands of our feeling toward him are allowed to take on new prominence. The contrast with the long, energetic, increasingly fantastic comic scene that has been interrupted, the relative stillness, our new awareness

From *Shakespeare and the Energies of Drama* by Michael Goldman. Princeton, N.J.: Princeton University Press, 1972, pp. 55–57.

that it is late at night, our growing certainty that a decisive return to the great world of politics and combat is imminent, all these tend to heighten whatever is protective and elegiac in our response. It is a good scene to meditate on.

Falstaff at this moment seems not only grandly self-indulgent and indifferent to crisis but particularly vulnerable. The Prince stands over him; Falstaff's life is in his hands in more ways than one. He has promised the Sheriff that the fat knight will make good his thefts. He makes Peto read aloud the ludicrous facts of Falstaff's internal economy. Falstaff's utter relaxation is enviable, his snorting and belching delightfully irreverent, but the guard that has been up so splendidly throughout the long tavern scene is down and the soft belly is exposed. We feel drawn to him and we see how easily we can hurt him; we know now that the wars have begun, that he won't do as he is. Falstaff must suffer. He must submit to the indignities of realism, of number and measure. Today his appetites are converted into arithmetic ("Item, Sack, two gallons . . . 5s. 8d."); tomorrow he must lead a charge of foot. ("I know his death will be a march of twelve-score. The money shall be paid back again with advantage.") We know that Falstaff will respond resourcefully; he is far from finished. But we have always known that finished he eventually must be.

Falstaff is not only endlessly inventive and delightful, audacious and dangerous, but vulnerable. This is also true about the things for which he comes to stand—our sensuality and our impulse to anarchy. The tenderness, broad humor, and absurdity that are mixed in this tableau come close to the mystery of Falstaff—or more correctly the mystery of the play, for our emotion here includes Hal, whose stance is the already familiar one of authority and detachment, and whose heroic career is plainly about to begin. The Prince of our reason stands over the attractive, grotesque, audacious, pathetically vulnerable body of our sensuality—an image for one of the many selves inside us, indeed for more than one—a sleeping child that we will have to punish, the silly, dying father we are destined to displace.

COPPÉLIA KAHN

# from *Man's Estate: Masculine Identity in Shakespeare*

In the course of the two *Henry IV* plays, Shakespeare presents a conception of the father-son bond and its part in the formation of a masculine identity vastly different from that in the first tetralogy. In place of the emphasis on repetition and the past there, with its taut emulation of the father and inflexible vendettas, Shakespeare conceives of a relationship with some give to it, literally some free play, some space for departure from paternal priority and for experiences fundamentally opposed to it. In place of the failures in transition from sonship to fatherhood represented by Henry VI, John Talbot, Young Clifford, and Richard III, he tries to portray a successful passage negotiated, paradoxically, as lawful rebellion and responsible play. He makes Hal the stage manager of his own growing up, the embodiment of a wish to let go—but to let go only so far, without real risks. In the end, Falstaff's regressive appeal is so dangerously strong for Shakespeare that he cannot afford to integrate it into Hal's character, and must, to Hal's loss, exclude it totally. From the sonnets to *The Winter's Tale*, the idea of remaining "boy eternal" exerts a powerful pull on Shakespeare's imagination that he strenuously resists. At the same time, however, he discovers new dimensions in the lifelong process of becoming a man; he begins to see how the father's identity is shaped by his

From *Man's Estate: Masculine Identity in Shakespeare* by Coppélia Kahn. Berkeley, Calif.: University of California Press, 1981, pp. 70–74.

son, as well as the son's by his father. In Henry and Hal
he uses the renewal of the principle of succession as a way
to validate Henry's kingship as much as Hal's; identity becomes a reciprocal process between father and son.

The relationship between the two men has three focal
points of overdetermined needs and signals at which crises
are defined or resolved. The first is the Boar's Head and
Hal's reign there as madcap prince under the tutelage of
Falstaff, who is usually seen as anti-king and anti-father,
standing for misrule as opposed to rule. But he is also the
opposite of the king in the sense of being his predecessor
psychologically, the king of childhood and omnipotent
wishes, as Henry is king in the adult world of rivalry and
care. Franz Alexander describes Falstaff as the personifica-
tion of "the primary self-centered narcissistic libido of the
child," commenting that

> the child in us applauds, the child who knows only one
> principle and that is to live. . . . Since the child cannot
> actually overcome any external interferences, it takes
> refuge in fantastic, megalomaniac self-deception.[1]

"Banish plump Jack, and banish all the world!" Falstaff
cries. Because of his sophisticated adult wit, however, he
makes social capital out of his megalomania; men love his
gloriously ingenious lies better than their own truth. Falstaff is a world unto himself, shaped like the globe and
containing multitudes of contradictions as the world itself
does; fat and aging in body, but ever young in spirit and
nimble in wit; a shape-shifter in poses and roles, yet always inimitably himself; a man with a curiously feminine
sensual abundance.

A fat man can look like a pregnant woman, and Falstaff's fatness is fecund; it spawns symbols. In the context
of Hal's growing up, its feminine meaning has particular
importance.[2] As W. H. Auden says, it is "the expression

[1] Franz Alexander, "A Note on Falstaff," *Psychoanalytic Quarterly*
2 (1933): 392–406.
[2] W. H. Auden, "The Prince's Dog," in his *The Dyer's Hand* (New
York: Random House), p. 196.

of a psychological wish to withdraw from sexual competition and by combining mother and child in his own person, to become emotionally self-sufficient." Falstaff is said to be fond of hot wenches and leaping-houses, but he is no Don Juan even in Part 2 when his sexual relations with Doll Tearsheet and Mistress Quickly are made more explicit. They are fond of him rather than erotically drawn to him. It is not only tactful regard for Hal's legendary dignity as the perfect king that keeps Shakespeare from compromising him by making Falstaff a lecher. Rather, Falstaff represents the wish to bypass women; he has grown old, but remains young, and yet in terms of women has "detoured manhood," as Harold Goddard says.[3] In the first tetralogy Shakespeare avoided treating the woman's part in male development by making women witches or helpless victims. In the second tetralogy he again treats the feminine obliquely, through its absence, as Falstaff's avoidance of sexual maturity. The fat knight desires food and drink more than he desires women. And though women are devoted to him, he cheats and deceives them, giving his own deepest affections to a boy. No wonder that, for Hal, Falstaff incarnates his own rebellion against growing up into a problematic adult identity.

Hal himself is unaware that his affinity for the fat knight constitutes rebellion; he conceives it, rather, as part of his long-term strategy for assuming a proper identity as king. That strategy reveals his likeness to his father, his ability to think and act in the same terms of political image-building as his father, his fitness for the very role he seems to be rejecting. Many parallels between Hal's first soliloquy (1.2) and the king's long admonitory speech to him (3.2) reveal the essential similarities between father and son. Both speeches dwell on the proper management of one's political visibility and the importance of avoiding overexposure. Hal pictures himself as the sun obscured by clouds and therefore more "wonder'd at" when he reappears, while Henry compares himself to a comet "wonder'd

3 Harold C. Goddard, *"Henry IV,"* in his *The Meaning of Shakespeare,* 2 vols. (Chicago: University of Chicago Press, 1951), vol. 1, p. 184.

at" because it is "seldom seen." He implies that his is that "sun-like majesty" that, when it "shines seldom," wins an "extraordinary gaze," and Hal says that his reformation "shall show more goodly, and attract more eyes" because of his fault. Both use clothing imagery to denote a kingliness they put on or off at will; Hal says he can "throw off this loose behaviour," and Henry says that he too dressed himself in humility, then donned his "presence like a robe pontifical." Hal's soliloquy implies that the Hal we have just seen with Falstaff is no more genuine and spontaneous than the self he will assume as king, and it is immediately followed by Henry addressing the Percys in equally ambiguous terms:

> I will from henceforth rather by myself,
> Mighty and to be feared, than my condition. . . .[4]

> (I.iii. 5–6)

Neither man can freely express his true self, whatever that is, because each has something to hide . . . Hal hides his sympathy with his father, while Henry hides his guilt over the deposition and murder of Richard. Nonetheless, that guilt is revealed in the way he splits his son into two contending images: the bad son, Hal the wastrel; and the good son, Hotspur the king of honor. For Hal to become his father's son personally (to be loved) and politically (to be trusted as fit to succeed his father), he must restore his reputation as heir apparent, triumph over Hotspur, and assume Hotspur's identity as the model of chivalric manhood in England. This he obediently promises and economically does, in the sum-zero terms of heroic combat:

> Percy is but my factor, good my lord,
> To engross up glorious deeds on my behalf
> And I will call him to so strict account
> That he shall render every glory up,

---

[4] A. R. Humphreys, editor of the new Arden text, glosses *condition* as "natural disposition."

Yea, even the slightest worship of his time,
Or I will tear the reckoning from his heart.

(III.ii. 147–152)

Thus Shrewsbury is the second focal point of the father-
son relationship, and constitutes Hal's and Henry's first
mutual reaffirmation of identity.

CLEANTH BROOKS AND
ROBERT S. HEILMAN

## from *Understanding Drama*

If *Henry IV, Part I* does have a principle of unity, it is obviously one which allows for, and makes positive use of, an amazing amount of contrast. Many of these contrasts have already been noted in the questions which come at the end of each act. There is the contrast between the king's hopes for his son and the life which Prince Hal has actually been leading; the contrast between the pomp and state of the councils at court which are called to debate the state of the realm and those other councils at the Boar's Head which take measures for the better lifting of travelers' purses. Moreover, as we have remarked earlier, Prince Hal and Percy Hotspur are obvious foils for each other; they are specifically contrasted again and again throughout the play. But one of the most important contrasts developed in the play is that between Falstaff and Percy Hotspur.

On one level, it ought to be pretty obvious, the play involves a study in the nature of kingship—not an unduly solemn study, to be sure—but a study, nevertheless, of what makes a good king. In this study, of course, Prince Hal is the central figure, and the play becomes, then, the study of his development.

On this level of consideration, Percy Hotspur not only

From *Understanding Drama* by Cleanth Brooks and Robert S. Heilman. New York: Holt, 1948, pp. 377–79.

is Hal's rival but also furnishes an ideal of conduct toward which Hal might aspire (and toward which his father, the king, actually wishes him to aspire). Falstaff represents another ideal of conduct—and here, consequently, finds his foil in Hotspur. (If the pairing of Falstaff and Hotspur seems, at first glance, forced, nevertheless we shall presently see that there is abundant evidence that Shakespeare thought the contrast important and relevant to his purpose.)

Indeed, as Mr. R. P. Warren has poined out, it is almost as if Shakespeare were following, consciously or unconsciously, the theme of Aristotle's Nichomachaean ethics: virtue as the mean between two extremes of conduct. This suggestion can be used to throw a good deal of light on the relationship of the characters of Falstaff, Prince Hal, and Hotspur to each other.

Consider the matter of honor. Hotspur represents one extreme, Falstaff, the other. Hotspur declares characteristically

> By heaven, methinks it were an easy leap,
> To pluck bright honor from the pale-faced moon, . . .
> (I.iii. 199–200)

Falstaff speaks just as characteristically when he argues in his famous speech on honor: "Well, 'tis no matter; honor pricks me on. Yea, but how if honor prick me off when I come on? how then? Can honor set to a leg? no: or an arm? no: or take away the grief of a wound? no . . . (V.i)

Falstaff's common sense is devastating; but it is also crippling—or would be to a prince or ruler. If it does not cripple Falstaff, it is because Falstaff frankly refuses to accept the responsibilities of leadership. Perhaps he chooses wisely in so refusing. By refusing he achieves a vantage point from which he can perceive the folly and pretentiousness which, to a degree, always tend to associate themselves with authority of any kind.

But Hotspur's chivalry is crippling too. He wants to fight for honor's sake: he will not wait for reinforcements

because it will beget more honor to fight without waiting
for them; but, on the other hand, he will not fight at all
(Worcester fears) if he hears of the king's mollifying offer,
for then his pride will be saved, his honor preserved, and
the political aspects of the rebellion can go hang; for Hotspur has little or no interest in them. Indeed, Hotspur can
rely on the obvious fact that he is fighting merely for
honor to gain the forgiveness of the king, though Worcester
fears that the forgiveness extended to himself will be only
a nominal forgiveness and that the king will be on the
lookout for later excuses to injure him.

If one assumes the necessity for leadership (and there
is little doubt that the Elizabethan audience and Shakespeare did), then Hotspur points to an extreme which the
truly courageous leader must avoid quite as clearly as he
must avoid the other extreme represented by Falstaff. True
courage, we may say, has as one frontier an unthinking
impetuousness like that of Hotspur: it has as its other
frontier a kind of calculation, which, if not cowardice, at
least results in actions which look very much like cowardice. Falstaff is too "practical"; Hotspur, not "practical"
enough.

### THE "IMMATURITY" OF FALSTAFF AND HOTSPUR

Yet Shakespeare does not give us an oversimplified picture of either extreme. Falstaff redeems himself for most
of us by his humor, by his good nature, by his love of life,
and perhaps, most of all, by a thoroughgoing intellectual
honesty. Hotspur also has his attractive side. There is a
kind of abandon, a kind of light-hearted gaiety—in his
whole-souled commitment to the pursuit of honor, in his
teasing of his wife, and in his laughing at the pompous
mystery-mongering of Glendower—which puts him, like
Falstaff, *above* the plots and counter-plots that fill up the
play.

Yet—if we assume the necessity for leadership and
authority—both Falstaff and Hotspur are *below* the serious concerns that fill the play. About both of them there is
a childlike quality which relieves them of the responsibility

of mature life, a frankness which is the opposite of the pretense and hypocrisy so apparent in the adult world.

This suggestion that there is something childlike and immature about Falstaff and Hotspur must, of course, be heavily qualified. There is a sense in which Hotspur is the epitome of manliness and aggressive masculinity, and certainly he thinks of himself as anything but childish. Moreover, Falstaff, in spite of the war cry with which he sets upon the travelers, "They hate us youth: down with them; fleece them," is old in the ways of vice, and indeed possesses a kind of wisdom which makes the solemn concerns of Henry IV's court appear callow and naïve beside it.

And yet, even so, the pair do not stand quite on the level of the adult world where there are jobs to be done and duties to be performed. They are either below it or else they transcend it; and Shakespeare is wise enough to let them—particularly Falstaff—do both. That is, they appear sometimes *childish* in their attitudes and sometimes *childlike,* for Shakespeare exploits both aspects of their characters in the play.

The childlike qualities, of course, are found predominantly in Falstaff—in his vitality and in his preservation of a kind of innocence. But Hotspur, too, has a kind of innocence which sets him apart from the more calculating of his fellow-conspirators. He is impulsive where they are Machiavellian; boyish, in his love of adventure, where they are playing coldly for high stakes. But the childlike innocence (or, if one prefers, the boyish impulsiveness) merges into childish foolhardiness when he insists on fighting the king at Shrewsbury before reinforcements can be brought up.

270 CLEANTH BROOKS AND ROBERT PENN
of mature life, a framework which is the threshold of
projected and imperfectly comprehensive relationships.
Thus expression that there is some of the collected entire
feature of Falstaff and Hotspur

SYLVAN BARNET

# Henry IV, Part One on Stage and Screen

This is a play which all men admire, and which most
women dislike. Many revolting expressions in the comic
parts, much boisterous courage in some of the graver
scenes, together with Falstaff's unwieldy person, offend
every female auditor.

Elizabeth Inchbald, writing in 1808

*Henry IV, Part One* has for most of its history been
immensely popular on the stage, not only in England but
also in the United States, probably because at least until
recently men rather than women paid for most of the
tickets. Perhaps because of Shakespeare's prestige and because Falstaff is usually seen as an evocation of Merrie
England, the play is considered a safe choice for opening
a new theater: it was the first play staged when the Shakespeare Memorial Theater (which had been destroyed by
fire in 1926) reopened in 1932, the first play staged when
the Royal Shakespeare Company moved into its new quarters at the Barbican Theater in 1982, and the first play
staged by the American National Theater, in 1985, at the
Kennedy Center in Washington, D.C.

This essay cannot hope to touch on all of the major
productions, but it will very briefly survey the early centuries and then will look a bit more closely at a few
productions since World War II.[1]

[1] For a concise survey of performances up to 1935, consult *A New
Variorum Edition of Shakespeare: Henry the Fourth, Part 1*, ed.
Samuel Burdett Hemingway, and for some corrections to Hemingway,

We have a few records of early performances—for instance, we know that it was staged as part of the entertainment offered to the Flemish ambassador in 1600—but the best evidence that *1 Henry IV* was popular in Shakespeare's day is the fact that it was published five times between 1598 and 1613. Another bit of evidence of its popularity in the theater is a line by Leonard Digges, written about 1623:

> let but Falstaff come,
> Hal, Poins, the rest—you scarce shall have a room.

About 1622 *1 Henry IV* and *2 Henry IV* were combined into one play, for a private performance. More precisely, Part 1 was slightly abridged (the only scenes completely omitted were II.i and IV.iv, both of which are short); three-fourths of the composite play comes from Part 1, and one-fourth from Part 2. (The taste for combining the two plays into one play persists. In 1964 Joan Littlewood directed *1 Henry IV*, with rearrangements and with additions from *2 Henry IV*, at the Edinburgh Festival, and, as we shall see, Orson Welles combined elements from several of Shakespeare's plays in a film.) But *1 Henry IV* continued to hold the stage in its original form until the Civil War broke out in 1642, when Parliament closed the London theaters and dramatic activity in England nearly ceased. Yet even under these severely adverse conditions *1 Henry IV* lived on the stage, in a highly abbreviated form called a *droll*. The drolls were comic extracts from plays, for instance the scenes of the grave diggers in *Hamlet* and Bottom the Weaver in *A Midsummer Night's Dream*. These brief plays were surreptitiously acted not only in London but in the provinces at fairs, in halls, and

Supplement to Henry IV, Part 1, ed. G. Blakemore Evans, also published in Shakespeare Quarterly, 7 (1956), 104–05. For a general yet erudite survey, see Arthur Colby Sprague, Shakespeare's Histories: Plays for the Stage, and for relatively full discussions of three stage performances in England (1964, 1975, 1982) as well as the BBC television version (1979), see T. F. Wharton, Henry the Fourth, Parts 1 and 2: Text and Performance.

in taverns. In 1662 a droll from *1 Henry IV* was published, entitled *The Bouncing Knight, or, The Robbers Robbed*,[2] in a collection of drolls entitled *The Wits, or Sport upon Sport*, with a preface by one Henry Marsh. In 1662 the book was reissued, this time by a bookseller named Francis Kirkman. It is not known who edited the individual drolls, but one can read them in J. J. Elson's excellent scholarly edition of *The Wits*.* A second droll, *The Boaster*, was published in 1704 in a collection called *The Theatre of Ingenuity*. It is based chiefly on Falstaff's description in II.iv of his fight with the men in buckram, with lots of cuts and rewordings.

The Commonwealth prohibition of theatrical performances ended in 1660, when Charles II was restored to the throne, and *1 Henry IV* was regularly performed during the rest of the seventeenth century. In 1682 Thomas Betterton played Hotspur (a role that since has been played by such eminent actors as Laurence Olivier and Michael Redgrave), but when Betterton revived the play in 1700 he took the role of Falstaff, establishing the tradition of putting the company's leading actor in this role. Judging from the acting edition of this production, published in 1700, Betterton did not heighten his part by making extensive cuts in the historical portions of the play, though later Falstaffs have done so when they controlled the company. His cuts were chiefly matters of decorum, though he also reduced Lady Percy's role and (because the end of III.i is cut) deleted the small part of Lady Mortimer, which is odd when one considers that actresses (having replaced boy actors in female roles) were now making an important contribution to the popularity of the theater. The Welsh scene with Lady Mortimer was abridged in most productions of the early eighteenth century, and omitted in the late eighteenth century, but it was restored in the middle of the nineteenth.

In the first half of the eighteenth century *1 Henry IV*

[2] For the record, *The Bouncing Knight* essentially consists of these parts of *1 Henry IV*: II.iv.113–284, 328–33, 376–485; III.iii.1–73, 84–157; IV.ii.12–49, 62–68; V.i.125–41; V.iv.101–28, 130–63.

seems (like *Hamlet*) to have been acted in London at
least once every year, and the evidence suggests that for
the entire eighteenth century *1 Henry IV* was more popular than any of Shakespeare's comedies. In the early
nineteenth it somewhat declined in popularity, possibly
because it has so few female roles, and possibly because
taste was moving in the direction of Mrs. Inchbald, quoted
at the start of this essay, though there were still some
important performances: praise was given to John Philip
Kemble and William Charles Macready as Hotspur, and
to Barry Sullivan and Samuel Phelps as Falstaff. In the
second half of the nineteenth century the play was rarely
performed in England, perhaps for the reasons just given,
or perhaps because Victorian taste preferred a nobler view
of English history than Shakespeare offered. What is especially puzzling is that from the end of the eighteenth
century to the last quarter of the nineteenth, the "play
extempore" of II.iv.380–481, in which Falstaff at first
impersonates the king and then (when Hal takes over the
role of the king) impersonates Hal, was usually omitted.
Abraham Lincoln was as puzzled as we are. When he
spent the evening of December 13, 1863, with the actor
James Henry Hackett (Hackett was the first American to
appear as a star in London, playing Falstaff in 1833),
Lincoln asked why this scene was omitted. Hackett replied
that it reads well but is not effective on the stage, a judgment that can only puzzle us further.

In 1905 Frank Benson, probably for the first time since
Shakespeare's day, staged *1 Henry IV* along with Shakespeare's three other plays related to the reign of Henry IV,
that is, with *Richard II, 2 Henry IV,* and *Henry V,* and in
1921 the Birmingham Repertory Company, under Barry
Jackson, staged the two parts of *Henry IV* in one day, a
practice occasionally repeated in recent years. Jackson's
production was given on April 23, supposedly Shakespeare's birthday, and we can detect here an implication
that *Henry IV,* far from being immoral or unpatriotic, is
quintessentially Shakespearean and by the same token
quintessentially English. In the following year Nugent

Monck's Norwich Players staged an Elizabethan-style *1 Henry IV* on a stage without a drop curtain, reflecting the belief (championed especially by William Poel) that Shakespeare's plays can best be performed on a stage that resembles the stage for which they were written.

Reluctantly passing over the 1935 production that cast George Robey as Falstaff (an especially interesting choice, since Robey was a music-hall performer, and the choice thus resembled casting W. C. Fields as Micawber in the film *David Copperfield,* or Bert Lahr as Estragon in *Waiting for Godot*), and even more reluctantly passing over the 1945 production with Ralph Richardson as Falstaff and Laurence Olivier as Hotspur, we can for a moment pursue the idea of performing the play on a more or less Elizabethan stage. In 1951 the four Henry plays were produced at Stratford-upon-Avon. A single setting was used for all four, which were viewed (partly under the influence of E. M. W. Tillyard's writings on the history plays) as a tetralogy. Tanya Moiseiwitsch constructed in the Shakespeare Memorial Theater a bulky scaffolding that served as a sort of Elizabethan stage with three chief acting areas: an upper stage or gallery, an inner stage (sometimes concealed by two doors) below it, and a main stage. Stairs curving down on each side connected the upper playing area with the main stage. The timber set, looking somewhat like the popular idea of Tudor architecture, was enlivened, when appropriate, with colorful banners.[3]

In this production Anthony Quayle (who with John Kidd directed Part 1) played Falstaff, Michael Redgrave played Hotspur, and Richard Burton played Hal. Reviewers pointed out that Quayle's Falstaff was both a courtier and a brute. A toady with his superiors, he was ruthless with his inferiors, especially with the recruits in Part 2. If we take a broad view of the stage history of the play, we

---

[3] For illustrations of the set, see *Shakespeare Quarterly,* 2 (1951), plate facing page 328; *Shakespeare Survey* 6, Plate 5; and all of the plates in J. Dover Wilson and T. C. Worsley, *Shakespeare's Histories at Stratford, 1951.*

can see that there are two kinds of Falstaffs: 1) the
convivial boozer, the lovable reprobate, a "huge bombard
of sack" irresistibly drawn toward the "sweet wag" Hal,
and 2) the shrewd—even depraved—contriver who plays
the role of the genial lush but who is much more than
mere physical appetite, or, to put it a bit differently,
whose appetite is for power as well as for sack and capon
and women. This second kind of Falstaff, uncertain of his
control over Hal but eager for advancement at court,
must continually keep an uneasy eye on the prince. Thus,
where the first kind of Falstaff (secure in the knowledge
that he has Hal's love) can be convulsed with laughter
when Hal in II.iv.224–67 denounces Falstaff's lies about
fighting men in buckram, the second kind—and Quayle
was of this sort—by no means enjoys the exposure.
Quayle seemed pressed, almost distraught, until he hit
upon a way out. Indeed, throughout, Falstaff's increasing
exaggerations seemed somewhat desperate attempts to win
a smile from an unsmiling Hal. George Robey apparently
had been a Falstaff of the first sort. Something of the
difference in the relationship between Hal and Falstaff,
between Robey's Falstaff and Quayle's, can be seen even
in the first scene between the two characters, II.ii. Burton's
Hal first appeared on the upper stage, stretched, washed
himself from a bucket, and then descended, violently
awakening Quayle's Falstaff (asleep in the inner stage) by
throwing a boot at the door; Robey's Falstaff woke up
Hal, and then listened to Hal's rebukes while laughing
and looking at the audience. Similarly, when we last see
Falstaff in *1 Henry IV*, carrying off the body of Hotspur,
he can (like Robey) seem comic—or he can (like
Quayle) seem disgusting and evil. It should be added,
however, that because in 1951 Part 1 was followed by
the much darker Part 2, there was (for the sake of con-
sistency) an inducement to darken even the early Falstaff,
thus making the rejection of Falstaff in Part 2 thoroughly
acceptable.

And Hal's rejection of Falstaff—though the final rejection of course comes only in Part 2—was evident in

Part 1. Burton's Hal was never the madcap prince. For instance, in the "play extempore," in II.iv.378–481, when Hal takes over from Falstaff the role of king, Burton did not play the role comically. It *can* be played comically, for instance with Hal continuing to use as a crown the cushion that Falstaff used. Burton's Hal, however, soon dropped the jesting; his indictment of the "old fat man," "that bolting-hutch of beastliness, that swoll'n parcel of dropsies," was an earnest denunciation. His Hal, in short, always kept Falstaff at a distance. (Quayle plays Falstaff also in the BBC television version, released in 1979, interpreting the role pretty much in the vein of the stage production. Hal, played by David Gwillim, is unamused by Falstaff's performance as the king, and, a little later in the scene, when he himself takes over the impersonation of the king, he delivers his insults with a straight face. As Hal ceases playing and becomes earnest, the on-stage audience ceases laughing; the camera focuses on Hal's unsmiling face and on Falstaff's hurt expression. After Hal's "I do, I will," Falstaff opens his mouth to speak, but no words come out.)

The tetralogy (to use an imprecise but convenient expression) was again presented at Stratford-upon-Avon in 1964, this time directed by Peter Hall, John Barton, and Clifford Williams, along with the three parts of *Henry VI* (though these three were combined into two plays). The set was in marked contrast to the "Elizabethan" set of the 1951 production, for now it was highly mobile (four tall structures that could be moved above separately), perhaps adding welcome variety to the eyes of those who witnessed the entire sequence of six plays. This Falstaff (Hugh Griffith) was chiefly in the tradition of the lovable rogue, full of Rabelaisian vitality. If that sounds a trifle too simple, it should be said that the play was complicated in other ways. Reviewers commented especially on the violence of the combats (for instance, Hotspur with a two-handed sword against Hal with sword and buckler), and on the influence of the Theater of Cruelty, especially at the end, when Vernon was hanged, cut down, and Worcester ascended the scaffold to take Vernon's place.

The Royal Shakespeare Company's production at the Barbican Theater in 1982 allows us to make a neat comparison with Griffith's Falstaff. Joss Ackland's Falstaff was conceived somewhat in Quayle's shifty manner. He was not a Rabelaisian comic figure, and indeed was not especially funny in any way. Rather he was by turns moody, manic, and savage. Ackland said he modeled his Falstaff on Orson Welles, a man whom he regarded as one who wasted his great talents. Hal, too, played by Gerard Murphy, was relatively joyless, something of a petulant hippie (long blond hair), irritable but also capable of giving affection. In the "play extempore," he put little weight on the banishment of Falstaff ("I do, I will," in II.iv.481); rather, after speaking these words, he gave Falstaff an affectionate hug, thus making the whole episode contrast strongly with those productions (such as at Stratford in 1964) that make this scene a key to the entire play.

Something has been said about interpretations of Falstaff and of Hal; it is time to say a word about Hotspur. After Falstaff's, the chief part has usually been regarded as Hotspur's; few actors of importance have wanted to play Hal. In the late seventeenth century Thomas Betterton was praised for those "wild, impatient starts, that fierce and flashing fire, which he threw into Hotspur," and in the early nineteenth century Macready was praised for his "impetuous declamation." A curious stage tradition has developed, giving Hotspur a stammer or some comparable speech impediment. The idea apparently is rooted in Lady Percy's comment, in *2 Henry IV*, II.iii.24, that her late husband was known for "speaking thick, which nature made his blemish." "Thick" here means "fast," as in "thick and fast"; that is, Hotspur crowded his words, but a misinterpretation of "thick" has given rise to the idea that his speech was impaired, or that he spoke with a northern burr or brogue. The earliest record of a stuttering Hotspur is in nineteenth-century Germany; Schlegel translated "thick" as *stottern*, and so German Hotspurs stut-

tered. In 1914 the English actor-manager Beerbohm Tree
told his Hotspur (Matheson Lang) to stammer, and the
impediment took root in England. Most effective of all
was Olivier's Hotspur at the Old Vic in 1945. This Hotspur could pronounce his *w*'s only after a slight hesitation.
His dying speech, in the last lines of which he addresses
himself, was thus given an added poignancy:

> O, I could prophesy,
> But that the earthy and cold hand of death
> Lies on my tongue. No, Percy, thou art dust,
> And food for—
> *Prince.* For worms, brave Percy.

In 1951 Michael Redgrave's Hotspur spoke with thick *r*'s,
suggesting northern speech, and in 1955 John Neville, at
the Old Vic, stammered on his *m*'s. There are still plenty
of letters left in the alphabet for actors to find fresh ways
of speaking "thick."

It has already been mentioned that *1 Henry IV* was the
premier production of the American National Theater, at
the Kennedy Center in Washington, D.C., in 1985. The
production was a failure (it was withdrawn after only five
previews and five performances), largely, it seems, because it was a rather sophomoric and highly inconsistent
exercise in assimilating the play to Brechtian drama. Thus,
the travelers who are robbed by Falstaff and his companions were represented by dummies on a wagon (shades
of Mother Courage's wagon); stagehands sometimes (but
not always) visibly hauled props; pieces of the set were
sometimes left on the stage, where they became irrelevant
in the subsequent scene; some battle scenes were done in
slow motion; a priest walked about on the battlefield at
Shrewsbury, providing the smoke of battle from his censer
(although in Shakespeare's play only in the brief scene
between York and Michael—IV.iv—is there anything
about the relation of politics to religion); and at the end
of the play, Hal and King Henry rode on carousel horses.
One other bit of mischief: the actor John McMartin

doubled as Falstaff and King Henry, thus needlessly emphasizing the idea that Hal has two father figures, and (worse) needlessly slowing down the play, since time had to be allotted for McMartin's costume changes, and (still worse) needlessly irritating the audience by using a double, his back to the audience, in scenes where both characters appear. It was all pretty silly. Less silly, but even more offensive, was Hal's conquest of Hotspur. He threw a knife into Hotspur, at a distance of some 20 feet.

A much more interesting American production, directed by Michael Edwards, was given at Santa Cruz in 1984.[4] The set in this Santa Cruz production was a mock-up of the Globe Theatre, but with a military helicopter crashed into the roof (stage right). The production was in modern dress: Hal (long hair, made up eyebrows, bright red lips, tight shiny blue trousers) was something of a Boy George, and Falstaff, in leather and chains, was something of an aging member of Hell's Angels. In Hal's interview with his father, however, the makeup was gone, and so was the flamboyant costume—though now, since he wore a kimono and was barefoot, there was still a suggestion of the rebellious youth. Henry IV was dressed at first in a three-piece dark suit, and later in the uniform of a five-star general. In the battle scenes Hal, too, wore the dress of a soldier (combat fatigues), and his hair was short. The king's opening speech was treated as a press conference for reporters, who were equipped with television cameras and tape recorders. Westmoreland was in attendance as a five-star general, and Sir Walter Blount, in a dark suit, as a cabinet officer. The last four lines of the play were yet another press conference. Staging of this sort usually leads to great liberties with the text, but in this production the text was scarcely tinkered with, though there were of course bits of business not specified in the text. For in-

---

[4] This production is discussed in some detail by Mary Judith Dunbar in *Shakespeare Quarterly*, 35 (1984), 475–78, and also by Alan C. Dessen in *Shakespeare Quarterly*, 36 (1985), 75–79. Since I have not seen this production my comments are based on these two sources.

stance, at the end of the play Falstaff, cigar in mouth, held his fingers up in a V sign.

The reviews indicate that the production was imaginative, intelligently conceived, and well acted. There is space here to illustrate only one example of its freshness. If we look at the text of V.ii.48–55, we find that when Hal asks Falstaff for his sword, Falstaff offers instead his pistol case; Hal opens the case and finds it contains not a pistol but a bottle of wine, and then, according to the quarto stage direction, Hal "throws the bottle at him." That is, Hal rejects the world of revelry and of escape from combat. In this production the case held a can of beer. Hal started to throw it, thought better, and carried it off. A little later, alone on the stage, he paused to drink some of the beer, and then found, to his surprise, that Hotspur was pointing a gun at him. Hal took a second drink and tossed the can to Hotspur, who also took a drink, and then cooled himself off by pouring the remainder of the beer over his head. Hotspur then tossed aside his own pistol, in order to fight Hal in equal combat. Dessen summarizes his impression of the business:

> A clear sense was conveyed here, albeit without the trappings of chivalry, of something shared between the two warriors, an unspoken code that, in modern as well as in Elizabethan terms, may be archaic and unrealistic (especially in the presence of high-powered automatic weapons and with a kingdom at stake), but is nonetheless appealing and moving. On the one hand, I missed the throwing of a bottle-can at Falstaff (one of Shakespeare's summary images), but I would not have wished to lose this moment where the imagery set up by the actors and the director clarified and developed something very important in the script that can easily be blurred in any production.

Finally, something should be said of Orson Welles's film, made in Spain in 1964, released in 1965 under the title of *Chimes at Midnight*, and retitled as *Falstaff*, with Welles as Falstaff. As a schoolboy Welles had assembled parts of Shakespeare's history plays into a single play, and the idea remained with him throughout his career. In 1960 he staged a work called *Five Kings*, made out of pieces of *Richard II, 1 Henry IV, 2 Henry IV,* and *Henry V,* and clarified by a narrator who read passages from Holinshed's *Chronicles*. (In the film, Ralph Richardson narrates these passages.) Welles made the film under difficult circumstances; to be specific, he could raise very little money, and he could get certain actors for only brief periods—and not always for the same periods as others who shared scenes with them. Jeanne Moreau (Doll Tearsheet) was available for only five days (perhaps it would have been better had she not been available at all), and Gielgud for only ten. This means that Welles sometimes had to use doubles, and his attempt to disguise this subterfuge by using long shots is transparent. Moreover, the soundtrack is very bad—when the voices are not inaudible, they are often out of sync. One often cannot tell who is speaking, sometimes because Welles dubbed in his own voice for other roles. Moreover, because he feared that his American accent would disturb the other actors, he recorded his own dialogue separately. Worst of all, however, is the basic idea of using pieces of several plays, and of distorting them. Hal, for example, is presented early as an effeminate bisexual, probably the lover of Poins. Still, there are some marvelous performances, especially John Gielgud as King Henry, and sometimes (when he is not a coy and mumbling Santa Claus) Welles as Falstaff. Almost all Shakespeare specialists detest the film, understandably and rightly; almost all cinema specialists admire at least portions of the film, especially the battle. No matter that the battlefield is hard and dry when we see cavalry, and muddy when we see footsoldiers. The scene, utterly unheroic, is visually beautiful and worthy of Eisenstein, Welles's inspiration here. Still, it must be said that the film is a mess, and is utterly unfaithful to Shakespeare, though Welles didn't see it that way. In a long interview, published both in *Cahiers du cinema in English,* #11, and in *Sight and Sound,* Autumn 1966 (the language differs slightly, but it is obvious that the interview is the same), Welles explains that the film is an elegy for a vanished Merrie England. It is about death—the death of Hal's youth, the death of Falstaff's friendship with Hal, and the death of joy. (Much of Shakespeare's comedy disappears in this film.) "Falstaff," Welles says, "represents a positive spirit, in many respects courageous. . . . He wages a struggle lost in advance. I don't believe he is seeking anything. He represents a value; he is goodness. . . . The film speaks too of the terrible price that the Prince must pay in exchange for power."

What is especially missing from Welles's *Falstaff* is comedy, a quality Welles said he did not greatly want in this film. "Comedy can't really dominate a film made to tell this story, which is all in dark colors." Dark interpretations of *1 Henry IV* are now the rule, partly because of our experience with war in the twentieth century, and partly because of academic criticism that has linked the play closely with the much darker *2 Henry IV*. The insights of our century should not (and cannot) be put aside; we cannot go back to the Falstaff who is merely a lovable jester. But perhaps it is time to remember that *1 Henry IV* is, among other things, a richly comic play. Even Mrs. Inchbald knew this truth almost two centuries ago, though (as we have seen) she found much in the comedy that would "offend every female auditor."

# Suggested References

The number of possible references is vast and grows alarmingly. (The *Shakespeare Quarterly* devotes one issue each year to a list of the previous year's work, and *Shakespeare Survey*—an annual publication—includes a substantial review of recent scholarship, as well as an occasional essay surveying a few decades of scholarship on a chosen topic.) Though no works are indispensable, those listed below have been found helpful.

## 1. Shakespeare's Times

Byrne, M. St. Clare. *Elizabethan Life in Town and Country*. Rev. ed. New York: Barnes & Noble, 1961. Chapters on manners, beliefs, education, etc., with illustrations.

Joseph, B. L. *Shakespeare's Eden: The Commonwealth of England 1558–1629*. New York: Barnes & Noble, 1971. An account of the social, political, economic, and cultural life of England.

Schoenbaum, S. *Shakespeare: The Globe and the World*. New York: Oxford University Press, 1979. A readable, handsomely illustrated book on the world of the Elizabethans.

*Shakespeare's England*. 2 vols. London: Oxford University Press, 1916. A large collection of scholarly essays on a wide variety of topics (e.g. astrology, costume, gardening, horsemanship), with special attention to Shakespeare's references to these topics.

Stone, Lawrence. *The Crisis of the Aristocracy, 1558–1641*, abridged edition. London: Oxford University Press, 1967.

## 2. Shakespeare

Barnet, Sylvan. *A Short Guide to Shakespeare*. New York: Harcourt Brace Jovanovich, 1974. An introduction to all of the works and to the dramatic traditions behind them.

## SUGGESTED REFERENCES

Bentley, Gerald E. *Shakespeare: A Biographical Handbook.* New Haven, Conn.: Yale University Press, 1961. The facts about Shakespeare, with virtually no conjecture intermingled.

Bush, Geoffrey. *Shakespeare and the Natural Condition.* Cambridge, Mass.: Harvard University Press, 1956. A short, sensitive account of Shakespeare's view of "Nature," touching most of the works.

Chambers, E. K. *William Shakespeare: A Study of Facts and Problems.* 2 vols. London: Oxford University Press, 1930. An invaluable, detailed reference work; not for the casual reader.

Chute, Marchette. *Shakespeare of London.* New York: Dutton, 1949. A readable biography fused with portraits of Stratford and London life.

Clemen, Wolfgang H. *The Development of Shakespeare's Imagery.* Cambridge, Mass.: Harvard University Press, 1951. (Originally published in German, 1936.) A temperate account of a subject often abused.

Granville-Barker, Harley. *Prefaces to Shakespeare.* 2 vols. Princeton, N.J.: Princeton University Press, 1946–47. Essays on ten plays by a scholarly man of the theater.

Harbage, Alfred. *As They Liked It.* New York: Macmillan, 1947. A long, sensitive essay on Shakespeare, morality, and the audience's expectations.

Kernan, Alvin B., ed. *Modern Shakespearean Criticism: Essays on Style, Dramaturgy, and the Major Plays.* New York: Harcourt Brace Jovanovich, 1970. A collection of major formalist criticism.

————. "The Plays and the Playwrights." In *The Revels History of Drama in English,* general editors Clifford Leech and T. W. Craik. Vol. III. London: Methuen, 1975. A book-length essay surveying Elizabethan drama with substantial discussions of Shakespeare's plays.

Schoenbaum, S. *Shakespeare's Lives.* Oxford: Clarendon Press, 1970. A review of the evidence, and an examination of many biographies, including those by Baconians and other heretics.

————. *William Shakespeare: A Compact Documentary Life.* New York: Oxford University Press, 1977. A readable presentation of all that the documents tell us about Shakespeare.

Traversi, D. A. *An Approach to Shakespeare*. 3rd rev. ed. 2 vols. New York: Doubleday, 1968–69. An analysis of the plays, beginning with words, images, and themes, rather than with characters.

Van Doren, Mark. *Shakespeare*. New York: Holt, 1939. Brief, perceptive readings of all of the plays.

## 3. Shakespeare's Theater

Beckerman, Bernard. *Shakespeare at the Globe, 1599–1609*. New York: Macmillan, 1962. On the playhouse and on Elizabethan dramaturgy, acting, and staging.

Chambers, E. K. *The Elizabethan Stage*. 4 vols. New York: Oxford University Press, 1945. A major reference work on theaters, theatrical companies, and staging at court.

Cook, Ann Jennalie. *The Privileged Playgoers of Shakespeare's London, 1576–1642*. Princeton, N.J.: Princeton University Press, 1981. Sees Shakespeare's audience as more middle-class and more intellectual than Harbage (below) does.

Gurr, Andrew. *The Shakespearean Stage: 1579–1642*. 2nd edition. Cambridge: Cambridge University Press, 1980. On the acting companies, the actors, the playhouses, the stages, and the audiences.

Harbage, Alfred. *Shakespeare's Audience*. New York: Columbia University Press, 1941. A study of the size and nature of the theatrical public, emphasizing its representativeness.

Hodges, C. Walter. *The Globe Restored*. London: Ernest Benn, 1953; New York: Coward-McCann, Inc., 1954. A well-illustrated and readable attempt to reconstruct the Globe Theatre.

Hosley, Richard. "The Playhouses." In *The Revels History of Drama in English*, general editors Clifford Leech and T. W. Craik. Vol. III. London: Methuen, 1975. An essay of one hundred pages on the physical aspects of the playhouses.

Kernodle, George R. *From Art to Theatre: Form and Convention in the Renaissance*. Chicago: University of Chicago Press, 1944. Pioneering and stimulating work on the symbolic and cultural meanings of theater construction.

Nagler, A. M. *Shakespeare's Stage*. Tr. by Ralph Manheim. New Haven, Conn.: Yale University Press, 1958. A very brief introduction to the physical aspect of the play-house.

Slater, Ann Pasternak. *Shakespeare the Director*. Totowa, N.J.: Barnes & Noble, 1982. An analysis of theatrical effects (e.g., kissing, kneeling) in stage directions and dialogue.

Thomson, Peter. *Shakespeare's Theatre*. London: Routledge & Kegan Paul, 1983. A discussion of how plays were staged in Shakespeare's time.

4. Miscellaneous Reference Works

Abbott, E. A. *A Shakespearean Grammar*. New edition. New York: Macmillan, 1877. An examination of differences between Elizabethan and modern grammar.

Bevington, David. *Shakespeare*. Arlington Heights, Ill.: A. H. M. Publishing, 1978. A short guide to hundreds of important writings on the works.

Bullough, Geoffrey. *Narrative and Dramatic Sources of Shakespeare*. 8 vols. New York: Columbia University Press, 1957–1975. A collection of many of the books Shakespeare drew upon with judicious comments.

Campbell, Oscar James, and Edward G. Quinn. *The Reader's Encyclopedia of Shakespeare*. New York: Crowell, 1966. More than 2,600 entries, from a few sentences to a few pages on everything related to Shakespeare.

Greg, W. W. *The Shakespeare First Folio*. New York: Oxford University Press, 1955. A detailed yet readable history of the first collection (1623) of Shakespeare's plays.

Kökeritz, Helge. *Shakespeare's Names*. New Haven, Conn.: Yale University Press, 1959. A guide to the pronunciation of some 1,800 names appearing in Shakespeare.

————. *Shakespeare's Pronunciation*. New Haven, Conn.: Yale University Press, 1953. Contains much information about puns and rhymes.

Muir, Kenneth. *The Sources of Shakespeare's Plays*. New Haven, Conn.: Yale University Press, 1978. An account of Shakespeare's use of his reading.

*The Norton Facsimile: The First Folio of Shakespeare*. Prepared by Charlton Hinman. New York: Norton, 1968. A handsome and accurate facsimile of the first collection (1623) of Shakespeare's plays.

Onions, C. T. *A Shakespeare Glossary*. 2d ed., rev., with enlarged addenda. London: Oxford University Press, 1953. Definitions of words (or senses of words) now obsolete. plement to *The Norton Facsimile: The First Folio of "Henry the Fourth."* London: Methuen, 1956. Reprinted in University Press, 1963.

Partridge, Eric. *Shakespeare's Bawdy*. Rev. ed. New York: Dutton; London: Routledge & Kegan Paul, 1955. A glossary of bawdy words and phrases.

*Shakespeare Quarterly*. See headnote to Suggested References.

*Shakespeare Survey*. See headnote to Suggested References.

*Shakespeare's Plays in Quarto. A Facsimile Edition*. Ed. Michael J. B. Allen and Kenneth Muir. Berkeley, Calif.: University of California Press, 1981. A book of nine hundred pages, containing facsimiles of twenty-two of the quarto editions of Shakespeare's plays. An invaluable complement to *The Norton Facsimile: The First Folio of Shakespeare* (see above).

Smith, Gordon Ross. *A Classified Shakespeare Bibliography 1936–1958*. University Park, Pa.: Pennsylvania State University Press, 1963. A list of some twenty thousand items on Shakespeare.

Spevack, Marvin. *The Harvard Concordance to Shakespeare*. Cambridge, Mass.: Harvard University Press, 1973. An index to Shakespeare's words.

Wells, Stanley, ed. *Shakespeare: Select Bibliographies*. London: Oxford University Press, 1973. Seventeen essays surveying scholarship and criticism of Shakespeare's life, work, and theater.

## 5. *Henry IV* [*Part One*]

Auden, W. H. *The Dyer's Hand and Other Essays*. New York: Random House, 1962, pp. 182–208.

Barber, C. L. *Shakespeare's Festive Comedy*. Princeton, N.J.: Princeton University Press, 1959.

Bradley, A. C. *Oxford Lectures on Poetry*. New York: Macmillan, 1909.

Brooks, Cleanth and R. B. Heilman. *Understanding Drama*.

New York: Henry Holt, 1945. A portion is reprinted above.

Charlton, H. B. "Falstaff," *Shakespearian Comedy,* 4th ed. London: Methuen, 1938.

Council, Norman. "Prince Hall: Mirror of Success," *Shakespeare Studies,* 7 (1974), 125–46.

Dickinson, Hugh. "The Reformation of Prince Hal," *Shakespeare Quarterly,* 12 (1961), 33–46.

Doran, Madeleine. "Imagery in *Richard II* and in *Henry IV,*" *Modern Language Review,* 37 (1942), 113–22.

Evans, Gareth Lloyd. "The Comical-tragical-historical Method—*Henry IV,*" *Stratford-upon-Avon Studies 3: Early Shakespeare.* J. R. Brown and B. Harris, eds. London: Edward Arnold, Ltd., 1961.

Hawkins, Sherman H. *"Henry IV*: The Structural Problem Revisited," *Shakespeare Quarterly,* 33 (1982), 278–301.

Hemingway, Samuel B. "On Behalf of That Falstaff," *Shakespeare Quarterly,* 3 (1952), 307–11.

Jenkins, Harold. *The Structural Problem in Shakespeare's Henry the Fourth."* London: Methuen, 1956. Reprinted in the Signet Classic edition of *Henry IV* [*Part Two*].

Kaiser, Walter. *Praisers of Folly.* Cambridge, Mass.: Harvard University press, 1963.

Kelly, Henry Ansgar. *Divine Providence in the England of Shakespeare's Histories.* Cambridge, Mass.: Harvard University Press, 1970.

Kernan, Alvin. *"The Henriad:* Shakespeare's Major History Plays," *Yale Review,* 59 (Autumn 1969), 3–32.

Kris, Ernst. "Prince Hal's Conflict," *Psychoanalytic Quarterly,* 17 (1948), 487–505.

McLaverty, J. "No Abuse: The Prince and Falstaff in the Tavern Scenes of *Henry IV,*" Shakespeare Survey, 34 (1982), 105–10.

McLuhan, Herbert Marshall. *"Henry IV,* a Mirror for Magistrates," *University of Toronto Quarterly,* 17 (1948), 152–60.

Ornstein, Robert. *A Kingdom for a Stage.* Cambridge, Mass.: Harvard University Press, 1972. A portion is reprinted above.

Palmer, D. J. "Casting Off the Old Man: History and St. Paul in *Henry IV,*" *Critical Quarterly,* 12 (1970), 267–83.

### SUGGESTED REFERENCES

Seltzer, Daniel. "Prince Hal and Tragic Style," *Shakespeare Survey*, 30 (1977), 13–27.

Spivack, Bernard. "Falstaff and the Psychomachia," *Shakespeare Quarterly*, 8 (1957), 449–59.

Sprague, Arthur Colby. "Gadshill Revisited," *Shakespeare Quarterly*, 4 (1953), 125–37.

Tillyard, E. M. W. *Shakespeare's History Plays*. London: Chatto and Windus, 1944.

Traversi, D. A. *Shakespeare: from "Richard II" to "Henry V."* Stanford: Stanford University Press, 1957.

Unger, Leonard. *The Man in the Name*. Minneapolis: University of Minnesota Press, 1956.

Waldock, A. J. A. "The Men in Buckram," *Review of English Studies*, 23 (1947), 16–23.

Wilson, John Dover. *The Fortunes of Falstaff*. London: Cambridge University Press, 1943. A selection from this book is reprinted in the present edition.

# POETRY THROUGH THE AGES

☐ **THE LOVE SONGS OF SAPPHO.** Translated by Paul Roche and with an Introduction by Page duBois. Arranged in six books, these epigrams, wedding songs, and elegies from Ancient Greece's greatest woman poet celebrate all the human emotions.        (525353—$4.95)

☐ **LEAVES OF GRASS by Walt Whitman.** These are the incomparable poems of one of America's greatest poets—an exuberant, passionate man who loved his country and wrote of it as no other has ever done. Emerson judged *Leaves of Grass* as "the most extraordinary piece of wit and wisdom America has yet contributed."        (524853—$3.95)

☐ **PARADISE LOST AND PARADISE REGAINED by John Milton.** Edited and with Introduction and Notes by Christopher Ricks. Chronology, Bibliography and Footnotes included.        (524748—$5.95)

☐ **IDYLLS OF THE KING and A Selection of Poems by Alfred Lord Tennyson.** Foreword by George Barker. Includes selections from *The Princess*, *In Memoriam A.H.H.* and *Maud*.        (524705—$5.50)

Price is higher in Canada

---